More Critical Praise for Barbara J. Taylor

for *All Waiting Is Long*

"[P]owerful . . . Every page is saturated with the 1930s milieu as the sisters navigate the adversities of their reality on a sea rough with the unrealistic expectations of well-intended idealists both religious and secular. As if to highlight those expectations, Taylor periodically interrupts her third-person narrative with Greek chorus-type commentary from the Scranton-based Isabelle Lumley Bible Class, including excerpts from a 1929 sex manual for women. The overall result is a thought-provoking book club discussion cornucopia."

—*Booklist,* starred review

"Set in the 1930s, Taylor's suspenseful and intricate follow-up to *Sing in the Morning, Cry at Night* tells the story of sisters Violet and Lily Morgan . . . Taylor delivers startling plot twists and incisive commentary on the social unrest of a coal-mining town during the Great Depression. Covering a six-year span, the novel reveals the consequences of arduous labor and widespread sterilizations that came with the eugenics movement. Among the prostitutes, mobsters, and miners is a web of interconnected lives that come together for a breathtaking ending in Taylor's fine sequel."

—*Publishers Weekly*

"A good selection for book clubs, *All Waiting Is Long* is set in Pennsylvania coal country in the 1930s, a time of tumultuous change and social unrest, including the rise of the eugenics movement. Barbara Taylor's characters—a cast of nuns and prostitutes, mobsters and miners, social activists and church busybodies—reflect the varying pressures and expectations of small-town life with rich, insightful prose and dialogue that rings true to each character's voice. Will the web of lies the two sisters weave around themselves survive? You'll have to read it yourself to find out. Recommended."

—*Historical Novels Review*

T0000558

"Barbara J. Taylor has created another suspenseful page-turner . . . revealing shocking details of enlightened thinking in the 1930s against the backdrop of political corruption, unions, rampant prostitution, coal mine strikes, and judgmental Christians. But it's Taylor's finely honed characters and plot twists that make *All Waiting Is Long* an unforgettable novel."   —*BookMark* on WPSU

"In this richly populated community, old ties are either torn or tightened, and the characters left behind when the sisters went off are nicely fleshed out . . . Ms. Taylor writes with total mastery of her craft. Her similes and metaphors are born of a highly developed abstractive sensitivity, and her dialogues are unerringly true to their respective speakers."   —*BookPleasures*

"Taylor deftly weaves a tale that quickly pulls you in wondering what will become of [Lily and Violet Morgan] and the lies they've propped up around themselves to make it all work. Will their relationship survive? And if the truth were to come out, what would their husbands, family, and the townsfolk think? . . . [Y]ou won't be disappointed with Taylor's newest novel."   —*A New Day*

"Taylor explores complicated issues with excellent prose and compelling characters. Her excavation of the religious and political context in this place and time is fascinating. She achieves depth and breadth, and tells a great story, too."   —*The Collagist*

"In *All Waiting Is Long*, Taylor once again performs the magic trick of making us fall in love with characters who live in her finely drawn, unforgiving past, and who grapple with the indelible consequences of honor and dishonor, hope and disappointment, and the mystifying nature of tragedy and love. I read this book in two sittings, flying through the pages, seduced."

—Robin Oliveira, author of *Winter Sisters*

for *Sing in the Morning, Cry at Night*

• A 2014 *Publishers Weekly* Best Summer Book/Pick of the Week

"[A] profound story of how one unforeseen event may tear a family apart, but another can just as unexpectedly bring them back together again."   —*Publishers Weekly,* "Best Summer Books 2014"

"This story is at once poignant and hopeful, spiced up by such characters as Billy Sunday, the revivalist, and Grief, the specter who haunts Grace to the very edge of sanity. A rich debut."
—*Historical Novels Society*

"Taylor's careful attention to detail and her deep knowledge of the community and its people give the novel a welcome gravity."
—*Columbus Dispatch*

"[A] fantastic novel worthy of the greatest accolades. Writing a book about a historical event can be difficult, as is crafting a bestseller, but Barbara J. Taylor is successful at both."   —*Downtown Magazine*

"An absolute gem of a book filled with beautiful characters and classical writing techniques rarely seen in modern literature."
—*Christian Manifesto,* "Top Fiction Pick of 2014"

"Like Dickens, the novel traces family tragedy, in this case the town blaming eight-year-old Violet Morgan for her older sister's death. As her parents fall victim to their own vices, Violet learns how to form her own friendships to survive."   —*Arts.Mic*

"One of the most compelling books I've ever read . . . [A] haunting story that will stay with the reader long after reading this novel."
—*Story Circle Book Reviews*

"No one without a heart as big and warm as Barbara J. Taylor's possibly could have written a story about a family tragedy that's

infused with so much hope and love, humor, mystery, and down-to-earth wisdom. This is a book I'll want to give to people. I could not put it down and can't wait to be captured again by the next book this wonderful human being writes."   —Beverly Donofrio, author of
Astonished: A Story of Healing and Finding Grace

"Not since reading Richard Llewellyn's *How Green Was My Valley* fifty years ago have I felt such empathy and love through fiction for a place, a time, and a people. *Sing in the Morning, Cry at Night* is a book of equal power and beauty, a bittersweet tale set in early twentieth-century Wyoming Valley, Pennsylvania, the heart and soul of America's anthracite coal mining region, a place where Grace and Grief—now, as then—walk hand in hand."
          —Sara Pritchard, author of *Help Wanted: Female*

"The world of Christian miners—the core of the anthracite mining industry in northeast Pennsylvania—is beautifully evoked by Barbara J. Taylor in this remarkable novel. I found myself drawn back to its pages, living deeply in its world as I read. The sense of place—a place I know well, as I grew up there—is vividly realized. This is a lyrical, passionate novel that will hold readers in its thrall. A first-rate debut."
          —Jay Parini, author of *Borges and Me*

RAIN BREAKS NO BONES

RAIN BREAKS NO BONES

BY BARBARA J. TAYLOR

KAYLIE JONES BOOKS

Published by Akashic Books
©2024 Barbara J. Taylor

ISBN: 978-1-63614-173-2
Library of Congress Control Number: 2023949610

First printing

Kaylie Jones Books
www.kayliejonesbooks.com

Akashic Books
Instagram, Facebook, X, Threads: @AkashicBooks
info@akashicbooks.com
www.akashicbooks.com

For Jeff, who always makes me laugh

I love to tell the story
Of unseen things above . . .
—Katherine Hankey

PROLOGUE

I'm gonna lay down my heavy load,
Down by the riverside . . .
—Pre–Civil War Negro spiritual

Ruth carried the chair in front of her like she was witching for water. Her fingers gripped each side of the seat's mahogany frame, palms up, thumbs tucked the way well-diggers worked divining rods. Not that anyone in Scranton had a need for such tricks. Water was plentiful and easy to find in spite of the dry summer.

It was a dining room chair with a common design—clawed feet, kneed legs, and a pierced splat in the shape of a vase. The front of the seat rested on a lip of flesh at Ruth's aproned waist. The back of the chair faced out, and its shadow stretched beyond hers, tandem ghosts skimming the flagstones. The Spencers' beagle tagged along for the first block, but when Ruth started down Linden Street, he abandoned her for an injured robin.

Crescents of sweat bloomed under her arms and breasts, staining the long gray dress she wore as a housemaid. The white trim on the sleeves and collar stood out against her chestnut skin. Had she been standing still, the full-length skirt might have concealed her clubbed right foot, but a hitching gait announces such afflictions.

Ribbons of August heat boiled up from the asphalt, bending the angles of road and houses. Just ahead, a blur of pigtails hopscotched from one sidewalk to the next. Ruth veered into the street and back again like water making its way around rock. Behind her, the Elm Park Church tolled the two o'clock hour. "I'm comin'," she said. The shrill whir of katydids swelled in response.

Ruth turned left onto Wyoming Avenue, where horses, streetcars, and the occasional Model T competed for a slice of road. Overhead, a banner proclaimed, *Scranton, Pennsylvania's Semi-Centennial, 1866 to 1916.* American flags waved from lampposts in an exuberant display of patriotism and pride. From atop a ladder, a man changing out a bulb in a string of electric lights, called down, "You're supposed to sit on that thing, not carry it." Ruth kept her head level and her feet moving as the man laughed at his own joke.

Farther along, a propped-up sandwich board read: *Whittall Rugs, an Outdoor Demonstration.* Drenched in reds and golds, an oriental rug spanned the length of the walkway outside the Poli Theatre. Ruth lifted and dropped her twisted foot onto the carpet, stepped forward with her good one, and repeated the process till she crossed. At the end, a second sign declared, *Rain, Snow, or Sunshine. Whittall Rugs Will Defy the Elements.*

Heavy with perspiration, the dress clung to her five-foot frame. Nonetheless, she carried the chair past the Jermyn Hotel, the Globe Store, and the Bee Hive Jeweler where *One dollar a week buys a diamond.*

And she carried the chair onto Lackawanna Avenue, toward wagons and warehouses selling produce and meats. Amid farmers and hucksters haggling for quantity and price. Around boxes and barrels blocking sidewalks and curbs. "Live fowl!" a poulterer shouted to passersby. Near the bridge that connected downtown to Westside, George W. Brown's Drayman Company advertised, *Hauling of all kinds,* on the side of his building. Red, white, and blue buntings hung from the windows.

Just before the river, Ruth put down the chair. A tumble of yellow roses poured over an iron fence, their thick perfume sweetening the air. She plucked a blossom from the spray, tucked it behind her ear, picked up her load, and started moving again.

Halfway across the bridge, she set the chair on the narrow

walkway, smoothed her dress, and shook out her apron. Nubs of embroidered huckleberries trimmed the white cotton panel. The roar of the river, forty feet below, landed on her ear as a murmur. "I'm comin'," she said a second time. With her good foot first, Ruth climbed the chair, stepped over the railing, and jumped.

PART ONE

CHAPTER ONE

Two weeks into the Scranton bus strike and still no progress. Violet rooted through her coin purse for thirty cents. If a courtesy car came along, she'd need to have two fares in hand, one for herself and one for her mother Grace sitting beside her on the bench.

"Whatever possessed us," her mother nodded toward the church across the square, "to take down that bell tower?" Strands of white hair pressed against the collar of her black dress as she lifted her chin to view the once steepled sky. "Providence Christian. Where I met your father. Did I ever tell you that story? I was selling Welsh cakes for Old Home Week." When Violet didn't answer, Grace mumbled, "Of course I told you."

"It had to come down." Violet cleared her throat, trying to scrub the impatience from her voice. "The city came in and declared it unstable. Must be seven years now." She studied the structure, a queen without her slatted crown. "Maybe eight." She turned to her mother as a streak of sun shone on her pale face. Violet noted the steel-blue veins coursing beneath her mother's papery skin, darkening the hollows under her eyes. Violet's last trace of irritability gave way to concern. "Remember?"

Grace laughed. "In all my days, I never saw a grown man so scared of a woman. Took your father three months to speak to me again."

"On Thanksgiving Day," Violet said.

"That's right." Grace's countenance brightened. "Thanksgiving Day."

Violet glanced at the bronze clock on the North Scranton Bank and Trust—half past ten. "We'll give it another few minutes."

"Enough time for a catnap," her mother said, settling into the bench.

Violet hoped someone would be along shortly. With the strike in full swing, bus drivers had begun using their own cars to pick up passengers. They offered the service as a "courtesy" in order to avoid legal troubles, but folks knew enough to pay. Striking workers had mouths to feed like everybody else.

Having come from a union family, Violet supported the walkout, but today she needed to get downtown. What she wouldn't give for a streetcar, but like so many other conveniences of her youth, they'd fallen out of favor. Buses, trucks, automobiles. Anything with a gas engine. That's how people got around. *And more's the pity*, she thought. When the last streetcar ran back in December, Violet and her daughter had taken the ride. No doubt Daisy had gone for her mother's sake, but Violet was pleased to have company.

"Is Daisy meeting us for lunch?" Grace's eyes remained closed. "The Purple Cow has their spaghetti plate on Saturdays."

"No." Violet searched the Market Street traffic for a courtesy car placard taped inside one of the windows. "She wants to be there when they move the piano."

The piano, a little red upright called a Tom Thumb, had been in the family as long as Violet could remember. She'd played some as a child, but abandoned it when she was eight years old. The instrument went untouched until her daughter Daisy had come along. Even before she could walk, Daisy would grab hold of the leg, pull herself up, pound on the keys, and hum along. Folks used to say she was born carrying a tune. Thanks to Violet's younger sister Lily, who'd twice married into money, Daisy had started lessons when she was seven years old, first in singing, then piano, and finally dance.

When Lily and her second husband Frankie had come up

from Atlantic City last Christmas, they offered to set Daisy up in her own music studio. Frankie, born and raised in Scranton, owned a few buildings in town, and one of his tenants, Antoinette Marinaro, of Miss Antoinette's Twirlettes, was planning to retire in the spring, leaving the second-floor baton studio on Lackawanna Avenue vacant. Violet had strong reservations because of Frankie's rumored ties to the mob, but in the end, her doubts couldn't compete with Daisy's enthusiasm. And Grace, caught up in the spirit of generosity, gave the piano to her granddaughter on the spot. Violet hated to see the thing go, so much so that she'd planned this little shopping trip. She didn't want to be home when the movers came by. Daisy could handle the matter on her own.

Grace sat up and opened her eyes. "Do you think she has a fella?"

"Who? Daisy?"

"I never hear her talk about a fella."

"You know as much as I do." There was that impatience. "She hasn't said. Not to me. Not in a long time."

"Wouldn't it be something if we could get her a television?"

"A what?" Violet half stood at the sight of a braking Studebaker, but sat back down when it continued past them. "We're getting her a dress."

"It would be some birthday." Grace's thin lips curled up as she shut her eyes again.

A television? They certainly didn't have that kind of money, and if they did, Violet could think of far more practical ways to spend it. The house needed a new roof, for one thing. And how much longer was that stove going to last? She had a heck of a time getting the back burner to stay lit. She shook her head. Where did her mother get these ideas? She knew very well they were going into town to pay off the dress Violet had put on layaway. And to buy a trowel. Somehow she had misplaced hers, and with Decoration Day a month away, she'd need one for the cemetery. She wondered about the pansies she'd started from seed. Would they be hearty enough to plant by then?

"How old will she be?" her mother asked.

"Daisy? Twenty-five on Wednesday." Born May 11, 1930. And here it was, 1955. Yet—Violet took a breath. Not three or ten or seventeen, but twenty-five. A number with heft. The age of a woman.

"It happens so fast," her mother said, as if concurring with Violet's revelation. "I remember the shock of it with you more than your sister. Lily's younger, so there's that. But you? I can tell you the exact moment." Grace straightened. "You won't want to hear it." In spite of the warning, she barreled into the next sentence: "It was the day you came home with Lily's baby in your arms."

"Mother!" Violet scoured the square for eavesdroppers and lowered her voice. "You promised."

"And I've kept my promise," Grace said, her response emphatic. "Still, I can see you walking through the door like it was yesterday," she smiled, "carrying that baby. Claiming her as your own. Not caring a wit about your reputation." Grace patted Violet's hand. "I knew you wouldn't leave her at the Good Shepherd with those old nuns." She wrinkled her nose. "That's why I sent you away with Lily."

"I certainly don't remember it that way."

"Doesn't make it any less true. Your sister was willing to adopt Daisy out to save herself. But not you." She nudged Violet's arm. "You were always a soft touch."

"I was terrified."

"You were strong." Grace smoothed out the skirt of her dress and sat up taller. "I'm seventy-five years old, and before I meet my maker, I want to tell you how brave a thing that was."

Brave? No one had been happy when she'd come home with Daisy, least of all her mother. And Violet's decision to claim her sister's baby had been anything but brave. She'd been scared witless for the first five years while raising the child alone. And shunned for being unmarried, because everyone in town assumed it was Violet's child. Everyone except Tommy Davies. Her Tommy.

Such a loving husband he'd turned out to be, and a wonderful father to Daisy, God rest his soul.

"Where to?" The driver of a black Chevy pulled in front of the bench, startling the pair.

Violet sprang up first. "Downtown." She peeked into the car and counted two men up front, and a mother with three young sons in back.

"Plenty of room." The driver motioned for the woman to hold one of the boys. "See?"

"It'll be cozy." Grace walked over to the car, slipped in next to the children, and pulled one of them onto her lap. When Violet hesitated, her mother said, "We'll be there in no time," then struck up a conversation with the woman.

In spite of her doubts, Violet paid the fare, climbed inside, and compressed her limbs like spokes on a closed umbrella. The driver managed to shut the door on the second try. "Plenty of room," he repeated before getting back behind the wheel.

Brave. Violet couldn't let go of the word. To show gratitude for the compliment was to accept the lie. Her mother's lie, but also her own. It was the part of the story only she and her sister Lily knew. Yes, Violet had returned to the Good Shepherd Infant Asylum that day, but not for the baby.

"The Lord be with you," Mother Mary Joseph had said before giving Violet and Lily one last squeeze at the door.

"And also with you." Violet's reflexive response amused her. What would the members of Providence Christian say if they heard such an expression coming from her Protestant lips? More to the point, what would they do if they knew where she and Lily had been these many months? Living with nuns in the Good Shepherd Infant Asylum for wayward girls, where only the Catholics were hidden away because clearly Protestants never had sex without the benefit of marriage. Or so they were told by every fire-and-brimstone preacher who'd graced their church's pulpit. Of course, Violet and the congregation only pretended to believe such nonsense. Protestants got themselves into trouble just as often, maybe more, and then they had to rely on the nuns for compassion. "Thank God for the Catholics." Violet laughed, realizing she'd said the words aloud.

Mother Mary Joseph seemed to share her amusement. "We'll make a nun out of you yet."

Violet's mirth proved short-lived. "And the baby?"

"She'll be much loved," the nun reassured as they embraced. "Now be on your way before you start me bawling again."

Laden with suitcases and traveling on foot, it took the sisters twenty minutes to get to the train station in downtown Philadelphia. Violet purchased two tickets to Scranton, and they sat on a bench to wait.

Lily caught her pasty reflection in a nearby window and smoothed her long dark locks. "Where's that hat you bought me for my birthday?" she asked, rummaging through their belongings.

"It's the only thing I asked you to remember!" Violet checked the clock—one hour before departing. "Don't move," she said, and hightailed it back to the Good Shepherd.

Mother Mary Joseph met her at the front door with a red hatbox in hand. "Something told me you'd be back." She hugged Violet, then went inside for a meeting with Jack Barrett, one of the asylum's benefactors. Violet stood on the porch a few moments longer. She didn't want to miss her train, but she couldn't help herself. She had to see her niece one last time.

As she passed by the front parlor, Violet heard snippets of conversation. "It'll be good for Mamie," and, "Something to clear her mind." Mamie Barrett, Jack's wife, had had a nervous breakdown after the death of their only child years before and never quite recovered. Violet continued down the hall, wondering what they could possibly do to help the poor woman after all this time.

A few doors away from the nursery, the crying started, Daisy's wails, and someone else's too. Violet stepped inside, and there was Lily's baby, inconsolable, dressed for travel, in Mamie Barrett's trembling arms. No matter how much pity Violet felt for the woman, she couldn't allow her niece to be raised by someone so broken. She scooped up the child, ran out the kitchen door, and made it back to the station right as the train to Scranton pulled in.

A horrified Lily understood immediately what Violet had done. "You've ruined my life!" she cried as the trio boarded.

"I swear I'll claim the baby as my own," Violet assured her, but nothing felt certain in that moment.

The courtesy car parked in front of the Globe Store, scraping its tires against the curb. Panic, she thought, not desire to be a mother, had driven her to take the baby. As much as she loved Daisy, that didn't make up for the fact that she'd have left her behind if circumstances had been different. If she hadn't gone back for that hat. Brave? Hardly. The shame of it settled over her eyes.

The driver opened the door, and Violet stepped out, rubbing her temples.

"You're getting one of your headaches," Grace said, grabbing the doorframe to pull herself out of the car. "I have aspirin in my purse. Let's go up to the ladies' lounge before we start shopping."

They each pushed through the revolving door into a heady brew of perfumed air. A sign on the fragrance counter announced, *Elevators closed for inspection. Our apologies for the inconvenience.*

"Of all the days," Violet said.

"I'll be fine. I don't mind the escalator one bit."

Violet knew her mother minded, but they didn't have much of a choice. "I'll be right behind you."

At the other end of the cosmetics aisle, Violet said, "You won't tell." When Grace didn't answer, Violet added, "About Daisy."

"No good would come of it. She's as much yours as you are mine. As much as all my children. You. Lily." Grace squeezed Violet's hand. "Our Daisy."

Always "our," Violet thought, whenever anyone in the family mentioned her sister Daisy. Violet had named the baby after her older sibling, who'd died as a child after her dress had caught fire from a sparkler one Fourth of July, the same day as her baptism. The "our" distinguished the first Daisy from her namesake. Soon Violet's Daisy would be twenty-five, while "Our Daisy" would be nine years old forever.

Once they reached the escalator, Grace stared up at it. "I heard Harrods department store used to give a shot of brandy to their customers when they reached the top."

A gentleman in line behind them chortled. "Oh, to be in London now."

Grace responded with a nervous giggle as she placed both feet on the emerging step and grabbed hold of the moving handrails.

"You're doing fine." Violet hopped on immediately after her. The scent of chocolate from the candy counter followed the pair all the way up to the second floor.

Relieved to be back on solid footing, Grace slowly led the way past the fur department and into the ladies' lounge. Two salesgirls sat at a built-in vanity that ran the length of the mirrored right wall; one blotted her lipstick while the other tapped a cigarette out of a pack of Chesterfields. Behind them, a woman dozed as she nursed her baby. A handful of other shoppers sat scattered among the clusters of couches and chairs, their pocketbooks and packages piled alongside them.

"I'll only be a minute." Grace padded through the lounge and disappeared into the lavatory behind it.

Violet sat on the closest couch and gazed at the glass display case near the entrance. A mink stole, she thought, always a mink stole, and expertly draped over the same wire torso. The Globe Store knew how to sell dreams. Every one of the dozen or so women seated in the room had pictured herself in that fur, if only for an instant.

Grace returned from the lav with a paper cup of water and two aspirin tablets. "Take these."

As Violet washed down the pills, both women settled into the plush cushions. Wisps of gossip and cigarette smoke drifted past them.

After a few moments, Grace asked, "Does she still come to you in your dreams?"

"Who?" Violet massaged her brow.

"Our Daisy," Grace said, repinning errant strands of hair into her bun. "When you were young, she'd come to you at night."

Violet thought for a moment. "I don't remember that." Sadness deepened her already somber mood.

"It was a long time ago." Grace dabbed her eyes and passed the handkerchief over. "Well aren't we a pair." She sat straight up and scooted to the edge of her cushion. "I know what'll give us a lift. A trip to the third floor to see the televisions."

"We don't have money for a—"

"It can't hurt to look. Besides, Johanna Lankowski knows a man who takes Green Stamps. Same as cash."

Violet thought about Mrs. Lankowski, their elderly neighbor from across the street and dear family friend. The widow, as she'd been known since Violet was a child, could get her hands on anything. She always "knew a man" who'd take payment in preserves or pies or mending and such. Truth be told, she'd been a great help, especially last year when the government cut the pensions in half for the miners' widows. Mrs. Lankowski found ways to help Violet and her mother make ends meet while her son Stanley, a local lawyer, petitioned the state for monthly stipends on their behalf. Violet didn't like to be beholden, but she was grateful for his efforts. Between the stipends and her work as a colorist for Walsh's Portrait Studio, she managed to keep a roof over the heads of her mother and daughter, and an eleven-year-old cocker spaniel named Archie.

Grace nudged Violet. "Did you hear what I said?"

"There aren't enough Green Stamps in the world for a TV." Violet stood up, reached discretely under her slip, and adjusted the garters on her girdle. "I've been saving for an electric sweeper for six months, and I'm still eleven books shy." She looked in the mirror and took stock, a habit she'd picked up since turning fifty. Streaks of gray tarnished her dark hair. Near her left temple, a quarter-sized liver spot stained her fair complexion. In just the right light, the skin on her neck showed signs of slackening. Violet had begun to think of herself as a faded garment at the back of the closet. Sunday best turned housedress. She picked up her purse and stretched a hand out to her mother. "We have shopping to do."

The women's department was around the corner. After paying off the layaway, Violet wrote her address on the delivery slip and handed it to the salesclerk.

"Spring Street," the girl said. "In North Scranton?" She ran her finger down the delivery schedule.

"Providence," Violet corrected. "One neighborhood over."

"Providence," the girl repeated. Her finger stopped halfway down the sheet. "Found it. Eleven o'clock Monday morning. Give or take."

"That'll be fine." Violet swung around to her mother. "Why don't you sit in the lounge? I'll go down to the basement for the trowel. Maybe the elevators will be running by the time I get back."

"Nonsense." Grace shuffled deeper into the women's department and stopped in front of a mannequin dressed in a red skirt over a navy romper. "Besides," she said, raising an eyebrow at the length of the shorts underneath, "we're going up to the appliance department first. They have a nice selection of televisions."

"According to whom?"

"Johanna Lankowski."

Violet stayed silent.

"It doesn't cost anything to dream."

"Dreams aren't going to get you to the third floor."

"I'll take you," a voice piped up from behind a white column. Violet and Grace stepped around to find a Negro woman, short-statured and big-bosomed, holding back a swinging door. Beyond it, a freight elevator stood open.

"See?" her mother said, as she gestured for Violet to follow. "Our friend . . ." She paused for the woman to offer her name.

"Zethray."

Grace closed one eye and squinted the other.

"Zeth," the woman's tongue held onto the *th* for the sake of clarity, ". . . ray. Last name's Long, as in *long-gone* like my ex-husband." She grinned and put her name all together: "Zethray Long."

"How strange." Grace's brow puckered.

"It's a lovely name," Violet said, embarrassed by her mother's remark.

"I shoulda said it that way from the start. White folks do better when I break it down." Zethray waved the women through. "It's Cherokee. Means running water. Least that's what Mama used to say." She limped toward the elevator, scraping the floor with a twisted right foot. "Her daddy had Indian blood in his veins."

Grace's hand flew to her mouth. "Don't tell me." She surveyed the woman, head to toe. "You're Ruth's daughter. Ruth Jones."

Zethray hobbled inside. "Yes, ma'am." Facing forward, she planted her feet shoulder-width apart and grabbed hold of an overhead rope. One good yank and a steel mesh gate thundered to the floor, causing the car's single light bulb to sway from the ceiling. Without looking, she reached over and lifted a wooden lever on the left-hand wall. They began to ascend.

"I saw you with that foot, and I said to myself, *That's Ruth's girl for sure.*" Grace inspected Zethray's worn-down orthopedic oxford. "I didn't know such a thing could be passed down."

"Mother!" Violet's cheeks burned red.

"Your mama don't mean no harm." Zethray pulled back on the lever just enough to line up the floor of the elevator with the major appliance department. "The foot always gives me away." She steadied herself and lifted the door with calloused hands.

"And the eyes." Grace stared at the woman. "You have her sparkle."

"Thank you for saying so." Zethray touched her hands to her cinnamon cheeks. "I'm blushing," she said. "Mama's eyes were her prettiest feature."

Grace and Violet stepped off the elevator only to linger in front of the open door.

"So you knew Mama," Zethray noted. "Must be what drew me."

"Oh, I loved Ruth!" Grace cradled her arms. "We worked together as housemaids for Colonel Watres when he still lived in town." She gazed beyond Zethray, conjuring a memory. "Did she ever tell you about the Christmas turkeys?"

"No, ma'am."

Grace snorted. "I can see it clear as day. Ruth standing at the sink yelling, 'They're getting away!' I look out and see a pair of turkeys making a beeline for the alley. Doesn't matter who forgot to lock the gate. We know who'll get blamed. Next thing, we're running after them. No coats. No hats in the middle of December. Just two fools chasing down next week's dinner. We finally catch up with them near the Jewish church, and they turn around, heads hung low, like kids caught out playing hooky. 'Time to go home,' Ruth says, and home they went with the two of us trailing behind." Grace pulled a handkerchief from her sleeve and dabbed her eyes. "Funniest sight you ever saw."

"That there's a gift," Zethray said. "Thank you, Mrs. . . . ."

"Where are my manners? Grace Morgan, and my daughter, Violet."

"A pleasure, Mrs. Morgan. Miss Violet." Zethray beamed. "A real pleasure."

"I remember running into your mother on the street a year or so after I married. She was working for the Spencers by then and had a baby in the carriage. I'm guessing it was you." Grace's face dropped. "I never saw her again."

Zethray grabbed hold of the overhead rope. "Time sure has a way of passing."

"Oh, I loved Ruth," Grace said again.

"Then we have that in common," Zethray said.

"And she made the best corn bread." Grace clasped her hands. "I've never had better."

"That she did. Used rainwater in her recipe. Made all the difference." Zethray held onto the rope, but she kept her eyes locked on the older woman.

"I remember seeing it in the paper," Grace bemoaned, "the summer of the semi-centennial."

"Gone almost forty years now," Zethray said.

"Tragic. I had my own family by then." Grace shivered. "I can't bear to think she took her own life. Such sadness. You must have been young."

"Just turned fourteen. Had to quit school the very next day. A shame too. I loved school, and I was good at it."

"I'm sorry for your loss," Grace said.

"And I'm sorry for yours." Zethray planted her feet and adjusted the rope in her hand. "No pain worse than losing a child," she said, as she yanked the gate closed and started to descend.

CHAPTER TWO

FINALLY, DAISY THOUGHT AS SHE STOOD on the porch listening to the truck chug toward her house. She watched the passenger, his bald head hanging out the window.

"A little closer," he directed. "A little closer. Closer. Stop!" Both men bounced as the right front tire jumped the curb and landed on the sidewalk. "Looks good," the passenger said, and the pair nodded.

Daisy winced. Thank goodness her mother and grandmother had gone to the Globe Store an hour earlier. Neither one would cross the street for the Summerlin brothers, let alone hire them. Daisy knew as much when she'd telephoned them about the piano, but what choice did she have? Professional movers didn't come cheap. The Summerlins did. Frick and Frack, as they were known in the neighborhood, worked just enough and not a minute more. In their case "just enough" meant being able to cover an assortment of bar tabs all over the city.

"I know. I know." Either Frick or Frack tumbled out from the passenger's side, banging his knee on the running board as he descended. "Son of a . . ." Instead of cussing, he smacked the side of the chalky-white milk truck, an old Step-N-Drive model from the thirties. Patches of rust spread across the fenders like measles. The words *Summerlin Brothers, Good in a Pinch* had recently been painted in black over a faded red Burschel Dairy banner.

"We woulda got here sooner," the driver called out, "but we stopped at Stirna's to do some figuring." From inside the truck, he pushed the back doors open, jumped out, and called his brother over.

A gin mill at this hour? Doesn't that take the cake! Daisy held her tongue for the sake of the piano. Side by side, she could now see the driver was a full foot taller than his sibling; otherwise, they'd pass for twins. Same bald heads. Same lined faces. Red cheeks, drinkers' noses. By the looks of them, neither man had lifted more than a beer bottle in some time.

Frick or Frack pulled a six-foot length board out of the truck, handed it to his brother, and grabbed a second one for himself. "Did you hear what happened to the blind guy who became a carpenter?" He angled his board lengthwise over the front porch steps. "He picked up his hammer and saw. And *saw*," he repeated, delighting in the pun.

"Did you hear the one about the mute guy?" The shorter brother set his board about two feet over, parallel to the first. "He picked up a bicycle and spoke." The men chuckled as they adjusted the ramps.

Daisy's annoyance melted into amusement. *Oldest jokes in the book*, she thought, tickled nonetheless. With the ramps in place, she noted the words *Property of Stirna's* scratched into the wood and chided herself for assuming the men had gone there for drink. "The piano and stool are inside." She held the screen door open and waved them through. As each one passed, the stink of beer relieved her of the guilt she'd felt for judging them so quickly.

The little red upright stood against the parlor wall, shorn of the photographs it had always held. As a youngster, Daisy used to play that piano at her grandparents' house next door. After her grandfather passed away, her Grandma Morgan moved in with Daisy's family, and she brought the Tom Thumb with her for sentimental reasons, Daisy assumed, since Daisy was the only one in the family who ever played.

She held her breath as the men wheeled the instrument to the front door and over the threshold. The piano was a third the size of a standard upright, but with its iron harp and plates, it still weighed in at over two hundred pounds and would test the limits of ramps intended for beer deliveries. "Whoever bought this piano didn't play a lot," the taller man said as he inched one of the boards over with his foot. "They only played a little."

"He came up with that one hisself," the other brother crowed.

This time Daisy's mirth didn't last long. Her mother would have her head if anything went wrong today. "Careful." She spoke the word as prayer.

Much to her relief, Frick and Frack guided the piano down the boards, across the sidewalk, back up the boards, and into the truck with the gentleness of nursemaids. One of the men climbed inside and tied the instrument in place while the other returned to the house for the little round stool. As soon as both pieces were secured, the shorter brother settled in next to the piano and grabbed the nearest leg. "In case the ropes don't hold."

"You can ride up front," the taller one said to Daisy as he strolled around to the driver's side.

Close up, she realized some of the truck's rust was actually caked-on mud. Good thing she'd put on dungarees this morning. She'd actually thought twice about her attire since people dressed for town, but now she could see she'd made the right decision. Daisy pulled herself onto the running board, and hesitated. She'd expected the steering wheel coming up from the floor and the tall saddle seat behind it. The design made it possible for milkmen to deliver from both sides of the truck. What she couldn't have imagined was the grass-green lawn chair bolted to the floor on the passenger side. It seemed sturdy enough, she thought, pressing her hand against the webbed fabric, tugging at the aluminum frame.

"She's safer'n Fort Knox." The taller brother climbed inside, perched on the driver's seat, and took the wheel.

After giving the chair another once-over, Daisy decided to take him at his word. "Corner of Lackawanna and Washington. Second floor. Right over the hairdressers—Bevy of Beauties." Daisy settled in and pulled a five-dollar bill out of her purse. "Beverly Hudson owns it. My best friend since grade school." She placed the money into the man's already open palm. "Half now, as promised." She sat back in the seat, pleased with her decision to hire the Summerlins after all.

Twenty minutes later, she waited on the sidewalk next to the piano. Behind her, the brothers stood in the doorway of a brick building, staring slack-jawed at the narrow staircase leading to the second-floor studio.

"Ramps aren't long enough," one of them said.

"Ain't that the truth."

They ambled over to Daisy, both scratching their bald heads. "This is gonna take some figuring," the taller man said.

"Gallagher's?" his brother suggested.

"As good as any."

"Wait!" Daisy yelled as the men set out for their second beer garden of the day. At the sound of her voice, they spun around. "What about my piano?"

They both considered the question. "It ain't going nowheres," the taller man finally said.

"No siree," the brother agreed, and they started walking again.

"We'll have this settled in no time," one of them called back.

"Thirty minutes at most," the other man offered.

"Fifteen!" Daisy shouted. "Not a second more!"

Frick and Frack each gave her a thumbs-up as they disappeared around the corner.

After waiting more than an hour, Daisy knew she'd been had. She stood inside the studio, chiseling her way around the first of four painted-shut windows with a hammer in one hand and a screwdriver in the other. Once the bottom half had a little give, she shimmied it up and set the screen in place. She needed a breath of fresh air to think. So much for holding back half the money. Five dollars could keep the Summerlins on barstools all day. Yes, they'd promised to come back, but as her mother always said, drink had a way of getting between a man and his word.

The second window went up more quickly. A couple of taps to the frame, and it slid open. Daisy leaned out to check on the piano. "It ain't going nowheres," she said. "No siree." She pulled her head inside and set the screen in place.

Daisy plopped down on a cobalt sofa abandoned by the previous tenant. Puffs of dust from the mohair cushions charged toward sunlight. She'd need to get rid of such a worn-out stick of furniture, but first she had to find someone to move the piano. The telephone wouldn't be installed till Monday, and Beverly was at home hosting her sister-in-law's baby shower, so the beauty shop downstairs was closed for the day. They had a phone booth across the street at Woolworths, but then again, who would she call? Frick and Frack down at Gallagher's Café? A professional mover whom she couldn't afford? Maybe it was better to stay put in case the men came back. Certainly, they wouldn't hang her out to dry. In times like these, she missed her father more than she thought possible. No doubt Tommy Davies would have found a way to get that piano up those stairs.

Enough fretting. She stood up and started sweeping out the studio. With each pass of the broom, she raised more dust than she contained, but the heavy varnish on the maple floorboards still shone through. She'd wait another ten minutes, and not a second more. That would give the Summerlins a chance at redemption, not that they deserved it. After that, she'd go over to the pay phone and call the widow Lankowski. Maybe she'd know what to do. Or her son Stanley. The poor man couldn't help Daisy himself, he'd lost his left hand in a mining accident as a boy, but maybe he could find a couple of able-bodied men and drive them over in his Oldsmobile. Of course, her mother would lose her mind if she found out. For some reason, Violet would rather die than ask Stanley for a favor, but desperate times meant desperate measures. And besides, Daisy was not her mother.

Even as a child, Daisy dreamed of a life bigger than Scranton. That's why she'd left home for good the day after high school graduation. No small-town living for her. She'd set out to perform onstage. And she'd made it too. Sure, it was only a chorus line in Atlantic City, but who knows how far she could have gone if she hadn't come back home when her father took sick? Not that she had any regrets. It's where she'd belonged. But now, here she was, over three years later, trading the stage for a studio. *When your dreams don't come true, you find different dreams.* She sighed. *And someone to move your piano.*

Those Summerlin brothers are going to get a piece of my mind, Daisy thought as she propped the broom against the wall and headed downstairs. Hopefully she'd figure out who to call by the time she made it over to the pay phone at Woolworths.

The instant her loafers hit the sidewalk, Daisy recoiled at the sight of a Negro man at her piano. Too tall for such a small instrument, he sat with his knees out and feet in, ready to work the pedals. Elbows on his thighs, his hands hovered over the keys like a praying mantis. Another time, Daisy might have found humor in such contortions, but the Summerlins had exhausted her goodwill.

"What're you doing?" Much to her annoyance, she sounded closer to tears than anger.

The man sprang up, toppling the stool. "No harm meant." He waved his hand as if to erase any misunderstanding. "Can't seem to pass by a piano without tickling the ivories."

Daisy took a deep breath to steady her voice. "This is my personal property."

"So it is." He righted the stool and coaxed it into place with the toe of his freshly polished shoe. "I'm very sorry."

The apology and the man seemed sincere, though Daisy's sudden need for grievance rendered her incapable of reason. "You think people just wheel their pianos outside for any Tom, Dick, or Harry to play?"

"No, ma'am." He buttoned the jacket of his gaberdine suit, fancy even by downtown standards, and adjusted his tie.

Daisy glistened now with perspiration in spite of her short-sleeved blouse. "And in this hot sun?"

"A fair point," he said, rocking back on his heels.

"Nothing's fair." Daisy dropped onto the stoop in front of the open doorway. "Not today." Her long dark hair fell forward, framing her watery blue eyes. "I have a piano that needs moving," she nodded up to the second floor of the building, "and a mother at home with an 'I told you so.'"

The man stretched over the top of the instrument and sized up the staircase before tossing his handkerchief to Daisy. "And here I am adding to your troubles," he said.

"No, you're not." She patted her tears. "You just showed up in the middle of them." Daisy stood and returned his hanky. "Thank you."

"We all have those days." The man turned to leave. "I hope yours gets better."

"Wait." Daisy measured him with her eyes, over six feet to be sure. She herself was five eight, and he appeared to be a good six inches taller. A sandstone skyscraper, the color of dark rum. Stately. Striking. What her friend Beverly would call a tall drink of water. "I'm sorry."

"No reason to be."

"Still." Standing at the back of the piano, she motioned for him to sit on the stool. "Why don't you play something?" A grudging smile passed her lips. "She's not going anywhere."

He hesitated for a polite second, then sat back down and folded himself into the instrument.

Daisy knew the song after the first few bars, number 219 in the church hymnal. "Just a Closer Walk with Thee." Surely that's what he was playing. The lyrics came to her, so familiar:

I am weak but Thou art strong;
Jesus, keep me from all wrong;
I'll be satisfied as long
As I walk, let me walk close to Thee.

She'd played that very song in church on countless occasions. She could see the page of music in her mind, the melody, the chords, and make them out as he performed; yet he went beyond the page, unearthing notes inside each measure, calling all fifty-eight keys for duty.

When the song ended, she wondered how long she'd been holding her breath. She held it a moment longer, staring at his now motionless hands.

"Holy mackerel," she finally said. "Now *that's* how you play a piano." Her gaze drifted toward his face. Jaw strong. Cheeks dimpled and full, especially with that smile. His eyes—dark, deep, round lakes—locked on hers, and she blushed. "I'm used to a more traditional arrangement."

"Whose tradition?"

Daisy had no idea how to answer such a peculiar question, so instead she said, "'A Closer Walk.' It's one of my favorites."

He began the song again, quieter this time, reverential, but with all the skill of his first performance. "My mama likes to say, 'Johnny, always start with a hymn. Let folks hear who you are.'"

"And who might you be?" she said, growing curious.

"Johnny Cornell. And you are?"

"Daisy Morgan Davies."

At that, Johnny began playing the main verse of "Daisy Bell," singing along for the first line, "*Daisy, Daisy, give me your answer do . . .*"

She surveyed him. "So, Johnny Cornell, where're you off to all spiffed up?"

"Went to see about a job down at the slaughterhouse." He pointed toward Washington Avenue, one of the streets connecting downtown to South Side.

Daisy's expression softened. "You must've been the best dressed man there."

"Let folks see who you are."

"And?"

"I got the job." He managed a seated bow. "Monday morning. My first day. Eight o'clock sharp."

"Glad to hear someone's having luck today." She gazed at the Summerlin brothers' milk truck parked on the street, then back at Johnny seated on the other side of the piano.

"I've been itching to sit down at a Tom Thumb ever since I saw Dooley Wilson play one in *Casablanca*." Johnny started in on the movie's most popular tune, "As Time Goes By."

"I always meant to learn that one," Daisy said.

Johnny's mouth dropped in feigned shock. "How long have you had this piano?"

"My whole life."

"And you've seen the film?"

"Every year it comes to town."

"Let me get this straight." Johnny arched an eyebrow. "You watched Humphrey Bogart and Ingrid Bergman fall in love to that song?"

"Again and again."

"And you never got the sheet music?"

Daisy raised her right hand. "Guilty as charged."

Johnny shook his head. "It's always the pretty girls who break your heart."

The compliment ignited Daisy's cheeks. "So, Johnny Cornell." She brushed off her blue jeans in an effort to avoid his gaze and suddenly regretted her casual attire. "Are you from around here?"

"Landed in Scranton a couple months ago. We were touring when the band broke up. Trombone player had a two-timing girl back home. Turns out she was two-timing with the saxophonist." He laughed. "Anyhow, here I was in a new town, not a plug nickel to my name, and Ferdie Bistocchi comes along and hires me for his band. Hell of a nice guy. Pays all his musicians fair and square. But man cannot live by music alone. Not yet anyways. I need to start saving up."

"For what?"

"New York City. That's the dream."

Daisy glanced up at her studio's windows. "What happens if you have to find a different dream?"

"I've got a few other ideas cooking. Sometimes I think about opening a club." Johnny scanned the buildings on Lackawanna Avenue. "Maybe here or Atlantic City."

Daisy's face lit up. "You know Atlantic City?"

"Yes, ma'am." He played the first line to the chorus of "California, Here I Come," but belted out the words "Atlantic City" instead. "Born and raised."

"Atlantic City, New Jersey." On Daisy's tongue, the words sounded more like a wish.

"You been there?" He sauntered through the rest of the tune with a lighter touch.

"Many times. I started out as one of Tony Grant's Stars of Tomorrow. Sang and danced on the Steel Pier the summer before my senior year."

He whistled his admiration. "You don't say."

"Mr. Wonderful. That's what they called him. Tony Grant. He liked giving young people a chance. A star-maker, he was." With one foot forward, she curved her right arm over her head, and angled her left in front of her, striking a ballerina's pose. "We performed three shows every day at the old Midway Theatre," she said, lowering her arms.

"Did you go all by yourself?"

"My Aunt Lily lives down there with her second husband. She promised to check in on me at the Franklin Hotel. That's where the talent stayed."

"And did she?"

"Not often," she laughed. "Then I moved down there after graduation. Danced in the floor show at the Rainbow Room of the Albion Hotel, much to my parents' dismay. Do you know it?"

"Never been inside myself. Not the kind of place someone

like . . ." Johnny glanced up at Daisy and traded one sentence for another: "I spent most of my nights over on Kentucky Avenue."

"At the Club Harlem?"

He blinked hard. "You know the place?"

"Been there often."

"How'd someone like you find out about it?"

"I go where the music takes me. That's my motto. Besides, everybody knows that place."

"Everybody?"

"Everybody I palled around with from the Albion. I once heard Mr. Louis Armstrong himself sing 'Blueberry Hill.' Didn't get to see him, though. The main room was full up, so we had to listen from the cocktail lounge. Still," Daisy beamed, "what a perfect thrill."

"Well, aren't you full of surprises."

"How's that?"

"Let's just say . . ." Johnny's head bobbed as he considered his words, "I wouldn't expect to see a white girl from Scranton on that side of the tracks."

"Is that so?"

"A lot of white faces in this town. I grew up in Northside, up from the Club Harlem. Negro families on every block. Businesses too. It's different here. Takes some getting used to."

"Not *so* different." Daisy felt compelled to defend her hometown even though she'd been eager to leave it. "I had two colored classmates in high school. A boy and a girl. I was friends with the girl, Mary Jane, before her family moved to Pittsburgh. Even went to her house a few times. My parents weren't too keen on it at first, but once they realized she didn't have any brothers, they let me go."

Johnny smirked.

"What's so funny?"

"Nothing. Nothing at all." He started singing her name again: *"Daisy, Daisy, give me your answer do."*

"All I'm saying is," she shook her hair, "Scranton might be more in step with the times than you think."

"Have you ever seen someone like me in South Side after sundown?" He dropped his eyes. "Scranton's no better, no worse than the rest."

Discomfort reared up in Daisy. "I never noticed . . ." She leaned against the building.

"Aw, come on," he said. "It's too beautiful a day for blues." His fingers took another turn at the piano. "Atlantic City," he said. "And a dancer no less. Now that's something."

Daisy perked up. "And a Tony Grant Star of Tomorrow." She bowed. "At the theater over by Steel's Fudge."

"I can taste it now." Johnny smacked his lips. "Best chocolate on the pier."

"Don't I know it."

"So what brought you back to town?"

"I was needed at home." Daisy looked down. "My father had a stroke. A terrible way to go."

"I'm sorry for your loss," Johnny said. "There's nothing like losing your daddy."

Daisy eyed his sad expression. "You too?"

"Yes, ma'am." He struck a handful of mournful notes. "A long time ago."

"My condolences."

Johnny bent his head, and they both held onto the sadness for a quiet moment.

"I loved Atlantic City though," Daisy finally said. "I'm not much for swimming, but oh, that ocean breeze." She closed her eyes and imagined the scent of salt water. "I felt so free. Nobody judging me."

"Did you ever see the diving horse? Now *she* was a sight to behold."

Daisy bristled. "That was cruel! Marching that poor animal up that ramp, making her jump into that pool." When she caught

Johnny smiling at her, she said, "How'd you like it if someone forced you to dive forty feet, day in and day out?" She folded her arms and waited for an answer.

"I would not." He squinted up at her. "Are you always this fiery?"

She peered over at the milk truck and back to Johnny. "Only when I have a piano that needs moving."

"Tell you what." He closed the lid, pushed back the stool, and stood. "I'll be back in a jiffy with reinforcements."

True to his word, Johnny Cornell returned half an hour later with a teenager covered in perspiration, his skin shining like polished cedar. "May I present James Williams."

"My buddies call me Chimsey." Sweat dripped off his face. "Been playing football over at the high school," he said by way of explanation, and if his broad chest and shoulders were any indication, he was good at it.

"And this," Johnny said, "is Miss Davies."

"Daisy," she said.

"How do." Chimsey turned his attention to the piano, lifting one end to get a sense of the weight. "You take the front."

"He's a bull," Johnny said, picking up his end. "This kid is going places."

"I can't thank you enough," Daisy said and scooted ahead of them.

Ten minutes later, Johnny and Chimsey had the piano up the steps and positioned against the opposite wall of the studio.

"You saved the day," Daisy said to them both as she rifled through her purse. "For your troubles." She held out a five-dollar bill out to Johnny. "Half for you," she said, "half for Chimsey. I'm sorry I don't have change."

"Your money's no good here," Johnny said. "Just helping out a fellow performer."

"I insist," Daisy said. "I had this for the movers. It's yours now. You two earned it."

"Tell you what," Johnny said, "Ferdie's band is booked at the Elks Club Saturday night. Grab one of your girlfriends, come hear us play. That'll be thanks enough."

Daisy's face flushed. "That's not much of a deal for you." She looked at Chimsey and pressed the money into his hand. "I'm paying *somebody* today."

Chimsey blinked, uncertain, but Johnny jumped in. "Just as well," he said, slapping the young man on the back. "You brought the muscle."

"I don't know what I would've done if you two hadn't shown up."

Chimsey made his way to the stairs. Johnny followed. When he hit the bottom step he called back, "Elks Club. Saturday night. Think about it."

"I will," Daisy said, when Johnny was out of earshot.

Well past nine o'clock, Frick and Frack stumbled up Washington Avenue carrying a spool of rope and a large pulley. When they turned onto Lackawanna, they stopped at the spot where the piano had been, glanced left, right, then at each other.

"Did you move it?" the taller man asked.

"Not me," his brother replied. "You?"

They stood for moment scratching their heads, climbed into the truck, and fell asleep.

CHAPTER THREE

SEVEN THIRTY IN THE MORNING seemed like an ungodly hour to be at the studio, but Bell Tell had said they'd send a man out on Monday to install the phone, and Daisy had forgotten to ask what time. Of course, most downtown businesses didn't open till ten. Nine at the earliest. Probably the same for the telephone company, but Daisy had more than enough work to do upstairs to justify the early start. Yet there she sat out on the stoop with a cardigan over her shoulders and a tin of fudge in her lap. She'd used her mother's recipe and the good baking chocolate from the back of the cupboard. Real cream too. If Johnny happened by on his way to the slaughterhouse, she wanted to have a proper thank you in hand.

Daisy glanced at the empty sidewalk and lit up at the memory of Johnny's long legs crammed under her piano. *Johnny*. Not John or Jay or some other amputated version of the name, but Johnny. It took a confident man to carry a moniker from his youth into adulthood. She liked that about him. Not that she knew him. But the thought of him and their mutual interests in music and Atlantic City had stayed with her these last two days. *Maybe he'll pass by*, she thought, drumming her fingers on the lid of the tin. She glanced up and down the empty block. *And maybe not.*

All the storefronts remained shuttered at that hour, including Bevy of Beauties. Across the street, a lady in the apartment above Dolitzky's Clothing began doing calisthenics in front of her open window. A minute later, an old red pickup, packed with bushels of produce, pulled around the corner. Laughing, the huckster behind the wheel honked his handheld horn, sending the woman running for cover.

And still no Johnny. Not that Daisy minded. No skin off her nose. She only wanted to make things right since he wouldn't take money for moving the piano. Just paying a debt. No more. No less. It's not as though she had any designs on him. Not to say he wasn't a fine man. He was, as far as she could tell. And a fine piano player too. But why court trouble? Assuming he even had an ounce of romantic interest in her. Not that she was entirely opposed to the notion in theory. Back in Atlantic City, a German girl from the chorus line dated a Negro boy who bellhopped at the hotel. Daisy was shocked at first. It had never occurred to her that people from different races might fall in love, but she got used to the idea after a while. You see the impossible become possible enough times, and it starts to feel ordinary.

Of course, that was in Atlantic City. Scranton might be another story. Sure, Daisy had felt obligated to defend her hometown to Johnny, but in truth, she worried he might be right about the backward thinking of her community. Not that it mattered. At least not as far as she and Johnny were concerned, because there was no "she and Johnny."

Daisy looked at the tin of fudge and suddenly felt silly. A few streets over, the courthouse chimed the quarter hour. "No time like the present," she said aloud and stood to go inside. As soon as she crossed the threshold, the sound of a whistled "Daisy Bell" caught her ear. She turned around and spied Johnny, this time in a work shirt and blue jeans, waving to her from a few doors down.

"It's good to see you," he said, trotting toward her.

"I made fudge," she called out, and immediately regretted her high-pitched enthusiasm.

"You don't say."

"By way of a thank you." She pressed the tin into his hands. "Probably nowhere near as good as Steel's."

"I'll be the judge." Johnny loosened the lid, grabbed a piece of fudge with his fingers, and took a bite. "Mmm-mm. Better than Steel's." He popped the rest of the square in his mouth. "Best I ever tasted. And that includes my mama's." He winked. "But I'll deny it if you tell her."

"Lying to your own mother," Daisy chided.

"Only when it comes to her cooking," Johnny said and grabbed another piece. "I may be a fool, but I'm not a *damn* fool."

"Lying and cussing," she teased. "It's a good thing you can play piano."

"Speaking of," Johnny leaned in and lowered his voice, "close your eyes."

Daisy's breath caught. Was he going to kiss her? Out on the public sidewalk?

"Have it your way," he said, when her eyes remained open. He reached around to his back pocket, pulled out a flattened roll of papers, and handed it to her.

Sheet music. Relief washed through Daisy, drowning out a whisper of disappointment. She uncurled the pages and examined the cover, a black-and-white close-up of Humphrey Bogart and Ingrid Bergman with the title *As Time Goes By* stretched across the top in a blue banner. "You shouldn't have," she said, delighted that he had.

"Didn't have a choice. You'd be ruined if people found out you couldn't play the one song that made Tom Thumbs famous."

"I would, would I?"

"That's not the kind of thing a man wants on his conscience."

"Well," Daisy rubbed her chin, "when you put it that way."

"I appreciate your understanding."

"How is it I keep finding myself indebted to you?"

"About that." Johnny put a hand in his pocket, trying for a relaxed pose. "Have you given any thought to the Elks Club this Saturday? I told them to hold two tickets for you at the door."

As Daisy considered the question, a green truck screeched to a stop in front of the building.

"Sorry." The driver stepped down from the running board, hurried around to the passenger side, and opened the door. "Brake pads are worn out." He plucked his tool belt off the seat and buckled it around his waist. "I keep telling 'em," he scrounged around till he found his notebook and a pencil, "but they don't listen." After slamming the door shut, he patted the large bell painted just below the handle. "Telephone company." His glance bounced from Daisy to Johnny and back again before checking his paperwork. "Davies?"

"That's me." Daisy raised her hand.

"Uh-huh." He eyed the pair for a long second, then walked to the back of his truck. "Have to grab a phone."

"What color?" Daisy wandered over to survey the inventory, hoping to find her local Bell Tell had started carrying some of the brighter models she'd seen in magazines.

"Any color you want," the man said, pulling out a box, "as long as it's black."

"Guess I'll take a black one, then."

"A fine choice." He tucked the box under his arm. "You lead the way."

When Daisy turned back, she found Johnny had disappeared.

C HAPTER FOUR

THE EARLY BIRD MAY CATCH THE WORM, Violet thought, but that didn't explain why Daisy had left for town hours before the stores opened. *She's a grown woman,* Violet reminded herself. *Time to let go. If only I knew how.*

With her mother still in bed, Violet tiptoed up to the attic, grabbed the card table, and carried it downstairs. After giving it a good scrub, she opened the legs and locked them into place. Now that the piano was gone, the parlor wall stood empty, save for the portrait of her sister Daisy, chalked from a sepia photograph taken the morning of her baptism, same day as the tragedy. The likeness captured the delicacy of her white dress and exuberance of the matching hair bow, but it didn't do justice to the child's beauty. Even so, the brass frame with its ribbon detail elevated the piece to a proper memorial.

Whether in this home or the one next door, the portrait had always taken pride of place over the piano. Now, without that anchor, Our Daisy appeared unmoored. Violet set the table against the wall, noted its flimsy appearance compared to the Tom Thumb, and said, "It'll have to do," as much to herself as to her sister's image. Besides, she thought, it would be good to have a permanent spot to do her work. No more setting up her paints in the dining room and putting them away for meals, as she'd done for years.

Violet unpacked her supplies—palette, brushes, pencils, paints, dyes, fluffs of cotton wool—and arranged them on the table. She'd started working as a colorist at Walsh's Portrait Studio the summer after high school graduation, hand-tinting sepia photographs into color. When she became a mother, Mr. Walsh allowed Violet to paint from home. She'd enjoyed the work, found it soothing in fact, and was sad to give it up for marriage, but Tommy wanted to support his new family, and a man's pride was more important than his wife's desires. However, two years later, Violet's father and Tommy's mother died a month apart, one from black lung, the other a gangrenous appendix. Grace moved in soon after, about the same time the coal mines began cutting back on production. Violet had set out to convince Tommy to let her work again. He bristled at first, but she softened the blow by referring to her wages as "pin money," and he relented.

Here she was all these years later, grateful to have a skill that could help make ends meet, though with the breakthroughs in color photography, she wondered how much longer she'd be needed. The work had slowed considerably in the last year, and Mr. Walsh's son, who'd taken over after his father's retirement, seemed eager to modernize the business. She should probably try to find a job outside the home, but the thought terrified her. For starters, she was no spring chicken. How would she keep up with women half her age? And if she went out to work, who would look after her mother or the widow Lankowski? And what about her duties as a church steward? Or her daughter? Yes, she was almost twenty-five, but not too old for worry. If only Daisy could find a man to support her. Then she wouldn't be tempted to take help from Lily or, more to the point, that husband of hers. Supposedly he'd cleaned up his act when they'd moved to Atlantic City, but Violet didn't buy that for one minute.

"She'll be glad to have the company." Grace stood in the doorway between the kitchen and the parlor, studying the portrait on the other side of the room.

"I'd like to think so," Violet said as she pulled a ladder-back dining chair over to the card table. "Didn't hear you get up."

"I was finishing my prayers." Grace patted her legs. "The old knees are shot, so it takes me awhile."

"Anybody home?" the widow called out as she pushed through the front door with her cane hanging from one arm and a blue-enameled bread box tucked under the other. A patch of rust bit through a bouquet of white tulips painted onto the lid. She elbowed the door behind her and it closed hard, sending several of Violet's brushes to the floor.

"Good morning, Mrs. Lankowski." Violet retrieved the brushes and dropped them into an empty canning jar. "What has you out so early?"

"We're all ready," Grace said.

"Ready for what?" The women now had Violet's full attention.

"The coast, it's clear?" The widow scanned the room.

Grace glanced behind her at the wall clock. "She's been gone over an hour already."

"Who's been gone? Daisy?" Violet followed the pair to the kitchen.

The widow placed the bread box in the middle of the table while Grace set sponges and bowls of water in front of three of the four chairs.

"Let's hope we have enough books," Grace said as she pulled an Acme grocery bag out from under the sink.

The widow peered inside. "I'd say more than enough." She turned back to the table and tried to lift the front corner of the bread box lid. "It's on there good," she said, moving from one corner to the next, her fingers permanently curled from a lifetime of lacework, first as a girl in Poland, then for decades here in the States.

Violet watched from the doorway. If the widow wanted help, she'd ask for it. At ninety-one, age may have robbed a few inches off her six-foot frame, but her independent nature remained intact. "I'm not feeble yet," the widow would say when anyone suggested she might not be up to a task.

With the corners loosened, the widow lifted the lid. "Ta-da!" Streamers of S&H Green Stamps sprung up as if startled from slumber.

"What on earth . . . ?" Violet's mouth dropped open. Since merchants issued one stamp for every dime shoppers spent, it had to have taken years to collect such a stash.

Grace beamed as she pulled handfuls of empty booklets out of the bag and put them on the table. "How many did he say?"

"How many did *who* say?" Violet asked.

"A hundred and fifty," the widow said as she sat down. "Give or take."

"Books?" Violet balked at the sheer audacity of the number. She could get a top-of-the-line sweeper for twenty-two. "Are you trading them in for a Cadillac?"

"They won't stick themselves," Grace said and tapped on the empty chair. "Now let's see if we can't get her a television."

"So that's it." Violet rolled her eyes as she sat down. "How'd she talk you into this, Mrs. Lankowski?"

"She can be very persuasive, your mother."

"Somehow, I don't think it took too much convincing." Violet glanced at Grace, who had settled into the work of pasting thirty stamps into the five-by-six grids on each of the booklet's forty pages. According to the instructions on the inside cover, completed books held a value of two dollars, to be redeemed for merchandise at the S&H Green Stamps store. "What's the point? They don't even carry televisions." Violet knew this for a fact. She'd practically memorized the catalog. Sweepers? Yes. Ceramic roosters? A matching pair. Ottomans? Three different styles, one of which would work perfectly in her parlor. They even had a four-piece set of TV tray tables, but no actual TVs. And as far as she was concerned, Daisy needed a television like she needed a hole in the head. That's what her Tommy would say if he were alive to see this. Violet picked up a loose stamp, licked the back, and winced at the taste of the glue.

"That's what the sponge is for," Grace said without looking up.

Violet reached for another stamp. "I'll be dead and buried before we reach a hundred and fifty."

The women ignored her ill humor in favor of their own conversation. Both Grace and the widow were known in the neighborhood for being tight-lipped, but when it came to each other, they shared gossip like missionaries spread the gospel. Fortunately, they'd both been to church the day before, a Protestant service for Grace, a Catholic mass for Mrs. Lankowski, so they had plenty of fodder.

"Myrtle's gallbladder flared up again." Grace fished out a strip of three stamps and pasted them into Violet's book to finish off her first row.

The widow peered over her glasses. "How many years since she had it out?"

"Seven, by my count."

"Her gallbladder . . ." the widow paused, as if to deny credence to that last word, "seems to act up every time Myrtle does."

"You certainly have her number." Grace completed her own book and placed it on the sink behind her.

"What set her off this time?"

"Potato salad."

Genuine alarm crossed the widow's face. "Spoiled?"

"In a manner of speaking," Grace smirked. "Pearl brought potato salad to Wednesday night's covered-dish supper, as did Myrtle. Folks favored Pearl's." She arched her eyebrow. "Myrtle took to her bed that night. Been there ever since."

"I don't know how that husband of hers puts up with it."

"My Owen never would have. God rest his soul."

Out of respect for the dead, the widow waited a moment before picking up the conversation. "Bad news about Mr. Katulis."

"Mr. *who?*" Grace asked. The glue made her fingers sticky, so she rinsed them in her bowl, and dried them on a dish towel.

"Katulis."

Grace shook her head as she picked up another book. "Don't know a Katulis."

"Sure you do." The widow eyed Grace's progress, looked back

at her own half-filled book, and frowned. "Katulis. From over on School Street."

"Not ringing any bells."

"Albert," the widow said. And then a little louder, "Katulis. You know him. From School Street."

Grace gave the matter serious thought. "Can't say that I do."

"Katulis." The widow plowed ahead: "He married that Lebanese girl from over in West Side." She waited a beat for a sign of recognition. "The one with the gold bracelets."

"Up both arms?" Grace nodded. "I know the one. What about her?"

"Not her. The husband."

"Albert?"

"That's right."

"What's wrong with him?"

"Shingles." Now that she had her story on its track, the widow delivered the worst of it: "Blisters bubbled up on his back," she lowered her voice, "but they're making their way around." She sorted through the bread box for a strip of six stamps, so she could complete a whole column at once. "And you know what they say."

Grace dropped her voice to match the widow's solemnity. "Shingles'll kill you if they meet."

"Exactly." The widow wet her stamps, slid them in place with her swollen knuckles, and fished out another strip of six.

"That's how Shirley met her reward." Grace scratched a spot on her own stomach to indicate where Shirley's shingles had converged.

The widow blanched.

Grace turned her attention to her now completed booklet. "Two down," she said as she started a pile. "One hundred and forty-eight to go."

The conversation shifted to Mr. Aukstones, who'd come over from England a dozen or so years earlier. He'd recently been stricken in a manner too delicate to spell out if the ladies wanted to stay in good standing with the Lord. Sufficeth to say, while Grace and the widow felt sympathy for the man, they also shared a sense of relief for his wife. After nine children, including a set of twins, she most likely welcomed the respite from marital relations.

Archie yelped in the backyard as if to contradict their conclusion.

"I'll let him in." Violet opened the kitchen door and watched as his butterscotch snout pushed through a hinged screened panel on the far end of a room that had once been a porch. Tommy had enclosed it in the forties. He'd wanted a place to pull off his boots and hang up his coat and overalls before stepping into the house proper. Since Archie was a part of the family by then, Tommy cut a spot at the bottom of the outer door, so the cocker spaniel could come and go as he pleased, provided the kitchen door stayed open.

"Where did you get to this morning?" Violet scratched the dog's neck as he poked his head farther into the house. Daisy must have let him out when she'd left for the studio. Archie liked to roam the neighborhood, sniff out a couple of cats, find the previous day's bacon grease spattered across a yard. Tommy had gotten him as a bird dog to flush out pheasants. He'd even built a doghouse and a run out back, but Daisy wasn't having it. The teenager was more concerned about the dog's comforts than his hunting abilities, so she took to sneaking him into her room. The first few times Tommy caught her, he'd tried to tell Daisy it's not right to make a house dog of out a hunter. It ruins the nose. But she didn't care about noses. She cared about Archie, her new best friend. It wasn't too long before Tommy gave up on having a bird dog and went back to shooting rabbits.

Now inside, the dog shook off the morning, followed Violet back into the kitchen, and curled up under the table at her feet. While her mother and the widow continued their chatter, Violet scratched Archie behind the ears and thought about what a godsend he'd been after Tommy's passing. Archie would nudge her awake in the first few months when waking seemed impossible. Slowly, she learned how to manage her grief. Begin with a wall calendar. Hang it prominently at the sink, so you can see the days coming. Brace for them. Holidays. Birthdays. Anniversaries. That was the trick of it. Get a running start. Throw yourself into preparation. Change traditions, or rearrange seating so his absence, any absence, isn't felt as keenly. No need to entertain in the dining room when a cozy kitchen will do. And the good china, a gift from his mother, didn't need to be pulled out this year. Make the day festive for the others, and you may just have a moment for yourself where you stop thinking about the thing you know you'll never forget, and maybe, if only for a minute, you can join the living.

As if sensing Violet's low mood, Archie stood up under the table and pressed his side against her thigh, allowing his warmth and steadfastness to be absorbed. Violet hugged him hard around the neck and cast her eyes toward the back porch. Even with its walls and outer door, they'd never stopped calling it the back porch. And there, on a hook alongside the washing machine, stood Tommy's overalls, because stand they did, in a manner of speaking. Three years after his death, the pant legs, slick with coal dust, stiff with sweat, held onto the form of the man who had worn them. The pyrite from the coal gave the fabric a metallic sheen that always put Violet in mind of the Tin Man. Had she ever told Tommy that? Had she ever thanked him for taking her and Daisy to see *The Wizard of Oz* the summer it came out? *Daisy was nine. Remember? We'd been married four years by then, and she was already your daughter in every way that counted. Hands down, the Tin Man was her favorite character in the movie. On the way home, she wondered if we could ask Doc Rodham about finding him a real heart.*

Archie gave a low growl as he curled up to sleep. Violet offered a tired smile to her tin man, hanging from a hook on the porch. He'd had the biggest heart of all, her Tommy, even after the stroke that shorted out his whole right side like a blown fuse. The doctor had said the hospital wouldn't be able to do any more for him, and besides, he'd be more comfortable at home. Nothing could make a difference but God's mercy. He'd last a week, maybe two. Even so, she left the overalls hanging on the hook. You can't take hope away from a man all at once. Hanging work clothes say, *You're not that bad off. Sicker men than you have recovered.* And it helped for a while. Eight months in all. It would have been a blessing too, if he hadn't suffered so.

Thank goodness for Daisy, though. She was the real blessing. Came home from Atlantic City right away. Didn't even have to be asked. And now she was getting ready to make her own way right here in Scranton. Violet lost herself in thought, dreaming a mother's dreams for her daughter.

As the morning wore on, Grace occasionally yelled out numbers like a bingo caller. "Sixteen books!" "Thirty-seven!" "Sixty-two!" At "Eighty-seven!" she got up from the table and pulled a cookie tin out of the cupboard. "I've been saving these for a rainy day." She dropped dozens of green strips, some as long as shoelaces, in or around the bread box.

A few loose stamps settled on Violet's booklet, bringing her attention back. "You've been holding out." Unlike the newer stamps with the red *S&H* insignia on front, her mother's had the word *Co-operative* written across the decorative oval. "How long have you had these?"

Grace aimed her chin at Violet. "Never you mind."

The widow grabbed several of Grace's strips to finish her book. "So what were you saying about Mrs. Henry's gout?"

"She hasn't had an attack," Grace said, "since her Chester stopped drinking."

"How'd that happen?"

"One night, she'd just had it. Beat him senseless with a sack of oranges when he was passed out. Woke up all black and blue the next morning. Hasn't touched a drop since."

"Where'd she get the oranges?" The widow finished her book and set it on the pile.

"She has a sister in Florida," Grace said. "Eighty-eight."

"I couldn't take that heat year-round." The widow fanned herself with an empty book and several stamps scattered.

"I'm always happy to see the next season when it comes."

"Funny how life works out. I'm forever grateful that my Stanley gave up the drink. Woke up one morning and said, 'Enough.' Went to his first . . ." the widow's voice dropped momentarily, "Alcoholics Anonymous meeting . . ." her volume picked up again, "that very day. Always had a strong character." Her voice cracked with pride. "Still goes over to the Polish Club now and again, but only for a soda."

And to meet Arlene, Violet thought. According to Evan Evans, who'd told his mother Myrtle, who'd told Pearl when they were on speaking terms, who'd told Violet. Arlene Wardell was a brazen one, to hear Pearl tell it. She'd sit right up there at the bar with him. Not even at a table. And according to Pearl, she'd park out front and skip the ladies' entrance. She had a husband somewhere. Never took measures to divorce him. Wanted to stay in good standing in the Catholic church. Violet groaned. She had to shake this peevishness.

"Ninety-nine!" Grace announced.

Really? Violet had no idea they were that close. She checked out the piles on the sink. "I'll be right back." She ran upstairs, grabbed a shoebox, and returned in under a minute. "I've made do with my push sweeper this long," she said. "Eleven more." She handed the already completed books to her mother.

"That's the spirit." Grace laughed. "One hundred and ten!" She pawed through the stamps. "I'll bet we have enough for at least six more."

The widow joined in: "And I bet he can find one for that."

"He who?" Violet asked. "How is it you always 'know a man' who's willing to bargain?"

Grace and the widow exchanged a quick look.

"A lady never tells her secrets." The widow crossed her arms.

"Whoever this one is," Grace said as she recounted the books, "we have to pay him what's due."

The widow scanned a nearby shelf. "Maybe we can sweeten the pot with a couple of jars of Violet's mustard pickle."

"If you think he'd take them." Violet allowed her excitement to catch hold. "And I still have a few jars of last summer's jam."

"Perfect." The widow started stacking the completed books inside the bread box while Grace pasted the last of the stamps onto an empty page.

"I'll carry that over for you," Violet said. "Or I can drop them off to your mystery man."

"All men are a mystery." The widow laughed. "He said he'd swing by before the birthday. I think he mentioned a Philco, if that's all right. People seem to like their Philcos."

"I don't know about brands," Grace said. "Any television will do, if you're asking me."

"What makes you think she even wants a TV?" Violet said. "I never heard her say one word on the subject."

"Then she'll be good and surprised." The widow collected her cane.

"One hundred and seventeen!" Grace called out. "All finished." She handed Violet the very full bread box and said, "I'll get the canned goods together after a cup of tea. Fingers crossed he's a man who barters."

"I think I can persuade him," the widow said. "He's a good man. Maybe someone for you, Violet."

"I've had my turn."

The widow shook her head. "You're young. Fifty."

"It's Daisy's turn. We need to get her settled," Violet said. "My dreams are for her now."

"That's the thing with dreams." The widow gave Violet's arm a squeeze. "You can have as many as your heart can hold." They moseyed into the parlor as a delivery truck from the Globe Store pulled up in front of the house.

"Daisy's dress is here." Violet set down the Green Stamps and opened the door.

"A package for Mrs. Davies," a deliveryman said as he climbed the steps.

"Right on time." Violet opened the screen door and reached for the box. "Thank you so much."

"I almost forgot." The man ran down to the truck and returned with a plate of something baked. "Mmm." He peeled back the waxed paper on eight thick wedges of corn bread. "A little bit of sunshine," he said, tucking the paper back under and handing her the dish.

"I didn't order . . ." Violet eyed the man.

He pulled a delivery slip from his shirt pocket and read a note on the bottom: *"For Mrs. Grace Morgan. A treat, by way of Zethray Long.* From the freight elevator," he clarified, "at the Globe Store."

"But how did she . . ."

"Well isn't that lovely." Grace stepped into the doorway and took the plate. "Please tell her we said thank you. Would you like a piece?"

"Already had mine. Zethray made me my own pan." He rubbed his stomach. "There's a note on the other side," he said, handing the slip to Violet.

"Wait," Grace called back as she headed toward the kitchen. "Give me a minute to put these on my own plate, and you can take Zethray's."

"You'll see her," the delivery driver said as he hurried down the steps and into his truck. "She's a fixture in that place!" he exclaimed, and pulled away.

Violet stood in the doorway long after the man drove off, long after the widow and Grace decided to sit back down in the kitchen to share a wedge of corn bread.

"Get it while it's hot." The widow aimed her words at Violet, still planted at the front door, reading the note: *You're the bravest girl she knows.*

The bravest girl? The message made no sense. Or it was some sort of a prank. That was it. A prank. Leave it to Violet not to get it. She never did like jokes. *You're the bravest girl she knows.* Violet balled up the paper and threw it in the dustbin across from her sister's portrait.

CHAPTER FIVE

DAISY STOOD ON A SIX-FOOT STEPLADDER, tacking half-moons of white butcher paper onto the tops of four arched windows overlooking Lackawanna Avenue. On the street side of each semicircle, bold red letters called out to passersby:

> *Song and Dance Studio*
> *Dance classes now forming*
> *Voice and piano lessons by appt.*
> *Call DI 4-0903*

She'd made the signs that morning after the Bell Tell man had finished installing her phone. Luckily, the paint had dried quickly, and it matched the color of the piano to a T, a nice touch since she could see a reverse image of the letters from inside the studio.

Daisy peered out the last window. Down below, the street teemed with shoppers bustling in and out of clothing stores, banks, and not one but two five-and-dimes on the same side of the block. Woolworths and Kresge's. Both had plenty to offer, but the downtown Woolworths reminded her of the one she used to frequent in Atlantic City.

And just like that she was back to thinking about Johnny. She'd spent the better part of the morning either delighted over his gift of sheet music, or disappointed because he'd left without a goodbye. If only she could settle on an emotion. *Better yet*, Daisy thought, *focus on the task at hand*.

From atop the ladder, she could see that the studio was almost ready. She'd already run a broom across the dusty ceilings, washed down the walls, tightened the screws on the ballet barre, and polished the floor and benches to a luster. Instead of throwing away the cobalt sofa, she'd scrubbed it down and covered the mohair cushions with an old hand-knotted bed quilt from home. Wooden folding chairs, in need of a good cleaning, waited against the wall—her last big chore before officially opening. Not bad for a week's work. Pleased with her efforts, she turned back and started down the ladder. Second rung from the bottom, her loafer heel caught, throwing her backward onto the floor. "Damnit!"

"Hello?"

Embarrassed by the fall and her language, she jumped up quickly and brushed herself off.

"Was you talkin' to someone?" A ginger-haired boy, no more than eight, appeared in the doorway.

"*Were* you," Daisy corrected as she fingered her scalp for the goose egg that was sure to rise.

"Not me." The boy snorted, puffing up his freckled cheeks. "I thought I heard you talking," he looked around, "but you's all alone." He stepped inside and ran his hand down the length of the ballet barre.

"*You are*," she said. "You are alone."

"Not anymore."

Daisy decided to ignore the boy's indifference to proper grammar and answer his original question. "I was talking to myself."

"Granny says that's where you get the best answers."

"Is that so." Daisy extended her hand to the boy. "I'm Miss Davies. I'm going to be the instructor here. And you are . . . ?"

"You're the dance teacher, right?" He kicked off his shoes and skidded across the hardwood floor in his socks.

"Dance. Voice. Piano for beginners."

He skated back. "Mickey McCrae, of the South Scranton McCraes. At your service." He doffed an imaginary cap. "We're part of a handful of Irishmen in a sea of Krauts and Pollacks. Granny says she don't mind. She can't eat too many foods because of her sugar, but she likes all the cooking smells. Says we're a regular United Nations down there in the Flats, and if you don't believe it, come take a sniff."

"Germans and Poles," Daisy corrected without much hope the boy would pick up on it.

"Exactly. With a few Guineas mixed in."

"Nice boys don't use such words."

"Don't mean no harm. That's how all the fellas talk at school."

"Well you're not with the fellas," she said. "Besides, what would your granny say if she could hear you right now?"

"Not a word." After a look of surprise registered on Daisy's face, Mickey grinned. "She'd probably be too busy washing my mouth out with soap."

"Exactly. And if she wouldn't use that language, neither should you."

"Granny treats all people the same. Says everyone's shite stinks. Ain't no exceptions."

Daisy dropped her head. "So what brings you here, Mr. McCrae?"

"Mickey."

"Mickey." She glanced at the clock on the wall behind the piano. "Why aren't you in school?"

"It's after school," he said, tapping his watchless wrist.

"But it's . . ." As she was about to call the boy out for his lie, she noticed the second hand frozen on the three. The hour and minute hands hovered near the eleven. "When did that stop working?" she wondered aloud.

"Around five to twelve by the looks of it," he answered sincerely. "Anyhows, Granny overheard Gertrude on the party line. She said something about you getting your dance school together, so Granny sent me up to give you a hand."

"Gertrude?"

"The old lady next door."

"Not old. *Elderly*. That's kind of your grandmother."

"She says it's good manners to offer help to spinsters."

"Spinsters?"

"Granny said it, not me."

"And what makes your grandmother think I'm a spin . . ." she forced her voice into a lower range, "not married?"

"Are you?"

"No."

"Figured as much." He threw his arms out at his sides and spun in place. "You'd be home having babies if you were." He twirled once more and wobbled to a stop.

"Your granny again?"

"Uh-huh."

"She sure has a lot to say." Daisy couldn't fault the boy for parroting his grandmother. Besides, at almost twenty-five and no steady beau in sight, the word *spinster* had a whiff of inevitability.

"Granny wants me to take dance lessons when you're up and running." He lifted his pant legs to reveal a slight bowing at his knees. "She thinks they'll straighten out with practice."

Daisy shook her head. "I'm not sure I . . ."

He smoothed his pants back down. "Granny asked her card club to recommend a dance teacher. Her friend Mrs. Beppler has a sister over in Providence who mentioned you. She says you come from a good Christian home, and that was good enough for Granny." He sat on the floor and tugged his shoes back on. "So?" Mickey surveyed the room. "What needs doing?"

"Well," Daisy glanced toward the far wall, "those chairs could use some elbow grease."

Mickey considered the task. "Looks like thirsty work," he said.

Daisy fished two nickels out of her pocket. "Run over to Woolworths and get us a couple of Cokes. We'll get to it after that."

"I can't accept," he said, scooping up both coins.

"You'll be doing me a favor. And we'll talk about those lessons when you get back."

As soon as she heard the door close, Daisy moved over to the bench along the wall and sat down. That had been a good hard fall earlier, and she wanted to check herself over for any injuries. A nice bump on the noggin, of course, and when she rolled up her sleeve, she saw another one on the elbow. She'd be sore tomorrow, but that was the worst of it, thank God.

What a day. First her fall, then Mickey. "He's something," she said out loud and laughed. "And the grandmother!" A smaller laugh started and stalled as if caught on a fish bone at the back of her throat. "A spinster, indeed." And how had she arrived at that conclusion? Small-town gossip, that's how. Daisy hated gossip, always had. Even when she was too young to grasp the meanness that fueled it, she saw it for what it was. Righteous people standing on other people's sins. Take for example that spring day she went out to play hopscotch in front of her grandparents' house. She couldn't have been more than five or six when she heard Myrtle Evans and her sister Mildred talking and scraping their chairs to the front of their porch to peer past their awning.

"It's the Morgan girl," one of them said.

The other one corrected, "Davies. He gave her his name when he married the mother."

Daisy had stopped playing hopscotch and begun chalking flowers on a clean piece of slate. She thought about the roses her mother had carried the past fall when she'd married Daisy's daddy. It was her first wedding. Her Grandma Morgan had made her a special dress, and someone had baked a red velvet cake for dessert. Daisy loved everything about that day. Her mother looked so beautiful. Her father so handsome. Someone took a photograph of them. It was meant to stay on top of the radio cabinet in the parlor, but Daisy liked to sneak it up to her bedroom sometimes.

"She roped herself a good one. I'll give you that." Myrtle this time. Daisy knew because she'd peeked over to see what had been roped.

"To think they took that little girl to the wedding." Mildred shook her head. "That's called a travesty in my book."

Both sisters had rested their elbows on the porch banister. Myrtle aimed her nose at Daisy. "Who do you think she takes after?"

"The mother, of course." Mildred craned her neck. "You can see it in the features, same dimple, same dark hair."

Daisy smiled. People often commented favorably on her likeness to her mother, though she had her Aunt Lily's blue eyes.

"She's going to be a tall one," Myrtle noted, and Daisy sat up a little straighter.

"Must get that from Tommy's people. Was his side tall? The father died so young I can't remember."

"Tommy? You think it's Tommy?" Myrtle snorted. "Too short. And look at her. Have you ever seen a Welshman with olive skin?"

"Are you suggesting . . ." Mildred's hand flew to her mouth.

"More than suggesting."

"I don't believe it. She has to be Tommy's. Why else would he have married her?"

"All I'm saying . . ." Myrtle shifted sideways as if to share a secret, but her volume remained unchanged. "The Tommy Davies I know wouldn't have waited five years to make an honest woman out of her. He's too good a man for that."

Long before Daisy had worked out the details of that conversation, she tried on the shame of it as she would a coat from her mother's closet, and, mistaking familiarity for fit, she made it her own. First, she stopped talking about the wedding. Something was off in the order of events. Other children had not witnessed their parents' nuptials. Other mothers hadn't waited to get married until their children were older. By third grade, when she'd heard the expression "born out of wedlock," she knew it belonged to her story. And her mother's.

She never looked too closely at her father's part in it. Mildred had been right. He was a good man, and more importantly, a good father. Daisy's father. No, this was her mother's doing. Whatever had happened, it was her mother's decision. Or her mistake. One that Daisy vowed not to make. She'd hold onto her virtue because her mother had given hers away.

"It's hotter than blazes out there!" Mickey yelled as he climbed the studio stairs. "Going to be a scorcher of a summer if this keeps up." He ambled over to the bench and handed Daisy an opened Coke. "May the good Lord take a liking to you," he tapped her bottle with his, "but not too soon."

Daisy grinned. "What am I going to do with you, Mickey McCrae?"

Two Cokes and twenty folding chairs later, Daisy wiped her brow on a clean rag while Mickey used his sleeve for the same purpose. "Should we stack them?" he asked.

"Let's leave them open. Give the polish a chance to dry. Besides," Daisy said, "it's getting late, and you need your supper."

Mickey stood up and stretched. "Granny'll be happy to hear about the lessons," he said.

"Remember: Wednesdays at four o'clock. Starting next week. Tell your grandmother the first month is on the house for all your hard work."

"Thank you kindly," he said, once again tipping his imaginary cap. As he turned to leave, barking erupted in the alley behind the building. Mickey ran over to the closest open window and leaned past the sill. "You all right down there?"

"Right as rain," someone responded.

Johnny. Daisy recognized the voice and kneeled next to Mickey, poking her head through the same open window.

"Saw this poor fella on my way to work," Johnny called up as he held out his hand to the dog. "Nothing but skin and bones. Thought he might appreciate a few scraps from the slaughterhouse."

"You thought right." Mickey stretched farther to see the stray. "His tail's wagging."

Daisy grabbed the back of the boy's shirt to keep him from falling as she addressed Johnny: "So that's where you disappeared to."

"Couldn't be late for work my first day. How's that song coming along?"

"Haven't gotten to it yet. My helper and I have been busy today." Daisy tipped her head toward the boy. "Johnny, this is Mickey, my very first dance student."

Johnny saluted. "Pleased to meet you, little man."

"Likewise." Mickey elbowed Daisy. "It's a regular United Nations around here too."

Daisy looked at the boy and determined he meant no ill will, so she picked up her conversation with Johnny: "We've been cleaning all day." She finger-combed her hair. "I'm an absolute mess."

"You mean it gets better?" Johnny said with a smile. "Hardly seems fair to the other girls in town."

Now that's a good compliment, Daisy thought. "Why don't you come up to see what we've accomplished?" As soon as the question left her lips, she chastised herself for being so forward.

"Not till I've had a good scrubbing." Johnny made of show of pulling the front of his shirt to his nose and grimacing. "Slaughtering sticks to a man. Only dogs can stand me."

She *had* been too forward. "Suit yourself." Her words sounded sharper than she'd intended. "Another time then." *A little better. What's the matter with me?* she thought as she moved back from the window. *Did you really want him to come up? Of course not. You were just being polite.*

Johnny yelled from the alley, "Will I see you at the Elks Club on Saturday night?" His words, like an unexpected gust of wind, swept her mind clean of reason.

"Yes." The answer slipped out before a second thought had a chance to catch it.

I'm gonna lay down my sword and shield,
Down by the riverside . . .

The Scranton Truth

AUGUST 9, 1916

DAUGHTER IDENTIFIES NEGRESS WHO LEAPED FROM BRIDGE

SCRANTON, WED.—The Negro woman who committed suicide in Scranton yesterday by leaping into the swollen waters of the Lackawanna River was identified as Ruth Jones, a housemaid for the family of gentleman farmer Arthur P. Spencer IV, one of Scranton's most prominent residents. Mr. Spencer's great-grandfather, Arthur P. Spencer Sr., was an early settler in Scranton, back when it was still known as Slocum's Hollow. The Spencer name is inscribed in the annals of our fair city's history alongside Abbott, Scranton, Slocum, and Tripp. According to Mr. Spencer, his wife's nerves are wracked over losing their faithful servant. Mrs. Arthur Spencer, the former Henrietta Wilson, is one of the founding members of the Women's Century Club. She currently serves on the committee for Scranton's semi-centennial parade. Though her spirits have been dampened, Mr. Spencer assured us that his wife intends to resume her committee duties early next week, a noble gesture given the shocking circumstances of her maid's demise.

The tragic death may have gone unnoticed, save for Patrolman Norman Barnwell who, while walking his beat, came upon a dining room chair on the Lackawanna Avenue Bridge. He quickly deduced the chair had been used as a means to climb up and over the railing.

Mrs. Jones's body was recovered by two rivermen with grappling hooks. She is survived by her daughter, Zethray, 14. A funeral announcement will be made later.

CHAPTER SIX

"Ruth," Grace said aloud to an empty kitchen as she finished the last wedge of corn bread, "your Zethray did you proud." She pressed a few crumbs onto her finger and into her mouth. "A day later and still moist. Heaven on earth." She set her dish in the sink, put on her gray cardigan, and ambled out to the front porch.

With Daisy at the studio and Violet on her way downtown to return Zethray's plate, Grace settled into the closest of two wicker rockers. A pleasant breeze carried the promise of budding lilacs and longer days. Grace was blessed, no question about it. After her husband Owen passed, she'd had family to take her in. Not everyone was so fortunate. Johanna Lankowski for one. There was Stanley of course, her rock, but he'd moved out after law school, so she spent most days rattling around that house by herself.

Grace was grateful for her situation, but she also appreciated a pocket of silence now and again. It gave her a chance to sort out her thinking. Lately, some unnamed truth had been vying for her attention, but at seventy-five, old memories had a way of cutting to the head of the line. What she needed was a breather—some fresh air and an hour alone to let her mind wander. An hour without Violet fussing over her. Grace shouldn't complain, she was loved to be sure, but sometimes her daughter was too careful, too attentive. Nobody treated the widow that way, and she was older by a long shot. Then again, Grace's family had always watched her for signs of decline, the hint of a backslide. And to be honest, she'd given them reason. After the death of her daughter Daisy, she'd danced with Grief a little too closely and had nearly made a home with him. As much as she regretted the pain it had caused her family, she never could figure out a right way to mourn. *Fill the void,* they'd said. *You have another child who needs you. Not everyone is so lucky.* But she didn't want to fill the void. She wanted to live in it with her grief and her daughter's memory.

She thought of the coal mines where Owen had spent half his life. No sunrise or sunset to mark time. No change in temperature to indicate seasons. Day after day, he worked deep in the earth, near where the dead resided. Where Grace resided after her daughter's passing. Not in the mines, but cozied up with the dead just the same. If she stayed still in a place that eluded the normal measures of time, then maybe time itself would cease.

But there was no escaping it. Even an instant was time enough to set a child's dress on fire, time enough to change the world.

An instant. The thought put Grace in mind of a day back in 1903, long before Daisy's accident. Owen had coaxed Grace away from her chores to see what he promised would be a spectacular sight. The roof of an abandoned mine shaft had given way in Olyphant, two towns over, causing one of the largest cave-ins in memory. Extra streetcars had even been added to the line to accommodate the swarm of gawkers.

When they arrived, Grace stood stunned at the extent of the horrific devastation. Houses, hotels, and a Chinese laundry had fallen into a half acre–wide hole. A few remaining buildings teetered at the brink, waiting their turn. The subsidence took seconds, according to those who'd survived to tell the story. Worlds had collapsed in the time it took to throw back a drink or drop off a soiled suit.

Grace shivered. Or clean up after spilling a huckleberry pie. That's what she had been doing when she'd heard her daughter screaming in the yard that Fourth of July in 1913. And in that instant, the earth opened up and swallowed Grace whole the way it did the dead, and there she stayed long after what others deemed an acceptable time of mourning. When Grace finally emerged—

pulled out by Owen and Violet and the birth of Lily—she brought back a piece of that earth and dressed herself in its colors.

And here she was, forty-two years later, still turning it over in her mind. Forty-two years? That couldn't be right. But it was. *Where does the time go?* She glanced at the empty rocker next to her. There sat Owen—at his best. Twenty-five, if he was a day. Boyish. Trim. Content. The cuffs on his trousers and shirtsleeves rolled. His feet bare. Those gray-blue eyes silvered by the sun.

"I miss our girl," Grace said, her voice low so the neighbors wouldn't hear her talking to her long-dead husband.

You'll see her soon enough, Owen told her.

"I imagine so." *I wonder how she'll look*, Grace thought, glancing at Owen, so handsome and spry. *Do people age on the other side?* A dozen or so years after Daisy's passing, Grace had walked up to Mr. Bonser's grocery store for a pound of flour. She'd noticed the dark windows before she got close enough to read the sign on the door: *Closed for Gloria's wedding.*

Gloria? Grace had thought. Daisy's best friend Gloria from third grade? It couldn't be. The Gloria that Grace knew wasn't anywhere near old enough to marry. She and Daisy were the same age, and Daisy was still nine years old. Grace had cried all the way home to Spring Street.

Life goes on, Owen said from his rocker.

"So it does." Grace's brow furrowed. "I just wish I understood why."

God's will, he said. *There's your answer.*

"Baloney." Grace hated that expression. What God would will such a tragic and painful death on a child? No. She dismissed the answer out of hand. She had to. Otherwise, she couldn't make peace with her God, and she needed to make peace with Him if she wanted to see her child in the hereafter. Grace wouldn't risk losing her a second time.

The breeze picked up, and Grace wrapped one side of her cardigan over the other like a bathrobe. How long had she worn this sweater? Long enough for the cuffs to pill. Long enough for the color to fade from slate-gray to ash. An easy fix, she thought. A little Rit dye would do the trick. She'd ask Violet to pick some up the next time she went to the Acme.

Violet, Owen said.

"I know." When they'd lost Daisy, Grace's grief kept her from grasping eight-year-old Violet's pain. She'd been in the yard when her sister's dress had caught on fire. That alone should have brought Grace to her surviving daughter's side, but nothing and no one could rouse her from her own despair. Worse yet, Grace not only ignored Violet, she'd blamed her for throwing the sparkler. Not for long, mind you, but a mother's betrayal cuts quick and deep. Grace had been out of her mind with grief, after all, but the child deserved to be comforted, not accused. Still, Violet had forgiven her.

In the time it took for Grace to come back to her senses, Violet had learned to ignore her own needs in favor of others, a lesson that would shape her life. When Lily was born to Grace eight months after Daisy's passing, Violet had assumed responsibility for her baby sister's care. She was nine by then and already knew she was stronger than her mother. Sixteen years later, when Lily became pregnant out of wedlock, it was almost natural that Violet had claimed the infant, sacrificing both her reputation and her future with Stanley.

Yes, Stanley.

Grace had known about their secret engagement, even if they'd never spoken of it to her. Mixed marriages between Protestants and Catholics had been taboo in those days. Still were in most circles. Owen thought Tommy was a better match when he started coming around, but that didn't erase Violet's hurt over losing Stanley. Lasting love doesn't take the place of first love. It moves in next door. If you're lucky, it grows into a sprawling mansion, but first love stays put—a warm cottage on a cold night.

You're too sentimental. Owen sighed.

"She hasn't had it easy, is all I'm saying." Grace peered at the rocker. "And then you up and die, and Tommy too."

Owen tipped his head toward hers. *It's a part of living.*

"I don't need platitudes."

What do you need, my love? He gave her a playful wink.

Grace's face lit up. "A television for Violet."

Owen straightened. *I thought it was for Daisy.*

"I watched one over at Pearl and Carl's last month. A program called *I Love Lucy*. We laughed like fools." Her buoyant moment turned heavy. "I want to put laughter back in the house."

Now that's an idea. Owen folded his hands in his lap and closed his eyes.

"And color," she said, picking at the sleeve of her ash-gray cardigan.

And color, Owen repeated.

No sense waiting. Grace got up from her rocker, went into the house, and returned to the porch with her purse on her arm. If she set out now, she'd be gone and back before anyone missed her. The Acme was sure to have a nice selection of Rit dyes. All she had to do was pick a color.

I always loved you in pink, Owen said, smiling as he drowsed.

CHAPTER SEVEN

THE PREVIOUS DAY'S GIFT OF CORN BREAD was a lovely gesture, but as Violet entered the Globe Store, she couldn't help feeling annoyed. It was as if Zethray had wanted to obligate Violet to come back downtown for the second time in a week to return the plate. And this wasn't just any plate. It was Haviland china. Violet recognized the pattern, with its clustered roses and coin-gold edge. It matched a plate in her own cupboard, the only one left from her grandmother's set. A dish like this would cost a pretty penny to replace.

Violet stopped in front of the fragrance counter, set down the plate, and wiped her brow. Only ten days into May, and the heat already felt oppressive. Since no one was around, she crossed her arms, pressing her blouse under her breasts to absorb runnels of perspiration. Was this the weather or her age? As she pondered the question, Violet smoothed her top, and in the process, caught the edge of a perfume bottle and knocked it on its side.

"Tabu. A daring choice."

Violet looked up to see a twentysomething salesgirl with a poof of red curls on top of her head appear in front of her. "I'm so sorry."

"According to the ad," the girl said as she picked up the perfume and dabbed a generous amount onto a small square of paper, "it's a forbidden fragrance."

"My husband doesn't like . . ." Violet thought to correct herself, *My husband* didn't *like*, but she decided not to put that burden on the girl. "He doesn't like perfume, so I never wear it."

"You don't know what you're missing," the girl said, handing the paper over. "For your purse or your drawer of unmentionables." She put a finger to her lips. "It'll be our secret."

"Thank you." Violet inhaled the scent, a potent blend of floral and spice. "Very daring." She picked up the plate.

"And forbidden," the girl teased.

Violet slid the paper into her dress pocket next to the crumpled note from Zethray. *You're the bravest girl she knows.* After much speculation, Violet had concluded the message wasn't intended for her. Zethray must have written the address on a delivery slip without knowing someone had scribbled something on back. That had to be it. So why had Violet taken the note out of the dustbin and tucked it in her pocket the morning it arrived? She shook off the question and continued down the aisle toward the ladies' shoes department on the right. Multiple tables of sandals, pumps, and flats lined the way to the freight elevator.

"You can't go back there," a gruff voice called out from the doorway of a nearby stockroom. "Employees only." A ruddily complected man kicked a cardboard box labeled *Decoration Day* out into the aisle and pushed it against the wall.

"I'm trying to find Zethray." Violet held up the plate as if to explain her purpose. "Zethray Long." *As in long gone*, she added in her head.

"She's in the storage area putting away the Easter decorations." He waved toward a stairwell. "Go down to the bargain basement. You'll see a pair of swinging doors past budget men's. She should be inside." He kicked out another box and lined it up with the first. "And when you find her, tell her to get a move on," he said, his brow slick with sweat. "Memorial Day is coming, and these flags won't hang themselves."

Violet couldn't decide if she should thank the man for his help or chide him for his rudeness. Instead she headed downstairs without a word, found the swinging doors, and pushed her way through. On the other side, a long concrete ramp stretched into a harshly lit subbasement brimming with Christmas. A pair of ten-foot toy soldiers stood watch over a large sleigh filled with plaster figures from the Globe Store's Nativity set. At the opposite end of the room, yards of old tinsel corralled at least fifty bowling ball–sized ornaments, and waist-high candy canes poked out from cardboard boxes. An assortment of carolers, elves, and angels stood at the ready, dusting the shelves with glitter. It was as if Violet had entered a wonderland straight out of Lewis Carroll's disordered imagination.

"I hope you're on his list." Zethray peered out from behind Santa's velvet-covered throne. "Only good girls and boys are allowed at the North Pole."

"A man upstairs . . ." Violet stammered.

"I'm teasing with you, Miss Morgan. Come on in."

"Davies. My married name." Embarrassed for correcting Zethray, she said, "But please, call me Violet."

"Well, Violet, Easter's all put up." Zethray wiped her hands on her smock, limped over to a tufted ottoman, and sat down.

Violet glanced beyond the Christmas trimmings and noticed painted wicker baskets carefully stacked on top of crates labeled *Eggs, Bunnies, and Flowers*. "It's funny. I've always admired the Globe's decorations, but I never once thought about where they were stored."

Zethray swept her arm around the room. "Hearts. Pumpkins. Horns of plenty. We got 'em all and then some." She motioned toward Santa's chair. "Go ahead. He won't be needing it for a while." When Violet remained standing, Zethray said, "I have to give my foot a rest from time to time," she bent down and untied her orthopedic oxford, "away from prying eyes."

"That reminds me. There's a man near the shoe department who asked me to hurry you along."

"Little guy with a sour puss?"

"He seemed angry."

"Good thing I don't scare easy." Zethray wiggled her twisted foot out of the shoe. "How's your mother?"

"I have your plate," Violet said, holding it out.

"I knew you was good for it." Under the glare of fluorescent lighting, Zethray's brown eyes sparkled like new pennies.

"She loved the corn bread. We all did. But her especially. It brought back good memories."

"Glad to hear it." Zethray set the plate on the floor next to her and rubbed her ankle. "Most days it's easier to mine the dark ones."

Violet considered the statement. "Why is that?"

"Unfinished business. We turn the dark days over and over, wondering our way to a different outcome. No need to chew on the good ones. They worked out fine on the first go around."

Violet considered the truth of the remark. How often had she brooded over her sister's accident? "Well, thank you." Violet shivered and changed the subject: "The corn bread was quite a treat."

"Taste and smell," Zethray said, "two straightest lines to the past. My mama taught me that."

"A wise woman." Violet turned toward the ramp. "Speaking of mothers, I better get back to mine."

"I once had a doctor who told me he could do something about this foot, but I said no." Zethray worked her shoe back on but kept it unlaced. "Not sure if I was more scared of having the operation or losing a part of Mama. I don't have much to remember her by. A paperweight with her picture. An old chair. One of her aprons. She liked to dress them up with a little embroidery. She was funny that way."

"I'm sure you miss her."

"Every day. I'm lucky, though. She comes to me. Never says a word, but I can guess what's on her mind."

"Comes to you?" Violet echoed.

"I get visitations now and again." Zethray took a beat before adding, "From the dead." She adjusted her stocking. "Had 'em as long as I can remember."

Violet gasped. "I don't know about that."

Zethray chuckled. "You don't have to."

"The Bible frowns on . . . I'd be drummed out of the church if they knew I was a party to such talk." She shook her head. "It's not God's way."

"You know His ways?"

"I know my Bible."

"And I know I'm a child of God, same as you." Zethray tied her shoe and stretched her legs. "He give me a gift, so I use it, is all."

"It's not real," Violet said. "It can't be."

"Funny how people always saying, 'Anything's possible with God,'" Zethray pointed left, "'except this here,'" and pointed right, "'and that there.' Either anything's possible or it's not, if you ask me."

"I'm sorry," Violet said, "I really have to go," but her feet wouldn't cooperate.

"Lately, she's been coming to me with a little white girl in a dainty white dress with a bow blooming from her hair. Couldn't figure out why. Mama never brought me no white girl before. I'll confess, it scared me a little. I like to keep with my people." She nodded to Violet. "You understand."

Violet nodded back.

"I assumed it was the same way on the other side."

"Why are you telling me this?" Violet patted her brow with her sleeve.

Zethray plowed on: "I couldn't figure it out, but then you and Mrs. Morgan showed up at the store, and that little girl got to jumping, excited as could be. And still, I wasn't having it. I said, 'Mama, don't make me go where I'm not wanted,' but she didn't listen. Never did. So I sent the corn bread. The rest was up to you."

Just for a moment, Violet's curiosity overcame her dismay. "How'd you know I'd show up?"

"Easy. You know the value of the plate." Zethray gazed past Violet, toward a far corner of the room. "You're too good a woman not to return it."

"This is all too much." Violet waved her hands.

Zethray's eyes dimmed. "You're the bravest girl she ever knew."

Violet patted the note in her pocket. "Don't say that. I'm not brave."

"And she's proud."

"Who?" Violet asked, blinking hard.

"The little girl."

"Of what?" Violet's legs started to give, so she dropped onto the velvet throne.

"Of you and the way you've lived your life." Zethray's eyes remained dull, but her tone sounded matter-of-fact.

"I've done no better, no worse than most," Violet said.

"Not true. Leastways, not according to her." Zethray studied the air. "She's pretty. Strong enough resemblance to be your daughter. But she's from another time."

"My sister." The words slipped through Violet's reluctant lips.

"Your big sister." Zethray chuckled. "'And don't you forget it,' she's saying."

A fleeting smile crossed Violet's face. "Is she really here?"

Zethray tipped her head. "What is it?"

Goose pimples peppered Violet's arms. "What's what?"

"Not you." Zethray bent forward. "I'm asking *her*. She's holding something."

In spite of her own beliefs, Violet turned to see what Zethray saw. Crates marked *Summer*. A few clothing racks. An old dress form. Nothing unexpected. She sighed, relieved, but a whimper of disappointment bubbled up on the end of her breath. She looked to see if Zethray had noticed, but the woman now sat still as stone.

Two long tubes of fluorescent light buzzed overhead. One of the bulbs flickered, and Zethray stirred. "It's some sort of flower. I can't quite make it out. An aster? No. A black-eyed Susan?"

"A daisy." The answer flew out of Violet's mouth before her mind had a say in the matter.

"Almost." Zethray squinted. "She's holding up two fingers."

"Two Daisys." Violet put her hands together as if in prayer. "Please. No more." She bolted up from her seat.

"She's said her piece." Zethray stood, appearing smaller somehow. "I've done my part." She steadied herself against the back of Santa's chair. "Lord knows I never mean any harm. They come to me, and won't let go till I speak their truth."

Violet opened her mouth but couldn't find words, so she headed for the ramp on shaky legs.

"She says it doesn't matter how or why," Zethray called out. "Only that you claimed that baby. She's yours. Don't let anyone tell you different."

Holding her breath, Violet pushed through the swinging doors and ran up the steps. Back on the main level, she found a bench near the baked goods counter and sat down to collect herself.

On the other side of the counter, out of Violet's view, Stanley stood at a metal easel, studying the store's directory. "Televisions. Televisions." He ran his finger down the list of departments until he landed on the word. "Third floor," he said to himself and headed toward the elevator.

CHAPTER EIGHT

A HEAVILY PREGNANT WOMAN sat in front of Stanley's desk, balancing an S&H Green Stamps catalog on her stomach. Other than an occasional "ooh" or "aah," she silently thumbed through the baby goods section, folding down pages that seemed to catch her eye. Diamond-shaped gussets, sewn into the side seams of a plaid housedress, accommodated her growing belly.

Stanley sat at his desk, mindlessly staring at the mirror image of his name and profession on the plate-glass transom over the front door of his office. From the street it read:

Stanley Adamski
Attorney-at-Law

Adamski. He'd kept the name for the sake of his father who'd died on the same day Stanley had lost his hand. Same coal mine too. What were the odds? Better than good, Stanley concluded. And because his mother had passed years earlier from rheumatic fever, the widow Lankowski stepped in and gave the orphaned ten-year-old a home. When the courts finally made the adoption legal, the widow encouraged Stanley to keep his last name. "It's all he had to give you," she'd said of his father, a generous sentiment considering the guy's quick temper and his taste for liquor. But that was Babcia—Stanley's nickname for the widow, Polish for *Grandmother*. She always looked beyond the sins of a man to see his worth.

"I don't know how we'll ever thank you," the pregnant woman

said as she folded down another page in the catalog. "He's been out of work eight months already."

"He never should've been fired." Stanley stopped himself from reciting precedent on the matter. He'd save that for his meeting with the husband.

"The timing couldn't have been worse." The woman shifted in her seat, trying for a more comfortable position. "I held onto my secretarial job as long as I could, but they let me go as soon as I started showing." She blushed.

"He had the legal right to unionize his fellow garment workers." Stanley's face reddened. "Guess they forgot about a little something called the National Labor Relations Act." He pounded the desk. "This is America, for God's sake."

The woman began crying for the third time in the half hour since Stanley had returned from the Globe Store. "This can't be good for the baby," she said, but the tears continued to flow.

"Tell you what, Mrs. Hinkley. I'll worry about the case, and you worry about the nursery." He glanced at the catalog. "Find anything of use?"

The woman wiped her eyes and pulled her chair sideways toward the desk, so she could lay the catalog out between them. "They have it all!" She flipped through to find the folded pages. "Here." She pointed to an aluminum-framed baby carriage in navy. "It can double as a bassinet." She beamed at her thrift while thumbing another page. "Bottles, diapers, receiving blankets, layettes . . ." Her finger hovered over an enamel sterilizer, then dropped. "I think we can boil the bottles in my mother's corn pot," she said, moving on to another item. "How many books?"

"One hundred and seventeen."

"How on earth did you save that many?"

"I'm a sucker for sweets. The Acme has the best gumdrops around." Stanley pushed out his stomach and patted it with his handless arm. When the front of his pinkish stump peaked out through his sleeve, the woman went pale. Stanley immediately dropped his arm and asked, "Can I get you some water?"

"This happens," Mrs. Hinkley said, holding a hanky to her mouth. "It'll pass." A moment later her color started coming back. "Everything sets me off these days. You should see me cleaning chicken. Don't know what's worse, the sight or smell of it."

"I have an idea." Stanley closed the catalog and handed it to the woman. "Take this home. Go through it good and make your list." He stood up, walked around the desk, and helped her up from her seat. "Your husband can pick these up," he said, holding an Acme bag full of Green Stamp books.

"I'd like to save him the trip."

"You're carrying enough." He gestured toward her pregnant belly. "Howard can grab them on his way to the S&H store. It'll give me a chance to go over his case with him."

After a silence long enough to make them both uncomfortable, she said, "He's a proud man, my Howie."

"No reason not to be."

"He doesn't believe in taking charity."

"It's a helping hand," Stanley said, "for the baby."

"Exactly. That's how I talked him into letting me come down here after you called about the stamps. But he doesn't want to face you. Not for this."

"Understood." Stanley escorted her to the door and handed her the bag. "Are you sure you can manage?"

The tears came back, but so did her smile. "You're a good man, Mr. Adamski."

Stanley opened the door, setting off a cowbell hanging over the frame. "I hope so," he said, walking outside with her. He contemplated the matter as she disappeared around the corner. A competent lawyer could make a case in Stanley's favor. Drunk or sober, he'd spent his career fighting for the rights of the downtrodden. That had to count for something. Then again, a priest could offer a different argument, given Stanley's penchant for loose women. Pride and shame had always been his faithful companions. A jury could be swayed in either direction.

"Am I late?" A man wearing a United Mine Workers pin on the lapel of his Sunday suit trudged up to the office door. "Legs don't move as fast as they used to." He covered his mouth to suppress a barking cough.

Stanley waited for him to catch his breath. "Right on time," he said, leading the man inside.

The sun blinked through half-open blinds. A quarter after three, Stanley guessed, before checking his desk clock. On the nose again. For someone with lousy timing, he sure had a knack for time. "May 10," he said aloud as he opened his appointment book and ran a finger down the page. He'd seen three more clients after Mrs. Hinkley, the miner with black lung and a couple of prostitutes out on bail, but they looked to be the last. "Guess I'll call it a day."

Stanley opened a door behind him, and took the stairs up to his apartment. He briefly considered going over to the Methodist church for their four o'clock AA meeting, but he'd already gone twice this week, and it was only Tuesday. Instead, he decided he'd go up to Providence, do a few chores for Babcia, and have an early supper with her. That would give Arlene time to get to the Polish Club for a couple of drinks after her shift at the Lace Works. He hadn't seen her in over a week, and he was hoping to go home with her at the end of the night. Of course, it all depended on whether or not that sister of hers was still at the house. She'd shown up on Arlene's doorstep out of the blue. Something about her husband making a rude comment after she'd burned his supper. According to Arlene, their spats never lasted more than a week, and Stanley hoped this visit was no exception. While he wouldn't say he missed Arlene, when she wasn't around he remembered he was lonely.

A beer would taste good about now, he thought as he grabbed a Crystal Club Cola out of the fridge. He'd been off the sauce almost three years already, and still, he missed that first beer at the end of the workday. He positioned the neck of the bottle between a set of cast-iron teeth mounted on the wall and pried off the cap, releasing a quick spray of soda. "Every time," he said, wiping his cheek with his sleeve.

The bottle opener had been left behind by a previous tenant. Stanley studied the place. Almost everything in his apartment had come to him secondhand. His kitchen table. The davenport sofa. Even his bed frame in the next room. Stanley didn't mind. *Waste not, want not,* as Babcia always said. She'd been a young widow, so she'd learned how to make do.

Stanley spied his leather Barcalounger, the only new piece of furniture he'd ever purchased for himself. He slept in it when his sciatica acted up. *Old age doesn't come alone.* Something his father had always said in spite of the fact that he died at thirty-two. Strange to think that at fifty-one, Stanley was almost twenty years older than his father would ever be. Most men in Scranton couldn't count on longevity, leastways not the ones who worked in the mines. If the accidents didn't get you, the black lung would.

Stanley had started out in the mines. Like father like son. He became a breaker boy at the age of nine, picking coal from slate twelve hours a day, six days a week. Soon enough, he was promoted to nipper, opening and closing the heavy airtight doors whenever mine cars full of coal passed through. One day, as he watched a mule pull her two-ton load up an incline, her leather harness snapped, sending the coal car hurtling toward a group of miners. Stanley jammed a wooden sprag into a wheel, stopping the car and saving the men, but he got too close and lost his hand in the spokes.

Babcia refused to let that hold him back. *Find the blessings,* she used to say whenever anyone referred the loss of his hand as a tragedy. And Stanley could count his education as one of those blessings. After he recovered, he went to school on a regular basis for the first time in his life. With a little prodding, he buckled down and earned a scholarship at graduation.

He looked around his apartment. *This may not be the Taj Mahal, but it's a decent life. Better than I had a right to expect, all thanks to Babcia.* Still, Stanley wondered what would have happened to him if his father hadn't died so young.

He downed his cola like he would a beer and settled into his Barcalounger. Babcia wouldn't be expecting him this early. No reason he shouldn't take a quick nap. As soon as he closed his eyes, the wall behind him began to pulsate with the drum of a distant stampede. He opened an eye and cocked his head. *Sounds like the Roosey's showing a Western.* Stanley shared a wall with the Roosevelt Theatre in Green Ridge, and while they took great pains to contain the noise, the movies still reverberated in his apartment, Westerns in particular. "Go get 'em, cowboy," he said, and started to drift off.

Inconvenience aside, Green Ridge made sense for Stanley. He could go to the movies anytime. The neighborhood also had heavy foot traffic, so business was good. And, since it butted up against Providence, he was three minutes away from the widow by car or fifteen on foot. All uphill, as Arlene liked to remind him. She hated Green Ridge, and refused to spend the night "all the way down there." In truth, Stanley preferred having a little elbow room between them. He and Arlene liked each other well enough, but that's as far as it went. That's as far as it ever went with Stanley. He'd keep time with a woman for a while. He'd miss them when they weren't around, but after a couple of hours together, he was always ready to be on his own again.

It hadn't been that way with Violet. He couldn't get enough of her back then. Best friends who fall in love. That's how the story's supposed to go, and it did, until that day.

He'd wanted to surprise her, so he lied and said he'd be home from law school a week late. That way he'd be back in Scranton in plenty of time to meet her at the train station. She and her sister Lily had gone to visit an aunt up in Buffalo for a few months, or so he'd been told, but as soon as Violet stepped off the train with a baby in her arms, he knew the score. Or thought he knew, so he didn't give her a chance to explain. It didn't help that he'd been drinking that day. She didn't know. He could still hide it back then.

They both got their hackles up. The pride of youth. Words, hurled like hand grenades, leveled them where they stood. *Fool, liar, coward, whore.* Over the next few months he'd tried to make amends, and so had she, just never at the same time.

Years later, after she'd married Tommy, Violet paid Stanley a visit. Time hadn't assuaged their anger, or their love. They spent the first hour defending their actions and the second one apologizing for them. Eventually, they made their way to a place so honest, it couldn't be sustained. The kind of honest that forces people to turn away rather than see their own truth in someone else's eyes. So she went back to Tommy and never spoke of it to Stanley again.

But God, how he had loved her. You get a love like that once in your life if you're lucky, and he'd been lucky. Or not.

"Whew." He shook his head to chase away the ghosts. A beer would do the trick, *like father like son*, but he'd made a promise to Tommy Davies, and he intended to keep it. "Quit the drink," Tommy had urged a couple of months before he died. Stanley and Tommy hadn't been close for years, but mortality has a way of diminishing old jealousies. "I need you to watch after my girls."

And Stanley had, from making Violet think the government paid those monthly stipends, to buying the family a television. He opened one eye and noticed the jars of mustard pickle and jam on his shelf. She'd be furious if she knew what was going on behind her back, and maybe she'd be right. Stanley didn't intend to find out. He'd keep his distance and rely on Babcia to tell him when and how to help.

Stanley needed to clear his mind. He reached over to the table beside him, turned on an old jade-green Bakelite Motorola radio, and tuned it to WARM 590 on the dial. "Up next," the disc jockey announced, "'I'll See You in My Dreams,' sung by every boy's girl next door, Doris Day."

What were the odds? Better than good, Stanley thought for the second time that hour. Of course, when he and Violet used to dance to that song all those years ago, Isham Jones was singing it. Since then, everybody took their turn, including Ella Fitzgerald, Stanley's favorite. But he had to hand it to Doris, she knew how to croon.

Although Stanley had a terrible voice, he used to sing the song to Violet on the last night before returning to school in Philadelphia. At least, he'd sing the parts that mattered.

I'll see you in my dreams,
Hold you in my dreams.

He'd hum through a few lines and pick up at the end:

Tender eyes that shine,
They will light my way tonight,
I'll see you in my dreams.

"I think you missed something," she'd always say.

"Only you," he'd answer, "when you're not in my arms."

"Only you would turn a torch song into a love song." She'd tease and sing the missing lines:

Someone took you out of my arms,
Still I feel the thrill of your charms,
Lips that once were mine . . .

And that's when he'd kiss her. Stanley remembered them dancing to it once, over at the Robert Morris canteen. He closed his eyes and imagined Violet in his arms. *That may have been the absolute best day of my life.*

Doris Day circled back to the chorus. This time the words sounded keen and sharp, more torment than song. *It's too much.*

It's all too much. Ever since he'd quit drinking, life came at Stanley a little louder, a little brighter, for better *and* for worse. Like the forty-foot weeping willow at the corner in Green Ridge. Stanley had passed that tree hundreds of times, maybe thousands, but one day, a couple of months into his sobriety, he stood before it marveling at the blade-shaped leaves. Veined and serrated, they hung from ropes of bark, mimicking the patterns of fish bones arranged head to toe. He'd felt gratitude at the sight of such beauty, and sorrow for having missed it all these years.

> *Lips that once were mine,*
> *Tender eyes that shine . . .*

Stanley reached behind him and yanked the radio cord, ripping the plug out of the socket. In his drinking days, this song would bump him up against the memory of Violet, but now it gutted the thing, laying bare his insides. Maybe he needed a meeting after all.

A loud knock roused Stanley from his ruminations.

"It's me." Arlene pushed through the door, past the kitchen, and dropped onto the davenport. "I'm never getting rid of her!" she screamed into a pillow.

Stanley kicked down the leg rest. "I wasn't expecting . . ." He shifted in place to shake off his sour mood.

"I wanted to surprise you." Arlene lowered the pillow, tossed her long dark hair, and waited for a reaction.

"You succeeded." He forced a smile and joined her on the couch.

"I can go," she said, not making a move.

"This is new." He fingered her short fringe of bang.

"You like?" She scooted around to face him. "The beautician said I look like that pinup girl, Bettie Page." Arlene put a hand behind her head and aimed her breasts at Stanley.

He sat back to take in the whole picture. "I like." He smiled for real this time as he lifted her bangs and kissed her brow.

Now that she had his attention, she turned the conversation back: "Seriously, what am I going to do about Doreen?"

"Doreen?" Stanley's lips trailed down her neck and lingered in the hollow of her throat.

"My sister." Arlene pushed him an arm's length away. "Are you listening to anything I'm saying?"

"Your sister," he whispered. "Doreen."

"She wants that husband of hers to stew a little longer, but hand to God," she raised her arm, "I can't take much more of it. Look at me. I had to come all the way to Green Ridge to get away from her."

Stanley tried to be sympathetic, but his earlier mood reared up again. "Put your foot down," he said. "You're not her keeper."

"I'd never hear the end of it." Arlene ignored his irritation. "And besides, she's family." Her tone softened. "Maybe you can think of a way to distract me." She struck her pinup pose again.

Stanley drank in the sight of her. *A man could lose himself in that figure.* He leaned forward, lips parted, eyes closed.

I'll see you in my dreams . . .

The lyrics filled the space between the pair, knocking Stanley back. His eyes broke open and settled on Arlene. He wanted to want her. He willed himself to want her, but it did no good. That damn song had him rattled. "I can't do this . . ." He'd meant to end with "now," but the word "anymore" finished first. "I'm sorry."

"Then more's the pity," Arlene lamented, her chin quivering with disappointment.

CHAPTER NINE

DAISY SAT AT THE PIANO, ELBOWS PROPPED on the closed lid, hands clasped at her chin as if in prayer. But she wasn't praying. She was trying to decide how to broach the topic of Johnny and the Elks Club with Beverly. Downtown businesses closed at five o'clock on Tuesdays, but the hair salon, Bevy of Beauties, was still open at a quarter to six. One of the regulars had arrived late for a shampoo and set, and since Beverly was Daisy's ride home, she had extra time to mull over her situation.

It wasn't that Daisy expected her best friend to give her a hard time. If anyone broke with convention, it was Beverly. Daisy just wanted to get the whole story out before she started asking questions. Beverly always had questions. "Vaccinated with a Victrola needle," people used to tease.

Daisy simply liked to speak her mind without interruption, so people would have all the facts before coming to conclusions. When she was five or six and wanted to ask her mother for something unreasonable, like a pony or a trip to the moon, she'd instruct, "Don't talk till I say 'ding.'" Inevitably, about halfway through the request, her mother would open her mouth to answer, and Daisy would hold up a finger and remind her, "I didn't say it yet." When she'd finally get to the end of her request, she'd sing out, "Ding!" and in exactly the same key her mother would sing out, "No." Even so, as long as Daisy had been able to give her whole spiel, she was satisfied.

In the case of Johnny, Beverly would ask about Daisy's intentions. She wouldn't bring up race right away. Instead she'd circle around to it. *You're not getting any younger,* she'd say. *You'll be twenty-five tomorrow. Let's suppose Johnny turns out to be Prince Charming. Perfect in every way. Do you see a future with this man? Would you marry him? Would he marry you?*

And Daisy would rear up because she'd know race was at the heart of those questions, and who was Beverly to be so judgmental? Beverly had certainly made enough iffy choices in life, and Daisy had always stood by her. Besides, a person's skin color shouldn't matter.

Except it did. Not to Daisy. Not really. Not in the same way it mattered to small-minded people who'd only lived in one place all their lives. But what would her mother say? Or worse yet, the gossips up and down Spring Street? Those women loved nothing better than a bone to chew.

After a little thought, Daisy settled on her father's *So what?* philosophy. Whenever neighbors talked about his grass being too high or his habit of sleeping in on Sundays after working six days a week, he'd say, "So what? If they're talking about me, they're letting some other poor soul alone."

Of course, Beverly wouldn't stop at race. She'd also poke at Daisy about her general lack of experience with men. *Do you even know what it means to be in love?* Beverly would ask, while claiming to be an expert on the subject. Daisy would be inclined to balk, but truth be told, she'd only been in love once, maybe, with Michael Lennon, a quiet Irish boy who'd walked the halls of their school with a notebook under his arm and a pencil behind his ear. He used to read her the stories he wrote, but to be honest, she probably loved the stories more than the boy.

Shortly after, Daisy swore off guys from Scranton altogether, not because of anything Michael had done, but rather, an incident with her crush, Teddy Ryan. Daisy winced remembering it. No need to go down that road now. She had enough on her mind.

During Daisy's time in Atlantic City, she'd dated off and on, but three shows a day left little time for serious romance. *And so what?* as her father would say. Beverly was twenty-five and just as unmarried as Daisy was, and she'd tell her that, if Beverly decided to get up on her high horse.

"Of all the gall," Beverly yelled as she climbed the stairs and strolled into the studio, "I stayed an hour late to do that woman's hair, and she didn't even tip me!"

"You should have told her you were closed."

"Not if I want to keep customers." Beverly bit a hangnail off her thumb. "You'll see, once you're up and running."

"Ah, so now you're an expert on business." Daisy pushed her stool away from the piano and stood up.

"Cripes," Beverly said, "who wound you up?"

"Sorry. Can we talk?"

"Sure." Beverly opened one of the folding chairs, sat down, and crossed her arms. "Talk."

"I met someone." Daisy took a breath. "Over the weekend."

"And you didn't tell me?"

"I'm telling you now."

"So who is this promising beau?" Beverly leaned forward.

"He helped me move the piano."

Beverly cringed. "Please, not one of the Summerlin brothers. The short one's awful, and the tall one's worse. I should know. I dated him."

"No! Somebody else."

"Thank God."

"Listen." Daisy glanced at the back window, remembering Johnny in the alley the previous afternoon. "He's sweet and kind and honest. After going to all that trouble to get my little Tom Thumb up here, he refused to take a penny."

"And handsome?"

"Very. Boyish dimples. Better yet, he plays piano."

"Better than dimples?"

Daisy ignored the comment. "And with such passion. I play what's on the page, but he has this way of heading toward a note, then skipping right past it for a better one. Like taking a scenic route you never knew existed." She took a beat. "He's playing with Ferdie Bistocchi's band at the Elks Club this Saturday. He asked me to come. And to bring a friend."

"And?"

"And you're my friend."

"What's his name?"

"Johnny Cornell."

"Cornell. Don't think I know any Cornells."

"He's not from around here," Daisy said.

"Well, that makes sense."

"What does?"

"Him not being from Scranton." Beverly scratched her brow. "He sounds too perfect. So what's the catch?" Her hand shot up. "I know. He's divorced. Well, that never stopped me."

"He's not divorced."

"Married?" Beverly feigned shock. "And people say *I'm* the wild one."

"No!"

"Then what?"

Daisy braced for Beverly's reaction. "Let's just say," she took a breath, "he's not Welsh."

"That makes two of us. I'm English and Irish." Beverly touched the side of her face and lowered her voice. "Orange Irish to boot." She smirked. "And you never seemed to mind."

"He's . . ." Daisy struggled with her word choice, "not white."

"Oh." Beverly's steady tone did not give away her opinion. "I don't suppose he's Italian."

"Nope."

"So am I to understand that Mr. Johnny Cornell, the world's greatest piano player, is a colored man?"

"Uh-huh."

"Anything else I need to know?"

"Isn't that enough?" Daisy offered nervously.

"*You* have to decide what's enough," Beverly said.

"I really like him."

"Oh, I can tell." Beverly peered into Daisy's eyes. "Honestly, I don't remember the last time I saw you this excited about someone. Maybe not since seeing Teddy Ryan at Rocky Glen Park, and we know how that turned out."

Daisy's cheeks flushed. "I told you I never want to talk about that again."

"After this, I won't. I promise. I just have to say one thing. You stopped dating boys in Scranton because of what happened that day."

"I hate to be the brunt of gossip."

"Well, you will be if you date this Johnny." Beverly shrugged. "I'm not saying it's right. I'm saying it's true."

"And unfair." Daisy toed a water stain on a floorboard under the window. "Why can't I be brave like you?"

Beverly snickered. "I'm flashy. That's different from brave."

"All of this silliness over a man I barely know."

"True. But you light up like Christmas when you talk about him."

"Because I think I like him," Daisy said.

"So?"

"So, what are you doing Saturday night?"

"Apparently, I'm going to the Elks Club. Maybe I'll get a new do for the occasion." Beverly patted her hair. "You better let him know I'll have a few questions."

"I'm sure you will." Daisy closed the windows. "Time to go."

The conversation stalled for the ten-minute drive home to Providence. "You're still coming over tomorrow, right?" Daisy finally asked.

"For your birthday? Wouldn't miss it." Beverly pulled up in front of the Davies's house, turned the wheels away from the curb, shifted into first gear, and set the brake to keep her old Pontiac from sliding back down the hill.

"And so you know," Daisy grabbed the door handle but stayed seated, "Rocky Glen? Teddy Ryan? That was all a long time ago."

"I know."

"And nothing happened." Daisy swung the door open.

Beverly rubbed her hands. "Time to let bygones be bygones."

If only it were that easy, Daisy thought as she stepped out of the car.

CHAPTER TEN

IT WAS TWENTY MINUTES TO MIDNIGHT according to the glow-in-the-dark hands on Daisy's travel alarm. She'd gotten the clock as a graduation present from her parents, a peace offering of sorts after months of trying to talk her out of leaving home. They'd had her initials, *DMD,* stamped on the lid of the pigskin case. Inside, her mother had pinned an old Welsh proverb, *Do good while time permits,* but it was a different adage keeping Daisy awake.

Let bygones be bygones.

Thanks to Beverly's earlier comment about Teddy Ryan, Daisy couldn't sleep. She turned on her bedside light, an old oil lamp that had been wired for electricity decades earlier. The lamp and the travel alarm sat on the small drum table she'd used as a nightstand since moving into her father's house at the age of five, the day of her parents' wedding. Daisy surveyed her room. Same dresser she'd had as a child. Same Shirley Temple doll seated on top. Same porcelain ballerina made in occupied Japan. Same trinket dish. Same mirror. Same ghosts.

Let bygones be bygones.

Daisy had buried the memory of Teddy Ryan long ago, but on the cusp of twenty-five, she finally understood that the deeper you bury pain, the more room it has to grow.

And yet, she thought, *nothing really happened. Well, almost nothing.*

In June of '46, Daisy and Beverly had celebrated the end of their tenth-grade year by taking the Laurel Line trolley to Rocky Glen.

The amusement park had recently added the Million Dollar Coaster, and the girls couldn't wait to see it for themselves. They got all dolled up in dirndls and peasant blouses, not for the roller coaster, but for the boys who were sure to show. Tuesday was Nickel Day, and the rides were half-price.

Daisy glanced around the trolley car to see if she knew anyone on board. No one looked familiar, but given the number of sun hats and picnic baskets, most of the passengers were bound for the Glen.

"It didn't really cost a million dollars." Across the aisle, an elderly man in a straw bowler folded his newspaper back in half. "Says it right here." He tapped at a picture of the roller coaster and the description underneath.

"Well, that's something," Daisy offered so as not to appear rude. Her upper body lurched forward as the conductor brought the car to an unusually hard stop. The man with the newspaper seemed unfazed.

The conductor cupped his hands around his mouth and hollered, "All aboard!" New passengers streamed in.

"A hundred thousand's nothing to sneeze at," the old man said, pointing to the actual cost of the attraction, "but it's not a million."

"Maybe they thought 'million' sounded better." When the man didn't respond, Daisy spoke a little louder, "Fewer syllables."

To Daisy's left, Beverly threw an elbow and whispered, "Forget Gramps." Her eyes landed on a trio of boys now holding onto the brass poles at the front of the car. "Teddy Ryan." The name slipped through the corner of her mouth like steam from a kettle.

Teddy Ryan. A dreamboat for sure, Daisy thought. Tall. Handsome. Sandy-blond hair. And he could charm you with a look. Any girl with sense swooned in his presence, and she and Beverly both had sense.

"The biggest coaster in the world, or so they say. Almost 4,700 feet long." The old guy whistled his admiration through a set of yellowed teeth. "Took two thousand gallons of paint to cover her."

"You don't say." Daisy's gaze pinballed between the man in the straw hat and her crush with his cleft chin. She willed Teddy to glance in her direction. Not that he knew she existed. He was two years ahead of her in school and had his pick of older girls.

"Says here its highest peak is ninety-six feet."

"Is that so?"

"You won't catch me on it. Not at my age." The old man rolled up the newspaper and tucked it under his arm. "Now, in my youth," he chuckled, "you couldn't hold me down."

Daisy swung around and faced him. "How high did you say?"

He counted on his fingers. "I'd say seven floors."

"Rocky Glen!" the conductor announced.

Daisy looked out the window, but all she could see were the latticed trusses supporting the coaster's tracks.

"Grab your purse," Beverly said as the trolley rolled to a stop. Passengers started gathering their belongings and moving toward the front and rear exits.

Daisy turned back toward the old man. "Seven stories high?" She gave a nervous giggle. "Well, now I'm scared."

The man straightened his straw bowler, retrieved his cane from between the seats, and pushed himself up. As he stepped into the aisle, he pulled a couple of nickels out of his pocket and pressed them into Daisy's hand. "Then do it scared," he said as he made his way toward the front of the car.

Do it scared, Daisy repeated to herself as she and Beverly followed the crowd past a row of benches, up over a footbridge, through the arcade, and into the park. Besides, she reflected, she'd been on the Pippin, Rocky Glen's other roller coaster, just last year. Really, how much scarier could the new one be?

A lot scarier, she thought as she and Beverly came face-to-face with the wooden beast. From where they stood, the coaster seemed to rise out of the spring-fed lake like an enormous, seven-humped Loch Ness monster. Daisy watched as the roller coaster cars click-clacked up the first incline. Why was she so afraid? The front car reached the top of the hill, and teetered for a split second before plummeting down the other side at a dizzying speed, dragging the rest of the train along with it. Screams filled the air. *That's why.*

"I'm pretty sure one of those nickels is mine," Beverly said. Daisy opened her palm, and Beverly scooped up a coin. "So you're never going on?"

"I never said never." Daisy put her nickel in her skirt pocket and pressed the side of her hand against her forehead to shield the early afternoon sun. The coaster flew along the curved track and the screaming riders threw their arms in the air. "I said I'd see."

"Never pegged you for a scaredy-cat."

"Sticks and stones," Daisy said.

"That's all right. Teddy'll take me for a ride." Beverly laughed. "On the rolly coaster, I mean." She scanned the park. "Now where did that boy get to?"

"Why you?" Daisy blurted out. "Why not me?"

"Because I called it."

"You can't *call* a boy like you call a seat at the movies."

"Sure I can." Beverly cupped her hands and hollered, "Teddy Ryan!"

"Doesn't work that way either."

"I'll tell you what. Maybe one of Teddy's buddies will take a shine to you. We can double date."

"What makes you think he's interested in *you*?"

"Teddy? He kept sneaking peeks at me on the trolley."

"How do you know he wasn't just staring in our general direction?"

"A girl knows. But no harm in sweetening the pot." Beverly slid her puffed sleeves partway down her forearms, revealing a pair of creamy shoulders and some ample cleavage. "Now let's see if we can't find those boys."

As Beverly zigzagged through the crowd, Daisy tried pushing her own sleeves over her shoulders, but her neckline had no give.

Not to be outdone, she untucked her blouse and tied a knot in front, exposing an inch or so of stomach. "We'll see who he picks," she mumbled under her breath before catching up.

Beverly threaded her arm through Daisy's. "Now where would you be if you were Teddy Ryan?"

Daisy studied the scene. "I'd say the Dodgems or, better yet, the concession stand. Boys are always hungry."

"Well look at you, Miss Nancy Drew. You'll make a fine detective someday." Beverly squeezed Daisy's hand. "Whaddaya say we go find him?"

Two hours later, Daisy took one last bite of her candied apple before tossing the core. "I cry uncle," she said, rinsing her fingers in the drinking fountain. "We've been on the Dodgems, the Tumblebug, the Whip . . ."

"Don't forget the new Duck Boat." Beverly took her turn at the fountain.

"New for Rocky Glen, maybe. I don't see the point. An amphibious vehicle from World War II is not an amusement park ride."

"You're just afraid of water."

"Not afraid," Daisy shot back. "Respectful."

"Uh-huh."

"So like I was saying." Daisy wanted to get back to the original subject. "We've covered every inch of this park. That boy doesn't want to be found."

"I'm not ready to throw in the towel." Beverly hopped up on a bench to get a better view of the crowd.

"If you can find him," Daisy curtsied, "he's all yours."

"You mean that?" Beverly jumped down and spun her around to face the Mammoth Fun House.

A large sign on the L-shaped building promised *25 Different Amusements Under One Roof.* "What am I supposed to be seeing?" Daisy asked.

"Over by the entrance."

"Well I'll be." Daisy's eyes landed on Teddy and his buddies at the front of the line.

"Come on," Teddy motioned the girls over, and lifted the rope to let them in.

"No cutting!" someone yelled from behind, and the boys snickered.

"Next," the ticket taker signaled the line forward.

"Ladies first," Teddy said.

Between Teddy's surprise invitation and the spinning barrel inside the door, Daisy fought to stay upright. Somehow the boys made it through the contraption with no effort. She grabbed hold of Beverly. They each stretched out an arm for balance and laughed like fools as the barrel revolved around them. Just when they got the hang of it, Teddy and one of his friends pulled the girls over the threshold to solid ground.

"How'd you get across so fast?" Beverly asked.

"Practice." Teddy winked and disappeared in the dark.

Daisy and Beverly linked arms and giggled their way through a maze of crazy mirrors and dozens of other attractions before reaching an oversized turntable called the Spinning Plate. The young man at the controls instructed, "Sit down and hold on." Thirty seconds later, someone in the shadows shouted, "Turn up the speed!" and the attendant obliged. Dizzy but determined, Daisy and Beverly managed to hang on for the next surprise, a jolt of electricity strong enough to startle them into letting go. Hearts pounding, they tumbled off, helped each other up, and burst into giggles that lasted all the way to the Alpine Slide, the last and steepest attraction in the whole fun house.

Beverly got in line first, and when her turn came, she let go of the handrail and started down the slide. Daisy counted to ten Mississippi before pushing off, but the mahogany surface proved so slick, she caught up to Beverly right before they landed. The two dissolved into laughter and only moved when an attendant yelled, "Out of the way!" to avoid a pileup of bodies.

Breathless, the girls pushed through the exit and paused to collect themselves.

"Give 'em the air!" someone ordered. A blast of wind rushed up from a floor grate, lifting their skirts past their thighs. Teddy and his friends sat on a bench in front of them, watching and whistling.

"You dirty dogs," Beverly scolded as she and Daisy hopped off the grate and smoothed down their skirts.

The boys stood up. Teddy offered Beverly a disarming smile. "See?" he said, putting his arm around her shoulder. "I knew you were the kind of girl who could take a joke."

Beverly's face radiated joy. "Oh, you'll pay," she teased and let him pull her in closer.

Daisy's throat ached with disappointment. Beverly always got the guy. She was braver. More daring. *Do it scared*. The old man's words came back to her, and she repeated them in her head. "I'm ready to try the coaster now."

"She speaks," Teddy said, and he and Beverly had a good laugh.

"The big one," Daisy said, scooting past them so they couldn't see her cry.

By the time they arrived at the Million Dollar Coaster, Daisy's tears had dried. No one would be the wiser to her sadness, including Teddy's two friends who tagged after him like puppies. She joined the line first, hoping her daring behavior would mask the fear rising up from her stomach.

The others fell in behind her, and the line moved quickly. Too quickly for Daisy's liking. As they stepped onto the loading station, she counted the heads in front of her. A baker's dozen. That meant she and her group would make it onto the next train, the one now whipping around a hairpin turn of track at the other end of the coaster. Thunderous screams swelled, receded, and swelled again as the cars shot down the final slopes. Daisy searched for a means of escape. *Shouldn't there be a way to get out of line if you change your mind?* She inadvertently caught Teddy's eye and thought for a moment he was gazing at her.

A train of jubilant passengers returned to the station and they exited in the opposite direction of those waiting to ride. An attendant on Daisy's side opened the gate and started ushering the line toward the now empty cars. Daisy willed her legs to carry her forward.

"How many in your group?" the attendant asked.

When Daisy didn't answer, Teddy piped up, "Five."

"Two to a seat." The worker pointed up to a sign without looking. "No singles."

"I need a partner!" a girl shouted from the edge of the platform, and one of Teddy's buddies hightailed it over to her.

"Move it along," the attendant barked. Now holding hands, Beverly pulled Teddy toward the car in front of them. She let go long enough to slide across the bench seat, and as soon she was in, Teddy stepped back.

"Moose here is going to do the honors," Teddy said, pushing his husky friend toward Beverly. "I promised Daisy I'd take her."

He'd made no such promise, but Daisy was too stunned to contradict him. "Let's go," Teddy said and directed her toward the last car. As soon as they sat down, he tugged the lap bar into place and squeezed her knee, sending a jolt of electricity through her body for the second time that day. "No turning back now," he said, putting his hands on the bar as the train pulled away from the station.

Terror and delight competed for Daisy's attention. As the coaster climbed the first incline, she felt the sensation of tipping back too far on a chair. She gripped the bar to keep from falling out and watched the lead car clear the crest. An instant later, she felt her body lift up off the seat as they flew down the first slope.

The train shot up again. Daisy opened her eyes, wondering when she'd even closed them. Worse, she suddenly realized she'd grabbed Teddy's hand at some point during the ride. Another time, she might have collapsed under the weight of embarrassment, but instead, she tightened her grip as they reached the second peak.

Swoosh! This time her body bounced higher, but to Daisy's surprise, she enjoyed the weightless feeling. In fact, as they rushed up the third hill, she started laughing in anticipation of the next drop.

Teddy yelled something to her. Daisy couldn't hear him over the roaring coaster, but she nodded agreeably. As soon as they hit the top, Teddy threw his arms into the air. Daisy caught on quickly and, in a moment of exhilaration, let go of the bar. They waved and screamed as the car plummeted down the other side.

When the train began its fourth ascent, it was Teddy who took Daisy's hand. The track leveled out over the lake for a turnaround so sharp Teddy fell into her, his forearm skimming her breast. Instead of sliding back over, he stayed pressed against her, and the coaster took another precipitous dip before three quick hills in succession brought them back to the station.

"So, what do you think?" Teddy asked when the train pulled up to the platform.

"Glorious!" Daisy answered.

While they waited for the attendant to reach their car, Teddy leaned toward Daisy to give her a smooch.

"Okay, Romeo." The worker disengaged the lap bar. "Keep it moving." As they disembarked, someone on the other side instructed, "No singles," to the passengers clamoring to get on the ride.

Daisy ran down the steps, excited to tell Beverly how she'd conquered her fear.

Beverly.

My best friend.

Who'd looked so happy on Teddy's arm. The image stopped Daisy cold.

"Something wrong?" Teddy placed his hand on Daisy's back and guided her toward a shade tree.

"Beverly," Daisy said, scanning the crowd. "I think we lost her."

"Would that be so tragic?"

Teddy was teasing. Daisy was sure of it, yet that truth didn't temper her guilt. "Of course it would." Her words sounded sharp. What was she doing? This was Teddy. Teddy Ryan. Standing with her. Rubbing circles into the small of her back. She tried again, softer this time: "I'm worried."

"Maybe she and Moose hit it off."

At the moment Teddy mentioned Moose's name, he wandered over, shoving a tuft of blue cotton candy into his mouth.

"Where's Beverly?" Daisy asked.

"Went home." Moose's blue lips made him appear sickly.

"What?"

Moose wiped his mouth with his hand. "Said you welshed on a deal."

"What deal?" Daisy tried to think while Teddy's fingers lightly grazed the inch of bare skin at her waist where she'd tied up her blouse. She struggled to still a purr working its way up her spine. She shook her head in an attempt to focus. *A deal?*

The words she'd spoken in front of the fun house came rushing back: *If you can find him, he's all yours.* That couldn't be it. Surely Beverly knew she was kidding. They both liked Teddy. Daisy had made that clear. *You can't* call *a boy like you call a seat at the movies.*

"Some friend," Teddy said. "Now Moose here knows what's what, don't you, pal? You'd never leave me high and dry," he winked at his friend, "unless I wanted you to."

Moose mumbled something about a swim, and trotted off toward the lake. Daisy only half heard because she was still fretting about Beverly. Yes, she wanted to feel bad about her friend, maybe even rush after her, she really did, but she also wanted this time with Teddy to last forever.

"How about an ice cream over at the Swiss Cottage?" he asked. "My treat."

"I'd love one," Daisy said, taking his arm.

* * *

Just short of the Kiddie Train, Teddy led Daisy off the pathway toward the woods. "I know a shortcut," he said and kissed the top of her head. Daisy hesitated for an instant, though Teddy seemed not to notice. "I'm trying to decide," he pulled her along by the hand, "if you're a rum raisin or butter pecan kind of girl."

"Not even close." She gave him a playful shove. "Strawberry's my favorite."

"Strawberry, huh?" He seemed to consider the matter. "Well, that settles it."

"Settles what?"

"I'm taking you to West Pittston for our first real date. Grablick's has the best strawberry ice cream around."

Our first date? Are we dating? Daisy's heart pounded. If it weren't for the cacophony of music and rides a few yards away, Teddy would hear it beating.

"We're almost there."

Deeper into the woods, the canopy of trees started crowding the early evening light, but Daisy could still make out Teddy's easy smile.

Close enough to hear music from the bandstand, but far enough from prying eyes, he stopped and danced Daisy up against a towering ash tree. Its pale-green leaves rustled against the intrusion. Before she had a chance to speak, Teddy laid a gentle finger on her parted lips. "Shhh. You're safe with me." He outlined her mouth with the tip of his finger. "Mmm."

"I'm not sure I . . ." Daisy's breath ran out as he nibbled on her ear.

"I'm falling for you, baby. Hard." He showered her neck with the most delicate kisses, and she shivered.

Daisy pulled back, though in her state, she couldn't remember why.

"No funny business." Teddy held up three fingers. "Scout's honor." He took those same fingers, slipped them under the bottom of her blouse, and caressed the flesh on her lower back. "You're my girl," he said, pressing inside the waistband of her skirt. "Nobody in the world but you and me."

Daisy's lips ached to be kissed. Her whole body ached, and as if reading her thoughts, Teddy put his free hand on the back of her head and pulled her mouth so close to his that she matched his breathing. "I could fall in love with a girl like you," he whispered. She let out the purr she'd stifled earlier. And he kissed her. Gently at first and then with abandon.

Daisy felt weightless in a way that was a million times better than any coaster. How were her legs holding her up? Did she even *have* legs? His lips traveled down the side of her neck to her throat. Moony-eyed, Daisy threw back her head and let his tongue find the hint of cleavage at the top of her blouse. Teddy looked up. "This your first time?" Without waiting for an answer, he returned to that most delicious spot.

Daisy didn't know how to respond. Sure, she'd kissed her share of boys during games of spin the bottle, but Teddy's kisses were something else. They made her forget everything and everyone she'd ever known. "Yes," she whispered, reacting more to his touch than his question.

He smiled up at her with his eyebrow cocked. "Well aren't you full of surprises." His lips found his way back to hers. "You're doing fine, baby. Real fine."

There are rules, she thought. *What are the rules?* Hadn't Beverly told her about them a thousand times? Something about bases and over the blouse.

Teddy parted her knees with one of his, and tangled his legs up with hers.

The rules. But it was no use. She didn't want to think about rules. Or to think at all. She only wanted to feel.

Teddy's kisses were so dizzying and deep she hadn't realized he'd untied the knot in her top till his fingers started working their way up her stomach to her brassiere. *Was it over the blouse or over the bra? Think.*

His free hand inched up the inside of her thigh, giving her the most exquisite sensation.

No! She tried to say the word. *Not there! But it felt so good. Why did it feel so good?* She couldn't think.

When he reached her cotton undies, his breath quickened.

No! No! No! Could he hear her? Had she actually spoken the words aloud?

He slid his hand inside her panties and his thumb grazed the split between her legs.

She tried to wriggle away from him, but he had her pinned to the tree.

"What's wrong?" His question had razored edges. "Don't be a tease."

"No!" She'd finally said the word out loud. "No more." She tried to push him off, but he pushed back.

"That's not how the game is played, baby." He yanked one side of her panties down over her hip. "You should know that," he said, cupping a handful of her bared behind. "You're your mother's daughter. Everybody says so."

Angry tears welled up in her eyes. "Don't you dare say that. Don't you dare talk about my mother!"

"Knock it off," he said, watching the tears roll down her cheeks. "You're taking all the fun out of this."

"No!" She pushed against him as hard as she could. "Get off me."

Teddy scoffed and gave her behind a painful pinch before inching away. "I never figured you for a cold fish."

Still flattened against the tree, Daisy tugged up her underpants without lifting her skirt.

"Go on." He shoved her. "Get out of here."

Daisy took a tentative step forward, and Teddy grabbed her arm. "Joke's on you." He smirked. "I'm going to say it happened anyway," he said and let her go.

* * *

Daisy ran out of the woods, through the park, slowing only when she reached the trolley stop. When she looked down the track for the Laurel Line, she spotted Beverly sitting on a bench. "I'm so sorry," Daisy said as she sat down and broke into heaving sobs.

"What happened?" Beverly asked, clearly concerned over Daisy's disheveled appearance.

"I thought you left." Daisy gulped for air.

Beverly pulled two handkerchiefs out of her pocket. She handed one to Daisy, who gave her nose a good blow, and spit on the other one to wipe the dirt off Daisy's cheek. "You had to come back here eventually," Beverly said, "so I waited."

"This whole time?"

Beverly shrugged. "I'd never leave you behind, no matter how sore I was."

"I'm really sorry," Daisy said, "really and truly."

"Me too."

Beyond them, a headlight came around the bend. Daisy stood to adjust her blouse and smooth her hair. "Promise me we'll never let a boy get between us again."

Beverly held out her hand. "Pinky swear," she said, hooking her finger on Daisy's.

The red Laurel Line trolley pulled into the station, and the conductor called out, "All aboard!" Beverly took Daisy's hand and led her to the car.

For the rest of the summer, Daisy laid low, but on her first day back to school, Moose and a couple of his buddies whistled as she walked past. Teddy had made good on his promise.

Daisy glanced at the travel alarm that had become a permanent fixture on her nightstand since her return to Scranton. Two minutes after twelve. Her birthday. The start of her twenty-fifth year. A turning point, if she'd allow it. Daisy switched off the lamp and focused her eyes on the clock's glowing hands till she fell asleep.

CHAPTER ELEVEN

"YOUR ANTENNA'S ALL SET," a man called out from the enclosed porch.

"Come on in," Violet responded, "Archie won't hurt you." At the sound of his name, the napping dog moved from the threshold to a rag rug in front of the sink.

The man brushed off his navy coveralls, stomped his boots, and stepped inside. "Looks like someone's having a birthday." He took off his peaked cap and aimed it at a two-layer cake with chocolate icing.

"My daughter," Violet said, as she finished wrapping a dress box in the previous day's newspaper. "Twenty-five today. Where does the time go?"

"You're lucky the weather held out." The man scrutinized the heavy gray clouds outside the kitchen window. "Can't work in a storm."

Lucky? Violet still wasn't sure she even wanted a television in her house, let alone an antenna on the roof. When they'd started popping up all over Spring Street, she found them unsightly. They looked like giant drying racks for clothes. On the other hand, the widow had gone to great pains to have the antenna installed that morning in preparation for the TV delivery later in the day. Violet might have been undecided about her luck, but she was firm in her gratitude to the widow. And to her mother, who'd instigated this surprise. A slice of sun pierced the dusty sky. "It may be clearing up," she said. "Then again, we could use the rain."

"Not in my business. I'll take sunshine all day, every day." The man pulled a schedule out of his pocket. "The delivery guy should be here by four, give or take."

"I suppose it's time we got a television. Everybody in Providence has one."

"Not everybody. Between you and me," he lowered his voice, "some a them antennas are for show."

"For *what?*"

"They want you to think they can afford a TV."

"Why on earth?"

"Keeping up with the Joneses," he said, pocketing the schedule. "Takes all kinds." He put his cap back on, patted the dog's head, and walked out the door.

Eight hours later, Violet, Daisy, and Grace sat shoulder to shoulder on the sagging couch, staring at the deliveryman as he began to set up the television. The coffee table in front of them held a folded newspaper, the instruction manual for the TV, and four dessert plates seemingly licked clean of the birthday cake they'd held. Next to the couch, the widow squirmed in a button-backed armchair.

"I was hoping you'd show up before the birthday girl got home."

"Like I said . . ." the man scooted behind the TV, "got a nail in my tire. Put me back for the rest of day."

"He's here now," Violet said to smooth out the tension. "That's what matters."

"You could've knocked me over with a feather when I came home and saw that antenna on our roof." Daisy grabbed the newspaper and turned to the program schedule. "If I live to be a hundred, I'll never be as surprised as I was today."

"Still," the widow started again, "when a man gives his word to be on time—"

"Is it true you'll go blind if you sit too close?" Violet interrupted.

"Nothing but an old wives' tale," the man called out from behind the set. "My boy, Roy Jr., sits with his nose right up to it, and he sees better than I do."

"Can we begin watching tonight?" Daisy scanned the listing. "I'd love to see *This Is Your Life*."

Roy Sr. poked out his head. "Yep."

"I used to listen to that show on the radio," Grace said.

"TV's different." Daisy kept her eyes on the paper. "You can see if they're really surprised."

"I'll have you up and running in a few minutes." Roy pushed the plug into the socket, wiggled out from behind the TV, and walked it back against the wall on its four tapered legs.

"I don't care for the show." Violet crinkled her nose. "That host . . ."

Daisy looked up. "Ralph Edwards?"

"He's the one," Violet said. "What makes him think people want their life stories aired like dirty laundry? Do they even get a choice? Some of them sound absolutely horrified when they finally figure out what's going on."

"He always sounded like a gentleman to me," Grace said.

Daisy folded the paper back and set it on the coffee table. "I heard he's handsome."

"I'm willing to give him a chance," the widow glared at the deliveryman, "provided the TV is working by then."

"Tell that to Laurel and Hardy," said Violet. All eyes landed on her. "He wasn't much of a gentleman with them." Now that she had their attention, she repeated a story she'd heard at Bible study a few weeks back: "Ralph Edwards ambushed the comedians, and they were none too happy. At one point, some woman from Oliver Hardy's past tells about how he tried—and failed—to save his drowning brother. Now you tell me, does that kind of thing belong on TV? Or the radio, for that matter?"

"They get prizes," Grace said. "Cuff links for the men, charm bracelets for the women. And he surprises them with people from their past."

"No one likes to be surprised." Violet stared at her mother. She'd been wearing that pink sweater for two days now. The burst of color brightened her pale complexion, so why did Violet find it unsettling? "I'm just saying, he always sounds a little disappointed when the stories are happy."

Roy polished the wooden console with a velvet cloth. "Blond mahogany," he said. "Our newest finish."

Grace aimed her chin at the TV set. "How does it turn on?"

"Glad you asked. This model has a fine-tuning system unique to Philcos." He swept a hand across a slim rectangle of controls between the screen on top and the speaker below. "It's our fingertip system, located on the front for your convenience. Most manufacturers hide buttons under trapdoors or on the back of the units. Not us. We're here to make your life easy." Roy twisted the first knob. "On," he said before rotating it in the opposite direction. "And off. You can hear the click." He cupped an ear with his free hand. "On." *Click.* "Off." *Click.* "Like a radio." He turned it on again. "It'll just take a minute for the picture to warm up." He tapped the convex glass. "Twenty-one inches. You got yourselves a beaut."

The longer Violet stared at the television, the more suspicious she became. "What about radiation? I remember reading some kind of warning about radiation."

"People say that to scare you off." Static blasted from the speaker as snow materialized on the screen. "Same knob works the volume," Roy said as he swiveled it back. "I maybe shoulda started there." He reached behind to adjust the built-in aerial.

Grace and Daisy sat mesmerized by the flickering dots.

Violet refused to be seduced. Radiation was nothing to fool around with. "What people?" she asked. "Who wants to scare us off from watching television?"

"Radio salesmen." Roy delivered the line with a serious expression, but he couldn't hold it long. "I'm pulling your leg," he said when Violet crossed her arms, unamused. Roy collected himself and addressed the group: "Listen, girls. Everybody's afraid of change, but rest assured. Philco uses aluminized picture tubes. Gives you a brighter picture and a safer one too." When Violet's eyebrows lifted in concern, he corrected, "A safe picture. Not safer. *Safe*. Safest available. Now this here," he pinched a knob at the other end of the control panel, "changes your channels." He turned the dial half an inch and landed on a rolling black-and-white image of what looked to be Perry Como, though Violet couldn't be sure. "Hang on." Roy adjusted a button near the middle of the panel and the picture stabilized.

It *was* Perry Como! They could see it for certain now. That dark hair. His friendly smile. Daisy beamed. She loved his records.

"Vertical hold," Roy said, pointing to a button. "Right next to the horizontal. Use 'em both to tune in your picture. It's all in the manual if you forget. Just takes a little practice to get the feel of it."

Daisy craned her head to see around Roy as a beautiful blonde joined Perry Como onstage. "It's Betty Hutton! Turn it up!"

Roy obliged, and for the next few minutes, they all sang along to a playful duet of "A Bushel and a Peck."

Even the widow knew the words from listening to the radio. When the song ended, Roy lowered the volume. "Any questions before I go?" He began packing up his tools.

Violet was sure she'd have more questions, but she was also sure they wouldn't come to her until the deliveryman was halfway home. "We're good for now," she said.

Roy held up a finger. "One more thing. When your picture tube burns out, we recommend you call a certified Philco dealer, somebody like me." He handed Violet a card with his name and telephone number.

The widow scoffed. "And will somebody like you be on time if we call?"

"She's one tough cookie," he said aloud, but he seemed to enjoy the ribbing. "As long as I don't pick up another nail in my tire, you have my word."

The widow glanced at the television. "Well," she said and pushed herself up from the chair, "my work here is done."

"You aren't staying to watch?" Daisy asked.

"Another time." The widow collected her pocketbook and cane while Daisy and Violet stood to see her off. "*Wszystkiego najlepszego z okazji urodzin*. All the best on your birthday."

"I'm so glad you came over." Daisy hugged the widow. "I can't thank you enough for what you did." She looked around the room. "What everyone did."

The widow took Daisy's face in her hands and kissed her forehead. "That smile is thanks enough."

"Hang on," Violet said, "and I'll walk you to your door."

"I already have an escort." The widow threaded her free arm through Roy's. "You won't mind getting an old woman across the street now, will you?"

He patted her hand. "It would be my pleasure."

As they crossed the threshold, Beverly rushed up to the porch. "Sorry I'm so late. Did I miss anything?"

"You're right on time," Roy said as they passed by. "Television's ready to go."

"Television?" Beverly stepped inside. "We can watch *Name That Tune*." She sauntered over to the TV, took off her hat, shook out her auburn bob, and whistled. "Well, isn't she something." Her eyes locked on Perry Como. "What a dreamboat." She shimmied her ample hips in front of the screen. "Now *that's* what I call a birthday present."

"Will you eat a piece of cake?" Violet asked.

"Well, I won't say no," Beverly said, taking a seat on the couch.

Daisy spotted two small, brightly wrapped packages. "For me?"

"Happy birthday. Thought you might like to try them out this Saturday night." Beverly punctuated her words with a wink before handing over the gifts. "Mrs. Morgan," she turned to Grace, "beautiful as ever. That shade of pink suits you."

"Thank you, dear. Not everyone's taken to it." Grace pushed her sleeves back to cool off her arms. "We're all in a bit of a rut around here. Sometimes you have to shake things up."

Standing halfway between the parlor and the kitchen, Violet

ignored her mother while she waited her turn to speak. "What's happening Saturday night?" she finally asked.

Before Beverly had a chance to answer, Daisy explained, "We might go to the Elks Club. Ferdie Bistocchi's band is playing."

"We have an itch for jazz." Beverly offered another exaggerated wink.

Daisy gave her friend an almost imperceptible shake of the head before ripping open the first gift. "A lipstick!" She pulled a bejeweled, gold bullet tube out of its navy box.

Beverly gently poked her elbow. "Read the front."

Daisy held up the box. "*Hazel Bishop no smear lipstick*."

"Keep going."

"*Won't eat off, bite off . . .*" Daisy laughed.

"Or kiss off!" Beverly slapped her knee in delight. "Now you're ready for Prince Charming."

Daisy examined the bottom of the tube. "*Secret Red.* How mysterious." She removed the cap, twisted the base, and spread a little lipstick on top of her hand. "It's a bold shade."

"For a bold woman," Beverly said.

"And it goes with my new dress!" Daisy pointed toward an opened box on the hall table.

"And nail polish to match," Beverly said, indicating the second package.

"Thank you!" Daisy gave her friend a hug. "So what happened?"

Beverly looked confused.

"You're an hour late," Daisy said.

"Oh." Beverly exhaled loudly. "That sister-in-law of mine. She's running me ragged. You'd think she was the first woman to ever carry a baby. 'Do this, Cinderella. Do that, Cinderella.' I'll tell you. She and my brother better find a house of their own, and soon. I've about had it."

Grace moved from the couch to the armchair. "My lumbago," she said. "It helps to change positions."

Violet handed a slice of cake and a glass of milk to their guest. "Hope you like chocolate." She went over to her mother, lifted her feet onto the ottoman, and draped the afghan over her legs.

Beverly continued with her complaint: "Tonight, as I was walking out the door, she starts whining about needing a York Peppermint Pattie. *Needing* it, mind you. And what does my mother do? She makes me go to the store for, not one, but two of them. I've never met such a delicate flower in my life." She looked at Violet, who was sitting down again. "How about you, Mrs. D? Were you this demanding when you were pregnant?"

"Well, I . . ." Violet stammered. "I don't really remem—"

"Buttermilk," Grace jumped in. "If I didn't have a full quart of it in the house, I'd make poor Owen go all the way over to Pritchard's on Wayne Avenue, where Taylor's Store is now. Couldn't get enough the whole time I was carrying. Funny how that happens."

"I better clean up before it gets too late." Violet stood and loaded the dirty dessert plates, forks, and glasses onto a black, round, metal serving tray with hand-painted roses, a wedding gift from her mother-in-law all those years ago.

"The dishes can wait," Daisy said. "*This Is Your Life* comes on in fifteen minutes."

"That's more than enough time." Violet kept her eyes on the tray as she headed for the kitchen. Behind her, everyone began singing along with Perry Como and Betty Hutton's rendition of "She's a Lady."

How about you, Mrs. D? Violet set down the tray and grabbed hold of the sink to keep her legs from buckling. *Were you this demanding when you were pregnant?*

Breathe, she thought. *Evenly, quietly, so no one suspects. That's how to hold back the tears*. But the tears came as she knew they would, so she turned on the faucet to mask the sound.

One lie. That's how it started. *Daisy is my daughter. Mine.* And it wasn't much of lie if you really thought about it. She'd raised that child as her own for twenty-five years, and if that didn't make Violet a mother, nothing would.

But it hadn't been just the lie. She'd committed what Mother Mary Joseph at the Good Shepherd Infant Asylum used to call "sins of omission" in service to the lie. Daisy was six years old the first time it happened. She asked if she'd lived in her mother's belly like Beverly's new baby brother, and Violet told her nice girls didn't ask such questions. Her answer was brusque and easy, too easy, but she'd had no choice. You don't burden a child with your own sins.

Yet, Violet hated to think the best part of her life was tied up in a lie. The more you lie, the darker you stain your soul. Every child in Sunday school knew that. And if Violet thought God drew a distinction between telling a thousand different lies or telling the same one a thousand times, well, she was kidding herself. A sin is a sin is a sin.

Nothing to be done about it now, though. Violet had told that lie to protect others, first her sister, then her daughter. Or was that the lie she told herself?

"Show starts in five minutes!" Daisy announced.

"Be right in," Violet said, untying her apron and using it to dab her tears.

CHAPTER TWELVE

"PUT A SMILE IN YOUR SMOKING," a gentleman proclaimed, causing Violet to glance at the TV on her way over to the card table. On the screen, a toothy blonde accepted a proffered cigarette and a ready light. "So smooth," the announcer continued as the woman inhaled. "So satisfying. Chesterfield."

"That actress is a dead ringer for Marilyn Monroe." Beverly patted her auburn hair. "What do you think? Should I go platinum?"

Daisy rolled her eyes before turning toward her mother. "Come sit with us," she said, pulling Archie onto to her lap. "There's plenty of room on the couch."

"I'm fine." Violet sat down at the table and held up a large manila envelope with the words *Walsh's Portrait Studio* stamped on front. "It's high school graduation time. I have photos to color."

"You're going to paint now?" Daisy's face dropped. "It's my birthday. We just got a television."

"I can work and watch at the same time." Violet angled her seat toward the screen. Grace dozed in the armchair alongside her.

"It's not a radio."

Violet ignored Daisy's slight. With Tommy's old penknife, she sliced open the envelope and pulled out the black-and-white portrait of a young woman. An accompanying note read: *Dark brown hair and eyes. Peaches and cream complexion. White sweater. Red neckerchief and lipstick.*

Wonder if it's Secret Red, Violet thought as she glimpsed Daisy. Why had she been so keen to get Beverly off the subject of

Saturday night? Violet may have been keeping a secret from Daisy, but her daughter seemed to have one of her own.

"Who do you think he'll surprise tonight?" Daisy asked.

"Maybe Gary Cooper." Beverly pretended to swoon.

Daisy crinkled her nose. "He's not my cup of tea."

"That's right," Beverly said. "You like them tall . . ." she hesitated, "daaark, and handsome. Isn't that what you told me yesterday?"

Daisy's eyes widened into a warning.

Beverly said, "I'm talking about Cary Grant, of course."

"What woman doesn't love Cary Grant?" Daisy's face slowly relaxed. "*The Philadelphia Story* is one of my favorites."

While the pair discussed the merits of the movie, Violet combed through tubes of Marshall's Photo Oils. *Peaches and cream complexion.* Over the years she'd learned to create every possible skin tone with the same four colors—burnt sienna, cobalt, cadmium yellow, and white. The differences lay in the proportions. She smeared a dollop of burnt sienna onto her palette and saw worlds in that shade of reddish-brown. An autumn of oak leaves. A wall of weathered brick. The apples of Zethray's cheeks.

Two days later and Violet still felt troubled by Zethray's words. *She says it doesn't matter how or why. Only that you claimed that baby.* Who was she to tell Violet what mattered? And, more importantly, how did she know what Violet had done all those years ago? Could she really speak to the dead? Impossible. Violet had gotten caught up in the moment, but time and distance had brought her back to her senses. It was some sort of parlor trick. She'd probably eavesdropped on Violet and Grace the day they'd picked up the dress.

She blended a dab of cobalt into the base while she tried to recall what they'd talked about that day in the ladies' lounge. If Zethray *had* been in there—though for the life of her Violet couldn't remember seeing her—would she have picked up enough of the story to guess at the rest? Maybe.

But why go to the trouble in the first place? Money? To be fair, Zethray hadn't asked Violet for a red cent. Influence of some sort? Violet was hardly in a position of power, and she knew few who were. So many questions swirled through her mind. And the worst one of all—who else might Zethray tell?

For twenty-five years, only a small number of people had known the truth about Daisy's birth. Violet's mother and the widow, of course, but they could be trusted to take that secret to their graves. And her sister Lily would never let on. She hadn't wanted the baby in the first place. Her husband Frankie was no threat. Anything to keep Lily happy. And with Tommy gone, God rest his soul, only Stanley remained. They'd had their differences over the years, but Violet considered him to be a man of his word.

Plenty of outsiders had speculated on the matter. Violet set tongues wagging the moment she got off that train with a baby in her arms.

Who's the father?

I heard she doesn't know.

How many men have there been?

Too many to count.

What kind of woman finds herself in such a predicament?

Violet's kind.

Having been the subject of gossip since her sister Daisy's death, Violet only hoped it wouldn't find its ugly way back to Lily. Fortunately, the eye accepts what it sees, and since everyone saw Violet mothering that child, they all took that part of the lie for truth. After all, so great was Violet's sin, no one ever gave Lily a thought. What woman in her right mind would bear that cross for another?

Violet mindlessly stirred specks of white and yellow into her paint. Even with the gossip, she had no reason to believe the truth would ever come out. No reason to tell her daughter about any of it.

She picked up her palette and held the blended color up to the light to see how close her mixture was to peaches and cream, but with all her fretting, she must have reversed the proportions. Violet had created a rich shade of walnut, perfect for the tops of Zethray's hands. But she wasn't painting Zethray. *Zethray Long.* *Zethray Long Gone.* She should have been long gone from Violet's thoughts by now.

Trumpets blared from the fabric-covered speaker, grabbing Violet's attention.

"It's on!" Daisy tugged her grandmother's foot. Grace murmured and her eyes remained closed.

"*This Is Your Life*," the announcer began. "America's most talked about program is brought to you by America's most talked about cosmetics, Hazel Bishop."

"Hazel Bishop!" Daisy held up her gifts. She and Beverly sat mesmerized as black-and-white pictures of lipstick, nail polish, and liquid rouge floated across the screen.

"And now," the announcer took half a beat, "Mr. *This Is Your Life* himself, Ralph Edwards!" The congenial host filled the screen.

"That's a sharp suit," Beverly whistled.

"He's handsome," Daisy said, "for someone his age."

For someone his age? Violet eyed the man and decided she had at least ten years on him. She turned back to her paints, but her eyes kept drifting toward the screen.

"Sitting here with me is a man whose life was changed as the hands of the clock reached eight fifteen one summer morning." The camera pulled back to reveal a Far Eastern gentleman, lost inside a double-breasted suit too large for his small frame. The host began, "Good evening, sir. Would you tell us your name, please?"

"Kiyoshi Tanimoto." He carefully articulated the syllables as if he were used to making himself understood.

At the sound of his accent, Violet blurted, "He's Japanese!"

"So?" Daisy kept her attention on the screen.

"So, World War II." Violet couldn't help but think of her old neighbor, Mrs. Craven, who'd lost her only boy at Pearl Harbor. She kept that gold star in her window till the day she died.

"Watch," Daisy said. "People are more alike than different."

"I doubt that." Violet studied the man's features—peculiar, to her thinking. Prominent forehead. Narrow eyes. She'd seen such faces in newsreels during the war.

Beverly piped up: "He's a Christian minister."

"Says who?" Violet asked.

"Ralph Edwards, just now."

A sleeping Archie shuddered hard as if shaking off fleas. Violet wished she could rid herself of her peevishness as easily. She thought about all the soldiers' pictures she'd painted during the war years. Some on their way to battle, others safely home with a chest full of hardware. Back then, Violet took pride in knowing the ribbon colors for each medal. It was her small way of honoring the men who'd risked their lives for democracy.

Enough. She plucked a brush out of the jelly jar. *Focus*, she thought, then continued to stare at the TV. The host shook hands with his guest, and Violet found herself wondering how she'd color the scene if this were a photograph instead of a moving picture. Raw sienna for the paneling, she guessed. Shades of viridian for the potted ferns.

Ralph Edwards addressed his guest: "You thought, of course, that you were going to be interviewed as a part of the work you are doing."

"What did I tell you?" Violet tsked. "Lured under false pretenses."

Daisy ignored her mother as the host encouraged his guest to explain the purpose of his visit to the United States.

"I brought a group of girls . . ." Reverend Tanimoto struggled to communicate in English, "who have terrible disfigurement . . ." He searched for the words. "On account of the atomic explosion on Hiroshima."

Violet gasped. She'd seen pictures in a magazine of some of the survivors. They'd looked like burn victims. Like her sister Daisy that terrible Fourth of July.

"We are hoping to have plastic surgery for them," Tanimoto said.

Edwards began explaining the show to his guest: "Through this archway," he motioned to a small curtained area, "will come many people who have shaped your destiny, and we hope you'll have some pleasant moments." He stared into the camera. "We hope, too, ladies and gentlemen, that you will have a better understanding of what it is to look into the face of atomic power."

That was exactly why Violet didn't want a television in her parlor. No one needed to upset their digestion at this hour of the night by watching a program about war. She wanted to get up and turn off the set, but Daisy and Beverly seemed glued to it. Thank goodness her mother was asleep in the chair.

In spite of her discomfort, Violet could not tear her eyes away. On screen, the camera swung over to the announcer from the beginning of the show. He instructed a woman next to him to run steel wool over her painted fingernails. "Not a sign of a chip anywhere," the man said. "Treat yourself to a professional Hazel Bishop manicure."

The camera returned to Edwards. "I've been briefing the Reverend Tanimoto on the show here. He's a little surprised." The host scratched his temple and rolled his eyes. Apparently, the guest had never heard of the program. "Now, Reverend Tanimoto, are you ready to turn the pages?" Edwards held up a leather-bound book with the title *Reverend Kiyoshi Tanimoto, This Is Your Life*.

The minister offered a tentative smile.

"August 6, 1945, Hiroshima, Japan." A map of the nation filled the screen. "The morning is perfectly clear as the warm summer sun rises above the mountains," Edwards read. "What were you doing at six a.m., Reverend?"

Tanimoto explained that he and a friend were moving some of the church's belongings to the country.

The host asked, "Were you expecting a bomb attack?"

"What kind of question is that?" Violet cringed. "I told you, he's awful."

Daisy and Beverly shushed her at the same time.

"At six in the morning you're lending a hand to a member of your parish, when suddenly . . ." Ralph Edwards stopped speaking. A moment later, an air raid siren blasted through the speaker.

Grace jumped in her chair and the afghan fell to the floor. She shifted her position and drifted off again.

"He's torturing that poor man." Violet stood up, covered her mother's legs, and sat back down.

Behind the curtain, the silhouette of a barrel-chested man leaned into a microphone. "At zero six hundred on the morning of August 6, 1945, I was in a B-29 flying over the Pacific, destination Hiroshima."

As confusion registered on Tanimoto's face, Edwards explained, "A voice of a man whose life is destined to be woven up in the threads of your own, Reverend Tanimoto. Now, we'll meet him later on in our story."

Violet went into the kitchen for a glass of water. The orchestra swelled to a crescendo, and as she walked back into the room, a mushroom cloud bloomed on the screen. "Can he see that?" she asked, appalled.

"I suppose he sees what we see," Beverly said without taking her eyes off the set.

The host continued to prod Tanimoto into talking about that day, his feelings of helplessness as he waded through the dead and injured in search of his wife and baby. Edwards brought his guest and audience right up to the brink of the tragedy before pulling everyone back to safety with the story of Tanimoto's early years. His birth. His schooling. His conversion from Buddhism to Christianity. Mrs. Bertha Starkey, the Methodist evangelist who inspired his spiritual transformation, came out from behind the curtain, primly attired in a hat, gloves, and high lace collar.

Tanimoto relaxed at the sight of a familiar face.

Edwards addressed the woman: "Kiyoshi enrolled in a Methodist theological school in Japan, didn't he, Mrs. Starkey?"

The woman delivered what appeared to be a well-rehearsed response: "Yes he did, and when he finally told his father what he had done, his father was so furious that he went to the town hall and struck Kiyoshi's name from the family register, thus legally declaring him no longer a member of the family."

"Look at them airing his dirty linen," Violet said.

"What dirty linen?" Daisy replied.

"How he disappointed his father. That's his business to tell." Violet shifted in her seat for a better view.

Daisy shrugged while Edwards invited others to come through the curtain, including a friend from divinity school and several parishioners from Tanimoto's first church.

Soon enough, the story caught back up to the day of the bombing. "What did you see?" Edwards asked.

Tanimoto struggled. "I saw the whole city on fire . . . their skin peeling off and hanging from face, from arm, but, strange to say, in silence. It looked like," he searched for the English words, "possession of ghosts."

Violet watched, in spite of the volcano in her stomach.

"Did you know," the host continued, "Hiroshima had been the first city to feel the force of atomic power?"

"What an awful question!" Violet could barely contain her distress over the poor man being forced to relive that awful time, especially in front of television cameras.

"He's a witness to history," Daisy countered.

Once again, the male silhouette appeared behind the curtain and spoke: "Looking down from thousands of feet over Hiroshima, all I could think of was, *My God, what have we done?*"

Violet's mouth hung open as Edwards spoke: "The voice again of a man whose second of eternity was woven up with yours, Reverend Tanimoto. Now, you've never met him. You've never seen him, but he's here tonight to clasp your hand in friendship."

Violet, Daisy, and Beverly exchanged looks of incredulity.

"Captain Robert Lewis," Edwards announced, "United States Air Force, who along with Paul Tibbets piloted the plane from which the first atomic power was dropped over Hiroshima."

With a cascade of notes from an offstage harp, the camera panned to Captain Lewis as he pushed through the curtain and grabbed the guest of honor's hand. Tanimoto, his expression stiff, returned the handshake to loud applause before backing away.

"I've had enough." Violet stood up and gently roused Grace. "Mother, are you ready for bed?"

"The show's not over," Daisy groaned.

"It is as far as I'm concerned." Violet took her mother's arm and guided her toward the staircase.

Grace called out to Daisy from the first step: "Was it a good surprise?"

"The very best!" Daisy jumped off the couch, kissed her grandmother, and ran back to her spot in front of the TV.

As Violet climbed the steps behind her mother, she thought about Captain Lewis. Hero or not, the pilot had no right to put Tanimoto in that position. Neither did the host. Violet pictured Tanimoto's face in that moment. Had he felt shame? No, she didn't think so. Sadness? Yes, but something else too. Deference? Not quite. Shock? That was part of it for sure. Forbearance? That was a good word. A sort of patient endurance, when others claim the moral high ground. Violet knew that quality well. She'd demonstrated her share of forbearance throughout her life—when at eight years old people blamed her for her sister's accident. When at twenty-five and unmarried she claimed Daisy as her own. Violet had remained stoic in the midst of accusation and innuendo. What choice did she have back then? What choice did Reverend Tanimoto have now?

By the time Violet got her mother settled, the program was long over and Beverly had gone home. Violet wandered into the kitchen to finish cleaning up and found Daisy at the sink doing dishes. "It's your birthday," Violet said. "I'll do that."

"You can dry." Daisy passed her a dish towel. "You should've waited," she said. "It had a happy ending. His wife and child survived unharmed. They flew in and surprised him."

"That's a relief." Violet pressed the end of the towel into a glass and swirled it around. "What about the girls who need plastic surgery?"

"They stayed behind the curtain. Ralph Edwards didn't want to embarrass."

"So he does have some sense."

Daisy set the last dish in the drainer and wiped the sink. "I'm sorry you didn't like it."

"This TV is going to take some getting used to." Violet put away the dried plates and pulled three cereal bowls out of the cupboard for breakfast. "The older I get, the harder change hits."

"You were right about one thing." Daisy set the silverware on the table.

"What's that?"

"I wouldn't want every detail of my life laid out like that."

Like what it is you're doing Saturday night? Violet decided to keep that thought to herself as she slid cups and saucers off the shelf. "Everyone has secrets."

"Tell me yours," Daisy teased, "and I'll tell you mine."

The two women eyed each other for an uncomfortable moment before breaking into nervous grins. Beads of sweat bubbled on Violet's neck. She fanned away the heat from the furnace rumbling to life inside her.

"What about that handshake?" Daisy said. "Now that was something."

"Something awful." Violet pressed her back against the sink.

"Maybe it gave that pilot a bit of peace."

"But that wasn't the minister's burden to bear." Violet's voice cracked. "He didn't start the war. He didn't drop a single bomb." She twisted the towel as if to wring it out. "He spent his life minding his own business, trying to do his best for others, ignoring his own needs," she took a breath, "and see where it got him."

"Well, look at you . . ." Daisy stared at her mother with wonder, "singing a different tune. What happened to . . ." She raised her voice an octave, "'He's Japanese! World War II!'"

Violet harrumphed. "I didn't say it like that." She turned and gave the sink another wipe.

"But you did say it."

"And I'm sorry for that. We're all God's children."

"You mean that?"

"I guess change doesn't have to hit so hard."

"What a relief." Daisy's shoulders relaxed.

"A relief?" Violet cocked her head.

"I just think we'd all be better off if we could put aside our differences. See people as people. Japanese, Chinese," Daisy glanced up as if searching for another example, "Negro." She bit her lip. "Like you said, we're all God's children."

Violet kissed her daughter's cheek. "Happy birthday, doll baby." She switched off the kitchen light and they moved into the hall.

"You used to call me that when I was little."

"I remember the day you told me you were too old for nicknames. You couldn't have been more than eight or nine."

"I'm not too old anymore." Daisy picked up the Globe Store box and tucked it under her arm.

"And you like your dress?"

"I love it." Daisy gave the box a squeeze.

"You had a nice birthday then?"

"Wonderful." She kissed her mother on the cheek.

"That's what I like to hear." Violet patted Daisy's thigh and Archie jumped off the couch. "Let's go to bed," she said, and the trio headed up.

I'm gonna put on my traveling shoes,
Down by the riverside . . .

City of Scranton, Pennsylvania
Bureau of Police

Witness Statement in the Suicide Death
of Ruth Jones, August 10, 1916

The chair's what stuck out. That and her limp. I was on a ladder in front of the Episcopal church changing out an electric bulb. I seen her with that chair and yelled, "You're supposed to sit on that thing, not carry it!" Kidding around like. Never gave her another thought. Next morning, I read it in the paper. Tore me right up. If only I knowed what she was thinking. Maybe I coulda done something.

Signature of Patrolman on Duty   Signature of Witness

NORMAN BARNWELL   Christopher West

C HAPTER THIRTEEN

JOHNNY SAT ON THE EDGE OF THE TUB, wincing as he clipped back his cuticles, swollen and torn after a week in the slaughterhouse. At the end of his first day, he'd marched straight over to Quint's Army Navy Store and bought himself a pair of work gloves. They helped some, but not enough. Blisters still formed. Still broke open on account of the way he held the knife. Not for slaughtering, thank God. That task fell to other men who could look a steer square in the eyes while stunning him with a bolt gun to the forehead. "Keep them calm or you ruin the meat," the floor butchers would say before slitting the animals' throats.

Johnny had been hired on as a hide-shaker, a backbreaking job, given the weight of the pelts, well over one hundred pounds apiece when saturated. Each one came to him from a rock salt bath, part of the curing process. It was Johnny's job to shake the water from the hides by slamming them hair-side down against a wooden horse, after which he'd take a broom to any caked-on salt. He also had to cut out the horse flies that had burrowed into the flesh. Gloved or not, salt water takes a toll on a man's hands. *Pickled* is what they called it at the plant. "They'll heal up," one of the old-timers had said. "Give it a couple of months." A lifetime for a piano player.

Johnny walked over to the sink, rubbed a little Black and White Ointment into his palms, and waited the minute it took to soak in. "It does wonders," Zethray had said when he'd shown her his hands. Zethray, or Mama Z as he'd taken to calling her, treated him more like a son than a lodger. When Johnny had first arrived in town, he'd found Mama Z's name and address in *The Negro Motorist Green Book*. Hers was the first of three tourist houses listed under *Scranton*. He'd only planned on staying a couple of days, but when the band broke up, she'd offered him the room until he could get back on his feet.

The bulb over the mirror sputtered and died. After he finished dressing, he'd see if Mama Z had a new one. Back in his room, Johnny put on his suit and tie and slapped a few extra drops of aftershave onto his cheeks. No matter how hard he scrubbed, the stench of blood stayed with him. Mama Z had assured Johnny it was in his head, not his pores. "The nose has a way of holding onto a smell."

He slid his feet into a pair of black-and-white wingtips and gingerly double-knotted the laces. All set, he thought, for Saturday night at the Elks Club with Ferdie Bistocchi and his Dixieland Band. And maybe, just maybe, Daisy would show up. All his life he'd been warned off of white girls, *no sense courting trouble*, but she lit a spark in him that could not be dimmed with reason.

After a look in the dresser mirror, Johnny headed downstairs in search of Mama Z.

"Sorry to interrupt," he said when he found her sitting in the kitchen, her eyes shut, an orange scarf with gold pineapples wrapped around her hair. "Light's burned out in the bathroom." When she didn't respond, he added, "If you have a bulb, I'll change it."

Zethray chuckled. "Where you off to smelling so good?" She aimed her nose at him and sniffed.

"Too much?"

She opened her eyes and took in the sight of him. "You clean up real good," she said. "That's one lucky girl."

"No girl. I'm playing with Ferdie tonight."

"Tell the truth and shame the devil." Zethray stood up, measured out a quart of water, and poured it into the percolator.

"That is the truth." Johnny caught his reflection in the window and evened out his tie.

Zethray cocked her eye. "The whole of it?" She scooped four heaping spoonfuls of coffee into the basket.

"The part you need to know." Johnny smiled. "Looks like you're getting company." He patted the kitchen table, a four-seater with chrome legs and a mint-green Formica top, set with two hand-stitched place mats, cups and saucers, napkins, and a couple of spoons.

"Marcella Madison from over on Pine Street. Tall woman. Silver hair." Zethray glanced at the back door. "Said she'd be here after practice."

"Don't think I've had the pleasure."

"She's the choir director at the African Methodist Episcopal Church on North Washington. Must be thirty years now." Zethray crossed her arms and rested them on her ample bosom. "'Course, you'd know that if you went to a service once in a while."

"Thought you were a member at Shiloh Baptist."

"I am, but I go over to the AME church when there's a visiting preacher. I like to hear a different voice now and then. They get a good crowd. Lotta nice girls at both churches, not that it's any of my business."

Johnny smiled again. "Lotta nice girls everywhere."

Zethray blew air into one cheek and then the other, as if biding her time while deciding whether or not to let that comment pass. "Marcella," she said, choosing the earlier thread, "is itchin' to talk to that husband of hers. He passed a couple weeks back. Sounds like she's ready to forgive him for something or other."

"I used to know a Hungarian woman who read palms down at the Steel Pier," Johnny said.

"That's a lot of mumbo jumbo."

"You think so?"

"I know so." Zethray put the percolator on the stove. "I know lots of things."

"Like what?"

"Like how you need to be careful. Big-city ideas don't always go over in a small town."

Johnny laughed. "Atlantic City's a lot smaller than Scranton."

"You know what I mean. It's best to go along to get along around here. That means keeping with your own kind."

"It's a great big world, Mama Z. I only want my piece of it. I'm tired of waiting. Anyway," he said, "times are changing."

"Your generation wants everything fast."

"We see how life should be, and we're not afraid to take what's ours."

"What *should* be is a long ways off from what *is*."

A car horn beeped out front. "That's my ride." Johnny turned to leave. "Don't you fret," he called back. "I'll be good as gold."

"Fool's gold," Zethray muttered as she waited for the coffee to brew.

Half an hour later, Zethray and Marcella Madison sat across from one another in mint-green chairs. "I'm telling you," Marcella said for the second time since she'd arrived, "it's a beautiful set." She lifted the place mat and ran her hand across the tabletop's faux mother-of-pearl design.

Zethray appreciated the compliment. She'd had her eye on this dinette since last year, knowing how good it would match her floral wallpaper. No need to mention, she could finally afford it because of a damaged table leaf and her Globe Store discount. That was her business.

"Now, like I told you when you telephoned," Zethray began, "I'll try my best, but I'm guessing your husband ain't been dead long enough to come through." When Marcella didn't respond, Zethray explained, "Some souls take months, even years, to settle in. Has nothing to do with him loving you. Your Otis is on his own journey now."

Marcella unsnapped her purse, pulled out a postcard with a sepia photograph on the front, and laid it on the table. "I'm not here for Otis."

Zethray studied the image of a soldier sitting in a wicker chair, calves wrapped in long strips of cloth called puttees, head topped with a garrison-style side cap. World War I, no doubt. A volunteer in one of the army's few Negro units. She eyed the contours of the young man's face. He couldn't have been more than eighteen.

"That the Starks boy?" Zethray said, remembering when his family got word of his death over in France.

"My daddy didn't want Walter coming around." Marcella stroked the soldier's capped head with her finger. "Said I was too young."

"Love don't care nothing about age," Zethray said.

Marcella kept her eyes on the photo. "When I turned sixteen, we took ourselves to Wilkes-Barre and found a preacher." She sat straight up. "I became Mrs. Walter Starks. Happiest day of my life." The corners of her mouth lifted then dropped. "Next day, he went off with a cousin of his and joined up. Said he wanted to make a proper life for us. The morning he shipped out, I cried and cried. Told him I'd never forgive him, and I never did."

"Did Otis know?"

"No, ma'am. I never told a soul until this very minute. At first, I figured I was better off keeping the wedding to myself while I waited for Walter to come home." She sighed. "Of course, he never did. After that, I didn't want to share my grief with anybody. It was all I had left of him."

In such a close-knit neighborhood, secrets were hard to keep. Zethray marveled at this woman's ability to hold onto hers.

"All these years, I thought maybe you knew," Marcella said, "given your talent." She dropped her head. "That's why I always kept a bit of distance."

"I only know what the dead tell me. And besides," Zethray said, "I'm not one to pry."

"I'd be tempted to if I had your gift." Marcella sat quiet for a moment. "Otis was a good man, treated me like a queen." She doled out her next sentence in pieces: "And I loved him . . . in my own way . . . but he was no Walter."

Zethray understood uneven love. She'd been fool enough to build a marriage out of it, thinking her flame could spark his. That never happened, but give Sam his due. As long as he put his feet under her table, he never strayed. He never grew to love her either. Five years in, he finally left, but not before fixing the loose stovepipe and patching a hole in the roof. Sam was that kind of man, and all this time later, her heart still swelled at the thought of him.

"Let me see." As Zethray picked up the postcard, she could hear the wicker groan under the man's weight. Her eyes swept across the words *Pvt. Walter Starks* typed in small letters on the top part of the photo. She inhaled deeply, taking in the warmth of his pride. "He's a fine-looking soldier," she said. "But you don't need me." She set the picture back down. "You can forgive him your own self."

"I want to hear *his* side of things." Marcella bit her lower lip. "Providing he shows."

"He will," Zethray said. "Back of my neck is already tingling."

"What's that mean?"

"Means he's on his way." Zethray shook out her arms and legs and rolled her shoulders. "Like when you put your hand on the railroad track and feel a vibration. Can't see the train yet, but you know it's coming." She sat up taller and closed her eyes. After about a minute of silence, her nose started to whistle.

"Walter," Marcella whispered, "you in there?"

Zethray gave a little snort. "He's playful," she said, her eyes still closed. "I can hear him teasing me about my scarf. It reminds him of his mother."

Marcella tittered. "She liked bright colors."

"Like a peacock, he's saying."

"That's her." Marcella sounded relieved. "Can you see him?"

Zethray looked down the dark tunnel that stretched out in front of her closed eyes. A bloodied figure stepped into the light, his chest sliced open with a bayonet. *Not like that.* She kept the words inside her head where only Walter could hear them. *Weak stomach.* The man bowed slightly, lifted his cap by its knife-sharp crease, and set it back again. His uniform suddenly immaculate, his body whole, Zethray nodded her thanks and answered Marcella's question: "I see him. He's holding a few strings of something in his hand. Something pinkish."

"This?" Marcella reached into her pocket and pulled out a three-strand necklace made of small, coral-colored glass beads. "He gave this to me on our wedding day. So he can see me?" The woman's curiosity gave way to regret. "I'm not the girl I used to be." She smoothed out the front of her sherbet-striped caftan.

"You were all arms and legs." Zethray laughed and opened her eyes. The walls of the kitchen had fallen away. Out where the parlor should have been, Walter sat on a rock near a river. "Says you hadn't finished coming into your womanhood yet."

Marcella sucked in her prominent stomach. "I'm fifty-six years old. I've grown into it and then some."

"He's tapping the side of his nose. That some kind of joke you shared?"

"You asking me or him?" Marcella's brow furrowed.

"He says you as beautiful as the day you met."

"Tell Walter that's one whopper of a lie." Marcella relaxed her belly. "And I thank him for it. Truly."

"He's showing me something." Zethray closed her eyes again, trying to bring the picture into sharper focus. "It's metal. Gold, I think. A coin? No." With her lids still shut, she leaned forward for a better look. "A star?" Her head tilted to one side then the other. "Stars mean anything to you?"

"Not that I can think of."

"It'll come." Summoning spirit brought with it a kind of tired Zethray felt in her bones. She suppressed a yawn and opened her eyes to avoid nodding off. "What's that? Something blue. The color of cornflowers. And more stars. Lots of them. White. Different from the metal one." She squinted. "And some sort of bird? I'm not sure what—" She broke off her sentence as the little white girl named Daisy skipped past Walter to take a turn up front. "I thought I was done with you," Zethray said.

"With me?" Marcella asked.

"Nah. Some souls don't wait to be called on. They show up on their own." Walter took a couple of steps back to give the child some room. "I already delivered your message," Zethray said to the girl. She found children exhausting, be they flesh or spirit. "My part's done."

Talk to my sister. Daisy twirled and the skirt of her white cotton dress filled with air. *She can tell you about the stars.*

"Violet? Trust me, baby, she wants nothing to do with me."

"Walter!" Marcella stared up at the ceiling. "Are you still there?"

"He's here," Zethray assured, "waiting for the girl to have her say."

"What girl?" The veins in Marcella's neck started pulsing. "If he had another woman . . ."

"Simmer down. She's not here for Walter."

"Then who?"

"Good question." If only Zethray could talk to her own mother. More to the point, if only her mother would talk to her. She came to Zethray all the time. And since her mother was the one who brought the child forward to begin with, she'd be the one to ask. But much to Zethray's dismay, her mother never made a sound.

Undeterred, Daisy said, *Violet can help. She likes to help.*

"I don't mean to be rude," Zethray said, "but this woman here is a paying customer, and she's wanting to speak to her first husband."

"Zethray! That was supposed to stay between us," Marcella huffed. "How do you know she won't tell the whole town?"

"'Cause she's spirit." Zethray rolled her eyes. "Who she gonna tell?"

"Otis, for one." Marcella put a hand to her heart. "He went his whole life not knowing about Walter, and I intend to keep it that way."

Zethray tried and failed to keep from grinning. "He'll know soon enough. That's how it works up there." She took a breath to rein in her amusement. "But he won't care. He's walked this earth. He's lived temptation."

"I don't like this one bit." Marcella snatched the postcard and slipped it back into her purse.

"That tickled Walter's funny bone." Zethray chortled along with Walter, who stepped forward again. "He says you always was quick to anger. Like that time the cake fell."

"It was for the church picnic," Marcella's voice rose with indignation. "I wanted it to be perfect. Wait, how'd you know about that cake?"

"Walter."

"What's he doing telling my secrets?"

"He's tapping his nose again. Mean anything yet?"

"Nothing comes to mind."

"He's showing me something." Zethray leaned in. "I see," she said before directing her words toward the woman: "A brown jacket and matching breeches. His wool uniform."

"Wet wool. I hate that smell." Marcella's eyes watered again. "It was raining the morning he shipped out. I ran to the station to beg him not to go, and I buried my nose in that wool coat. The odor stayed with me long after the train pulled out. To this day, I think of him when I smell it." The instant the words crossed her lips, understanding struck. She tapped her nose and attempted a smile.

"I knew it'd come to you," Zethray said. "And he knows you love him."

Marcella pulled a handkerchief out of her purse. "I do. I really do."

"He loves you too."

"How can he?" She gave her nose a quick blow. "I swore I'd never forgive him."

"He didn't take that to heart." Zethray yawned loudly. "You were young, scrappy, full of affection." She stretched her arms. "Passionate, he's telling me." A second yawn. "He's whispering it again. *I love you.*"

Marcella's shoulders relaxed. "He loves me." She glanced at Zethray. "Are you all right?" She reached for the percolator. "Let's get some coffee into you," she said. "You're nothing but a dishrag."

"You get what you needed?" Zethray put her elbows on the table and dropped her face into her hands.

"Yes, ma'am." Marcella poured coffee for each of them. "I was coming here for peace of mind, and I'm taking true love home with me." She passed a cup and saucer to her host. "I'll be forever grateful."

The first sip of the coffee roused Zethray to the point of sitting up. She watched, fuzzy-headed, as the papered kitchen walls slowly materialized around her. "He's gone now."

"Will he come back?"

"Not tonight," Zethray said, "but they're never far from us. Take comfort in that."

"I do." Marcella sounded unsure. "I will," she corrected. "It's easy to get lost in the past."

"So long as you don't get stuck there." Zethray poured a spoonful of sugar into her coffee. "So what're you going to do with yourself now that Otis is gone?"

"Anything I damn well please." Shocked by the boldness of her own answer, Marcella's hand flew to her lips. "I can't believe I . . ."

The pair locked eyes and giggled like young girls. "No shame in honesty," Zethray said.

"Nothing like a husband to make demands on a woman's time." Marcella fanned her face and returned to the original question. "Maybe I'll take a trip to see my sister out in Harrisburg. What about you? I don't see a man keeping you down."

"Not that I wouldn't like a good roll in the hay once in a while." Zethray winked and both women roared.

"I hear that." Marcella pulled a flask out of her purse and poured a finger of whiskey into each of their coffees. "To Walter." She lifted her cup and Zethray followed suit. "And Otis." They toasted again.

"To Sam." Zethray held up her drink. "He married me for my eyes. Said they were my best feature." She tugged at the bottom of her left lid. "Mostly brown with specks of copper, but if you look real close, they're rimmed in green. Sam fell in love with these eyes." Zethray sat back and took a swallow of coffee. "Wish he could've fallen for the rest of me."

"To Sam," Marcella said, and she added a touch more whiskey to each of their cups.

CHAPTER FOURTEEN

WITH A TOOT OF THE HORN, Beverly pulled up in front of the Davies's house as the sun was setting.

"You may as well park," Violet called from a rocker on the porch. "Daisy's still upstairs getting ready."

"Slowest poke in Scranton," Beverly responded through her open window. "Has been since first grade." She got out and slammed the door.

Violet peered around the post and watched as Beverly came toward the steps. "Your hair!" she shrieked, startling Archie who'd been snoozing at her feet. "It's so short! And so blond!"

"And all the rage. Not everyone can pull it off though." Beverly put her hands on her waist and swiveled her hips. "You have to have the figure for it," she laughed.

"It's . . ." Violet clicked her tongue till she landed on a word, "daring." She tipped her head from side to side, examining the style from both angles.

"Platinum glamour waves like Miss Marilyn Monroe. Not *Gentlemen Prefer Blondes* Marilyn. *The Seven Year Itch* Marilyn. It's coming out next month." Beverly tucked a few curls behind her ears. "They're showing it in all the magazines."

"Turn around." Violet studied the back of the cut. "Well," she said, "if it's all the rage."

"You're next." Beverly snipped the air with her fingers. "Though I see you as more of the Elizabeth Taylor type."

Violet stood up and opened the screen door opened for Beverly. "Are you saying I don't have the figure for Marilyn?"

Before Beverly had a chance to respond, Violet surprised her with an awkward shimmy, and they both cracked up.

"Violet, is that you?" Grace called out from her chair in the parlor.

"Yes, Mother. And Beverly."

"Tell her to come say hello."

"I'm right here, Mrs. Morgan." Beverly poked her head into the room. "It's Saturday night. Get your dancing shoes on."

"Look at you!" Grace clapped her hands. "Very snazzy."

"You like?" Beverly gave her curls a shake as she bent to hug Grace.

"I'm afraid my dancing days are over," Grace said. "Not that I was ever much of a dancer. My Owen used to dance me around the kitchen from time to time." She began swaying in her chair. "Violet, remember him dancing me around?"

"Can't say I do." Violet sat on the couch and Archie jumped up beside her.

"How're you ladies enjoying the television?" Beverly asked. "Ever watch *Search for Tomorrow*?"

"I'm not much for soap operas," Violet said. "Takes 'em a week to turn a page."

"My mother's obsessed. As soon as her program starts, everybody has to get quiet or get out."

"Beverly," Daisy shouted from her bedroom, "I need your help!"

"That's my cue." As Beverly stood up, she could hear Grace say, "Violet, you remember. He'd dance me all around the kitchen."

"Yes, Mother," Violet gave in. "All around the kitchen."

"I can't believe it!" Daisy screamed when she saw Beverly's hair.

"You like?"

"Love!" Daisy stood back in awe. "You'll be fighting the men off with sticks tonight."

"Let's hope so. Now what about you?"

Standing in her strapless bra and petticoat, Daisy held out two pairs of earrings, imitation pearls and rhinestones. "Which ones?"

"I have to see you in the dress first." Beverly dropped onto the bed and admired her reflection in the bedroom mirror. "I may have put your mother into an early grave with this hair."

"She's not one for change," Daisy said, pulling a garment out of her closet.

"How do you think she'll react when she finds out about this Johnny of yours?"

Daisy stepped into the gathered skirt of her red taffeta dress, slipped her arms through the narrow straps, and lifted the boned bodice into place. "He's not mine," she said, backing up to the bed unzipped.

"Not yet." Beverly pulled the zipper up.

"Let's not borrow trouble." With a little dab of Vaseline, Daisy polished a few scuffs out of her patent-leather flats. "I'm not sure he even likes me that way."

"Don't try to kid a kidder." Beverly glanced at the mirror again. "Just make sure I'm not here when you drop this bombshell on your mother. I almost swallowed my teeth when you told me, and I'm broad-minded."

"Can we just get through tonight?" Daisy shook out her petticoat, planted her hands at her cinched waist, and swooshed. "What do you think?"

"I think you'll drive him mad."

Daisy dabbed a little Shalimar on her wrists and behind her ears. "I'm not trying to drive anyone mad." She turned away from Beverly and added another drop of perfume to the V of cleavage visible at the notch, centered on her squared neckline.

Beverly handed her the rhinestone earrings. "You're a regular Anna Sage."

"Who?"

"The Lady in Red. The girl who betrayed . . ." Beverly snapped her fingers, trying to recall the name. "You know. The gangster who robbed all the banks. They made a movie."

"Dillinger?" Daisy said, clipping on her earrings.

"Dillinger. He's one of those dangerous men," she lowered her voice, "like this Johnny of yours."

"Johnny's not dangerous." Daisy fumbled through a drawstring bag of makeup, pulled out a compact, and powered her face. "You should have seen him helping me with that piano."

"But you haven't told your mother."

"Well, no."

"Then he's dangerous," Beverly concluded.

"You're incorrigible." Daisy applied rouge to the apples of her cheeks. "Besides, there's nothing to tell yet." *Nothing*, she repeated to herself. So why were her insides shaking? And not only her stomach. Her head too. That woozy feeling she'd get as a child playing blindman's bluff. Daisy remembered taking her turn at being "it"—the blindfold covering her eyes, the neighborhood kids spinning her till she lost her bearings. That first step, an act of faith that her foot would land safely. Scared and excited, she'd stagger toward the laughter in the hopes of tagging someone out.

Daisy opened her new tube of Secret Red and carefully dotted the cupid's bow of her upper lip. *When you're young,* she thought, *that kind of scared doesn't stop you. It keeps you coming back. But now?* She steadied her hand to color in her lower lip.

"Remember hygiene class? Mrs. Chapin?" Beverly jutted her chin and raised her voice an octave. "*Any girl who can put lipstick on without a mirror is too social.*"

Daisy couldn't help but howl at Beverly's spot-on impression. "*And never put lipstick on in front of a boy.*" She batted her mascaraed lashes. "*It'll give him ideas.*"

"I wouldn't mind giving a man a few ideas. Does this Johnny of yours have a friend or two?"

Daisy blotted her lips and threw the tube into her purse for touch-ups. "We'll find out soon enough." She took a deep breath, but still felt woozy. No matter. She was scared, but *good* scared. The kind of scared that accompanied big change. Moving to Atlantic City. Coming back home. Opening a studio.

Falling in love? Maybe. A shiver of possibility surged through her like a gust of wind on the cusp of a new season. She tucked a handkerchief into her clutch. "Ready?"

"And able." Beverly smirked and they started for the stairs.

As soon as they reached the bottom, Violet came over. "Two beauties."

"We're hoping to break a few hearts tonight." Beverly adjusted the straps of her slip so they wouldn't show under her sleeveless sheath.

"Blue's a good color for you," Violet said, "especially with that hair."

"See? It's already growing on you. And what about Daisy's dress? Fits her like a glove."

"I picked it out," Violet bragged. "Not bad for an old lady."

Daisy glanced over at her grandmother, snoring lightly in her chair. "Guess I'm too late to say good night."

"I was just getting ready to wake her for bed," Violet said.

A hint of sadness pulled at the corners of Daisy's eyes. "She's sleeping more and more."

"She's fine," Violet assured. "We had a busy day."

"It's getting to be every day," Daisy said.

"I know." Violet blinked back her emotion. "But she's a tough old bird. She's not going anywhere for a long while."

Daisy walked over to her grandmother and gently kissed her cheek. "Sweet dreams," she whispered.

"Now get going, you two." Violet led the girls over to the door.

"I can stay home," Daisy offered, "if you need me."

"I think Beverly might have something to say about that. We're fine here. Go. Have a good time. But not *too* good a time. And be careful."

"We will," they echoed as they stepped onto the porch.

Out of earshot, Beverly said, "And if we can't be careful, we'll name it after you," cracking herself up all the way to the car.

"I have to get cigarettes," Beverly said as she dragged Daisy into the drugstore across the street from the Elks Club, "and a roll of Life Savers."

"Skip the cigarettes," Daisy said, "and you won't need the mints."

"But I look sexy when I smoke. Like a woman of mystery." Beverly puckered her lips and kissed the air.

"You look like a chimney. There's no mystery in that."

"I think someone's nerves are getting the best of her." Beverly grabbed both items from the same colorful display at the cash register and handed the clerk a one-dollar bill. "See? Easy as pie." With one quick sweep of her forearm, the Life Savers, cigarettes, and change fell into her open handbag.

"I just don't want them giving away our tickets after he went to all that trouble," Daisy said as they stepped outside.

"I don't think it was any trouble," Beverly said and the pair linked arms. "All kidding aside, are you sure you know what you're doing?"

"What do you mean?"

"You said it yourself. I'm the wild one. You're the good girl."

"I said you're the brave one. And you didn't see me in Atlantic City," Daisy explained as they crossed North Washington Avenue. "I lived free as a bird. And my dance card was always full."

Beverly lowered her voice. "Did you ever have any colored names on that card?" She put up her hands. "Just wondering how far you're willing to go."

Daisy ignored the question. "Club Row is all lit up tonight," she said, referring to a trio of architectural gems in the same downtown block. With its elegant limestone and brick facade, the Elks Club held its own between the Masonic Temple and the Scranton Club. She took Beverly's arm as they strolled up a wide set of concrete steps, stopping briefly to admire dozens of bearded irises blooming from a pair of urns on either side. "I'll cross that bridge when I come to it."

"I think we're crossing it now," Beverly said as they passed under the patinaed copper awning and through the front door. Once inside, she stopped to take in the beauty of the foyer with its marble floor and barreled ceiling. "Those Elks know a thing or two about class."

"How many?" a male voice asked.

Daisy turned to her right to find a man at a desk distributing tickets. Behind him, members of the club wandered in and out of a heavily paneled room called *Men's Reception*. "Two," she said, "for Daisy Morgan Davies."

"Davies." He thumbed through an envelope. "Downstairs in the ballroom," he said, handing over the tickets. "Give these to the usher. He'll take you to your table. Enjoy your evening."

"He didn't forget," Beverly said as they followed the crowd down a grand marble staircase. "That's a good sign."

Inside the ballroom, people clustered around cabaret-style tables, talking, laughing, drinking. While the pair waited for someone to take their tickets, Daisy marveled at the splendor of clothing before her—a garden of dresses in vibrant shades of red, blue, green, and yellow, and delicate tones of pink, mint, lilac, and lemon chiffon. The men's suits reflected a more sedate palette of browns and grays, as if to complement the women and allow their colors to sing.

"Next," an usher said and Daisy handed him the tickets. He led the young women through a maze of round tables. Each time they neared empty seats, Daisy expected the man to stop, but he kept going till they arrived up front.

"Swanky," Beverly said.

Daisy glanced at the stage. No Johnny yet. Just a set of drums and an upright piano.

"What would you ladies like to drink?" a waiter asked as soon as they were seated.

"Two sloe gin fizzes," Beverly answered. "We need a little liquid courage tonight."

Daisy raised her hand to object before dropping it back on her lap. "Maybe you're right."

After peeling off the cellophane wrapper, Beverly opened the cardboard lid on her pack of Lucky Strikes, tapped out a cigarette, and held it between her fingers. She surveyed the room and let her eyes settle on a gentleman sitting alone at the next table. "Would you mind giving me a light?" she asked with a girlish lilt in her voice.

He ogled her as he pulled a lighter from his breast pocket. "Always happy to help a damsel in distress."

"I'll *damsel* you," a woman said as she strutted up to his table from the direction of the ladies' room. "And to think I gave you that lighter for our anniversary."

As the man stammered out an apology to his wife, Beverly slinked back around in her seat. "Can I pick 'em or what?"

"Or what," Daisy joked, grabbing one of several matchbooks scattered on their table. "Would the damsel like a light?"

Daisy struck a match and touched the flame to Beverly's cigarette. The paper caught, but as Beverly tried to take a puff, the scent of burnt sugar filled the air. "What in the . . ."

They examined the pack. Same red circle. Same gold and black trim. Same words—*Lucky Strike, King Size*—but there in small letters on another line, *Milk Chocolate*.

"You're right," Daisy said giggling. "Nothing sexier than smoking a candy cigarette." She tapped one out of the pack and held it between two fingers like a pro. "May I have a light?"

Beverly held her cool long enough to take an exaggerated drag before bursting into a very unladylike snort.

"We look like two fools," Daisy said in an effort to gain control of herself.

"We better pull it together," Beverly managed, "before they kick us out."

Both young women stared at their laps to avoid eye contact and took a few deep breaths.

Just then, the waiter returned with their drinks.

Beverly lifted her glass as if to toast. "For the fizzy broads up front," she said, and they broke into stitches again.

Daisy checked Beverly's wristwatch. "It's five after." She glanced up at the empty stage. "Shouldn't the band be here by now?"

Beverly peeled the paper off her Lucky Strike and popped the chocolate into her mouth. "Maybe they stopped for cigarettes."

"I'm serious."

"You're nervous." Beverly grabbed her drink and pushed Daisy's toward her. "Down the hatch. He'll be here any minute."

"That's what I'm afraid of," Daisy said, picking up her glass.

"So let me get this straight," Ferdie said to the stage manager holding open the back door. "You're saying, me and the boys . . ." with his bass case in his left hand, he pointed to the four other white musicians with his right, "are welcome to play . . ."

"More than welcome," the stage manager assured.

". . . as long as Johnny here sits this one out."

"That's what I'm saying."

Ferdie squinted in mock confusion. "You have something against piano players?"

"Don't get cute."

"Says here," Ferdie propped his bass against the building and pulled a handwritten contract out of his houndstooth sport coat, "you hired Ferdie Bistocchi and his Dixieland Band." He put his hand on Johnny's shoulder. "This young man is part of the band."

"Not tonight."

"Understood." Ferdie slapped Johnny on the back as he turned to face the white musicians. "I heard the Ron-Da-Voo's in need of a band tonight."

"The club in South Side?" the trumpeter asked.

"At the bottom of Cedar Avenue," the drummer offered. "The old Shangri-La."

"That's the one," Ferdie said. "Let's go and surprise them." He looked at Johnny. "They've got themselves a nice piano."

"What the hell is going on?" a man bellowed from the open doorway. "I have a full house and no band!"

"Emmett." Ferdie turned and shook hands with the Elks Club's leader. "I was wondering when you'd show." He put his arms in the air. "Your buddy here's turning us away."

"Only him." The stage manager hooked his thumb at Johnny. "I knew you wouldn't want a darkie in the house."

"I don't give a rat's arse what color he is," Emmett bellowed. "I have paying customers inside, and I need a band!" He looked at Ferdie. "Can the kid play?"

"Six ways to Sunday."

"Then let 'em in." Emmett glared at the stage manager. "All of 'em."

"You heard the man." Ferdie grabbed his instrument and waved Johnny through the door first. "It's showtime."

CHAPTER FIFTEEN

FERDIE STRODE ONTO THE STAGE and over to the microphone as the band members took their places. "Sorry for the delay, folks. We'll only be a minute."

Swells of cigarette smoke ebbed and flowed as the first few tables applauded.

Ferdie got to work unpacking his bass. The other musicians followed suit. After a double set of clicks, the trombone and clarinet players pulled their instruments out of velvet-lined cases while the trumpeter plucked his horn from a paper bag. Johnny helped the drummer carry his snare and cymbals over to the house drum kit before continuing stage right to the piano.

"Jesus, Mary, and Joseph!" a gray-haired man with a stubbled chin yelled from the bar, "and all the rest of the goddamn gang!"

Save for a few clanking glasses, the room fell silent. An enraged Emmett stormed over, grabbed the loudmouth's arm, and said, "Let's go."

"You're kicking *me* out," the man pointed at Johnny, "instead of that louse?" He pulled free. "I won't soon forget this," he said, beating it for the door.

Quiet gasps rippled through the crowd as they all swung back toward the band. After a moment, Ferdie leaned into the microphone and said, "Good riddance to bad rubbish." Most of the audience applauded. To punctuate the sentiment, the trumpeter picked up his plunger mute and played a descending *wah wah wah wah*.

"For ten dollars," Beverly called out, "Name. That. Tune!"

Everyone laughed, and the man with the trumpet gave her a cheeky grin.

Daisy took in the entire scene from her front-row table. The band. The man at the bar. Johnny. As a young girl, she'd gone to see *The Wizard of Oz* with her parents. Years later, her father had told her that before seeing the movie, someone had tipped him off to its dazzling transformation from black-and-white into color. He'd known enough to watch his daughter watching the movie, so he could catch her reaction. She thought about that as she watched Johnny watching the events unfold.

He sat at the piano, a black-lacquered upright set perpendicular to the edge of the stage. She could only see him in profile now, but when he'd first walked out, he'd given her a smile that had set her heart racing.

Then that awful man had to spoil the moment with his ugly behavior. Thankfully, the band and Beverly broke the tension. Leave it to Beverly to loosen up the crowd. Daisy watched Johnny watching the bandleader for the signal. Ferdie said something only the musicians could hear. Their quizzical expressions turned to nods in Johnny's direction. After a quick shuffle of sheet music, Ferdie stepped up to the microphone.

"What a night." He shook his head. "And we haven't even got started." He glanced at the band and back to the audience. "A change in our song list. A little treat for all your troubles. 'Tiger Rag,' ladies and gents." He snapped his fingers, counting off.

All of the musicians seemed to stand down except for Johnny, who straightened his back, extended his forearms, held his wrists high, and curved his fingers.

No intro. No pickup. He dug right in, squeezing every drop out of a note, using it up completely. The juice. The pulp. A couple of seeds. The zest in the rind for good measure.

His ravenous style, his syncopated rhythms, set Daisy's heart afire. She angled her seat to get a better look. Johnny's hands skittered up and down the ivories, a pair of blue crabs on white sand. In the piano's black-lacquered fallboard, a second set of mirrored hands kept up the same wild tempo.

New musical phrases dovetailed with old melodic lines. Johnny was both playing the song and creating it. For a moment, he switched to a lighter touch, skipping notes like stones across a pond.

Daisy remembered to breathe.

Moment over, the tempo surged to a dizzying clip. As Johnny neared the end of the song, sharps and flats flew off of his fingers, crashed to the floor, and scattered like marbles.

Loud. Harsh. Barbed. Seemingly chaotic.

Pure. Bright. Clear. Maddeningly honest.

A beat of silence, and then Johnny played a simple glissando, a shiver of descending notes to finish the number, cleanse the palate, reset the heart.

Daisy sat in awed silence.

Ferdie addressed the stunned crowd: "That's Johnny Cornell. Remember the name, ladies and gents."

The audience broke into exuberant applause.

Ferdie and the boys started on "Tiger Rag" a second time, layering in the warm, rich, deep, crisp sounds of their instruments. Ferdie proved to be a generous bandleader, giving every man a chance to shine.

Daisy half listened, still savoring Johnny's performance. His kind of talent made you happy to be alive and sorry for all the time you'd wasted. Such beauty. Such pain. A good cry set to music.

"Let's dance." Beverly grabbed Daisy's arm as the band slid into "Sweet Georgia Brown."

"Did you hear him?"

"Oh, I heard him," Beverly said. "Now let's go."

"I can't." Daisy's face tensed into an apology. "Not yet."

"Suit yourself." Beverly used her thumbs to pull the straps from her slip back into place. "I need to take this dress out for a spin."

"I'll stay here and watch the purses."

"Why? Do they do tricks?" Beverly laughed at her joke all the way to the dance floor.

A dozen songs later, Ferdie mopped his brow. "That was 'Honeysuckle Rose,' ladies and gents. Give it up for the boys." The crowd clapped loudly. "We're going to take a little break," he said. "Be back in two shakes of a lamb's tail."

Daisy watched as the musicians disappeared into the wings. Four out of the six, including Ferdie, reappeared through a side door that opened to the ballroom.

"Thanks for taking care of that clown," Ferdie said as he caught Emmett's eye.

"There's ladies present," Emmett said. "We'll not tolerate profanity in here."

"Just the profanity?" The drummer shook his head, grumbling, and headed on to the bar.

Daisy watched the side door for another minute, but when Johnny failed to emerge, she scraped her chair back around to the table.

"You're missing all the fun." Beverly sat down and drank up the last slivers of melting ice in her sloe gin fizz. She motioned to the waiter. "Two more."

Daisy tapped a chocolate cigarette out of the pack and peeled off the paper. "Where is he?" She snapped the candy in two and popped one of the halves into her mouth.

"Excuse me, ladies." The trumpeter, a string bean of a man, pulled up an empty chair, sat down between the women, and set his paper-bagged horn on the table. "Top-secret mission," he said, his voice low. He lifted a blond eyebrow and gazed at Beverly. "Kenny Wilkens."

"Beverly Hudson." She extended her hand. "Pleased to make your acquaintance."

"Don't you mean Miss Marilyn Monroe?" Kenny squeezed

the tips of Beverley's fingers. "The pleasure is mine." His eyes settled on hers and lingered.

"So what's with the grocery sack?" Beverly asked.

"If it's good enough for Dizzy Gillespie," Kenny patted his trumpet, "it's good enough for me."

Daisy gave a little tug on his jacket sleeve. "You said something about a secret mission."

"That's right. I get distracted in the presence of beauty." He threw Beverly a flirty grin, then turned to Daisy. "Duke Ellington over there," he gestured toward the opposite wall, "would like to have a word with you."

Daisy swung around and saw Johnny standing near a side exit, his knee bent, a black-and-white wingtip planted against the baseboard. He tilted his head toward the doorway and winked an invitation. A thrilling mix of fear and delight charged through Daisy's body. She swung back. "Tell him to come over *here*."

"A guy like Johnny can't be too careful," Kenny said.

A guy like Johnny? Daisy surveyed the ballroom. Earlier that evening, she'd marveled at the garden of colors in the crowd, but now the sea of white faces gave her pause. Kenny was right about Johnny's situation, but she also had to be smart about a man she hardly knew. Daisy's eyes widened to the size of half dollars as she looked to Beverly with a silent plea for guidance.

Beverly nodded her understanding. She stiffened her spine and folded her hands on her lap. "Any reason I shouldn't let my friend go off to talk to that very eager man?" she asked Kenny.

"Besides the obvious? Nah."

"What's that supposed to mean?" Daisy bristled, annoyed with the man's insinuations.

He shrugged. "A white woman and a colored man? Not saying it can't happen, but this ain't Paris."

Beverly scooted her chair back and crossed her arms. "Why'd you come over here then?"

"Don't get me wrong," Kenny said. "Johnny's a hell of a nice guy." He turned to Daisy. "Hell of a nice guy."

"But . . ." Beverly nudged.

"No *but*. I was happy to do him the favor. Volunteered, in fact."

"What favor?" Beverly batted her eyes.

"Keeping you company . . ." He pulled his chair a little closer, "while he talked to his girl."

His girl? Daisy glanced over her shoulder to steal a quick look, but Johnny had already vanished into the hall.

"Turns out he's doing *me* the favor," Kenny said, as he touched Beverly's elbow.

Beverly shivered but stayed the course. "This Johnny, he's a stand-up fellow?"

"Best of the best," Kenny said. "Honest to God."

Beverly studied the trumpeter for a moment and announced, "He's telling the truth," before offering him her hand again.

"If you're going," he said to Daisy, "go now." He eyed his wristwatch. "And remind Count Basie over there," he glanced toward the spot where Johnny had been standing, "we're back onstage in twenty. I'll give him a signal."

Daisy stood up, fluffed her skirt, and drew in a breath. "If you'll excuse me." She felt a thrum of excitement bubbling up inside, despite her attempt at nonchalance.

"I'll watch the purses," Beverly said.

Kenny slipped his unoccupied hand onto Beverly's knee. "Whataya say we make these twenty minutes count?"

As Daisy crossed the ballroom, her heart beat twice for every step she took. Once in the hallway, she glanced left and right. With no Johnny in sight, she headed toward the marble staircase.

"You're getting colder."

Daisy turned and saw Johnny holding open one of two swinging doors into the kitchen. His dimples cut valleys into his cheeks. "Come on," he said, already pushing through the door.

Daisy followed him through a cloud of steam, past a couple of cooks who seemed not to notice the intruders. One of the men set a silver cloche over a pungent plate of ham and cabbage before carrying it over to the dumbwaiter. "Where's it going?" he shouted as he grabbed the rope.

"Third floor, room two," the other man answered, not looking up.

Johnny stood at the bottom of a staircase at the opposite end of the kitchen and called out playfully, "You're getting warmer." He raced ahead of her, taking the steps two at a time.

Scared and excited, Daisy slowly made her way up, each stair an act of faith that her foot would land safely. Once again, she had that dizzy sensation she used to get when playing blindman's bluff.

"You're getting hotter," Johnny goaded.

The stairwell filled with his laughter, generous and bright. Daisy smiled. He made her smile. She picked up her pace and soon found herself on the top floor of the building, in front of a door that opened to the roof.

"Hotter! Hotter!" Johnny roared as Daisy followed.

Johnny stood against the waist-high parapet at the front of the building. "You're burning up," he teased.

"Five stories," she said, a little breathless. "Good thing I didn't wear heels."

"Come see."

Daisy sashayed toward him. "See what?"

"Scranton at night." He held up his arms as if presenting her with a gift. "Best show in town." He turned to face the street, bent forward, and rested his elbows on the concrete railing.

"After the performance *you* gave?" She came up alongside him. "I'd say second best, tops."

Johnny beamed.

"Truly." Daisy's face lit up. "Hearing you play tonight made me think, *Why bother?*" When Johnny tried to protest, she put up her hand. "I mean that in the best possible way. I can play piano. I'm even good at it. But you have a God-given talent."

"Aw, shucks, ma'am," he said, imitating the drawl of a movie cowboy.

"'Tweren't nothing," she responded with a fake twang of her own. "Seriously, though, everyone in there loves you."

As long as they can see my hands on the keys. Johnny shook off the dark thought. "Listen," he said, cupping an ear. "She's singing to us." He faced the street, closed his eyes, and caught the call-and-response of a car horn blasting and tires screeching. A window scraping open and a phone slamming down. An accordion pushing and pulling out a polka in the club next door and couples stepping, half stepping, stepping in time.

"Every city has a sound." He opened his eyes.

"And what's ours?" Daisy asked.

Before Johnny could answer, a boy on the corner yelled, "Extra! Extra!" He pulled a newspaper out of his bag and held it over his head. "Bus drivers reject offer! Strike still on!"

Johnny chuckled. "A fight song, I'd say."

"And you'd be right," Daisy said. "We have coal dust in our veins."

"How do you mean?"

"Miners have always fought for workers' rights. My father was a union man, and my grandfather before him. We're generous to a fault around here, but don't try and take advantage."

"I wouldn't think of it." Johnny held up his right hand in a show of sincerity.

"I didn't mean *you*." Daisy laughed.

"I knew you were a firecracker the first time we met." He playfully pressed his shoulder into hers.

"I guess I get passionate about some things." Daisy lowered her eyes.

Johnny tipped his head to see her face. "Such as?"

"This view." Daisy broke away from his gaze and looked out.

On the downtown side of the river, headlights, streetlights, spotlights, and marquees clamored for attention. With storefronts closed till Monday morning, restaurants, theaters, clubs, and hotels brought the shine to Saturday night. Every few blocks, church steeples stretched toward the heavens, but atop the *Scranton Times* building, a 301-foot radio tower seemed to reach them.

Across the bridge, hundreds of lamps flickered in distant houses like heavy-eyed children fighting off sleep.

"She's something to behold," Daisy said, delighted.

Johnny studied her in that red dress. "Yes, she is. I'm real happy you showed up tonight. It was good to see a friendly face out there." He tucked a piece of hair behind her ear. "And a beautiful one at that."

Daisy took a sharp breath and mumbled a thank you. "That guy at the bar could use a lesson in *friendly*."

"Forget him," Johnny said.

"I don't know how you stayed so calm."

Johnny had stayed calm because he'd had no choice, like he'd had no choice when the stage manager tried to dump him from the act. But Johnny didn't want to talk about any of that. He'd come to the roof to clear his mind. To fall in love with the city. And maybe with Daisy. He shrugged off the night's insults. "Sticks and stones."

"May break my bones," Daisy singsonged the next part of the adage.

"But rain will never hurt me."

"Rain?"

"When I was a kid, I heard it as *rain* not *names*. Even after I got it straightened out, rain always stayed with me. Funny how that happens."

"Rain breaks no bones," Daisy said, glancing up at him.

"Haven't heard that one."

"It means a little discomfort never hurt anybody. It's Welsh. My father used to say it whenever I complained about a church service going too long."

"Into each life some rain must fall." Johnny began humming.

"Name. That. Poet." Daisy slapped her hand on the railing like she would a buzzer. "Henry Wadsworth Longfellow," she called out, laughing. "Do I win?"

"I was thinking the Ink Spots and Ella Fitzgerald, but we'll accept Longfellow." Johnny listened to the music of her laugh. *A cure for what ails you.* "You look beautiful tonight." He stepped back and took in the sight of her. "That's a good dress."

Daisy held onto the parapet as if to steady herself. "How much time do we have?"

"Kenny'll let us know." Johnny inched closer.

"My high school!" Daisy hurried over to a corner of the roof. "Where?"

She pressed up against the railing and pointed past the Masonic Temple to the end of the block. "See that lamppost?"

"Barely," Johnny said as he caught up to her.

"That's the public library. Central is across the street. My alma mater." Her tongue raced. "It takes up the whole block. The girls' entrance is on the corner. There's a copper spire on top, but you can't see it from here. They have an auditorium inside. That's where I played Emily in *Our Town*." She closed eyes and plucked a line from memory. *Oh, earth, you're too wonderful for anybody to realize you.*" She opened her eyes, glanced at Johnny, and blushed. "That's from the play. Do you know it?"

"Keep going," he said.

She closed her eyes again. "*Do any human beings ever realize life while they live it—every, every minute?*"

Johnny kissed her lightly on the lips. "*No.*" He took a beat. "*Saints and poets, maybe . . . they do some.*" When she opened her eyes, he winked. "I played the stage manager my junior year."

Daisy smiled at the coincidence, and he gave her another peck.

"Look!" She grabbed Johnny's hand and pulled him to the other side of the roof. "I can see it." She scooted a few feet left, then a few feet right in search of the best angle. "City Hall's in the way, but I can spy a piece of it."

"Of what?"

Daisy lifted their clasped hands toward the back of the forty-foot sign on top of the Pennsylvania Power and Light Building. An intricate pattern of interlaced ironwork supported the massive structure.

Johnny craned his neck. "You can't see the front from here."

Daisy persisted. "But we know what it says. Scranton. The. Electric. City. Each word on its own line. Each letter four feet tall." She gestured toward the sky with her free hand. "A beacon of welcome to passersby." She giggled. "My sixth-grade essay for Scranton's seventy-fifth anniversary is serving me well."

Johnny grinned. "I thought maybe you were with the Chamber of Commerce."

"When I was seven years old, my father woke me up from a sound sleep, wrapped me in his hunting coat, and brought me downtown. They'd remade the sign and were testing the bulbs that night, all 140,000 of them. He wanted me to see that. We were making a memory, he said."

Johnny let go of Daisy's hand, wrapped his arm around her waist, and pulled her in. "What do you like most about the sign?"

"The sunburst on top. It's really an eight-foot light bulb with rays, but I always thought it looked like one of those rhinestone brooches women pin on their coats for sparkle."

Johnny curled his finger around a lock of Daisy's hair. "All I see is sparkle." He pulled her in for a kiss, and she melted into him.

A few seconds later, they heard five round notes floating up from Kenny's trumpet. With her lips lightly touching Johnny's, Daisy whispered, "Name that tune."

"'When I Fall in Love,'" Johnny whispered back. He kissed the tip of her nose. "That's our cue." They both sighed as Johnny took Daisy's hand and led her back downstairs.

CHAPTER SIXTEEN

VIOLET SAT ON THE GRASS tending one of the flower beds beside the front porch steps. The geraniums were already a little leggy, and it was only the middle of June. She'd have to spend more time snipping off spent blossoms if new ones were going to grow. *And watering*, she thought, pinching a marble of dirt into dust. Spring had been dryer than usual, and summer seemed to be following suit.

Archie sauntered into the yard from his midafternoon stroll and sniffed at an old woodchuck hole near the coal-bin window. "Where'd you get to?" Violet asked, picking up her pruning shears to cut a burr out of the dog's fur. He barked a response before stretching out on a sunny patch of grass.

A ragtag pack of boys, second grade, maybe third, ran up the middle of the street playing kick the can. When they got as far as Violet's house, Archie jumped up, chased down the can, and brought it back to the last kicker. "Come on," the smallest member of the group said to the dog, scratching his ears. "Don't worry, Mrs. Davies," he hollered over, "I'll keep an eye on him."

Violet waved. *One of the Powell boys*, she thought, though at that distance she couldn't tell which one. A gaggle of girls followed the pack at about a six-foot distance, far enough away to suggest indifference, but close enough to eavesdrop on any conversation.

"Must be the last day of school," Grace said as she pushed open the screen door.

"Looks like," Violet said, pulling tufts of white clover from between the river rocks that bordered her beds.

"Wish I could get down there with you." Grace settled into a rocker. "I'm afraid my gardening days are behind me."

"I'm just happy to have the company." Violet tossed the weeds onto her pile of rusted geraniums. She squinted up at her mother.

Grace tilted her head toward the empty rocker. "She's eyeballing me again."

"I'm not eyeballing you." Shears in hand, Violet scooted over to the flower bed on the other side of the steps.

"It's going to be a good summer," Grace said. "Don't you worry."

Violet couldn't help but worry. For the better part of forty years, the onset of summer meant the beginning of the "before time" for Grace. Before Our Daisy's death. Before her accident. Before her baptism. Soon enough, Grace would start talking about the days leading up to *the day*, July 4, 1913. The story of the pie. Or the hair bow. Or the dress—the one she'd bought for Daisy's baptism when, as Grace told it, they didn't have two pennies to rub together. "Your father and I had a little spat over the cost," she'd always say. "I'm so glad I put my foot down. She loved that dress."

Violet could remember her sister twirling in it, the white pleats opening like petals on a rose. Violet had been jealous of that dress, and of her sister's special day. Sure, at fifty years old, she knew better than to blame herself for a child's envy, but the sting of shame could be easily summoned.

Violet didn't begrudge her mother the stories, but she dreaded where they led. *To everything there is a season*, and the beginning of summer marked the season of Grace's despair.

"I'm done with all that," Grace said.

"With what? I didn't say a word."

"You didn't have to." Grace bent forward and stared down at Violet. "I said I'm done with all that."

"That's good to hear." To change the mood, Violet said, "I sure wish I had your green thumb."

"Your thumb's not the problem."

"What is?"

"Slugs." Grace pushed herself up from the rocker, groaning from the arthritis in her crackling knees. "They're chewing up your leaves," she said, stretching over the railing.

"So what do I do?" *Scatter eggshells or coffee grounds*, Violet thought, but she kept quiet. She liked to give her mother a chance to feel needed.

"Put out a saucer of beer."

"That's news to me!" Violet laughed.

"Your father taught me that. They drown in it." Grace's eyes twinkled with delight. "But they die happy."

Violet laughed harder and Grace joined in. It felt nice to laugh. Maybe her mother was right. Maybe it would be a good summer.

"Hello, Stanley!" Grace called out.

Stanley? Violet's cheeks instantly flushed. She hadn't even heard his car pull up in front of the widow's house. And besides, it was Wednesday. He usually worked late on Wednesdays. Not that she kept track.

"Mrs. Morgan." From across the street, he waved with his good arm. "You're looking well. And Violet," he said. "I didn't see you down there."

Violet motioned to him with her shears. She was too good a Christian not to acknowledge the man, but she didn't have to put the welcome mat out for him either.

"We could use a favor," Grace called from the porch. "Are you still off the liquor?"

"Mother!" Violet stole a glance at Stanley but didn't dare to look him in the eye.

"I am indeed." Stanley chuckled as he made his way across the road.

Grace's face fell. "Beer too, I suppose."

"Beer too, Mrs. Morgan."

"Well, that's a shame."

Stanley approached the house with a pair of binoculars

dangling from a strap around his neck. "How so?" He flashed a quick grin at a cringing Violet.

"We need beer. A quart should do it."

"For the slugs," Violet clarified, her hands now covering her face.

"No reason to report you to the church elders, then." When neither woman laughed at his joke, Stanley held out his binoculars. "I'm headed to Leggett's Creek."

Birdwatching. Violet remembered him teaching her how to call sparrows when they used to play hooky in grammar school. At Leggett's Creek, come to think of it. Birds, rabbits, dogs, mules— Stanley had a good soul when it came God's creatures. She'd give him that.

"I'll swing by the Polish Club tonight," he said, "and pick up some beer."

And that floozie Arlene, Violet thought, cutting short her moment of sentimentality.

Grace's brow furrowed. "Will they let you do that?"

Stanley hesitated. "Will *who* let me do *what?*"

"That organization of yours."

"AA?" Stanley cupped his hand around the side of his mouth. "It'll be our secret."

"I don't want to get you in trouble," Grace said.

Stanley patted the banister. "No trouble at all," he said and started up the street.

Astonished, Violet stared at the steps where Stanley had just been standing, then up at her mother.

"That's a good job done." Grace wiped one palm against the other. "Time for a little nap," she said.

Violet stayed in the yard long after the screen door snapped shut. Maybe if she yanked the weeds harder or raked the soil deeper, she could shake loose those mortifying words. *Are you still off the liquor?* Instead they stuck to her like a burr in Archie's fur. What was her mother thinking? Violet stewed for another half hour before going inside.

* * *

As Stanley strolled up Spring Street, he wondered if Violet had spotted his heart jumping out of his chest. How long had it been since he'd stood that close to her? More than a few years for sure. He'd seen her in passing on countless occasions, and in those moments, he'd tried to conjure the smell of her hair, the taste of her lips, the feel of her waist in the crook of his arm. Sometimes he even succeeded, provided he'd had a few drinks under his belt. But today he was sober, and she'd been a foot away, close enough for him to catch the scent of her Juicy Fruit gum.

So she still has a sweet tooth. Everything changes and everything stays the same. He passed a row of paper birches on his ten-minute walk to the creek. Thin sheets of bark curled away from their bleached trunks. Stanley pinched a piece of what a young Violet used to call "tree skin," ripped it off like a half-picked scab, and slipped it into his shirt pocket. Back when he was in law school, she used to tuck a peel of bark into her letters. A reminder of home, she'd say. And it was. A reminder of home and Violet and the certainty of love that comes with youth.

Stanley tossed a handful of unshelled peanuts onto the bank of the half-dry creek and waited. Moments later, a blue jay swooped in, his sapphire tail feathers skimming the ground like a king's robe. Stanley lifted his binoculars for a closer look, startling the bird back to his perch with a peanut in his beak. As much as Stanley loved to watch blue jays, he'd come today to check on a cardinal's nest he'd spotted the previous week. By his count, the trio of green-speckled eggs should have hatched by now.

He squatted near a patch of scrub, trained his binoculars on the center of the thicket, and whistled the *chew chew* of the cardinal. Inside a cup-shaped nest, the mother, a brown bird with a red crest and beak, replied with a *chip chip chip* of warning. After a few seconds of silence, she resumed feeding a pair of open-mouthed hatchlings.

A pair. Stanley tipped his binoculars down and found the third hatchling, lifeless on a mossy rock below the nest. *Anything could have gotten to it*, he told himself. *It's nature way.* But somehow, none of that mattered. Nothing could stem the sadness rising inside him.

I don't want to die alone.

He thought about Violet, and how, other than while he was at law school, she'd always been within walking distance. Growing up, she'd lived across the street; in later years, just across the river; and yet the span between them seemed insurmountable. Until today. Today he'd crossed the street and stood alongside her, and for a moment, their souls touched in the way of old friends whose memories match up. Did she feel it too? When she stole a glance at him, did she see the nine-year-old boy who pulled her out of the elderberry bushes after that bully, Evan Evans, pushed her into them? Better yet, did she remember how Stanley had taught her to fish at this very spot? It had been fall, and the water considerably higher than it was now, but the sight of the creek could still spark a powerful memory, Stanley thought as he lowered himself onto a log.

Thanks to Mrs. Morgan, he'd crossed the street today. Would he have the nerve to do it again unprompted? Maybe start up a conversation when he saw Violet on her porch? *You'll never guess who I ran into the other day.* Or better yet, *Remember the time the widow caught us cutting school?*

And she'd reply, *Yes, I remember. I was shaking in my boots.*
And what did she do?
Offered us cookies.
And they'd laugh.

And maybe she would look at him and ask, *What made you think of that?*

I've been thinking about a lot of things lately. Life. Love. Regret.

If that didn't scare her off, maybe he'd take the opportunity to work "the steps." The fellows in AA were always preaching about amends. If he was going to apologize to anyone, it should be Violet. Maybe she'd forgive him, or at the very least hear him out. And then, if he felt encouraged, he could accidentally on purpose run into her another day, say at the farmers market one afternoon. He'd offer to buy her a cherry pie, a treat for her mother. Knowing Violet, she'd probably invite him over later for a slice and a thank you.

Maybe.

Of course, there was still the matter of the beer. Stanley could drop it off before Violet settled in for the night, but he really didn't want her to see him with a bottle in hand. Not that he had any intention of drinking. None at all. *I will not drink*, he thought. "I will not drink," he repeated, this time aloud. No, Stanley hadn't touched a drop of alcohol in three years, two months, and four days, and he wasn't going to give up on his sobriety. Not today. And hopefully not ever. He set his binoculars on his lap and fished through his pocket for his three-year coin, a simple red poker chip. The men who ran the Methodist meeting didn't have the budget for anything fancy. Stanley didn't care. He'd earned his "coin" fair and square, and it meant more to him than gold.

Instead of the chip, Stanley pulled Violet's Scranton Central High School valedictorian medallion from his pocket. Class of 1923. It had been at home on his dresser the day she'd stepped off the train with a baby. They'd broken off their engagement in the middle of the station, and rather than return the medal, he'd begun carrying it around. A talisman of sorts, or maybe a spoil of war. *Either way*, he thought as he fingered the raised gold lettering, *it couldn't hurt to make amends for holding onto it all these years.*

Something crashed into the water on the other side of the creek, flushing a pair of doves out of hiding and into the scrub that held the cardinals' nest. Stanley turned toward the commotion and saw Archie happily slogging his way across and onto the bank. "No!" Stanley yelled as the dog pointed his snout toward the thicket. Archie stopped short, but remained vigilant, and soon his patience paid off. The doves took flight, and he resumed the chase.

With the cardinals out of harm's way, Stanley tipped his head toward the sky. "I'm not one for signs," he said, "but that one was a dilly." He glanced along the creek bed.

"Archie," he called out, "let's go home!" When the dog didn't come running, Stanley hiked up the path in search of him. Faint yelps rose up near a pile of old fencing someone had dumped over the embankment. Stanley ran down and found a bloodied Archie tangled in a rusted nest of barbwire. "Hang on." The panicked dog tried to extricate himself by twisting his head back and forth, causing the barbs to dig deeper into the flesh. "Easy, boy." Stanley sat down and set his leg over the dog's side to keep him from wriggling. Next, he used his stump to loosen a dangerous bit of wire at Archie's throat. "I'll take care of you." With his right hand, Stanley gingerly extracted the barbs from Archie's face, one at a time. His snout had a couple of nice cuts but his ear had taken the real brunt.

With no first aid kit, Stanley scooped up the wet cocker spaniel with his right hand and crossed his left arm under the belly to form a cradle. He inched his way up the bank and onto the road toward Violet's house. Archie couldn't have weighed more than thirty pounds. Thirty-five tops. Definitely less than the bushel of apples he delivered to Babcia every fall for pies and canning. Then again, a bushel of apples never squirmed while being carried. "Easy, boy" he said again. Stanley hated to see anyone suffer, man or beast.

I hope he doesn't lose that ear. Stanley thought about his own loss, forty-one years earlier. "Listen," he said aloud, worried the dog might be picking up on his fear, "if I can manage with one hand, you can make it with one ear."

And Stanley had gotten along fine with just one hand. Not that he'd had a choice, but he'd also never let it stop him. Fishing, baseball, even driving. When he'd first gotten behind the wheel, he'd learned to steer with his stump and shift with his right hand. And he'd still be doing that now if Oldsmobile hadn't come out with Hydra-Matic Drive back in '48. No more gears. No clutch.

Put the car in "hi," turn the key, and go. Stanley splurged on a maroon sedan as soon as it hit the showroom. He could've kept driving a car with a manual transmission, but why not choose comfort? He'd made the same choice years earlier when he'd finally given up on his artificial hand. Best of the best, German-engineered, in fact, but no matter how many times Stanley tried to use the prosthesis, it only got in the way. He kept at it longer than he should have for the comfort of others, but eventually his own comfort won out.

Stanley crested the hill and saw Violet's house a few doors down. *Just in time*, he thought, as his lower back began to pinch.

"Anybody home?" he shouted when he got to the yard.

"Good lord!" Violet yelled as she opened the door and ran down the steps. "You're bleeding!"

Stanley glanced at his bloodied shirt. "It's Archie," he said. "Got caught up in some barbed wire." The dog lifted his head as if to confirm the story. "His ear's busted," Stanley said. "And his snout's sliced up pretty good."

"Bring him inside." Violet ran up to hold the door. "How bad is it?"

"Hard to say."

Violet darted into the kitchen, filled a bowl with warm tap water, and placed it on the floor.

Stanley gently set the dog down on the rag rug in front of the sink. "Ears can bleed like a son of a gun," he said, stretching his arms to loosen his elbows.

Violet grabbed a couple of clean dish towels out of a drawer and plunged them into the water. "Hold the ear up," she said, dabbing at the blood.

Stanley wrapped his arms around the dog to keep him still. "Looks like someone took a cheese grater to it."

"Put pressure on it." Violet handed Stanley a dry rag. "At least the ear canal's intact," she said. Archie whined as she gave his snout a quick swipe with the wet towel. "I know," Violet comforted the dog.

"It won't stop bleeding." Stanley's face drained of color.

"Grab the cornstarch," Violet said, taking over for Stanley with the ear. "It's on the top shelf." She lifted her chin toward a cupboard. "Good. Now make a paste."

Stanley poured a cupful of the powder into a bowl and mixed in water. "Here you go."

Violet smeared the concoction onto Archie's wounds. The bleeding slowed some but not enough. "Hold this." She pressed Stanley's hand against the dog's ear and ran upstairs. A minute later, she returned with a roll of gauze and wrapped it around Archie's head to keep the ear pinned and elevated. "Hopefully he'll keep it on long enough for the cuts to scab over."

"Thank God it's not worse."

"Thank you. You saved him." Violet patted the top of the dog's head. "He saved you, didn't he, boy?"

Stanley stood up and stretched. "He looks like Marley's ghost in *A Christmas Carol*."

"Or Old Mrs. Daniels," Violet laughed. "Remember her? She wore a kerchief around her face whenever she had a toothache."

Roused by the cheery banter, Archie added his stifled bark to the conversation.

"How on earth did that help her tooth?" Stanley chuckled.

"You've got me."

Archie nuzzled against Violet in front of the sink.

"Where's his water dish?" Stanley asked, figuring the dog would be thirsty.

"On the back porch." Violet inspected the bandage. "Did she even have teeth?" she called out to Stanley? "I swear I never saw that woman smile."

Before Stanley could find the water dish, his eyes settled on Tommy's overalls still hanging on the hook three years later. As Violet continued talking, Stanley slipped out the back door without a word.

* * *

At ten o'clock that night, Stanley stopped by the Polish Club for that promised quart of beer. An easy purchase. Too easy. Set a few dimes on the bar, and a bottle of Gibbons appeared. No questions. No mention of his sobriety. Just an ice-cold beer.

Stanley's arms ached a bit from carrying Archie, so the bottle felt more burdensome than he'd expected. The ten-minute walk to Violet's house may as well have been a year. Those overalls. The dog. Violet. It was all too much, too loud in his head. The beer would take care of that, though, wouldn't it? Just a sip. Enough to quiet the freight train charging through his mind. *God grant me the serenity to accept the things I cannot change . . .* Stanley shifted the bottle to the crook of his handless arm, *courage to change things I can, and wisdom to know the difference.* He shifted the bottle back. *God, grant me the serenity . . .*

The next morning, Violet went out to the front porch and spotted a quart of beer alongside the milk box. *Stanley*, she thought, not sure what to make of the man or the gesture. She bent down to pick up the capped bottle and noticed something pinned underneath—a piece of bark from a paper birch tree. *Tree skin*, she said to herself, tucking it into the pocket of her housedress.

I'm gonna put on my long white robe,
Down by the riverside . . .

CHAPTER SEVENTEEN

"IT SMELLS LIKE A GIN MILL IN HERE." Dressed in her robe and slippers, Grace shuffled into the kitchen and took her place at the table. White feathers of unpinned hair skimmed her stooped shoulders.

Over at the sink, Violet continued to pour Stanley's beer into a half-dozen wide-mouthed jelly jars. After the sun burned off the dew, she'd take them out to the front yard. It was barely seven o'clock, and she was already out of her nightclothes and into one of her shapeless housedresses. The only hint of her figure came from the apron at her waist. She tipped her head toward a flowered teapot in the middle of the stove. "Give it another minute."

Grace picked at a loose thread on her sleeve. "How long've you been up?"

"A while."

"What'd you do," Grace snorted, "wet the bed?"

As though in on the joke, Archie barked from his nest of blankets in the far corner of the room.

"The milkman woke me up with all his clanking." Violet set the empty beer bottle on the drainboard and grabbed the teapot from the stove. "I couldn't get back to sleep. It's a shame too. I was dreaming something happy." She filled two cups and set one in front of her mother.

"What about?"

"Not a clue." Violet carried her tea over to the other side of the table and sat down. "He chased it off with all his racket. I should start getting my milk at the Acme. It would serve him right."

"So how do you know it was happy?" Grace spooned a little cream off the top of the milk and stirred it into her cup.

"Just do. Have you ever read a book, one you really enjoyed—you laughed or cried—but it's been so long, you don't remember a thing about it except how it made you feel?"

"Many times." Grace took a long sip of tea.

"It's like that." Violet tapped at her forehead. "I keep feeling like I'm on the verge of remembering, but it won't come."

"*How Green Was My Valley*."

"What?"

"My favorite book. It came out a couple years after your father passed on. And now I couldn't tell you a thing about it."

"We saw the movie a few Christmases ago."

"If you say so."

Concern settled into the corners of Violet's eyes. "Over at the Rialto. They had that papier-mâché Santa in the lobby with that silly wig."

"When you're seventy-five," Grace said, "you forget more than you remember."

"With Walter Pidgeon," Violet nudged. "And Maureen O'Hara."

Grace's face brightened. "We should read it."

"We?"

"My eyes may be shot, but my ears work fine."

Violet smiled. "I'll pick it up next time I go to the library."

"Perhaps it'll come back to you."

"What?"

"The dream," Grace said. "They do that sometimes." She looked out the window and watched as a robin hopscotched across the outside sill. After he took flight, Grace's gaze landed on the drainboard and the empty bottle of beer. "Glad to see he came through again."

"Who?"

"Stanley."

Violet scrunched her brow. "Again?"

Grace took a long sip of tea, and Archie bounded to her side dragging the bandage that had previously been wrapped around his head. "That's right, boy." Grace picked up the gauze, tossed it in the waste bin near her chair, and rubbed the dog's back. "If it weren't for Stanley, you'd still be stuck in that fence."

Violet patted her thigh, and the dog sprang over to her side of the table, his tail wagging. She carefully lifted his ear, loosening the last of the cornstarch paste. Much to her relief, the gashes were starting to scab over. "You gave us quite a scare," she said, rubbing the fur at his neck. His proffered paw suddenly sparked Violet's memory. She closed her eyes to press for an image. "It was her hand."

"Whose hand?"

"Daisy's." Violet opened her eyes. "Our Daisy."

Grace scanned the kitchen. "Where?"

"My dream." Archie barked and Violet let go of his paw.

"Oh," Grace whispered, "how did she look?"

Violet shook her head. "I don't know." She squinted toward the opposite wall. "I only see the hand."

"Doing what?" Grace peered at the wall as if she might see what Violet was trying to recollect.

"Stretched toward me."

Grace turned back and settled in her chair. "What did she say?"

"Nothing. She wanted to show me something," Violet took a sip of her tea, "but I was afraid to move."

"Why?"

Violet shrugged. "I think I thought she'd disappear."

"So what happened?"

"I took her hand and I was . . ." Violet shut her eyes again, "home." She hesitated. "Happy. Whole."

Grace nodded.

"I remember now. She pulled me out the door and down Spring

Street, but also, not Spring Street." She looked at her mother. "You know how it is with dreams."

"And?"

"That's all I remember. Our Daisy pulling me along. The softness of her hand." Violet drew in a long breath and examined her own hand. "The weight of it."

"I wish we could ask her."

"Ask her what?"

"Where she was going." Grace thought for a moment. "Wouldn't it be something if we could talk to them on the telephone?"

Zethray can talk to the dead. Violet shivered off the thought.

"Operator?" Grace stretched her thumb and pinky into a mock receiver. "I'd like to place a call to the great beyond."

"Think of that party line." Violet shook her head. "We're already sharing with three other neighbors."

"And they're all talkers," Grace grumbled. "Especially that Myrtle. The other day, I picked up the phone six times to call Reverend Meade, and six times Myrtle was yapping on the other end. I don't know how that woman gets any housework done."

"She doesn't," Violet said, and they both smirked. "Speaking of housework," Violet stood up, gathered the dishrags from breakfast, and added them to one of the clothes baskets near the back door, "I better get on with mine."

"Bronwyn and Ivor!" Grace shouted.

"Who?"

"They married each other in *How Green Was My Valley*. Bronwyn and Ivor Morgan—same names as my own dear parents, God rest their souls." Grace folded her hands. "It's a wonderful book."

Just after ten o'clock that morning, Daisy bounded into the kitchen. "Looks like you two had a wild night." She nodded toward the empty beer bottle on the drainboard.

"Stanley brought it over for the slugs," Grace said.

"A likely story," Daisy teased.

"Did you strip your bed?" Violet went over the stove and poured her daughter a cup of tea.

"No time." Daisy kissed her grandmother's cheek. "Good morning."

"It's wash day." Violet set the cup and saucer on the table.

"I meant for tea," Daisy said.

"What's your hurry?" Grace patted her granddaughter's hand. "We've hardly seen you lately."

"I'm giving a piano lesson," Daisy checked the clock, "in less than an hour."

Violet spied another dishrag and tossed it in a basket.

"Is my turquoise skirt clean?" Daisy walked over to the counter and grabbed an apple out of a wooden bowl.

"Did you put it in the hamper?" Violet pulled a bar of Fels-Naptha soap out from under the sink.

"It's on my bed."

"Then I didn't wash it."

Daisy sweetened her tone. "I mean, would you? Please? I want to wear it tonight."

"Who's the lucky fella?" Grace chimed in.

"Can't a girl have a good time without a fella?" Daisy took a bite of apple.

"I would think she'd have a better time *with* one," Grace said.

"Grandma!" Daisy covered her mouth to keep from spitting while she feigned shock.

"So you won't be home for supper?" Impatience gave way to annoyance as Violet worked the bar of soap into a grease stain on her good tablecloth. "Again?"

"I have a new student coming tonight at seven o'clock. A soprano from the First Christian Church." Daisy put a playful finger to her lips. "It's on the q.t. Doesn't want anybody to know. She's hoping to get a solo in the Christmas pageant."

"And will she?" Grace asked.

"With the right teacher."

"That doesn't answer my question," Violet said.

"I'm only coming back to get changed. It's Thursday. Town's open late tonight. I'll grab something to eat there."

Grace tried to steer the conversation away from Violet's growing irritability: "Daisy, how's that little bowlegged boy you told us about? The Irish one."

"Mickey?"

"That's the one."

"His legs are fine," Daisy said. "His two left feet are the problem. I love having him around. He's smart as a whip and tries hard, but he'll never be a dancer."

"What does the grandmother have to say?" Grace asked.

"I've tried telling her. I don't want to waste her money, but she won't hear of it. Thinks he's going to be the next Fred Astaire."

"At least her child makes an effort," Violet said.

Daisy bristled. "Are you saying I don't?"

"All I know is, you're coming in late every night . . ." Violet's words matched the rhythm of her scrubbing, "and sleeping away half the day."

Grace jumped in: "She's running the studio. That's hard work. And besides, she's young. She should be living it up."

"I'll never catch a courtesy car if I don't leave right now," Daisy said.

"Why didn't you go with Beverly?" Violet asked.

"She's already at the shop."

"If you'd gotten up earlier," Violet rinsed off her hands and sat down, "you wouldn't have to pay for a ride."

Daisy rolled her eyes. "I'll be home later." She headed out the door.

As soon as they were alone again, Violet said to Grace, "She's not pulling her load around here."

"What load?"

"I'm not running a hotel."

Grace waved her off. "Why would she want to spend her time with a couple of old crows like us?"

Violet's mouth dropped open. "Old crows?"

"Let her have fun."

"She doesn't appreciate the sacrifices I've made."

"She doesn't know about them," Grace said gently.

Violet ignored her mother in favor of her own rising anger: "She comes and goes as she pleases. She never spends time with you."

"Don't pull me into this."

Archie ambled over to the table and pressed up against Violet's leg. "Good boy," she said, scratching his head.

"The change of life hits some women harder."

"What? I'm talking about Daisy," Violet snapped. "Why do you always take her side?"

"Remember Alice Harris from up the street? Poor woman suffered something awful. She'd soak through a dozen pairs of dress shields in a day."

"It's not the change!" Violet lifted her hair to fan away the perspiration on her neck. "Well, not all of it," she said sheepishly.

"Then what?"

Everything, Violet thought. *Daisy. Hot flashes. Strange dreams. That curl of bark in my pocket.* She glimpsed the piece of trim on the doorway where Tommy had ticked off Daisy's height every New Year, and finally asked, "When did I get so old?"

"Fifty's nothing. Wait till you're my age." Grace stared at a set of chrome canisters on a shelf. "Sometimes I get startled by my own reflection." A budding smile withered on her lips. "I married your father just yesterday. Truly. That's how close it feels." She cast her eyes through the doorway to the spot in the parlor where the piano used to be. "He got that for me as a wedding present," she said, as if the instrument was still there, "because he wanted us to have music in our house." She shook off the melancholy tangled in that memory. "He never did tell me where he got it. I can picture him now, pushing that thing up Spring Street with his buddy Graham. What a sight." She laughed. "Have I ever told you that story?"

"Many times," Violet said and immediately regretted her answer.

"That's because I like to tell it." Grace sucked in her cheeks and shifted her chair toward the window.

"I'm sorry," Violet said.

Grace's expression remained unchanged.

Violet's guilt loosened the words she'd been trying to hold onto: "Stanley disappeared yesterday in the middle of a conversation. No goodbye. No 'I'm late for an appointment.' Poof. He was gone."

"So that's it." Grace studied Violet. "When did you start caring about Stanley?"

"I don't care. It's just . . ." Violet gave the dog a careful squeeze. "We were having a nice conversation, and for a split second, I thought maybe we could be friends again. Then he ran out, and I spent the rest of night wondering what I'd done wrong." She patted her pocket. "But then this morning . . ."

"Go on?"

Violet stopped short of mentioning the bark. She needed time to sort out its meaning. "I'm being silly," she said

"This morning?" Grace tried again.

"Nothing." Violet stood up and poured Daisy's untouched tea into the sink. "The beer," she said to satisfy her mother's curiosity. "When I found it on the porch, I thought, *Maybe he's not mad after all.*"

"Only one way to find out."

"Like I said," Violet rinsed the cup and kicked the full clothes basket onto the porch, "I'm being silly. "

"Maybe it's time for you to clear the air. My two cents," Grace said.

"And how do you propose I do that?"

"You're a grown woman, you'll figure it out." Grace pushed herself away from the table and stood up. "I'm going to get out of these nightclothes."

"Will you grab Daisy's skirt on your way down? I want to put it in the wash so I can get it out on the line in time to dry."

"That's my girl," Grace said. "Will do."

CHAPTER EIGHTEEN

"ONE MORE TIME," Daisy said from her stool at the piano. "You want to *hit* the high note," she punched toward the ceiling, "not slide up to it."

A few feet away, seventy-year-old Opal Lutz shook her newly permed hair and grimaced. "You're sure you can't smell this?" she asked for the third time that hour. "I'm not supposed to wash it for at least three days," she shook her gray head, "or the curl won't take."

Daisy chuckled. "I can't smell a thing over the Aqua Net coming up from the beauty parlor downstairs. I swear Beverly uses a whole can on every customer." She glanced at the clock. "It's five after eight. Why don't we call it a night?"

"May as well." Opal collected her pocketbook and hat from the sofa. "I have to get to the corpse house before they close up shop," she said, smoothing the quilt on the cushions.

"Oh no." As Daisy stood to comfort Opal, the pungent smell of the perm stung her eyes. "I'm sorry for your loss." She took a step back. "Is it someone close?"

"Hardly, but I fancied her husband when we were in junior high, and I hear he still drives. I'm not saying he'll be ready to date anytime soon, but what can it hurt? I'll show up to Kearney's, reintroduce myself, talk about the old days." Her eyebrows popped up. "Maybe offer him a shoulder."

"Kearney's?" Daisy was trying to keep up with this conversation so she could repeat it to Beverly.

"The funeral parlor over on Clay Avenue. That's where the wife's laid out."

"Well, I'm not sure what to say." Daisy considered her options. "Good luck? Godspeed? Break a leg?"

Opal smirked. "I'll take the luck. I want to see if time has been kind to him. I don't mind a bald head, but I do like a full set of teeth or a decent pair of dentures."

"Opal, you're a pip. You better get yourself over there before the ladies from the choir steal your idea."

"Speaking of the choir," Opal said, "remember, mum's the word. I'm tired of being passed over for the Christmas solo. Come hell or high water, I'm singing 'O Holy Night' this year," she tugged on Daisy's sleeve, "with a little help from yours truly."

"You'll be hitting those high notes in no time, assuming you don't run off and get hitched after the viewing."

"Then I'll sing at my wedding." Opal sashayed toward the doorway. "Either way, I'm getting a solo this year."

Daisy laughed. "Same time next week?"

"Thursday," Opal said, "seven o'clock sharp. And I won't be late again." She stopped short on the landing and blurted out, "There's a colored man on your stairs!"

Daisy ran over to find Johnny frozen on the bottom step, his hands in the air. "I know him, Opal."

"I'm sorry, young man." The woman clutched her chest. "You gave me a fright. I wasn't expecting to see anyone down there, let alone . . ." Her voice trailed off.

"No harm done." Johnny lowered his hands and slowly took one step up.

"This is Johnny Cornell," Daisy said. "Johnny, Opal Lutz."

"Pleased to meet you, ma'am." He took another careful step.

"Likewise," Opal said, backing up into the studio, giving Johnny a wide berth.

"I didn't mean to scare you," he said, entering the room. He pivoted toward Daisy. "I didn't know you had company."

"It's not your fault," Opal said. "With that sun going down, you and those stairs are black as pitch."

Daisy's eyes bounced back and forth between them as she wondered where to start. "The light's burned out," she said to Opal. "Johnny offered to change it for me." She looked at Johnny. "Opal's lesson ran long."

Johnny grabbed the light bulb sitting on the counter and set the stepladder up on the landing.

"I was late." Opal tossed her head. "My permanent wave took longer than expected."

"No problem," Johnny said. "Give me a minute." He replaced the bulb, climbed down from the ladder, and turned on the switch. "Let there be light."

"And now I'm off," Opal said loudly. She leaned into Daisy and whispered, "Unless you want me to stay."

"Good luck tonight," Daisy said, ushering the woman toward the stairs. "I can't wait to hear all about Kearney's."

"You're sure?" Opal rested a couple of fingers on her top lip as if to camouflage the movement of her mouth. "I can always go over to the corpse house tomorrow." She peeked over at Johnny putting away the ladder. "They're viewing the body for three days."

"No need. Now remember," Daisy put her arm around the woman's shoulder and gave her a squeeze, "mum's the word. We want you to knock the socks off those ladies from the First Christian Church when it's time to audition."

"We do, indeed." Opal glanced at Johnny one last time before starting down.

Daisy waited until the woman opened the door to the street before turning back to Johnny. "I'm sorry."

"About?" He ambled over to the piano and sat on the stool.

"Opal. I didn't think she'd be here this long." Daisy pulled a chair alongside him and pouted. "No kiss?"

"And that's it?"

"What?"

"I'm not the handyman," he said.

"I never said you were."

Johnny trained his eyes on the sheet music for "As Time Goes By," propped prominently on the piano. "You never said I wasn't."

"You told me you'd change the bulb."

"Because I was coming over anyway. Coming to see *you*."

"What was I supposed to say? 'This is Johnny, we're having a torrid affair'?"

"Torrid?" Johnny's jaw loosened into a smile. "That's news to me."

Daisy wasn't ready to let go. "Next time I'll say, 'Sure, he's changing that light, but not as hired help. He's here of his own volition.'" She pursed her lips, particularly satisfied with that last word, but then she thought of one more thing to say: "It's what a boyfriend does."

Boyfriend. Her cheeks immediately caught fire. She'd gone too far. Yes, they'd been out a dozen or so times in the last month, but that didn't make them an item.

Johnny quipped, "Now, when you say 'torrid affair,' how torrid are we talking, because I think I missed that part." He kissed her cheek. "Not that I'm complaining. I just remember a certain someone telling me she wanted to 'take it slow.'"

Daisy's defensiveness turned into worry about her own motives. *Did I purposely mislead Opal about Johnny?* "What *should* I say if there's a next time?"

"If?"

"When." She shook her head. "Never mind next time. What are we going to say, period? My mother's starting to wonder why I'm always out so late."

"Tell her it's the price you pay for having a . . . boyfriend . . . who's a *musician*."

"I'm being serious."

"So, I take it you still haven't told her about us?"

Daisy dropped her eyes. "I was waiting."

Johnny bristled. "For what?"

Because I don't know how she'll react, Daisy thought, but she couldn't say the words aloud. "I'm working on it."

"Makes me sound like some kind of chore."

Daisy felt guilty enough without Johnny adding to it. She moved her chair to put a foot of distance between them. "And have you told *your* mother?"

"It's not the same." He sounded more confident than he looked. "She's all the way in Atlantic City."

"It's the same."

"I know." Johnny took a couple of long breaths. "My mama always says we're better off not mixing. I suppose that's one way to see it."

"Is that how *you* see it?"

"I don't want to."

A train rumbled through the crossing behind the studio. As if by agreement, Daisy and Johnny sighed in time to its plaintive whistle. Outside, a last gasp of sun surrendered to the manufactured light spilling from Kresge's, A.S. Beck, and Woolworths. Stores stayed open till nine on Thursdays to accommodate shoppers who couldn't get downtown during the day. In another half hour, the electric light too would be extinguished, so the moon and stars could take a turn.

With the train now out of earshot, Johnny asked, "What're we doing?"

Daisy crossed her arms. "Having our first fight, though for the life of me, I'm not sure why."

"No." He swallowed hard. "I mean, what are *we* doing?"

"Spending time together, I thought. Getting to know each other."

Johnny scraped the piano stool a few inches closer to Daisy. "And what if we're kidding ourselves?" He pressed his dark forearm against Daisy's pale one and held it there.

"Why are you making such a big deal out of this?" Daisy

pulled away and sat up in her seat. "Opal just caught me off guard."

"Maybe that's the problem."

"What?"

"We'll always have to be on guard." Johnny sat back. "I'm not sure you're strong enough for this."

"What about you?"

"It's different for me." He kept his eyes locked on hers. "I know what's a stake."

"So do I."

"We don't know what we don't know." Johnny reached over and gave her hand a squeeze. "How are you going to feel when we're out in public?"

"I see you in public at the clubs all the time."

"You watch me from the audience."

"And we go out to Tony Harding's after every show. Are you saying a diner isn't public?"

"And why do you think we always go to Tony Harding's?"

"Because they're open all night."

"And?" Johnny waited, but when Daisy didn't answer, he said, "Because they won't give two people like us any trouble."

"Well, how was I supposed to know?"

"That's my point."

"Look," she said, "you're right. I don't know what I don't know. I've never been in this situation before."

"Situation?"

Daisy stroked the side of his freshly shaven cheek and inhaled the scent of his cologne. "I do know that every time I hear your footsteps on those stairs or see you sit down at a piano, my heart races. I've never known anyone like you, Johnny Cornell, and all I can think about is getting to know you better."

Johnny took her hand. "What if we end up breaking each other's hearts?"

"I'm willing to take that chance. Are you?"

Johnny pressed his navy pant leg against her turquoise skirt, creating a moody blue ocean. He touched her mouth and traced the length of her lips until they parted.

She closed her eyes, eager to feel the heat and hunger of his kisses.

He obliged, over and over and over again.

After a few minutes, Johnny exhaled loudly. "This 'taking it slow' is harder than I thought." He kissed her one more time and turned back to the piano.

Daisy sat very still, steadying her breathing.

Johnny curled his hands over the keys, twin bridges spanning the octaves. "Name this tune," he said. He started to play the first line of the opening to "Daisy Bell."

Four notes in, Daisy sang along:

There is a flower within my heart,
Daisy, Daisy.

"Well, look at you," Johnny said. "Nobody ever remembers that verse."

"I've spent my entire life being called Daisy Bell after that song." She rolled her eyes. "I know every verse ever written, even the naughty ones we sang as kids."

Johnny played the entire opening and somehow turned that simple piece of music into art.

"How do you do it?" Daisy asked, watching his hands.

"I sneak in a few blues licks." He played a handful of rueful notes before heading back to the melody. "A touch of bitter brings out the sweet."

"What a gift."

"How did I get so lucky?" Johnny gazed at Daisy with an intensity that made them both shudder. He swiveled back to the piano, played a few bars and crooned:

Daisy, Daisy, give me your answer, do.
I'm half crazy all for the love of you.

Daisy smiled, remembering the first time they'd met on the street, at this very piano.

It won't be a stylish marriage.
I can't afford the carriage . . .

He tugged her chin and kissed her nose.

But you'll look sweet upon the seat
Of a bicycle built for two.

Daisy got up and stood behind Johnny as he played the tune again. She rested her hands on his shoulders and sang sweetly in his ear:

Johnny, Johnny, here is your answer true.

He grinned at the sound of his name.

I'd be crazy to marry a lad like you.

She walked to the side of the piano, laughing.

There won't be any marriage
If you can't afford a carriage

He slapped his hands to his chest, feigning a broken heart, before returning to the keys.

'Cause I'll be damned
If I'll be crammed
On a bicycle built for two.

"So that's your idea of a naughty verse?" Johnny shook his head, and they both broke cracked up.

"What's so funny?" a voice came from the doorway.

Daisy looked up to see Mickey dressed in his baseball uniform from school. "How long have you been standing there?" she said, finger-combing her tousled hair.

Mickey kicked off his shoes, glided to the center of the room, and spun. "Long enough to hear you say *damned*."

Daisy blushed. "What are you doing out so late?" Before he could answer, she added, "Mickey, you remember Johnny."

"You're the guy who likes dogs."

"Not all dogs," Johnny said, "just the strays."

"What's the difference?" Mickey asked, sock-skating across the maple floor to the far wall.

"Nobody around to give them orders."

"Now *that's* a thing worth remembering." Mickey glanced in Daisy's direction and held up a paper bag. "My granny sent me over to Woolworths for bread. She can't have more than a slice because of her sugar, but she always likes to have a loaf on hand. Anyway, thought I'd come up and say hi."

"At this time of night?" Daisy said.

"Your light's on."

"Little man," Johnny chuckled, "she wants to know why you were at Woolworths so late."

"If you get there at closing," Mickey scanned the room to make sure no one else was listening, "they sell the bread as 'day old' and knock a nickel off the price."

Johnny tapped a finger against his forehead. "Something worth remembering."

Still holding onto the bag, Mickey bent over and walked his feet up the wall into a handstand. Soon he was steady, crossing over to the piano on his palms, dragging the bread with him. "So what are we singing?" he asked, still inverted.

"'Daisy Bell.'" Johnny started the song up again.

Mickey let his legs drop down so he could stand. "Do you know the verse about the barkeep and the beer?"

"Never heard that one." Johnny slapped his knee.

"I think that's enough singing for tonight," Daisy said.

Now that Mickey was upright, Johnny noticed the boy's face. "Where'd you get that shiner?"

Mickey fingered the purple bruise circling his left eye. "Got into a fight at school." He winked with his good eye. "You should see the other guy."

"Mickey!" Daisy pulled the boy over so she could examine his injury. "Fighting never solves anything."

"I don't know about that," Johnny said. "It depends on what you're fighting for."

"Just a couple of bullies having a good laugh." Mickey did another spin and bumped into the piano.

"They're trying to get a rise out of you," Daisy said. "When they laugh at you, ignore them. They'll get bored and move on."

"Not me," Mickey said. "Mary Lou Doyle, a girl from school. Her back's bent, so she's gotta wear a brace. Makes her walk real stiff, so the boys took to calling her Frankenstein. I got tired of hearing it. A joke's not funny if it hurts someone's feelings."

"Good for you," Johnny said, patting the boy on his back. "It's important to be on the right side of laughter."

Daisy couldn't decide where she stood on the issue of fighting, so she asked, "What did your grandmother say when she saw your bruise?"

"She gave me what for, for fighting, but after that, she told me those boys are fools. When Mary Lou's back straightens out, she'll be a real beauty." Mickey blushed. "I can already see it."

Daisy turned toward the window just as the storefronts on Lackawanna Avenue went dark for the night. Clerks drifted out of buildings, some packing into courtesy cars for a ride home, while others headed over to the Casey Hotel for a drink and a spin around the dance floor.

"It's late," Daisy said. "I think we'd better walk you home."

"I can take care of myself." Mickey grabbed a chain at his neck, pulled a silver pea whistle from under his shirt, and blew. "Loud enough to scare off a deaf man."

"He's not wrong." Johnny tugged at Mickey's ear good-naturedly. "Where do you live, little man?"

"In the Flats." Mickey pointed toward the windows on the alley side of the building. "At the bottom of the hill."

Johnny crossed his arms in thought. "Whereabouts?"

"Birch Street."

"Okay, then." Johnny said. "But let's be quick about it."

Mickey skated back across the room to put on his shoes, then Daisy locked up and followed the pair out the door.

"So which one is Birch?" Daisy asked as they walked down the hill past the army's towering ammunition plant with its imposing stone walls. "I swear, every street in South Side is named after a tree."

"Between Hickory and Beech," Mickey said.

"See what I mean?"

"Just past the bridge by Goodman Silks," Johnny offered, "Anthracite Plate Glass is across the street."

"Near where Roaring Brook empties into the Lackawanna River," Mickey said. "A lot of good fishing, or there will be if we ever get some rain. Granny says she's never seen a drier summer."

"I work at the slaughterhouse a couple of blocks over," Johnny said. "Eat my lunch on that very riverbank."

"Howdy, neighbor." Mickey shook Johnny's hand. "Maybe you know the house. Brown asphalt siding. Two front porches, one up and one down."

"Go past it twice a day," Johnny said, "coming and going. Always in the daylight though."

"We're on top. The Secoolishes live under us. I'll watch for you in the morning. If you hear . . ." Mickey pulled out his whistle and blew two high pitched notes, "you'll know it's me."

Within ten minutes, the trio had crossed the railroad tracks and turned right onto Birch Street. Mickey ran ahead and led them to the first house on the block. In front, a large streetlight cast a yellow beam toward the brook. "You want to come in?"

"Not tonight, little man," Johnny started to turn back, "but I'll keep an eye out for you in the morning."

"Hey, Bertie," Mickey called out as a burly man with a crooked nose staggered onto the sidewalk. "How's tricks?"

Bertie lurched forward and leered at Daisy. "Who do we have here?"

Johnny whirled around and stepped into the light.

"What the . . ." Bertie tripped back as he eyed Johnny. "You lost, boy?" He bent down and grabbed a baseball-sized rock at the edge of the yard. On his way up, he teetered like a top till he braced himself against the lamppost.

"That you, Gilbert Heerman?" a woman shouted from overhead.

"Hey, Granny." Mickey waved.

Bertie squinted up at the second-story porch. "Why if it isn't Mrs. McCrae." He dropped the rock and offered a shaky bow. "How are you this fine evening?"

"When I put my foot up your arse, you'll know how I am." Mickey's grandmother pulled her chair up to the banister. "Your saint of a wife is waiting for you at home." She clapped her hands as if shooing a cat. "Get going."

"Yes, ma'am," Bertie said as he stumbled into the street.

"I'll never understand what that woman sees in you," Mrs. McCrae said.

"Nor will I, Mrs. McCrae." He started up the road. "Nor will I." He disappeared into an alley.

"Who's down there with you, Mickey?" the woman called out.

"Mrs. McCrae, it's Daisy, Mickey's dance teacher. And this is Johnny Cornell."

The woman leaned over the banister for a better look. "Well there's your problem." She pointed a finger at Johnny before addressing Daisy: "You're not doing him any favors, you know."

Daisy glanced at Johnny then back up at the porch. "Ma'am?"

"Think it through." The woman shook her head. "With you on his arm, he's a sitting duck."

"Times are changing, Mrs. McCrae." Johnny squeezed Daisy's hand.

"Time moves slow in Scranton," Mrs. McCrae responded. "Young love. Do what you want. You're going to anyway." She addressed her grandson: "Did you get the bread?"

Mickey held the bag in the air.

"Will you come up for a sandwich?" Mrs. McCrae asked the couple.

"Another time," Johnny said. "We really need to be on our way."

"Mr. Secoolish!" Mrs. McCrae grabbed a nearby broom and hammered the handle into the porch floor.

Dressed in nightclothes, the first-floor tenant opened his screen door and called up, "What can I do you for?"

"How's that car of yours running?"

"Like a clock."

"I need a favor." Mickey's grandmother pointed her broom over the banister at Johnny and Daisy. "Will you give these two lovebirds a ride up the hill?"

"Let me put my robe on." Mr. Secoolish's screen door snapped shut.

"Mrs. McCrae," Daisy said, "we're fine to walk. It's a beautiful night."

"You never know if Bertie'll come back around. No sense tempting fate." Mrs. McCrae pushed herself up, using the broom as a cane. "Thank you for watching out for the lad. Mickey's good to his old granny."

Mr. Secoolish came back out to the porch and headed over to an old DeSoto at the curb with a ladder strapped to the roof rack. "Hop in," he said, double-knotting the tie on his robe. "Watch out for the paint cans." He gestured toward the floor on the passenger side. I'm a house painter by trade."

"Come back anytime," Mrs. McCrae called out. "You're always welcome here. The pair of you," she said before going back inside.

CHAPTER NINETEEN

IT WAS TOO QUIET IN THE HOUSE. With Daisy out gallivanting, Grace asleep upstairs, and Archie curled up in the kitchen, Violet found the silence as oppressive as the mid-June heat. If only it would rain. Her garden could use a good soaking, and Violet loved to hear the drops spatter against the windows, but they hadn't had more than a drizzle in weeks.

She could turn on the television, after all it was only nine thirty, though she didn't want to get into the habit of using it for company. Instead, she fished a few gingersnaps out of the tin and went out on the front porch. She passed up the rockers in favor of the swing Tommy had made long before they'd courted. Unbeknownst to Violet at the time, he'd hoped to woo her with his handiwork. After they'd married, the two spent countless summer nights outside, shoulder to shoulder, softly swinging. Tommy wasn't much of a talker, but that never mattered. There was comfort to be found in the silences they shared.

Now Violet sat alone, glancing at her neighbors' houses. An hour earlier, Spring Street had been teeming with children playing stickball, hopscotch, and tug-of-war, but as soon as the streetlights came on, they knew enough to hightail it home.

Violet noticed the glow in Mrs. Lankowski's upper window. At ninety-one, she still read her Polish Bible before bed like she'd done every night for as long as Violet could remember. She was eight the first time they'd met. Forty-two years later, it wasn't lost on Violet that she was now around the same age as the widow was then. *And we thought she was so old.*

Mrs. Lankowski wasn't the only one on the block to lose a husband. Violet glanced right, toward a nearby kitchen window where Mrs. Sweet sat under a single lit bulb, enjoying her cup of warm milk. To the left, Myrtle Evans's house had been dark for an hour already. One door down, Myrtle's sister Mildred's television cast its light into the street. Violet used to feel sorry for these women, and now she was one of them. Coal-mine widows, all.

Tommy's death had surprised Violet more than it should have. The mines always took what they wanted. It was just a matter of when. Some men died young in cave-ins or explosions. The older ones succumbed later in life to black lung. *Older*, she thought. *Never old*.

Other lamps in other homes blinked on or off, according to their routines. Violet had lived on this street her whole life and knew its habits. Even when houses changed hands, they usually stayed in the family. They'd gotten a few newcomers, like the Nisselbaums, the family who'd bought Grace's house next door after she'd moved in with Violet, but even they'd adapted, drifting along on the same current as the rest of the neighborhood.

Of course, with the mines in decline, people would start leaving soon enough. Last week, Mildred's son Pete mentioned something about a factory job in Jersey. Daisy had already left once, only to return when her father took sick. She'd leave again. Violet felt sure of it. And she couldn't begrudge her daughter for wanting to go. Violet just didn't like being left behind, not anymore. Her sister Daisy had left her behind when they were children. Stanley, too, when she'd brought the baby home. Lily had abandoned her by running off to Atlantic City with Frankie. Sure, it made sense to want a clean break after divorcing her first husband, George. *What a miserable man*. But Frankie was no prize either—made his money outside the law, Violet was certain of that—though at least he'd kept Lily's secret. It had taken Violet years to work out that Frankie, not George, had fathered Daisy. Leave it to Lily to get pregnant by one man, then complicate matters by marrying another. Not surprisingly, Lily had gone back to Frankie when things went south with George. That was Lily's style. Always take the easy way out.

Meantime, Violet was left holding the bag. She was the one who nursed the dying. Her father, Owen. Her mother-in-law, Louise. Her husband, Tommy. Not that she'd have had it any other way, but an extra pair of hands might have lightened her load. And here she was now, tending to her mother who, in spite of Violet's very best efforts, had started her decline.

Then there was Daisy, the love of her life. Violet got down on her knees every night and thanked God for making her the mother of this child, even if it meant being the subject of neighborhood gossip. Lily had never asked Violet to claim Daisy as her own, so Violet had no right to expect sympathy or gratitude from her. Still, she wanted them all the same. Or did she? Violet didn't know what she wanted anymore.

Across the street, Mrs. Lankowski turned off her bedroom lamp. A sliver of moon winked in the dingy sky.

I'm tired of following the rules, Violet thought. *Tired of putting everyone else's wishes ahead of my own. Tired of this view from this porch on this street. Tired of myself.*

Archie nudged his way through the screen door and lay down at Violet's feet. She offered him gingersnaps, one by one. "I'll never get tired of *you,* boy." She bent down to check his injured ear. "Let's call it a night." As they both stood up, a breeze brushed past, rousing the leaves on the poplar tree in the corner of the yard. "Maybe it'll be good sleeping weather," she said.

Archie responded with a muffled bark as the two went back inside.

The morning sun sliced through the upturned slats of the kitchen blinds. "What's next?" Violet asked, tapping a teaspoon of nutmeg into a mixture of flour, sugar, baking powder, and salt.

Grace peered into the bowl. "A cup and a half of lard, give or take."

Violet scooped a lump of fat out of the can and slid it on top of the other ingredients.

"Now mix it all between both hands like you would a pie crust," Grace said.

After all these years, Violet could make Welsh cakes, or what the church called "old country cookies," in her sleep, but she wanted her mother to feel needed. And she *was* needed. Just not in the ways she was used to.

"That's good," Grace said. "Where are your currants?"

Violet glanced behind her. "Soaked and drained." She held up her greasy hands. "Would you grab them for me?"

Grace shuffled over to the sink, gave the colander a good shake, and set it on the table. "Now don't be stingy," she said.

Violet had to hand it to her mother. No one could ever accuse Grace Morgan of skimping on the currants. People used to always request her cookies for the church's bake sales. Violet slowly stirred the fruit into the mixture by hand. "What's next?"

"Three eggs," Grace said, "but you already know that." She glanced toward a trio of eggs crowded on a saucer. "And a splash of milk. Nothing worse than a dry Welsh cake."

Violet finished up the dough. She rolled it out on a heavily floured board, cut it into dozens of perfect circles with the mouth of a water glass, and placed the raw cookies on a platter, ready to be cooked. She turned toward the griddle, which straddled two unlit burners on the stove.

"I've got it," Grace said, scooping two fingers of lard out of the can. She greased every inch of the cast-iron surface and reached for a light.

"Let me," Violet said, quickly taking the matches from her mother. "That back burner can be tricky."

"Wait till the grease starts to spit," Grace said as she washed her hands.

Both burners caught on the first try. "How long?" Violet asked when the griddle began hissing. She laid out three rows of eight cookies with the deftness of a card sharp.

"A few minutes on one side," Grace flipped her palms up, "and then the other. Like you're making pancakes." She carried a cup of tea over to her chair and sat down. "Oh how your father loved pancakes." She smiled.

"So he did," Violet said, picking up her spatula.

An hour later the dishes had been washed and the griddle put away in time for a late breakfast. "So what's the occasion?" Grace reached for the cookie plate in the center of the table.

"Thought they'd make a nice change. And it doesn't hurt that they're Daisy's favorite. I've been short with her lately."

"Well, that's a relief." Grace gave her brow an exaggerated swipe. "What is?"

"I thought I might be dying."

"Mother! Why would you to say that?"

"You only make Welsh cakes for birthdays and funerals, and since nobody's having a birthday soon," Grace took a bite of cookie and smacked her lips, "I thought you might be trying to tell me something."

"Don't talk like that, even if you're only teasing." Violet searched for an optimistic angle. "Last time Dr. Gustitis made a house call, he said your heart sounded pretty good, considering." Why couldn't she have stopped at *pretty good*?

"He also said I have a bad ticker, and it could give out any moment. I've made my peace with that. You should too." Grace brushed a few crumbs off the tablecloth and onto her plate. "Not that I'm in a hurry, but when the Lord does call me home, I'll be tickled pink to see my Owen and Our Daisy."

Unsure how to respond, Violet took the conversation back to safer territory: "And I make Welsh cakes all the time. Last month, I cooked a double batch for all the shut-ins from church."

Grace ignored Violet's claim in favor of a question: "Any more dreams about Daisy?"

"Afraid not."

"Hmm." For a few seconds, Grace seemed sad, but she perked up again. "I can't wait to see Louise and my sister Hattie. And oh! Do you know how long it's been since I've seen my own dear mother and father?"

Violet knew it had been many years; her grandparents had passed long before she was born.

"I sure miss them." Grace's smile budded and bloomed. "That'll be a reunion for the ages." Then, with the earnestness of a child, she lowered her head and said, "I hope I did them proud."

"Not a doubt in my mind." In order to keep her mother from getting anymore lost in the past, Violet said, "And you're still making them proud." She held up a cookie as if to toast and took a bite. "Not a bad effort."

"Best ones yet," Grace said. "Make sure we have enough for Daisy when she gets home."

"We made plenty."

"By the way, I threw a few of those embroidered tea towels onto your ironing pile." Grace pointed to a basket of clean laundry on the porch. "I'd like to use them as runners on my dresser."

"That's fine," Violet said. "I'll get to them tomorrow."

Grace's face burned with embarrassment. "Have I mixed up my days again?"

"Not at all."

"But you washed clothes yesterday."

"I did."

Grace gave Violet a sideways glance. "That means you iron today."

"I'm going to play hooky instead." Violet shook her whole body as if throwing off a chill. "I have to do something to change my mind."

"But tomorrow's cleaning day," Grace said, her confidence returning.

"So it is."

"And Sunday's a day of rest."

"If you consider two church services and a pot roast with all the fixings a day of rest, then yes."

Grace studied the basket of laundry. "But when will you iron?"

"It'll get done. Don't you worry."

"I know what," Grace said. "I'll do the ironing."

Violet shook her head. "I don't want you on your legs that long. They'll swell up in this heat."

"Then what are you going to do with yourself today?"

"Whatever I want. Maybe I'll go to the library and get that book you asked for. And I still need a trowel. I bet I can get one at the Handy Dandy."

"The five-and-dime in Green Ridge?"

"The one on Market Street."

"You may as well stop and thank Stanley for the beer. He's only a few doors down."

"We'll see." Violet chewed on her lip. "I think he's mad at me."

"He'll get glad again." Grace's brow furrowed. "What about all those graduation pictures?"

"What about them?"

"How are you going to get them finished when you have all that ironing to catch up on?"

"I'm done." Violet grabbed two more cookies.

"With the ironing?"

"No," Violet said. "Coloring the photographs."

"Already?"

"I only had thirty-two this year. Time was, I'd get a few hundred. All anyone wants now is color film." Violet pushed her plate aside. "If this keeps up, I'll need to find other work."

"What would you do?"

"Not a clue."

"Maybe Stanley will have an idea," Grace said. "You can ask him when you see him."

"*If* I see him. I told you I haven't decided."

"You tell me a lot of things," Grace said. "Why don't you go get changed, and I'll wrap those Welsh cakes."

"I'm already dressed." Violet looked down at another of her shapeless shifts, blue gingham today.

Grace eyed her daughter. "Those dresses aren't doing you any favors."

Violet bristled. "I'm going to Green Ridge, Mother, not the Taj Mahal."

"You won't want to hear this, but I'll say it anyway. You're not dead. You're fifty." Grace hesitated. "But you're also not getting any younger."

"Thanks." Violet pushed her chair back a little too hard and stood up.

"I'm saying, live a little. Turn a few heads while you still can. You're not going to the big reunion," Grace peeked up at the ceiling, "anytime soon. Stop acting like you're already there."

Her mother was right. Not that Violet had any intention of telling her. Instead, she pulled up the blind to watch the birds as she wrapped the cookies in waxed paper sleeves.

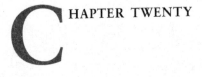

CHAPTER TWENTY

THE AUGUST BEFORE TOMMY'S STROKE, Violet had bought a madras skirt from Donis's Dress Shop. Its muted plaid caught her eye, and the half-price sale assuaged her conscience. She'd worn the piece several times that summer, but after Tommy passed away, she never put it on again. The sherbet colors seemed too cheery for a widow.

Three years later, Violet stood in front of her vanity's mirror in a cream slip and a white blouse. *I need a little cheer*. She carefully stepped into the skirt, full all around, cinched at the waist. *And a little luck*, she thought, struggling with that last inch of zipper. A combination of sucking in her stomach and tugging on the pull finally did the trick. She opened her top drawer, rummaged through her underwear, and pulled out the small square of Tabu-infused paper she'd gotten at the Globe Store's perfume counter. After rubbing the scent onto her wrists, she looked in the mirror and gave her reflection a modest nod.

Violet tiptoed down the stairs and into the kitchen. With a sleeve of Welsh cookies tucked into her purse, she listened for her mother's snores before slipping out the door. She wouldn't be long, a couple of hours, and her mother would be napping for most of it. Violet moseyed down Spring Street, then right onto North Main Avenue. A few blocks later, she crossed over to the Silkman house, a grand two-story structure with four looming columns supporting a gabled roof. Years earlier, the city had purchased the home and turned it into the Providence Library, but Violet would forever think of it as the Silkmans' house because that's who lived there when she was growing up. In recent years she'd picked up her mother's habit of calling places by their old names. *Funny how that happens.* Atlas's for Furman's. Varnele's for Trader's. The Palace instead of Bill's Sporting Goods, even though it hadn't been a theater since she was a girl.

The Silkmans' front porch spanned the length of the yard. Violet climbed the first of two steps before turning back around. No sense carrying that book all the way to the Handy Dandy in Green Ridge and back when she could pick it up on her way home. Up ahead, the North Scranton Bank and Trust cast its long shadow into the road. At a height of forty-five feet, the marble and limestone edifice dominated Providence Square. Violet especially loved the ornate clock suspended over the bronze door, but she also had a soft spot for Murray's, the general store they'd razed in the twenties to build the bank. As kids, she and Stanley had spent a small fortune in pennies buying gumdrops and peanut brittle at Mrs. Murray's candy counter.

Stanley. He'd been such an important part of her life, until he wasn't. *Water over the dam*, she thought.

When she reached the bank, she glanced up the hill. Not all the businesses from Violet's youth had disappeared. Stirna's Restaurant, Wilensky's Men's Shop, and Leonard's Drug Store remained. And the Providence Christian Church, of course. Other than removing the steeple, not much about the building had changed over the years. Same red brick. Same circle of stained glass above a pair of wooden doors. No matter what else might transform with time, she'd always have her church.

Violet started down Market Street toward Green Ridge, but stopped as soon as she reached the bridge. Below her, the Lackawanna River lazed past like a careless line of cursive. It had been years since she'd seen the water so low. Many were the times Violet and Stanley had traipsed along those banks. The summer after fifth grade they'd even tried to build a fort near a sharp elbow of river in the Plot, one neighborhood over, but a few days into the project, a good rain and a fast current washed away the wood they'd managed to filch from a nearby scrapyard.

Well before Violet was born, the church had used this very river for baptisms. Given the stew of coal ash and sewage they were submerged in, the congregants must have been desperate for salvation. Then again, she understood desperation. After Our Daisy's death, Violet longed for redemption. Neighborhood gossip had perpetuated the lie that she'd thrown the sparkler that had killed her sister. What a horrible thing to blame on an eight-year-old girl. Still, it was true that a spark from Violet's firework had caught on her sister's hem and set the dress aflame. That kind of guilt felt an awful lot like sin.

Violet had to wait over a year to be baptized. Finally, on the first Sunday in September, she'd made her way to a changing room behind the pulpit, stripped down to her bloomers, and put on the smallest of the long white robes hanging in the closet. Even so, a gratuitous amount of fabric swallowed her four-foot frame.

Reverend Halloway, who was already standing in the baptistry wearing his own white vestment, called for Violet to join him. She pushed through a velvet curtain, walked down the steps into a chest-high pool of water, and faced the congregation. Almost every pew was full, save for one where her family always sat. This day her mother was home with baby Lily, and her father was talking a neighbor into giving up the drink.

Violet refused to allow her disappointment at their absence to divert her from her purpose. She'd waited too long for this moment. In a matter of minutes, God would wash away her sins, and she'd rise up with a soul so clean, even the people in the back row would see it shine.

After a brief profession of faith, Violet crossed her arms in front of her chest. Reverend Halloway recited a verse from Colossians: "*When you were buried with him in baptism, you were also raised with him through faith in the power of God, who raised him from the dead.*"

In a motion both quick and practiced, the minister covered her mouth and pinched her nose with one hand while reaching behind her with the other. Violet's spine stiffened, but he managed to bend her body back till she was completely immersed. He'd only held her down for a few seconds, but underwater, time seemed to slow its gait while panic took the lead. Violet's chest tightened around her racing heart. She opened her eyes to a billowing sleeve shrouding her face. *I need to breathe!* She thrust her elbow toward the fabric cloud, and connected with the minister's arm just hard enough to throw his balance off, sending him into the baptistry wall. Her nose and mouth filled with water as she emerged, gasping for air.

The congregation held its collective breath while Reverend Halloway righted himself and slapped Violet's back till she coughed out all the water. Mortified, she spun around and marched up the steps as quickly as her sodden robe would allow. Once she was safely behind the curtain, she heard the minister joke, "Now I know how Jacob felt when he wrestled that angel." A round of amused amens rippled through the church as the organist started the closing hymn.

Even now, as Violet stood on the bridge staring at the river, she remembered trembling in that changing room. No one had seen fit to leave her a towel, so she pulled another robe out of the closet and used it to dry off. Her drawers were soaked. Why hadn't she thought to bring an extra pair? With no time to waste, she slipped her dress over her soggy underwear. By the time the organist reached the last verse, Violet was already out the back door and on her way to Spring Street. When she reached her house, she found Stanley waiting for her on the front porch. He eyed her damp dress and tangle of wet hair. "Do you feel any different?" he asked.

She dug a little hole in the dirt with the toe of her unlaced boot. "I don't think it took."

"How come?"

"Maybe some sins can't be forgiven."

"I don't know about that." Stanley sat back against the post. "Do you know Mr. Flynn?"

"From over on School Street? My father's at his place right now."

"Good," Stanley said. "Maybe he can talk some sense into the man. Every Friday night he gets soused and beats up that wife of his."

"How do you know that?"

"Evan Evans's mother. I was over there playing ball, and she was passing gossip over the fence, as Babcia likes to say."

Violet shook out her skirt, trying to get it to dry faster. "And?"

"I'd call beating your wife a pretty big sin. The kind that might not get forgiven. But every Saturday morning, like clockwork, he shows up at the parish for confession and gets that slate wiped clean."

"What's confession?" Violet dropped down next to him on the step.

"It's how we Catholics get rid of sin."

Violet pondered the answer. "What happens if Mr. Flynn gets run over by a train on his way to the parish?"

"I don't think there's tracks between here and there."

"I'm saying, what happens if he dies after he gets drunk and beats up his wife but before he gets to confession?"

Stanley tapped his index finger against his lip. "Now that's a good question."

"I thought so."

The pair sat side by side in quiet contemplation. A minute later, Stanley yelled out, "I almost forgot!"

"What?"

"I came over to tell you I found a hornets' nest in a tree along the river. Biggest one I ever seen."

"Bigger'n the one we found in Alice Harris's barn?"

"Twice that size." He jumped up. "Wanna see?"

"Okay." She gave her dress another good shake before stepping off the porch.

Well past Evan Evans's house, Stanley reached for Violet's hand and said, "I'm sure it took."

Violet squeezed his fingers, grateful for his certainty, since she had none.

Over forty years later, her heart still quickened at the memory. She may not have known where she stood with God, but for most of her life, she did know where she stood with Stanley. Even after their falling-out, he'd never had an unkind word to say about her. If he had, any number of neighbors would've come knocking at her door. Now, she didn't have a clue what he thought of her, and suddenly, on this bridge, on this day, that mattered. Violet had loved two men in her life, Tommy and Stanley, often at the same time, much to her chagrin. Yet try as she may over the years, her love for one never diminished her love for the other. She felt both discomfited and liberated by this revelation.

Maybe she would swing by Stanley's office after all. She could thank him for helping Archie. And for getting the beer. And for leaving that slice of bark. And maybe she'd find the courage to ask him why he'd run off in the middle of their conversation. Violet took one more look at the river for luck before continuing on to Green Ridge.

CHAPTER TWENTY-ONE

STANLEY NEEDED TO STRETCH HIS LEGS after sitting behind his desk for the better part of the afternoon. Outside his door, he watched as a young usher from the Roosevelt Theatre put up posters for their newest movie. "What's playing?" Stanley called out, hoping for something a little quieter than the Westerns they'd been showing lately.

"*Blackboard Jungle*," the boy yelled back.

Stanley strolled over to the first sign for a closer look. *Starring Glenn Ford and Anne Francis.* Stanley liked Glenn Ford. He'd seen him in *The Man from Alamo* more than a few times. *This could be promising*, he thought as he moved to the next poster. *The most startling picture of the year.* He wasn't so sure about that claim. It would have to be pretty startling to outdo *The Night of the Hunter.* Stanley shuddered as he recollected Robert Mitchum's character with the words *love* and *hate* tattooed on his fingers. Pure evil.

The usher closed the glass cover on the third *Blackboard Jungle* poster and pointed to a young actress striking a suggestive pose in the lower left-hand corner. The words *Introducing Margaret Hayes, temptation in a tight skirt* curved around her jutting hip.

As beautiful as she was, Stanley was more interested in another photo, the one in the upper right. "Who's that fella?"

"A Negro actor by the name of Sidney Poitier."

The world's changing, Stanley thought. If only he could figure out a way to change with it. Here he was, alone again since his breakup with Arlene. At least when he'd been drinking, he could blame the bottle. Nothing and nobody to blame now except himself. He bowed his head and offered a quick, "*God, grant me the serenity . . .*" but that's as far as he went. He and God had an understanding about shorthanding prayer in public, and besides, they both knew how this one ended.

Stanley took another gander at the posters. Yes, he had a pile of work sitting on his desk, but it would be there in a couple of hours. Meantime, maybe the critics were right about this movie. *Only one way to find out*, he thought, pulling open the first of the Roosie's six front doors. A blast of conditioned air confirmed his decision.

"That'll be ten cents." The girl at the ticket counter held out her hand.

As soon as she said the words, Stanley remembered emptying his pockets of change at the AA meeting that morning. One of the newcomers needed a little help with rent. Stanley held up a finger to the girl. "I'll be right back."

He ran out of the theater and over to his office, setting off the cowbell over the door as he entered. A couple of steps in, he noticed a woman sitting near his desk with her back to him. It took a split second for his brain to register what his heart already knew. "Is that you?"

Violet gave a nervous laugh as she turned around with a pen in one hand and a piece of Stanley's letterhead in the other. "I was leaving a note."

"I wasn't expecting . . ."

"I had to borrow the widow's trowel." Flustered, Violet tried again: "I lost mine, so I've been using hers." She put the pen and paper back on his blotter. "I wanted to see if they had any trowels at the Handy Dandy."

Stanley suppressed a grin. When they'd get into trouble as kids, Violet always started her excuses at the end and worked her way back. "And did they?"

"What?"

"Have any trowels?" His eyes skimmed the room for a package.

"I came here instead." She corrected herself: "First, I mean."

Violet half stood, but she sat back down as Stanley crossed behind his desk and dropped into his leather chair. "You look good." He shouldn't have said that, but he couldn't help himself. She always looked good.

"I have something for you." Violet reached into her pocketbook and pulled out the Welsh cakes. "A little thank you for all your help with Archie." She took a beat. "And the beer. I still can't believe my mother asked you to do that. She's getting brazen in her old age."

"You want to talk about brazen . . ." Stanley opened the waxed paper and offered Violet a cookie. When she declined, he took one for himself and continued: "Last week, Babcia made me drive her to Gertrude Hawk's candy shop, so she could take back a chocolate Santa. Apparently, in the six months since she'd gotten the little fellow, he'd turned waxy." Stanley arched his left eyebrow. "Surprise, surprise."

"And did they take it?"

"You know the widow. She always gets her way. I was so embarrassed I bought two pounds of gumdrops to make up for it. Would you like some?"

"They were always your favorite."

Stanley took a bite of a Welsh cake and hummed his satisfaction. "Boy, does this bring back memories."

"Speaking of, do you remember that big hornets' nest down by the river?"

Stanley flung his arms out. "It was this big around!"

"And you, throwing rocks at it."

"If I remember correctly, you didn't believe me when I said it was an active nest." Stanley feigned outrage. "A guy has to defend his honor."

"Oh, it was active all right. It's a wonder we didn't get stung to death."

"We can thank my lousy aim for that."

"How did we ever make it through in one piece?" Violet asked.

"Umm." Stanley pointed to the shirt cuff pinned over his stump. "*Almost* one piece."

"You're terrible," Violet chided. "Do you miss it?"

"You get used to it. Half the people I meet these days call me Lefty. I don't think they'd recognize me if I had two hands."

"I would."

Stanley smiled. "That's because you knew me before. When I was whole."

A wistful expression settled across Violet's features. "I wish you knew *me* when I was whole."

"How do you mean?"

"Before we lost my sister Daisy."

"I knew you then."

"You saw me around the neighborhood. I'm talking as a real friend."

"So am I. Remember the day you climbed that old oak tree in the schoolyard?"

"Not the best time to discover my fear of heights."

"I'm the one who went up to get you down."

"And everybody started singing, '*Violet and Stanley, sitting in a tree.*'" She laughed. "I was mortified."

"I wasn't."

Violet thought for a moment. "But that was after Daisy passed. I'm sure of it."

"Nope. You were in second grade, and your sister was yelling at you to come down. She was wearing a new dress and didn't want to ruin it climbing up after you."

"Robin's-egg blue." The recollection seemed to surprise Violet. "A gift from Aunt Hattie."

"I saw my chance to impress the Morgan sisters, the two prettiest girls on the playground, and I took it." Stanley stretched his arms. "Best day of my life to that point."

"I could have sworn that happened a year or two after."

"The mind plays tricks," Stanley said, "especially with time."

"So you remember Daisy." Sadness tugged at Violet's mouth. "We knew each other whole." She glanced again at Stanley's handless arm.

"It's fine," he said. "To tell the truth, I was well on my way to living and dying in those mines. Losing my hand probably saved my life." The second the words left Stanley's lips, he thought about Tommy, who'd spent more than forty years digging coal. Stanley gazed across his desk at Violet. Her face had collapsed into sadness. Surely she was having the same thought. "Tommy was a good man," Stanley finally said.

"Salt of the earth. And as honest as the day is long."

Stanley's heart dropped. When he'd seen Tommy's overalls hanging from that nail on the porch the other day, he realized how loyal she still was to his memory. And why wouldn't she be? Tommy was a man of integrity, and honesty mattered to Violet almost as much as love. Stanley had spent the last three years since Tommy's death telling one lie after another. Tommy had asked him to take care of Violet, but instead of including her in on the decisions, Stanley had gone behind her back. It started with the stipends he'd pretended to secure when the government cut the widow's pensions in half. He just had to remember to put the money into Violet's bank account each month. The mortgage payments were a little trickier. Stanley had to convince Violet that Tommy had enough life insurance to pay off the house, when in truth, he didn't have a penny to his name when he died. And the TV; well, that was Grace's idea, though Stanley went along. Helping Violet was how he showed love.

A loose S&H Green Stamp in the corner of his blotter caught Stanley's eye. It must have fallen out of one of the books he'd given to Mrs. Hinkley for the baby supplies. *Did Violet notice?* He swiped it up with the crumbs from his Welsh cake and tossed all of it in the waste tin.

Stanley could rationalize his sneakiness. Violet needed his

help, and she would have been too proud to accept it outright. He had no choice but to lie. He acted out of love for Violet and loyalty to Tommy. Stanley had almost convinced himself his behavior was justified, when Violet spoke up.

"Honesty matters."

Wow. Does she know? Is she somehow reading my mind? The thick flesh at the end of his stump started to itch.

"I'm at a crossroads." Violet took a breath.

Stanley opened his mouth to speak. Maybe if he could explain himself before she confronted him, he'd have a better chance of getting her to see his side of things.

"Over Daisy," she said.

Suddenly befuddled, Stanley stared at Violet. "Daisy? Your daughter?"

"What was I thinking?" Violet closed the clasp on her pocketbook and smoothed her skirt in preparation to leave. "You certainly don't need to hear my troubles."

"Sit. We're friends." Stanley thought about pulling his chair next to her on the other side of the desk, but fear got the better of him.

"You're one of the few people in this world who . . ." she lowered her voice, "who knows the truth about Daisy. I can't talk to my sister. Lily'd be furious if she knew what I was thinking. I have my mother and the widow, but at their age, I hate to burden them. If only Tommy were here."

Stanley loved the man, but every time Violet said his name, guilt and a little jealously burned its way up to his throat. He swallowed hard. "What's the problem with Daisy?"

"I am. I promised Lily I'd never tell a soul that she was Daisy's mother. I swore to it."

"Don't I know." Stanley's words sounded sharper than he'd intended. Violet seemed not to notice.

"I didn't even tell you, and we were . . ." Violet trailed off.

"Engaged," Stanley said.

"I'm sorry."

"I know."

"I never should have waited." Violet shook her head. "I should have told you the truth the second I got off that train."

"No. I'm the one who jumped to conclusions. What's done is done. And I'll never tell."

"I'm not worried about that," Violet said. "I've always trusted you."

Ugh. Stanley's guilt over lying to Violet reared up again. He wouldn't let her leave the office until he'd had a chance to make his confession. "So you gave your word and you kept it. That's admirable."

"But in order to keep my promise to Lily," Violet sank in her seat, "I have to lie to Daisy."

"You're not exactly lying." Why hadn't he pulled his chair over to hers when he'd had the chance?

"Keeping the truth from someone is as good as lying," Violet said.

"I know."

"She asks questions sometimes." Violet squirmed. "When she was little I could change the subject, but now . . ."

"Did you ever try to tell her?"

"I thought about it. Tommy and I discussed it, but the timing was never right. When does 'too young for a little girl to handle' become too late to tell her?" Violet's brow furrowed. "Sometime before twenty-five, by my count." She rubbed at her temples. "If I keep my promise to Lily, am I betraying Daisy? Worse yet, what if someone else tells her? Someone outside the family."

"Do you think that's possible?"

"I didn't till recently." She searched Stanley's face. "What do I do?"

Stanley thought about his own intention to come clean. "You tell her," he said, "before she finds out on her own."

Violet grasped at a thin strand of hope: "Maybe she'll never find out?"

"People always find out," Stanley said. "And speaking of . . ." He pulled his chair over to Violet and took her hand.

The clank of the cowbell stopped all conversation. Stanley and Violet swung around as a woman struggled to push a baby carriage through the front door. "Let me help," Violet said, hopping up from her chair. Stanley stayed frozen in his.

"No need," the woman said as she cleared the threshold. "I hope I'm not interrupting."

"Mrs. Hinkley," Stanley said. "Well, actually," he managed to get on his feet, "we're in the middle of—"

"What a beautiful baby." Violet peered into the carriage. "A little girl?"

Mrs. Hinkley beamed. "Katie. After my own dear mother." The woman addressed Stanley: "I won't keep you. I can see you're busy."

"Not at all," Violet said. "I'm the one who dropped by unannounced."

"I wanted to show off the baby," she caught Stanley's eye, "and say thank you for all you did."

"No thanks necessary, Mrs. Hinkley." Stanley slowly made his way across the room. "Now you tell Howard the case is going well. I expect to have news for him soon."

"He's a true saint," the woman said to Violet as the pair maneuvered the carriage around.

"A good friend to all," Violet said.

"Hang on." Stanley opened the door and lifted the front wheels over the threshold.

"Don't know where we'd be without him," the woman said. "Gave Howard and me 117 books of Green Stamps to use for Katie here. Can you believe it? A true saint," she said again and started up the sidewalk.

Violet stiffened as soon as they stepped back inside. "Green Stamps?"

"I can explain," Stanley said, gesturing for her to sit back down.

"A hundred and seventeen books? That's a rather specific number." Violet picked up her purse and locked eyes with Stanley. "Did you happen to throw in a few jars of mustard pickle?"

"And what was I supposed to do?" Stanley pushed aside his guilt for blame. "You've always been too proud to ask for my help."

"You never even gave me the chance."

"You would have turned me down."

"Maybe so. I guess we'll never know." Violet squeezed past him, her expression grim. "You were right about one thing, though," she said as she opened the door. "People always do find out."

PART TWO

I'm gonna put on my starry crown,
Down by the riverside . . .

Went by the Spencer house today for Mama's rolling pin. Mrs. Spencer said, "Zethray, your mama never brought her own pin into my kitchen."

That's a bare-faced lie.

I said, "Check again, please. My stepdaddy burned her initials into the handle. *RJ* for Ruth Jones."

She left the front door open, but didn't say, *Come in.* I could see two white ladies sitting in the parlor, and they could see me. One had yellow feathers on her head like a parrot.

"Shame about that colored girl," the parrot woman said. She was talking about Mama. "When I saw it in the paper last week, it gave me a start. With a name like Jones, I thought she was one of *ours*."

The ladies looked out at me, and I looked right back.

"Still," the one without the feathers chimed in, "you have to feel pity. Surely her people must grieve same as we do."

They both kept staring, but I could tell they didn't see me anymore.

"Poor Henrietta," the parrot woman said. "She's beside herself over the loss."

"Can you blame me?" Mrs. Spencer called out from the kitchen. "That dining room chair was part of a set."

I gave up waiting and went home.

CHAPTER TWENTY-TWO

"I SEE YOU," ZETHRAY SAID, her voice flattened by fatigue. Across the room, the little white girl named Daisy played hide-and-seek. Her hair bow poked out from behind the oak sideboard. "I ain't got time for no nonsense today." She threaded a pair of newly washed curtains onto a rod. "Got company coming."

Daisy clapped her hands. *Who?*

"You guess good as me." Zethray stopped and spied the child. "Maybe better."

Your mama knows. Daisy came out from behind the sideboard and started twirling.

"Well, she ain't speaking to me, is she?" With her good foot first, Zethray stepped onto a stool and hung the curtains over two French doors between the parlor and dining room. Former dining room. She used it as a bedroom now. No sense climbing those steps every night with that limp. Just because she could didn't mean she had to. That's what her husband Sam had said the week before he left. And he was right. She'd let him trade her table and chairs for a bed and mattress, but she'd kept the sideboard for a dresser, so she could rent out their upstairs bedroom fully furnished.

When's she coming? Daisy asked.

"Who?"

Your company.

"So it's a *she*." Zethray fussed with the heavy chintz panels till the folds lay right.

Today?

"Nah, baby. Sometime this week." Back on the stool, Zethray

ran a rag across the top of the doorframe. "But I do my heavy cleaning on Saturdays."

Daisy skipped down the length of the sideboard, eyeing the contents on top.

"Shoo." Zethray stepped down and brandished her dust rag. "That ain't none of your business."

Where'd you get those crosses? Daisy disappeared, then reappeared near the swinging door leading to the kitchen.

Zethray shuffled over to the sideboard and picked up one of three small crosses woven out of fronds, given to parishioners on a long-ago Palm Sunday. *Clarence*, she thought, but didn't dare speak the name aloud. She might not be able to keep the little white girl from filling her head, but she damn sure wasn't going to invite another spirit in on purpose. Not on cleaning day. Not in this heat. Six days into August, and it was already the hottest month of the summer. And the driest. What she wouldn't give for a cooling rain.

Your mama thinks it's funny you saved them, Daisy said, *considering.*

Considering Mama killed herself over the man who made them. Zethray held her tongue as she moved everything from the top of the sideboard onto her bed. She picked up a second rag, one dampened with a mixture of boiled linseed oil and turpentine, and polished a shine into the oak.

Zethray never took to Clarence, not that he hadn't tried. He'd tried. Hard. Too hard. When you marry a woman with a child, you have to give her time to come around. Zethray had had her mama to herself for ten years. They'd loved each other truly and solely. And Mama had a way of making Zethray believe she was worthy of all that love. Once, when she'd come home from grammar school sobbing because some white boy had said her skin was made of mud, her mother had kissed her cheek and savored the taste. *More like dark cherries*, she'd said. *And them makes the sweetest jam.*

Then Clarence came along, and her mama broke off a piece of that love and handed it right over. Suddenly he got the thickest slice of corn bread, the fattiest pork chop, the top scoop of mashed potatoes with the chunk of melting butter. Somehow Mama had forgotten about her own daughter liking butter too.

After draping a clean runner across the sideboard, Zethray dusted off the items it once held and set them back in place. A hurricane lamp. Her rose-colored candy dish with the hand-painted lid. Three woven crosses. A clear glass paperweight with her mama's picture glued inside and the name *Ruth Jones* scrawled across the back. The Old Spice aftershave lotion Sam had left behind. With a quick whiff and a wistful expression, Zethray set the bottle down along with an Avon catalog from her neighbor, Alice Blue, and a pink jar of cream sachet named Elusive. Next, she brushed the beginnings of a cobweb off the tail feathers of a lovebird, one of two Clarence had carved from a piece of black walnut. *No denying it,* she thought as she put the pair back on their perch, *Clarence could turn straw into gold with those hands.* Once, he took a broken-down wheelbarrow out of a burn pile at his boss's house, turned that wood into the finest-looking cradle you ever saw, and sold it right back to the man, who was none the wiser.

Zethray moved the candy dish over to make room for her Bible, a gift from the church after her first baptism, when Mama was still alive. A year later, they hauled her back to the river, after the maiden aunt who'd taken her in saw fit to report her to the congregation for "seeing the dead." Since Zethray had already gotten a Bible, they gave her a small plaque with the inscription, *Blessed are the pure in heart: for they shall see God,* which she now propped up against the lamp. Six months after her second baptism and with no gift in hand, they dunked her a third and final time. When that didn't take, the elders decided to forget they'd ever known about her affliction. And soon enough, their wives started lining up at her back door to hear from loved ones who'd crossed over. On those occasions, Zethray's aunt refused to step inside for fear of appearing ungodly. Instead, she sat on the porch, cigar box in hand, charging five cents a person for her niece's time.

Come with me. Daisy held out her hand. *There's a breeze by the river.*

In spite of the sweat streaming down her back, Zethray said, "Can't go for no walk." She shuffled over to a mahogany chair to the left of the sideboard. "Not on cleaning day." Since the chair had a cracked back leg, Zethray stored what she called her "treasure chest" on the seat, to keep folks from sitting down. She picked up the maple box and carried it over to the bed where she buffed the tiger-striped wood with her polishing rag.

For Christmas one year, Clarence had cleaned up an old maple toolbox, tacked in a velvet lining, and added a brass handle to the hinged lid. "There's treasure inside," her mother had said, opening the top. Three foil-wrapped chocolates winked in the light.

Over the years, Zethray filled that box with remembrances. Newspaper clippings about her mama's demise. An envelope with a carbon copy of the only witness statement given to the police. Zethray's diary from 1916, the year her mother died, the last one she ever kept. Condolences from neighbors tied up in a ribbon. Recipes and Bible verses in her mother's hand. Three letters from the life insurance company. The first one denied Zethray's claim outright on account of her age. Four years later, the second notice acknowledged her eighteenth birthday before refusing her again. Northeast Casualty had her best interests at heart, or so the agent had said. With no husband to manage her affairs, the money would become a millstone around her neck. After she married Sam, the company sent a third letter agreeing to pay her fifty cents on the dollar, take it or leave it, since the claim was so old and the deceased was a Negro woman. Zethray took their offer, and Sam went right out and put that money on a house. A man needed something to own, he'd said. Zethray looked around. *It's modest,* she thought, *but it's home.* Sam never fought her for it when he left. That policy was her inheritance, not his, and besides, he didn't want to risk a run of bad luck. He'd spent enough time with his wife to know the dead keep tabs.

Zethray opened the lid of the box. Her mama's apron lay on top. The one she'd worn the day she'd jumped. The undertaker had washed it out and given it to Zethray graveside. Not the dress she was wearing. Or the boots. Only the apron. Zethray never knew what to make of that. Lost in thought, she ran her fingers lightly across the blueberries her mother had embroidered onto the fabric.

Huckleberries, Daisy piped up.

"You think you know better?" Zethray shook her head.

I'm just telling you what your mama's saying.

"She can tell me her own self. I'll listen."

Will you?

"I don't need sass."

What do you need?

"Nothing, baby." Exhausted, Zethray nodded toward a broom propped up next to the broken chair. "Unless you can figure out how to give this floor a good sweep."

Daisy giggled.

Zethray turned her attention to the chair—mahogany frame, clawed feet, kneed legs, and a pierced splat in the shape of a vase. At least once a week, she found herself taking the measure of that chair with her eyes. Low enough to climb. Tall enough to be of use. Had her mama done the same before carrying it down to the Lackawanna Avenue Bridge? Was she sure the seat would hold her? Had she already stepped on it countless times to wash a window or dust a ceiling?

Daisy's hand shot up as if she were in school. *Why'd you take it?*

Why, indeed. Even at fourteen years old, Zethray knew better than to take something belonging to someone else. But in the hours after they'd pulled her mama's body from the river, Zethray didn't have the will to suss out right from wrong.

They left the chair behind. Zethray had heard those words deep in her soul that first night. At least she thought she'd heard them. As confident as she was in the messages she passed along to others, she could never be certain of the ones intended for *her.* Maybe she was too close to make out her own truth in the same way a pretty girl can't always see her own beauty.

Near midnight, Zethray had hobbled back over to the bridge where, sure enough, the chair lay on its back like a dead june bug. Setting it upright, she felt the weight, heavier than she'd imagined. Still, she grabbed hold of the seat and carried that burden back along the same sidewalks her mother had traveled, deviating only when the road broke off toward the colored neighborhood.

"It was the last thing of service to Mama," Zethray finally said as she got up and carried the chair over to the bed.

Just the same, stealing's stealing, Daisy responded, *even when there's a good reason.*

"Tell that to the woman who kept Mama's rolling pin." Zethray sat on the edge of her mattress rubbing circles of turpentine and linseed oil into the wood.

Didn't you already have the chair by then?

Zethray used her knuckles to knead away the pain working its way up her neck. She'd asked herself these same questions a million times and never could find the right answer. Yet, for all her uncertainty, she knew one thing to be true: her mama loved Clarence so hard, she'd followed him into the grave two weeks after his own passing.

Back then, Clarence played outfield for the Electric City Giants, one of two colored amateur baseball teams in Scranton. They'd gone up against the Dunmore Independents at the Athletic Park that day. Funny how Zethray remembered the opponents' name but not who won the game. Afterward, the Giants went over to the Newport Hotel on Center Street to celebrate their victory, or drown their sorrows. Either way, according to witnesses, Clarence was itching for a fight after a couple of dollar bills went missing from his back pocket. Halfway through the night, he pulled a knife on a fellow who pulled his out faster.

When the policeman showed up to give Mama the news, she started wailing and dropped to the floor on her hands and knees, a posture so heart-wrenching to a girl of fourteen, Zethray still saw it in her dreams thirty-nine years later.

She loved you, Daisy said.

"But she died for *him*." Zethray carried the chair back across the room and set it down, careful not to damage the cracked leg any further. She took a step back to admire the craftsmanship. Beautiful but broken, she thought, like her mother's body. Like Zethray's own spirit.

None of it's your fault. Daisy gave one more twirl.

"I know that, baby."

None of it's her fault either.

"Never said it was. Now scoot." Zethray picked up the broom and swept under the sideboard.

Never said it wasn't, Daisy whispered before she disappeared.

CHAPTER TWENTY-THREE

FOR THE THIRD TIME IN A ROW, Violet fed her card into the Scranton Lace Company's time clock, without result.

"There's a trick to it." The next woman in line reached over Violet's shoulder and wiggled the card till the machine chomped *7:51 a.m.* onto the line for Monday, August 8.

"You're a real lifesaver," Violet said.

The woman brushed off the gratitude. "Name's Doreen."

"A pleasure. I'm Violet."

Doreen reached into the pocket of her dress, pulled out a peppermint, and popped it into her thickly lipsticked mouth. "Do people ever call you Vi?"

"Not often."

"When'd you start?" Doreen asked.

"Five weeks ago. They made me a temporary utility girl. Put me anywhere I was needed. Mostly over in lace." The pair hung their purses in side-by-side employee lockers before heading out the door and up a flight of steps. "When they shut down at the end of July for vacation, I prayed they'd bring me back."

"Well, Vi, I'd say those prayers got answered."

"Talk about relief. The foreman called last night to say he'd found me a permanent spot in the Vinylite department."

"Not for nothing," Doreen said, "but as short as we are on help, you were always coming back. Heck, they'd let Lizzie Borden take a shift, providing she left the axe at home." They both laughed. "So what do they have you doing?"

"I'm going to be a cutter," Violet said.

"Makes sense." Doreen walked through the doorway to the factory floor and Violet followed. "We've been down one since Roxanne ran off with the barber."

"Roxanne?"

"I'll fill you in at lunch. Let's just say her husband got the surprise of his life." Doreen stopped at a bank of sewing machines. "This here's my stop. You're at the end of the line." She cast her gaze to the far side of the long room where large bolts of colorful vinyl fabric waited to be cut into shower and bathroom curtains. "Have Arlene tape your fingers before you start using those machines. It'll take a good week for your hands to callus up."

"Arlene?"

"Arlene Wardell, my older sister. Know her?"

Stanley's married girlfriend, Violet thought. At least she was this past spring, but there'd been talk in the neighborhood of a falling-out. One thousand employees at the Lace Works, and Violet got assigned to the same department as Stanley's Arlene. Talk about a kick in the teeth. "I know the name. She was a couple of years behind me in school."

"Arlene's the floor lady. Runs a tight ship, but she's fair. You'll get on with her, as long as you make your quotas." Two more women came in and sat down at sewing machines. Doreen turned and faced them. "Annie, Babs, this is Vi. She's taking Roxanne's place."

"Pleased to meet you." The seamstresses nodded.

Violet smiled. "Likewise. Thanks again," she said to Doreen before continuing on.

"Find us at lunch," Doreen called out. "I'll save you a seat."

As Violet approached the cutting tables, she recognized Arlene standing near an office, clipboard in hand. Her Bettie Page bangs framed her heavily made-up eyes.

"Mrs. Davies," Arlene said while staring at her paperwork, "I'm Mrs. Wardell." She aimed her clipboard at a piece of equipment that resembled an oversized drill press with a long wavy blade instead of a bit. "I'm starting you on the straight knife cutter. Doesn't take much skill." She set down her notes and stood the machine on its base so the blade hung vertically. "Watch what I do." With the switch turned off, she gripped the handle and mimicked a skater's figure eights on top of the bare table.

After Violet saw the trick of it, her eyes followed the knife's cloth-covered cord from the back of the motor, up to a series of electric sockets in the ceiling beams. Rows of pendant lights with black-enameled shades dangled alongside them. Violet returned her attention to the cutter before glancing at the clock. Eight on the dot. Suddenly, scores of machines roared to life inside the room.

"Let's see what you can do!" Arlene yelled over the din. She handed the device to Violet for practice while she grabbed a stack of four-by-four vinyl squares already cut from the large bolts.

Once Violet got a feel for the knife, Arlene set the pile on the table. "I'm starting you off easy. Window tiebacks and trim. Top one's marked," she said, in reference to the pattern traced onto the first ply. "Let that be your guide." She took the machine, turned on the switch, and cut through the layers as smoothly as she would a devil's food cake. "Your turn," she said, handing the cutter over and grabbing another vinyl stack.

As simple as the process looked, it took Violet the better part of half an hour to figure out how to keep the fabric from bunching up at the knife. It didn't help that Arlene's mouth pinched tighter with each failed attempt. When Violet finally managed to produce her first clean edges, Arlene scribbled something on her clipboard and scurried into her office.

At ten o'clock, a bundle boy came by with his cart and started tying Violet's work off with twine and tagging it for the seamstresses. "First day?" he asked.

"In this department, yes!" Violet shouted to be heard over the clanking of the die cutter one table over. "How long have you been here?"

"Two summers," he said. "I graduate next year, then I'm

joining up. Air Force. Going to be a paratrooper." He replenished Violet's station with four-by-four piles. "I want to jump out of planes like the boys at Normandy."

"A noble calling." Violet grabbed a stack of vinyl fabric and set it in front of her. "I remember when they made parachutes here during the war."

"In the old part of the factory," the young man said. "My Aunt Nancy told me all about it. Worked here forty years. Earned herself a gold watch."

Arlene stepped out of her office and peered into the bundle boy's cart. "Curtains aren't going to walk themselves." She nodded toward the seamstresses at the other end of the room.

He snapped to attention. "Yes, ma'am. On my way."

I'm sorry, Violet mouthed to the boy as she turned her knife back on.

At noon, the Lace Works's steam whistle blew from the clock tower, signaling the lunch hour. Violet made her way back through the room, to the doorway, and down the steps. Once she reached the cafeteria, the collective scents of turkey, dressing, and carrots delighted her senses and conspired to make her homesick. Her mother loved a hearty midday meal. Violet felt a twinge of guilt for leaving Grace alone, especially with her health such as it was, but what choice did she have? Her work for Walsh's Portraits had all but dried up, and she refused to accept more help from Stanley. Anyway, her mother wasn't really alone in that house. They had a telephone and a television, and besides, the widow promised to check in on her during the day.

Violet scanned the tables and found Doreen waving her over to a bench. As soon as Violet sat down, the woman launched into her promised story: "So, about Roxanne and the barber . . ."

Violet opened the sandwich she'd brought in her purse. Minced ham and pickle. Tommy's favorite.

Had he really asked Stanley to watch out for her and their

daughter Daisy? Yes, according to the widow who'd come over to the house in June to clear the air with Violet after she and Stanley had had their latest falling-out. Truth be told, Violet could believe it. Tommy was the kind of man who'd want to provide for his family even in death. She should have been mad at him too, for making the arrangements without her say-so, but it was easier to find fault with the living. With Stanley.

Doreen cackled. "So before she runs off with the company barber for good . . ." She studied Violet to make sure she had her attention.

"Wait." Violet put her hand up. "They have a barbershop here?"

"They do, indeed," Annie answered. "And a beauty parlor." She started ticking off some of the factory's other amenities on her fingers: "Basketball court, bowling alley, billiards—"

Babs jumped in: "Club rooms, lounges, a theater."

As Annie opened her mouth for another turn, Doreen sighed heavily. "I didn't know I was finished with my story."

"Go on," Babs said. "Violet needs to hear the ending. It's a humdinger."

"Does she now?" Doreen clenched her jaw. "Didn't sound that way when you and Annie decided to monopolize the conversation."

"That's my fault," Violet said. "I asked about the barbershop and got us off track. I'm sorry."

"Apology not necessary, but much appreciated." Doreen cleared her throat and tried again: "So, before Roxanne runs off for good, she drags that husband of hers to the barbershop for a trim and a shave from the very man she's leaving him for. Thinks she's doing him some kind of favor. Tells him he'll have a better shot at finding a new wife if he's all cleaned up."

"And he went along with that?" Violet couldn't imagine Tommy, or Stanley for that matter, putting up with such foolishness.

"Here's the topper." Doreen slapped the table. "The very next day, that son of a gun ran into his high school sweetheart. Turns out she was in the middle of a divorce her own self. He hasn't looked back since."

"And he shaves regular now," Babs added.

"Shame about all those broken marriages though," Violet said between bites of her sandwich. "Grass isn't always greener."

"Truer words," Annie said.

"Well," Babs said, "I think it's a real-life fairy-tale ending."

"Or a miracle," Doreen offered. "Not one broken heart in the whole lot."

"You're forgetting about Ethyl," Annie said. "Married to the barber almost twenty-five years, a few of them happy." She checked the wall clock.

"Still makes for a good story." Doreen stood up and looked at Violet. "If you need to use the little girls' room, do it now."

Violet balled up her waxed paper and followed the women out the door, wondering about the kind of man who'd leave his wife after twenty-five years, happy or not.

When the whistle signaled the end of the workday, Violet secured her straight knife cutter and swept up the last few scraps of Vinylite. "Shame to waste good fabric," she said to Arlene standing next to her with her clipboard.

"And what would you have us do with it, Mrs. Davies?"

"Oh, I don't know." Violet picked up a triangle of vinyl fabric with cheery stripes. "How 'bout a rain bonnet?" She put it on her head like one of the widow's babushkas.

"Piecework takes both speed and accuracy," Arlene said, ignoring Violet's suggestion. "I'm not sure you have what it takes." She pulled a pencil from behind her ear. "Time will tell." She noted something on her clipboard and turned away.

What were you thinking? Violet took off the makeshift hat, threw it in the waste basket, and walked across the now empty room. Even though she'd worn crepe-soled shoes, her feet hurt from so much standing. And her calves, she discovered on the stairs.

Once she made it outside, Violet found a bench near the original part of the plant and sat down. She had a mile-long walk ahead of her, mostly uphill, and between her aching legs and her flagging morale, she needed a few minutes to collect herself. *I'm not sure you have what it takes.* That had been Violet's fear all along. So much for teaching an old dog new tricks. Then again, she'd gotten better as the day progressed. The bundle boy had said as much on his last run.

But not Arlene, Stanley's old girlfriend. Bile burned in Violet's throat. Could he be the reason for her supervisor's sharp remarks? Ridiculous. Violet wasn't even a part of Stanley's life. She took in a deep breath and exhaled loudly. Not then. Not now. No reason at all for Arlene to have any opinion of her other than today's work performance. *Time will tell.*

Violet closed her eyes and listened for the burbling river on the other side of the road. Her ears buzzed from eight hours of machine racket, but she preferred to credit the katydids. And the dragonflies, she thought, imagining their iridescent wings. After a minute, she opened her eyes and caught her reflection in the gently arched windows. She looked older than she cared to imagine. Unfamiliar, even.

On the other side of the glass, two-and-a-half-story cast-iron looms, capable of creating the most delicate lace, sat idle. Eight o'clock each morning, master weavers brought them to life like Geppetto's Pinocchio. Violet thought about the afternoon she and her sister Daisy had visited the factory. The clock tower and the newer part of the plant had yet to be built, though to Violet's eye, the redbrick building looked the same now as it did in 1912.

Back then, everyone in town knew Benjamin Dimmick, president of the Lace Works. His niece attended No. 25, the grammar school in Providence, so Dimmick had arranged for all the grades to tour the plant. Violet was only six, but over forty years later, she still had a clear memory of the enormous looms thundering in a room so hot her petticoat clung to her body. She couldn't catch a good breath. The room started spinning.

Seeing Violet's distress, Daisy had slipped away from her own class, taken her sister's hand, and begun singing:

Jesus wants me for a sunbeam.
To shine for Him each day.

The sisters had sung the song in church on Children's Day.

In ev'ry way try and please Him . . .
At home, at school, at play.

Daisy had a beautiful voice. Violet had struggled to hear the words over the clanking machinery, but nonetheless felt soothed. Her sister was with her. No harm would come. Soon enough, Daisy had drawn her attention to a weaver whose very long cigar ash was about to fall into the loom. "Shit!" the man had barked as the ash dropped onto a half-finished panel of lace. "Shit. Shit. Shit."

The children giggled as their first-grade teacher hastily ushered them out the double doors. *These* doors, Violet thought, as she tried to picture her sister standing next to them in her lemon pinafore, the hulking looms visible through the window.

"Mechanical spiders."

"I'm sorry, what?" Violet glanced around.

Arlene sat down on the bench and stared at the looms inside the building. "Some guy in the paper called them that once, and it stuck with me." She plucked a cigarette and lighter out of a leather pouch inside her purse. "Fourteen-ton, forty-foot-long, lace-spinning spiders."

"My mother's home alone," Violet said. "I should be going."

"How're your hands?"

"Blistered a bit." Violet studied her palms. "Nothing a sewing needle and some castor oil won't fix."

Arlene's lips clamped onto the cigarette like the jaws on a vise. "You catch on quick, Mrs. Davies." Her thumb spun the lighter's striker three times in quick succession before it flamed. She took a shallow drag and the cigarette caught. "I owe you an apology."

"For what?"

"Have you ever tried to *not* like someone?" Arlene fanned away the smoke, and the flesh on her upper arms jiggled as if made out of pudding.

"I don't think so."

"I really wanted to not like you. For the record," she poked her chest, "I am di-vorced." Both syllables dropped from her tongue like hard pebbles. "I know people say I'm not, but I am. Took awhile, but it had nothing to do with me wanting to stay in good with the church. Trust me," Arlene snickered, "the church never did me any favors."

"Well, *I* never said . . ." Violet's face flushed. She may not have spread the rumor, but she'd accepted it as truth.

"And I had grounds," Arlene pressed on. "Abandonment. But I didn't have the money for a lawyer."

"I'm sorry," Violet said, and she meant it. Sorry for Arlene's situation. Sorry for thinking ill of the woman.

"Then Stanley came along and helped me file the papers. Hard to resist a knight in shining armor."

So this was about Stanley after all

"Spends most of his time fighting for the little guy, or gal." She took a long drag on her cigarette. "I fell hard," she finally said. "But not him. That man loves *you*."

"Why would you say that?"

"Because it's true."

"How do you know?"

"How do you *not?*" Arlene stood up and dropped her cigarette to the ground. "Stop by the office tomorrow and I'll tape up those hands," she said, stubbing out the smoldering butt with the toe of her shoe.

CHAPTER TWENTY-FOUR

EARLY TUESDAY MORNING, Johnny heard the commotion as soon as he crossed the tracks into Mickey's neighborhood. People conferring with passersby, some heading in the direction of the slaughterhouse along the river, others away from it. A fire truck siren wailing a couple of blocks over. Mr. Secoolish's horn honking as he backed his DeSoto onto South Washington Avenue from Birch.

"Mine cave-in!" Mickey called out from his second-floor porch. He punctuated the news with two high-pitched chirps from his pea whistle. "Hold up!" he hollered as he pounded down a set of steps on the side of the house.

"How bad?" Johnny asked, his eyes following the crowd.

"Not too, from what I'm hearing," Mickey said as he approached, "but the water main's busted. Fire department's checking the gas line now." He tugged at Johnny's arm. "Let's go see!"

"Thought you had vacation Bible school."

"Huh? Oh, you mean First Holy Communion class? That's not for another half hour. Besides, I'm not sure I'm going back."

Johnny studied the boy. "Why's that?"

"Every time we get to the door, Sister Maria yells, 'The heathens are here!' because we all go to public school." Mickey stopped cold and dropped his voice. "Speak of the devil," he said, dropping his eyes as a woman in a long black dress and veil followed the onlookers.

"Be careful!" Mickey's grandmother instructed from the second-floor window.

"I will, Granny."

"He's with me, Mrs. McCrae," Johnny said. "I'll watch out for him."

"See that you do. Last thing we need is another Jule Ann Fulmer around here."

"Another who?" Johnny asked Mickey as they joined the crowd.

"Jule Ann Fulmer," Mickey said. "Two years old. Out walking with her aunt and brother, sucking on a tangerine. She's looking around and ends up a few steps behind them. Next thing you know, her aunt sees that tangerine roll by. She turns around and Jule Ann's gone. So's the sidewalk where the girl was walking. Mine subsidence, forty feet deep. Ground just broke open and swallowed her up. May she rest in peace."

"That's awful." Johnny tugged at Mickey's shoulder to slow his pace. "How'd you know her?"

"Didn't. Happened in Pittston a few years before I was born. But I hear about it all the time. 'Mickey,'" he said, mimicking his grandmother's earsplitting inflection, "'watch out when you're playing near those mines. You don't want to end up like Jule Ann.' Every kid in town's grown up on that story."

"Show's over, folks!" a uniformed policeman shouted through his bullhorn. "Go on back home!"

"What's the damage?" a man called out.

"We got lucky this time." The officer sounded relieved. "Only four, maybe five feet down."

"How about the gas line?" Johnny yelled from the back of the crowd.

"Just the water main," the policeman said. "Houses are safe. Check your cellars though." He aimed his bullhorn toward rivulets of water running toward the storm grates along the street. "Drains could back up. They haven't had a good cleaning in ages."

As the people started to disperse, Johnny made his way forward. "I work at the slaughterhouse."

"Not today," the officer said. "Nothing's shored up yet."

"Guess I'm playing hooky," Johnny told Mickey as they headed back toward the house.

Mickey jumped into a few inches of streaming water with his rubber-soled sneakers. "Think I will too." The boy lifted a foot. "Keds are soaked right through."

"I'd think again!" someone boomed behind them.

"Dammit," Mickey mumbled as he turned toward the voice. "Sister Maria, I was only kidding around."

"Then you won't mind accompanying me on my walk to St. Mary's."

"Yes, ma'am. I mean no, ma'am. Yes, I'll join you. No, I don't mind one bit." Mickey rolled his eyes at Johnny. "Be seeing you," he said, and fell into soggy step alongside the nun.

Johnny started to formulate a plan for the day as he made his way over the bridge and back up the hill. No sense stopping by the studio this early. Daisy wouldn't be in for a couple of hours yet. He could swing by a phone booth, but he didn't dare call her at home. She still hadn't told her mother about him. He wanted to be mad, but as she'd pointed out on more than one occasion, he hadn't told his mother yet either. Instead of resolving the issue, they'd ignored it for months, though that wasn't going to work too much longer.

Johnny was falling for Daisy. Hard. He was willing to stand up to his family, if it came to that, but what about *her?* He needed to know before it was too late. Who was he kidding? He'd passed "too late" weeks ago. Still, it was time to find out where she stood. After six months in Scranton, Johnny realized he'd always be a small fish in this town. With the love of a good woman, he might be able to temper his ambitions and stick around. Without it, he should probably try his luck in a bigger pond. He'd bring up the subject with Daisy when he saw her today. But first, he had to convince her to play hooky. Maybe they could catch a matinee. There were four movie theaters within walking distance. He'd have to see what was playing, but in this heat, the air-conditioning alone would be a treat.

"Well, if it ain't Jelly Roll Morton!" Kenny Wilkens shouted from the Woolworths side of Lackawanna Avenue.

Johnny darted across the street. "I prefer to think of myself as the Art Tatum of Scranton."

"You've got to think bigger, my friend."

"Bigger than Art Tatum?"

"Bigger than Scranton. In fact," Kenny patted Johnny's shoulder, "I was planning on running an idea by you this week."

"Run it by me now."

"I thought you were a working man."

"Water main break. Slaughterhouse is closed for the day. I'm hoping to go out with Daisy this afternoon. Maybe take in a picture."

"Surely you can do better than that." A courtesy car pulled up to the curb and dropped off a couple of salesgirls. Kenny whistled as they headed over to A.S. Beck's, the shoe store next door. "Mm-mmm," Kenny said to Johnny, "I may have to see about a pair of nubucks when I get back."

"Back from where?"

"Grab a coffee with me," Kenny pointed to Woolworths, "and I'll tell you. Train doesn't leave for another hour."

"Train?" Johnny peered down the street to where the sun hovered over the Lackawanna Station's limestone facade.

"Going to the Big Apple." Kenny lifted his bagged trumpet and pretended to play. "A friend of mine runs a nightclub in the Village. They're looking for a new house band. Auditions are sometime this month." Kenny propped his elbow on Johnny's shoulder and struck a casual pose. "Thought I'd sign us both up."

"That's quite the idea," Johnny replied. "When you coming back?"

"Midnight. So what about that coffee?"

"You buying?"

"I'll do you one better." Kenny pulled a ring of keys out of his front pocket and tossed it to Johnny. "Take my car. Show your girl a good time today."

"I couldn't." Johnny tried to return the keys, but Kenny put his hands and his trumpet behind his back. "It's only going to sit in that parking lot all day. Just remember to pick me up."

"I wouldn't even know where to go."

"How 'bout Rocky Glen? Take your girl up in the Ferris wheel. Ride the Million Dollar Coaster. Best amusement park around." As if intuiting Johnny's next question, Kenny added, "Everybody's welcome, if you catch my drift. In fact, the colored church down the road holds its Sunday school picnic there every summer."

"Coffee's on me," Johnny said as he pocketed the keys and opened the door to Woolworths.

An hour later, Johnny parked in front of Mama Z's house, half wishing she were home to see how good he looked behind the wheel of a 1952 two-tone, surf-blue and sky-gray Buick Roadmaster. *Just as well*, he thought, sliding out of the car. She'd probably have given him the third degree about his plans. She was a lot like his mother that way. Only difference, Mama Z would ask her own questions—and a few more from the great beyond. Or so she'd say. That was the problem with seers. If you accused them of being too nosy, they sidestepped the blame by claiming a spirit was directing their words, like some sort of phantom ventriloquist. A floating Edgar Bergen holding his Charlie McCarthy dummy in one hand and a crystal ball in the other. At least that's how Johnny pictured it when Mama Z claimed to conjure the dead.

Johnny made his way upstairs to wash and change into a dress shirt and a pair of gaberdine pants. He knew enough to put his best foot forward. Rocky Glen might welcome everyone, but that didn't mean everyone at Rocky Glen would welcome *him*.

At ten after eleven, Johnny called Daisy at the studio and cajoled her into canceling her classes so they could spend the day together. He didn't mention the car. He wanted that to be a surprise, so he told her to meet him in front of Woolworths at noon. In the meantime, he sat on the porch, admiring the Buick like he would a famous painting, or better yet, a beautiful woman. The body's gracious curves. The grille's toothy smile. Maybe after Rocky Glen, he'd swing back home and show the car off to Mama Z after all. Now that he thought about it, he could kill two birds and introduce her to Daisy as a kind of dry run. Let Daisy see he meant business without bringing his own mother into it just yet.

Not a bad idea, he thought as he pulled a pair of sunglasses out of his shirt pocket and put them on. *Not bad at all.*

Daisy never should have said yes to Johnny. It was hard enough to get classes up and running without canceling them on a whim. Not that it mattered to the Belisario sisters whose ballet lessons she'd called off. They'd yipped for joy on the other end of the phone, something about a birthday party they could now attend. And Opal seemed just as happy about postponing that evening's falsetto work. The widower she fancied went to bingo on Tuesday nights, and she was eager to make an appearance.

Rearranging the schedule is not the problem. Daisy sighed. *It's having so little to rearrange.* After three months' time, she only had a handful of voice students and three dance classes, two ballet and one tap. She'd scrapped modern dance altogether since no one had shown any interest. No one had signed up for her piano lessons either, a genuine disappointment after the trouble it had taken to get the instrument up the steps.

Well, trouble with the Summerlin brothers. Johnny had been a godsend. If he hadn't come along, that little Tom Thumb might still be sitting on the sidewalk. And Daisy might still be pining for Atlantic City. When she'd come home to help with her father, she hadn't intended to remain in Scranton, yet that's how life goes sometimes. She'd mustered the courage to leave once. She couldn't break her mother's heart again. Thankfully, Johnny seemed content to stick around. Daisy closed her eyes and pictured him standing in front of her.

Startled by a sudden surge of desire, Daisy opened her eyes and surveyed the empty room: a stack of oak folding chairs, the old cobalt sofa, that little red piano—a wedding gift from her Grampa Owen to her Grandma Grace. "May you never want for music," he'd told his bride. Daisy loved that story, but there were others. Like how, as a little girl, her mother's feet couldn't reach the pedals. And how she'd offer to play hymns to get out of chores.

Or how she'd given up the piano after her sister's death. Twin tragedies, to Daisy's thinking. She couldn't imagine life without music.

That's why she'd fallen so hard for Johnny. He needed music as much as she did. Maybe more. When he laid hands on a piano, it was like watching a prophet saving souls.

When she was a child, Daisy had thought an awful lot about souls. The way the minister used to talk about them, she was sure they were nestled deep inside a person's chest, but no one ever mentioned what they were made of, or how they looked. Sometimes she'd imagine them shaped like hearts on a frilly valentine. Or cut like teardrops in a crystal chandelier. Then again, maybe souls were like the flame of a candle or a wave in the ocean. Or malleable, like jellyfish but without the stingers. In all those years, she'd never settled on an answer, though when Daisy thought of Johnny, she was sure his soul was split in two, each half stretching from his palms to his fingertips like rays on a starfish.

So, Daisy thought, *if a man has not one but two hand-shaped souls, you clear your calendar to be with him. The studio be damned.* She'd rearrange the schedule in a day or two, and in another week she'd start advertising for fall classes. Most new students signed up in September, anyway. She should have thought about that when she'd opened in May. And surely the bus strike would be over soon, so the students she'd had in Providence could catch a ride into town. Moreover, her Aunt Lily's husband, Frankie, had given her the studio rent-free for a whole year, plenty of time for Daisy to get on her feet. All in all, her future in Scranton looked promising.

Daisy glanced at the clock. Five minutes till noon. She hurriedly tucked the tails of her blouse into her fuchsia pedal pushers and grabbed her clutch. After a quick swipe of Secret Red, she dropped her lipstick in the bag, ran down the steps, and out the door.

On the other side of the street, Myrtle Evans and her sister Mildred walked arm in arm toward A.S. Beck's. Leave it to Daisy's busybody neighbors to come downtown today. She waited until they crossed the shoe store's threshold before darting over to Woolworths. Almost immediately, a blue and gray Buick drove up to the curb and Johnny jumped out.

"Your chariot awaits," he said, opening a door.

Daisy slipped into the leather passenger seat. *Yes*, she thought, as Johnny closed her door, the future looked promising indeed.

CHAPTER TWENTY-FIVE

"You can open those beautiful peepers," Johnny said, ten minutes after asking Daisy to close them so she'd be surprised when they arrived at their destination. "Ta-da!" Hand over hand, he steered the car into Rocky Glen's lot.

"Wow." It took Daisy a second too long to smile. "Rocky Glen."

It wasn't as though she hadn't been back since the Teddy Ryan incident. She and Beverly had come on Class Day every June during high school, and Daisy had always had fun, but something about this moment felt different, wobbly, like she'd just stepped off a tilt-a-whirl, and her brain still thought her body was in motion. *Spot*, she told herself. Finding a focal point was a ballerina's trick to keep from falling while doing pirouettes. Daisy fixed her gaze on the main entrance in the distance. Nothing really happened with Teddy. And if it had, she'd been long over it by now. A breathless heat settled itself inside the parked car.

"Something wrong?" Johnny's voice reached across the seat and steadied Daisy.

"Nothing," she said. "The sun. It's blinding."

The keys jangled against each other as Johnny turned off the engine. "I can fix that." He turned her face toward his and kissed the tip of her nose. "Better?"

"All." This time her smile came easily.

"Good." Johnny hopped out of the car, ran around to the other side, and opened the door. "Because I heard they have a million-dollar roller coaster here."

"It only cost a hundred thousand," Daisy said, fumbling through her clutch for her sunglasses as she stepped out.

"*Only*," Johnny joked as they strode across the parking lot, their stunted shadows taking the lead.

Inside the entrance, Daisy stopped. "Give me a second to get my bearings. I used to come here on the streetcar. Station's at the north end of the park. So's the coaster."

"We arrived in style today. Nothing but the best for my girl."

Daisy started to reach for Johnny's hand. *He's a sitting duck with you on his arm.* When Mickey's grandmother had uttered that warning almost two months earlier, Daisy had dismissed it as well-meaning but out of touch. Times were changing. Johnny had said so himself. No one ever gave them a problem at Tony Harding's. Same with the movies, though to be fair, Johnny always waited for the lights to go down before putting his arm around her. "We can't be too careful," he'd say. With all the strangers milling about the park, Daisy decided to defer to caution. She dropped her hand, hoping Johnny wouldn't notice, and headed for the center path.

"That's different," she said, spotting a ride called Love in the Dark.

"*Good* different?"

"*New* different. That's where they used to sell the Duck Boat tickets."

"Duck Boat?"

"An old army truck that could drive on water."

"Wonder where it went."

"They sold it off last month. Someone got hurt and sued the park. They've had a couple of fires here too." Daisy glanced over to where the Mammoth Fun House used to be. Where she and Beverly had finally managed to track down Teddy and his buddies that fateful summer. "A lot's changed."

"Change is good."

"Sometimes, I suppose. Half my life, all I wanted was change.

New me. New city. Then I followed you up to that rooftop and fell in love with Scranton all over again."

"Just Scranton?"

"Come on." Daisy blushed. "You know I'd already fallen in love with you by then."

"You don't say."

"I was a goner the second you pulled that sheet music out of your pocket."

"What took you so long?" He gave her a playful nudge. "I knew I loved you the day we met. There you were, so serious, asking me if I thought every Tom, Dick, and Harry should be allowed to play your piano."

"You're making that up."

"I pretended to straighten my tie so I wouldn't bust out laughing."

"I really said that?" Daisy hid her face in her hands. "I was so out of sorts that day."

"I knew right then and there you'd always keep me on my toes."

Simultaneously embarrassed and amused, she said, "You can't tell people that story."

"But it's the best part! Speaking of telling people things, I think it's high time I introduce you to Mama Z."

"You mean it?"

"I do."

Daisy beamed as they continued along the path.

"Step right up!" a barker called out from the shooting gallery at the top of Game Row. A sign with Buffalo Bill's likeness hung over the stand. "Ten shots a nickel. Every bull's-eye wins a prize."

Johnny walked over and examined the menagerie of stuffed animals straining the limits of their plywood shelves. "What's your pleasure?" he asked Daisy.

"Don't you have to win first?"

"Any Tom, Dick, or Harry can beat this game."

Daisy laughed and looked up at all the kitschy prizes on display. "Okay, then. The hot-pink dog with the purple spots."

Johnny turned to the boy working the stand. "What'll it take to win Spotty up there?"

"Twelve outta twenty," he said, pushing a .22 pump-action short rifle across the counter. "All crows."

Daisy studied the game, four rows of moving targets hinged upright on conveyor belts. One-dimensional ducks, rabbits, squirrels, and crows; bottom to top, large to small, easy to near impossible. She purposely picked the foot-and-a-half-high dog, one of the shooting gallery's more modest prizes, to give Johnny a winning chance.

"All crows?" She eyed the boy. "That hardly seems fair."

Johnny fished out a coin and tossed it on the counter. "How 'bout ten outta ten?"

The boy snickered as he scooped up the money. "You can kiss that nickel goodbye."

Ping! The first shot slammed into the closest crow, knocking it flat.

"Beginner's luck!" the barker shouted, while at the same time waving people over to watch the action.

With a brisk *clack-clack*, Johnny ejected the spent ammunition and chambered another round. *Ping! Clack-clack. Ping! Clack-clack.* Johnny worked the fore-end under the barrel like the slide on a trombone.

By the eighth shot, a crowd had formed. "Holy cow!" the boy yelled out from behind the counter. "Two to go."

Ping! Johnny winked at Daisy, chambered his last round, aimed up at the crows, and fired. *Ping!*

The onlookers cheered. The boy grabbed a hook and pulled the stuffed dog off the shelf in a puff of dust. "That was some shooting." He took the rifle and gave the prize to Johnny. "You earned him."

Johnny lifted an imaginary cowboy hat off his head, gave a nod to Buffalo Bill, and handed the dog to Daisy.

"She's with *him?*" a woman screeched, the words scaping across her tongue like Brillo pads.

Daisy turned toward the voice and found a thickset thirty-something with beads of sweat rolling down her scarlet cheeks.

"Best to move along," the barker whispered in Daisy's ear before returning to his duties. "Step right up!" he shouted to passersby. "Ten shots a nickel. Every bull's-eye wins a prize."

Johnny and Daisy quietly slipped away from the crowd. With more than a foot between them, they wandered farther into the park. All around, delighted screams rose and fell with the rhythms of the rides, but no amount of merriment could drown out the voices inside Daisy's head. *She's with* him? *Best to move along.* Daisy had followed the barker's advice, but now she couldn't help wondering if, in doing so, she'd let Johnny down.

"I should have given her a piece of my mind," Daisy finally said.

"I'm glad you didn't."

"Why?"

"Same reason you decided not to hold my hand."

"You knew?" Daisy's voice cracked. "I'm sorry. I let Mickey's grandmother get in my ear."

"No sorrys." Johnny handed her his hanky. "I'm saying you were right both times. We can't be too careful."

"I wish people would mind their own business."

"People are always going to have opinions about us. That's how the world works."

"Then we'll just have to change the world." Daisy fanned her brow with her purse.

"That's a pretty tall order. How 'bout we get a couple of birch beers first." He pointed to a refreshment stand a few yards away.

They walked to the back of a long line, and Daisy asked, "So how'd you do it?"

"What?"

"Win Spotty here." She held up the stuffed dog. "I always thought those games were rigged."

"They are." Johnny put a finger to his lips. "When the fix is in, most people think if they try harder, shoot straighter, they'll beat the odds. Doesn't work that way."

"How does it work?"

"You have to play *their* game, not yours. Figure out how they're cheating, and adapt."

"So how'd they cheat?"

The pair took a few steps forward.

"Loose barrels," Johnny explained.

"How could you tell?"

"Experience. The Steel Pier has every game known to man. I ditched enough school in my day to learn all the tricks."

"Good old Atlantic City."

"And not a coal mine in sight," Johnny said.

"Next!" a girl called out from inside the refreshment stand.

"Two." Johnny put a quarter on the counter and grabbed a couple of freshly opened bottles. "Let's find a seat." He led them toward a handful of benches in front of the carousel where parents could sit and see their children as they passed. Daisy sat down and slid over to the middle of a bench. Johnny handed her a soda but stayed standing.

In front of them, an attendant invited the next pack of riders up onto the platform. Boys and girls raced toward the outside horses to get a chance at the brass ring. A pair of tired-looking mothers with babies in arms settled into the golden chariot at the back of the herd. As the carousel whirred to life, a steam-powered organ began cranking a quick-tempoed waltz.

Daisy took a drink of her birch beer, then pressed the ice-cold glass against her forehead. "So what did you mean when you said 'not a coal mine in sight'?"

"Just that." Johnny put his foot up on the bench. "Mickey told me the craziest story this morning about a kid who got killed when a mine caved in."

"The girl with the orange or the boy playing marbles?"

"The girl, but I think you're missing the point."

"What's that?"

"Why would anyone want to live on top of coal mines?"

"I thought you loved Scranton," Daisy pouted.

"I love you, and you're in Scranton."

"So you're saying you'd rather be someplace else?"

"Not without you." Johnny dropped down next to her on the bench.

Daisy's eyes narrowed. "You never did tell me why Kenny was going to New York today."

"He heard about a club that's looking for a trumpeter."

"And might they also be looking for a piano player?"

"He may have said something about it." Johnny stared straight ahead. The carousel and the music slowed to a stop, and the attendant signaled the next group of riders forward.

"I call the pinto!" a boy hollered from the middle of the pack.

Johnny poked Daisy's arm and gestured toward the ride. "My money's on the steed."

"You're changing the subject."

"He's the lead horse," Johnny said. "Bigger than the others. More ornate. Look at the curls carved into his mane. The jewels on his saddle. The silver on his bridle. Of course, we're only seeing the romance side, the half of the horse that faces out. Lots of flash to catch your eye."

"So what's on the other side?"

"Nothing fancy, just a horse."

"You sure learned a lot by skipping school."

The organ and the carousel started up again.

"He's also known as the wishing horse. *Take a ride*," he said, mimicking a barker's cadence. "*Make a wish*."

"I wish you'd be straight with me about Kenny and New York City," Daisy said as she gathered her purse and the stuffed dog.

"There's nothing to tell." Johnny grabbed Daisy's empty bottle, and they began walking back to the refreshment stand.

"But what if . . ."

"No sense wasting our time on what-ifs." Johnny returned the empties to a soda crate and collected his deposit. "Not when there's a perfectly good roller coaster out there in need of our attention."

Daisy tried to smile.

"Stop worrying. You're stuck with me."

"In Scranton?"

"If that's what you want."

Neither one took the other's hand as they made their way up the path. Daisy wanted to believe Johnny could truly be happy in Scranton because she couldn't imagine leaving a second time. *Am I kidding myself?* As if in response, the high-pitched song of the cicadas intensified in the unrelenting heat.

Close to the lake, concession stands offered up caramel apples and cotton candy. The sweet scent of sugar, burnt and spun, clung to the heavy air. "Hungry?" Johnny asked, breaking the silence.

"No. It's too hot."

Johnny veered off in the direction of a nine-foot display case made of oak and glass. The sign on top read, *Grandmother's Predictions*. Inside sat a mechanical woman wearing a lacy white blouse and purple shawl. A shock of white hair framed her heavily painted face.

Insert a coin, receive a card below, the instructions read. An arrow pointed down to a slot with the words, *Your answer here*.

"Let's see what the future holds," Johnny joked as he pulled some change out of his pocket.

Daisy grabbed her own penny out of her purse and dropped it into the machine. "Will Johnny stay with me in Scranton?"

With the click of a motor, the automaton's head bobbed up and down as her gloved hand wobbled over a spread of tarot cards. A moment later, a rectangle of paper poked through the slot, and the woman sat motionless again.

Daisy grinned when she saw the message. "*The odds are with you*," she read. "*Insert another coin and I will tell you more*."

"That's how they get you." Johnny fed his own penny into the machine. The head bobbed, the hand wobbled, and the prediction appeared.

"Wait," Daisy said. "You didn't ask her a question."

"Don't have to." Johnny picked up the paper. "She'll tell me what I need to know." He glanced at the card and read aloud, "*Sometimes the calm comes after the storm.*"

"Great." Daisy glanced at the cloudless sky. "The one summer without a drop of rain."

"I wouldn't worry." Johnny laughed and the pair began walking again. "The odds are always in your favor."

"Let's hope so." Ahead of them, the coaster loomed over the lake. Daisy took a few steps back and examined the latticed frame. Here and there, replacement trusses had been added at odd angles. "It's a little worse for wear."

"Water takes a toll," Johnny said, "especially on wood."

"Still want to go on?"

Johnny stepped up to the line in front of the ticket booth. "We may as well while we have the chance. I'm not sure she'll be running too many more summers."

"What stinks?" a voice rasped.

Someone behind them started sniffing loudly.

That vile woman from the shooting gallery. Daisy turned around, intending to have her say.

Still facing forward, Johnny touched her shoulder. *Don't,* he mouthed.

"Honey," the woman said to a bearded man Daisy hadn't noticed at first, "get a load of this."

The man spit loudly: "In all my days, I ain't never seen nothing so dirty."

Johnny's hands curled into fists.

"And that piece of filth with him. Probably pushing out babies black as night," the man said. "Nothing but a cheap whore."

Johnny whirled around so fast, he kicked up a cloud of dust

and gravel. He grabbed the man by the front of his shirt and snarled, "Say it again."

Although he had an inch or two on Johnny, the man's bearing withered. "Just having a little fun," he said, raising his arms. "Didn't mean no harm." The woman cowered behind him.

Daisy shifted so Johnny could see her expression. "He's. Not. Worth. It." She spoke each word gently, evenly, as if tossing pebbles at a window.

Johnny relaxed his grip and took a tentative step back.

Daisy clutched his hand. "Let's go home," she said, and pulled him out of the line. Under the glare of an unyielding sun, the pair walked back to the car in silence.

CHAPTER TWENTY-SIX

THE BUICK'S GUNSIGHT HOOD ORNAMENT pierced the puckered air rising from the roadway's sunbaked surface. "I never should've listened to Kenny." Johnny hadn't intended to say those words out loud, but his frustration proved too powerful for restraint.

"About what?" Daisy rolled her half-opened window all the way down to catch the breeze.

"I wanted to take you to an air-conditioned movie. Rocky Glen was *his* idea."

Daisy pursed her lips while she held onto her spotted dog. "Kenny sure has a lot of ideas."

Johnny tightened his grip on the steering wheel and mentally replayed the scene near the roller coaster. "He had a point."

"Who? Kenny?"

"No. That son of a bitch from the park." Johnny made a sharp left turn past the Ron-Da-Voo Club. "As awful as that was for us, it'll be ten times worse for our kids."

"Our *what?*" Daisy swung around, bracing herself against the dashboard with a palm.

"You don't want kids?"

"Sure. Maybe." She sat back in the seat and hung her elbow out the window. "Talk about putting the cart before the horse."

"I meant," Johnny said as he coasted down the hill, "assuming we get married."

"That's a pretty big assumption."

"Is it?"

"I'd say. Considering no one's even asked me."

"What if I ask?" To avoid misunderstanding, he quickly added, "Down the road."

"If I remember correctly, I'm not supposed to waste my time on what-ifs."

"I'm trying to say, how would you feel about bringing mixed children into this world?"

Daisy considered the question long enough for the traffic light onto South Washington to cycle from yellow to red to green. "Scared."

"Too scared?"

"It's funny. I always thought I'd have a little girl someday who'd look just like me. The women in my family bear a strong resemblance to one another. No matter where I go around town, people come up to me and say, 'You must be a Morgan.'" She reached across the seat and stroked Johnny's cheek. "Where'd you get such deep dimples?"

"My daddy," he said, "and his daddy before him."

"Then you understand."

"I do." Johnny's shoulders dropped.

"I'm scared. No doubt about it. But I wouldn't miss seeing your dimples on a child of mine for all the tea in China."

"You mean it?"

"Assuming you ask me to marry you," she paused, "sometime down the road. And assuming I say yes."

"We won't have an easy time of it. The world will make sure of that."

"Then we'll just have to change the world."

The first time Daisy had said those words, Johnny was charmed by her optimism. Now, all he could hear was her naivete. For her own good, he needed to set her straight. "What happened at the park—that'll be our life."

"Sometimes."

"More often than not. Of course, we'd be less conspicuous in a bigger city."

"So this is about New York?" Daisy's eyes darted from the

view through the window to Johnny and back. "What if I need to stay here?"

"I'm not going anywhere without you." They turned onto Lackawanna Avenue and continued on past the studio. "Now how 'bout we pick up this conversation after I introduce you to Mama Z."

"We're doing that *now*? When were you planning to tell me?"

"I told you today."

"You told me you had the idea today."

"Don't worry, we'll be quick. We won't even go inside. And I'll take you to Tony Harding's right after. You must be starving. I know I am."

Daisy pulled a plastic comb out of her purse to tame her dark locks. "What if she doesn't like me?"

"Of course she'll like you."

"She might not."

"Won't change my feelings." Johnny reached across the seat and caressed Daisy's neck.

"You sure?"

"I could ask you the same thing. What if your family doesn't approve of me?"

"They will." Daisy grabbed his hand and held it tight.

"And if they don't?"

"They *have* to." Daisy sounded more desperate than certain.

"They will," Johnny said, trading honesty for reassurance. "Anyway, I heard the odds are in your favor today."

"That's true. Those mechanical grandmothers never lie." She took a tube of lipstick out of her purse. "Do you really think she'll like me?"

"I do." Johnny turned onto Olive Street, pulled halfway up the block, and parked in front of a weathered gray house shoehorned between its neighbors. "Be right back," he said as he hopped out of the car. When he reached the sidewalk, he took off his sunglasses, leaned into the passenger window, and whispered, "She's going to love you as much as I do," before charging up the front steps.

* * *

Daisy studied the house. Two stories. Wood siding. Covered porch. Not unlike the homes in Providence. A scooch taller, perhaps; a bit thinner, for sure, as if someone had instructed her to stand up straight and hold her breath. Along the foundation, scores of geraniums flamed like Roman candles. What Daisy's mother wouldn't give to learn this woman's secret. Most of the gardens on Spring Street had already given up the ghost.

Several young boys rounded the corner, laughing, joking, besting each other. As soon as they saw the Buick, they stopped short. A few of them whistled their admiration just as Daisy decided to step out of the car. All of the boys scattered but one. "You lost, miss?"

"You scared me." Daisy's hand flew up. "Not lost." She grabbed her purse from the car and fanned her face. "Hot."

"This your car?" he asked, studying the finned taillights.

"Friend of a friend's." She turned toward the house just as the screen door creaked open.

The boy looked up. "Hey, Mama Z!"

"Hay is for horses, young man." She hobbled down the steps with Johnny at her side.

The boy corrected himself: "Good afternoon, Mama Z."

"And a good afternoon to you, Charlie. Closer to good evening. Now, what are you up to this fine day?"

"Talking with your friend here."

"Not *my* friend," Mama Z said, "yet." She and Johnny reached the sidewalk at the same time. "We haven't been introduced."

Charlie's glance skipped from Mama Z to Daisy and back again before landing on Johnny. "Huh," he said, as if figuring out a riddle. "Well, I'll be darned." The boys who had run off reappeared at the bottom of the hill, and Charlie called out, "Wait up!" He waved to the unlikely trio of adults standing in front of him. "See you later, alligators." Chuckling, he sprinted down the street.

With Charlie gone, Johnny began making the introductions:

"Mama Z, I'd like you to meet Daisy Morgan Davies. Daisy, this is Mama Z."

"A pleasure to meet you, Mama Z."

"Call me Zethray."

"Zethray," Daisy repeated, certain her cheeks were turning as red as the woman's geraniums.

Johnny tensed. Something he was trying to say seemed to have lodged in his throat.

"You have two beauties here." Zethray pointed first at Daisy and then the car. "Only one of them's precious," she said. "Take good care of this girl."

"Yes, ma'am, I will." Johnny's body relaxed. "Any other advice?"

Zethray looked at him dead on, her features tight. "None you haven't already ignored." Her expression loosened into something more cordial. "Now, if you'll excuse me, I've had a long day, and this foot of mine could use a good soak."

"Why don't you let us run and get you some Epsom salts?" Daisy offered. "My father used to swear by them."

"Well, aren't you sweet. I'm fine, but thank you. Now you two run along. Enjoy that car. I hear it turns into a pumpkin at midnight."

"It was a pleasure to meet you." Daisy patted Zethray's arm.

"The pleasure was mine." Zethray put her hand on Daisy's and held it there. "You're both good people. Time will tell if you're good for each other." She turned back and started climbing the steps. Halfway up, she stopped and called out, "You wouldn't be Violet Davies's kin now, would you?"

"Yes, ma'am. Violet's my mother." Daisy's voice shook a little. "How is it you know her?"

"Our paths crossed at the Globe Store," Zethray explained. "My mother used to work with your grandmother a lifetime ago."

"Small world," Daisy said, her face now ashen.

Zethray eyeballed Johnny. "And getting smaller by the day."

* * *

Tony Harding's was hopping for a Tuesday. Instead of holding out for a table, Johnny guided Daisy toward an empty pair of stools at the far end of the counter. As hungry as he was, the promise of quick service trumped the privacy of a booth. Besides, Daisy hardly seemed in the mood for conversation. She'd barely said a word in the ten minutes since leaving Mama Z's.

Johnny couldn't blame Daisy. Mama Z's reception had been a little cooler than he'd expected. *Cool, but not unfriendly*, Johnny reasoned. He'd point that out to Daisy when she was ready to talk.

A sprite of a waitress appeared in front of them with her pad at the ready. "What'll it be?" she asked loudly enough to be heard over the chattering patrons and a sizzling grill.

"An open-faced roast beef sandwich," Daisy said. "And a Coke."

"Same, with extra gravy. And mashed potatoes."

"Comes that way." The waitress slid her pencil behind her ear and scurried off.

The couple sat quietly for more than five minutes. Johnny studied Daisy, her eyes focused on a thirty-foot mural spanning the wall on the other side of the counter, a tribute to the *Phoebe Snow*, a well-known passenger train on the DL&W Railroad. "A penny for your thoughts?" he eventually said.

"William J. McHale."

"Who?"

"The boy who did the painting," Daisy said.

"He's good."

"I went to school with his cousin."

"I can't decide if that train's coming or going."

"Wish I knew." Daisy bit her bottom lip. "Could be he's just passing through."

Johnny crossed his arms and drew back. "Are we still talking about the train?"

"Ice-cold Cokes." The waitress set the glasses on the counter before turning around to grab two steaming plates. "Save room for dessert," she said and scooted away to take another order.

Daisy passed a shaker over to Johnny. "Always needs a little salt." She returned her attention to her own meal, cutting her sandwich into bite-sized pieces and spreading the gravy over the top like she was icing a cake, making sure every inch of bread was covered.

"That's some technique," Johnny said.

When Daisy did not respond, they spent the rest of their meal in silence.

Back at the studio, Johnny opened the arched front windows to clear out the stale air. What a day. The park had been a disaster, and Mama Z's hadn't gone as planned. On the bright side, he had introduced Daisy to someone other than the band. That had to count for something.

"I have to look at this schedule," Daisy said as she dropped down on the old mohair sofa with a pencil in one hand and a calendar in the other. "I have to figure out a way to make up today's lessons."

"Do you want me to leave?"

"No."

"Good." Johnny smoothed the quilt covering the worn cobalt cushions and sat down beside her, trying to think of something soothing to say. "Mama Z was right to call you precious." He reached over and stroked Daisy's cheek.

"Don't you mean *Zethray?*" Daisy kept her voice even and her eyes on her work.

"*That's* why you're mad? Because she told you to call her Zethray?" Johnny half whistled with relief. "I thought it was something serious."

"I'm not mad." Daisy flipped her hair over her shoulders in a show of indifference.

"I should have introduced you to her by her given name. She'll warm up. You'll be calling her Mama Z in no time."

"She's not my mama." Daisy scowled. "And she's not yours either. Don't think I don't know what you were up to. Trying to pass her off as family, so—"

"She is like family," Johnny cut in.

Daisy barreled on: "So you could guilt me into telling mine."

She was onto him. Any argument Johnny might make would be a lie, so instead he took a more humble approach. "I should've told her we were coming. No one likes to be caught off guard."

"That's what happens when you rush into things."

"Rush?" Johnny backed up to the far end of the couch. "We've been dating almost four months now.

"What's that supposed to mean?"

"Just what I said."

Daisy flipped through the calendar with her thumb. "I canceled paying students to be with you today, and this is my thanks?"

"I didn't know being with me was such a sacrifice."

"You're twisting my words."

"Or maybe I'm really hearing them for the first time." Johnny got up and walked over to the piano. "I'm the one who put everything on the line with Mama Z. What have you done to prove *your* love?"

"Prove?"

"I didn't mean—"

"It's not enough that I love you? I have to prove it now?"

"So this is how I get treated for taking a risk," Johnny said.

"I never asked you to risk anything."

"Someone has to. You're certainly not telling people about us."

Daisy's voice swelled with indignation: "I told Beverly!"

Johnny glared at her. "And who have you told since?"

"There's the phone." Daisy gestured toward a small table against the wall. "Feel free to give your mother a call. You're *actual* mother." Her eyes narrowed. "Or maybe you want to wait until you get to New York City."

A dusty wind blew through the open window. Johnny stared out at a cluster of clouds moving in. "I never said I was going."

"You didn't have to."

The cords in Johnny's neck tightened. "So because you're too afraid to cut the apron strings, I have to stay in Scranton?"

Daisy's mouth fell open. "Of all the gall."

"At least I could be my own man in New York City and have a real life."

"Now who's looking at the romance side of things?"

"You don't have any idea how hard this is going to be."

"It'll be hard no matter where we are."

He snorted. "Not this hard."

"Then go," Daisy said. "That's what you want to do anyway. Find Kenny. Move to New York. Have a ball, for all I care."

"Maybe I will."

"Good. Chase after your stupid dream."

"At least I never gave up on mine."

"Get out."

A bolt of lightning split the cheerless sky, and a boom of thunder rattled the building's windows. Large drops of rain began pelting the glass.

"Gladly." Johnny stomped out of the studio and into the storm.

The rain passed as quickly as it had started, leaving behind a deep mugginess. Despite the heat, Daisy pulled the hand-knotted quilt up over her tensed body. In the dusky light, the cobalt couch had the mottled appearance of a fading bruise.

Good riddance! Daisy fumed, her breathing rapid, shallow, loud in such an empty room, like a bull preparing to charge. *Who is he to judge me for wanting to stay in Scranton? I'm not a child anymore. I don't have time for impractical dreams. I have a mother and a grandmother who need me. I have a studio to run. And a fine one at that.*

Daisy glanced around the room, proud of what she'd

accomplished in a few short months. Even in the shadows, she could make out the maple floors, ballet barre, window signs.

And, of course, the piano.

Her heartbeat quickened and her hands and feet started to tingle. *What have I done?* The tears she'd damned up during her fight with Johnny now stung her sunburned cheeks. How could she have driven off the only man she'd ever truly loved? She should have made him turn around as soon as he'd pulled into Rocky Glen. That was her first mistake. No good ever came from that place. Not for Daisy. And she should've put her foot down about going to meet Zethray. The short notice had put them both at a disadvantage. Poor judgment on Johnny's part, but that didn't excuse Daisy's over-the-top reaction. She yanked the quilt up under her chin.

He was right. She hadn't found the nerve to tell anyone other than Beverly about him. And the fact that something like that would take nerve on her part only made her feel worse. Ashamed, in fact. Johnny was finally seeing her for the coward she was. It served her right that he'd stormed out.

Fearing she'd never see him again, her tears turned into sobs.

The door at the bottom of the staircase scraped open and shut. Daisy wiped her eyes, threw back the quilt, and leaped off the couch while Johnny sprinted up the steps two at a time. The pair rushed toward each other and embraced.

"I didn't mean a word I said," Johnny whispered in her ear.

"You're right. I need to be brave."

"No." He rubbed his cheek against hers. "I'm too impatient. Always have been."

"I love you, Johnny Cornell." Daisy leaned back to see his eyes. "It's time people know."

"I love you too." He pressed his palm into the small of her back and pulled her close. "And I'm not going anywhere. Everything I need is right here in this room."

"Right here," she repeated, resting her head on his shoulder.

Johnny started humming a tender tune. "May I have this dance?"

"I'll talk to my mother," she murmured.

"Mm-hmm." Johnny set an easy tempo with his hips.

"Soon," she said.

"Only if it's what you want."

Daisy brushed her parted lips against his ear. "I want you."

Johnny shivered. Evening approached, casting its streetlamp glow into the unlit studio. He drew back and searched her face.

A most delicious ache rendered Daisy incapable of speech. She simply nodded.

Johnny took a few steps back but never broke his gaze.

"Should I not have said . . . ?" Mortified by her immodesty and Johnny's hesitation, Daisy drew back and turned toward the window.

Johnny walked up behind her, laid a hand on each of her hips, and started her swaying. Once she fell into the rhythm, he pressed his body against her back.

"I need to know you're sure," Johnny whispered. "I can't be clearheaded tonight." He slid his hands to her midriff. "Not with you looking so damn beautiful."

Her tongue, thick with anticipation, curled around her only thought. "Don't stop."

Still swaying, he unbuttoned her blouse and slipped it off. His fingers traced the bottom curve of her lace-covered breasts before wandering to the clasp. Hands trembling, he clumsily worked the hooks and eyes, to no avail.

They both laughed, and somehow this made Daisy love him even more. She reached around, pinched open the band, and shimmied the straps off her shoulders. The brassiere fell silently to the maple floor. Daisy arched her back as Johnny fondled her breasts and kissed her neck, her ears, her shoulders. She lifted her mouth to his, her tongue hungry to explore.

Johnny's left hand drifted toward her waistband. He pressed

his fingertips into the space between fabric and flesh, then pulled down her zipper and slid his hand into her cotton panties. Slick with desire, Daisy moaned as he slipped his fingers inside her. On the brink of losing all reason, she gasped. Johnny pulled his hand away and peeled her pedal pushers and panties all the way off. In the blinking light of a now dying streetlamp, he turned her around.

"My God." His eyes glistened. "You are so beautiful."

Caught in Johnny's gaze, Daisy felt exposed. "I'm not the kind of girl who . . ." Her voice dropped to a whisper. "I've never been with a man before. Not like this."

"Shhh." He put a finger to his lips, took her hand, and led her to the couch. As soon as she lay down, Johnny covered her with the blanket. "I love you," he said, standing over her, unbuttoning his shirt, unbuckling his pants, kicking off his shoes. Soon he stood naked in front of her. "Marry me," he said, kneeling down to kiss her.

"Yes. Yes. Yes." The words dropped from her mouth like summer rain. "Yes," she said again, as Johnny lifted the cover and climbed on top of her.

Afterward, draped with an odd angle of quilt, Daisy and Johnny spooned for well over an hour, dozing, dreaming, remembering. Daisy shuddered as another spark of pleasure flamed up inside her.

"We should get dressed," Johnny mumbled as he pulled her in tighter. A couple of blocks away, the courthouse chimed the hour.

"It's midnight!" Daisy bolted upright. "You have to pick up Kenny."

The pair jumped off the couch and scavenged for their clothes, all the while stealing glances at each other.

"I'll take you home first," Johnny said, putting on his pants, "and go back for Kenny."

"I can come with you." Half-dressed, Daisy turned her blouse right side out and slipped it on.

"No."

"No?" Daisy's hands froze on her last button.

"I didn't mean that to sound sharp." He kissed her forehead. "Half the time those trains are late." He sat down to lace up his shoes. "And besides, Kenny might want to go straight home."

"If you're sure."

"I am. I love you."

"I love you too." Daisy grabbed her purse from the piano. With her back to Johnny, she tried for a casual tone: "Just drop me on the corner. I'll walk up the hill."

"But I thought you were going to tell—"

"I am," she said cheerfully, turning around and taking his arm. "This weekend. Saturday. It's my mother's next day off."

"Promise?"

She stood up on her toes and delivered a long, deliberate kiss. "Promise."

Outside, the streetlight's bulb popped and shattered. Johnny took Daisy's hand in the pitch-dark room and led her to the door. "Good thing I don't believe in signs."

"Good thing," Daisy said, wishing she could have seen Johnny's face when he'd said those words.

Daisy stretched the three-minute walk up Spring Street into ten. *Easy enough to do when you're floating on air.* She laughed at herself. *I sound like a silly school girl.* She laughed again, louder this time, then looked around to see if anyone had heard. *So what.* She no longer cared about other people's opinions of her. She had Johnny. A man who loved her exactly for who she was. Sure, there were obstacles to overcome, but tonight she only wanted to remember the magic. Johnny's hands on her body. His proposal of marriage. Making love.

"Daisy?" Myrtle Evans dragged her chair to the front of her porch.

"Mrs. Evans? You scared the life out of me." Daisy took in the dimmed neighborhood. "You should be in bed by now."

"Too hot to sleep. Thought I'd get some air."

"Well don't stay up too late," Daisy said.

"That you I saw getting into a Buick this afternoon?"

Daisy stopped cold. "Yes, ma'am," she said, not willing to lie about Johnny. *So what?* she added in her head. If only she had the courage to say it out loud.

"And did I see a colored man behind the wheel?"

Be strong, Daisy thought. "Yes, ma'am." She braced for the worst of it. If Myrtle had seen her and Johnny together, everyone in the neighborhood knew by now. The thought terrified her. She wasn't ready. She needed time. She peered up at the moon for a miracle.

"I didn't know they let his kind drive courtesy cars."

Daisy gulped. "Yes, ma'am." On jellied legs, she continued on to her own house and dropped into the porch swing. *I should have corrected her.* Regret swept through Daisy's heart like an angry storm. *Next time.*

Johnny scooted across the bench seat as Kenny got behind the steering wheel. "Hard to let go of a beauty like her." Kenny patted the dashboard.

"She drives real good," Johnny said. "Thinking about getting one of my own someday."

"Someday soon. Our tryouts are in two weeks, but my buddy who runs the nightclub says we're shoo-ins. Steady gig. Six nights a week."

"About that . . ."

"Weekly paycheck. Good money too."

"Daisy's not too keen on leaving."

"So change her mind."

"I'm not sure I—"

"We're talking New York City money. You'll be doing her a favor."

"You think?"

"I *know*. This is our big break, buddy. You and me. Time to take our bite out of the apple. The Big Apple. Whaddya say?"

"I'm in." Johnny rolled down his window to take in the breeze. Somehow he'd figure out a way to convince Daisy to leave Scranton.

C HAPTER TWENTY-SEVEN

FOR ONCE, VIOLET WAS GRATEFUL for the milkman's early morning racket. After another night of restless dreams, she welcomed a sooner-than-expected start to her day. A thin stripe of sun ignited the horizon as she settled into her kitchen chair with her cup of tea and a copy of *Lace Yarns*, the company's monthly newsletter. The headlines were easy enough to make out, but she had to hold the four-page paper at arm's length just to skim the articles.

Jean Mitchell, a hem stitcher in the finishing department, joined the "Stork Club" with the birth of an eight-pound, eleven-ounce baby boy.

Lawrence Scott, a weaver's apprentice, won a 5-dollar "Bright Idea" prize for his suggestion to catalog the lace-pattern punch cards.

Bob Kenia, the head cook in the employee cafeteria, manned the grill at the Fourth of July picnic. Families gathered for wholesome entertainment and . . .

Violet turned the page. The article continued in the first column, but something else caught her eye—a photo of a blond-haired boy with a lit sparkler in his hand. Violet recoiled as if someone had set the thing off in front of her.

"For goodness sakes," she said aloud, "it's only a picture."

Archie popped up from his bed of blankets to make sure nothing was wrong, then curled back to sleep. "Sorry," Violet whispered, going over to the stove to reheat the kettle. It took three matches to get the burner to catch. Time to ask the widow for the name of a good repairman.

Violet waited at the stove for the water to boil, thinking about her sister, Our Daisy. Folks in town still talked about her accident, still used her tragedy as a cautionary tale about the dangers of fireworks. And this many years later, Violet still brooded over that day. Their father had hidden the Fourth of July sparklers behind the wash tin on the back porch. Violet had found them after she and her sister had been kicked out of the kitchen for spilling a pie. She knew better than to light them. They both did. One spark. That's all it took for the dress to catch on fire. For their world to shatter.

Violet had felt awfully alone these last few years. What she wouldn't give to have her big sister back. Grown, of course, as she would have been by now, not the nine-year-old Daisy who'd been showing up these past two months in Violet's dreams.

The dreams always started the same way. Daisy taking her hand, pulling her down Spring Street. Some nights they ended there too. Other times, Daisy would lead Violet toward the church or the school or the gate at the mine where they used to meet their father to walk him home. Last night, though, Daisy had brought her to the river. For what, Violet couldn't say. She wished she could take comfort in these visitations, yet they only left her feeling unsettled.

With the water heated and the tea brewed, she sat back down at the table to read the rest of the newsletter. There was that boy again. All smiles. Oblivious to the perils of sparklers.

His body twitched. Impossible, but Violet saw it with her own eyes. She looked closer, and for a split second she glimpsed her sister. Clear as day. White dress. Frilly bow on top of her head. Not instead of the boy, but layered into the photograph like a double exposure.

And then she was gone.

Violet shivered. *A trick of the eyes,* she thought, carrying her teacup over to the sink and pouring it out. *Nothing a good night's sleep won't fix. Or a pair of glasses. That's what you get for putting vanity over necessity.* She snatched the newsletter off the table and flung it into the dustbin. She'd see about getting her sight checked next week. For now, she needed to get dressed for work.

By the time the lunch whistle blew at the Lace Works, Violet had already cut through so many bundles of Vinylite she'd almost met her quota for the day. Just inside the cafeteria, she found Doreen standing in front of the employee bulletin board reading a newly posted flyer:

Dinner Dance
Sponsored by the Scranton Lace Service Club
Saturday, September 3
The Hotel Jermyn
Arabian Ballroom
Tickets: $5.00 per couple

Proceeds to benefit the Scranton School District
to help defray the costs of administering
the Salk Polio vaccine to students.

"What's today?" Doreen asked as they made their way over to a table.

"Thursday, August 11." Violet took a seat across from Annie and Babs.

Doreen counted on her fingers. "That gives us twenty-three days."

"For what?" Babs said, a butterscotch Tastykake in one hand, and a folded copy of the *Scranton Times* in the other.

"To find Violet a date for the dinner dance."

"A date's the last thing I need," Violet assured.

"That so?" Doreen unwrapped her sandwich. "What's the *first* thing you need?"

"I'd give my eyetooth for a good night's sleep."

"Haven't had one of those," Annie said, stirring sugar into her coffee, "since I went through the change."

"Ah, to be young again," Babs mused.

Mouths full of food, they all chuckled in agreement.

Doreen tapped the back of the newspaper. "What's the word on Hurricane Connie?"

"Coming up the East Coast," Babs said. "Expected here sometime tomorrow."

"Bad?" Violet wasn't concerned about flooding. The river was low enough to take a month of rain, and besides, her house stood on high ground. It was the power of the wind that gave her pause, especially with a roof as old as hers.

"Not necessarily." Babs ran her finger down the paper as she scanned for details. "Could be no more than a soaking rain by the time it hits here."

"Amen to that." Doreen clasped her hands in prayer.

Annie piped up, "I heard there's another storm behind her."

Babs scanned the article. "Hurricane Diane."

"That's the one," Annie said, sipping the last of her coffee.

"Not close enough to predict yet," Babs said, reporting as she read. "May just go out to sea."

"Connie? Diane?" Annie shook her head. "Why can't it ever be a man's name?

"It'll never happen," Violet said.

"Ain't that the truth," Doreen said. "The guys like to think *we're* the ones causing all the trouble."

"How about Hurricane Darwin?" Annie said.

"Hey," Babs looked over her paper, "wasn't that the name of your first husband?"

"Sure was." Annie smirked. "And like most hurricanes, he

turned out to be a lot of hot air and no action." She elbowed Babs in the ribs.

Doreen snorted. "You might say he *petered* out."

Violet had never heard such blue talk come out of the mouths of women, and God forgive her, she couldn't help but laugh along with them.

At the end of the workday, Violet decided to walk the riverbank for part of the way home. Knowing back-to-back hurricanes were brewing on the Atlantic coast, she peered at the cloudless sky and thought, *You can't tell by looking*. She'd try to remember to bring the rockers in off the porch. As for the roof, all she could do was pray it would hold through another storm or two.

On Violet's side of the Lackawanna, hemlocks, pines, and elms towered over a tangle of wild rhododendron. Having already flowered, the waxy leaves curled lengthwise into green cigars. Ivor Jones, one of Violet's grandfathers, had caught a lot of brook trout in this spot. He'd died decades before Violet came along, but her mother liked to talk about him. "You have to remember the dead," she'd say. "You have to tell their stories." Violet wondered what he'd think if he could see the river now. The trout had been fished out long ago. Runoff from the mines had turned the water to rust. Channels of silt, the color of clay pots, flanked the wasting river. And then there was the smell. The greening and decaying musk of vegetation. The fetid bite of sewage and heavy metals. A give-and-take between the living and the dead, made all the more pungent by the unforgiving heat.

Still, Violet could find beauty. She sat down on the grass and watched a blue heron skim the water with its long, thin legs. *Magnificent*, she thought. Maybe that was what her sister had wanted her to see when she'd brought her to the river in last night's dream.

Something scurried through the thicket on the opposite bank. A beaver or a fox or a deer.

Or a child.

Clear as day, in spite of the forty-foot span and Violet's aging eyes. "Get back!" she yelled as a pair of small feet scrambled toward the shoreline. The river may have been tempered by the lack of rain, but it had not been tamed. In spite of Violet's warning, the child, a little girl, walked straight into water.

"No!" Violet screamed, skidding down the embankment to save her. As soon as Violet reached the river's edge, the girl, in a beautiful white dress with matching hair bow, dissolved into a million pinpoints of shimmering light.

CHAPTER TWENTY-EIGHT

GRACE SAT ON THE PORCH, eyeing her old house next door. Her husband Owen slowly rocked his chair alongside hers. *Lotta good years spent there.*

"And a few not so good," Grace said. "But what can you do."

Not a thing, my love.

"The Nisselbaums seem to like it. The wife wants to get my roses going again."

She'll need new trellises. Owen leaned over the railing. *That wood's all rotted.*

"The mister's handy. He'll make quick work of it." Grace pointed to the mezuzah on the doorframe and lowered her voice. "That means they're Jewish. Told me when they bought the house." Grace pushed her shoulders back and sat up a little taller. "Never bothered me for a minute. Just like when the Catholics started moving in. I never cared."

If that's how you remember it. Owen smiled.

"It is."

You were always more accepting, my love. I had a harder time.

"Stanley." A hint of sadness pulled out Grace's features.

I couldn't see past the differences in their religions. Thought Violet would be better off with someone from her own faith.

"Tommy."

Yes.

"He was a good man."

Salt of the earth.

"But he wasn't Stanley."

The pair sat quietly, staring at their old house. Owen finally said, *What time does Violet get home these days?*

Grace opened her palm and showed Owen his gold pocket watch. "Not for another half hour. Plant closes at five."

I wondered if you'd kept it.

"I let go of a lot when I moved over here." She closed her fingers around the watch. "But I'd never part with this."

Telephones started ringing simultaneously in four side-by-side houses. Grace turned her ear to listen through the screen door. "Not us," she said. "We're two shorts and a long."

I don't know how anyone keeps track. We got along just fine without.

"You get used to it. Most people on a party line only pick up when they hear their own ring pattern." She cast her glance in the direction of Myrtle's. "Most people."

Owen stood up. *I'll see you soon, my love.*

"Where're you going?"

"Going?" the widow responded as she crossed the street, her cane in one hand, her crocheting bag in the other. "I'm coming to see you." She grabbed hold of the banister and pulled herself up. "And look. The rocker's already started for me. Like you knew I was coming."

"That's bad luck." Two porches down, Myrtle poked her nose out her front door as she checked for the mail. "An empty rocker, moving on its own, is nothing to fool with," she called over, before going back inside.

"Wasn't empty, was it?" the widow asked Grace.

"You caught me." Grace blushed. "Talking with my Owen again. But that stays between me and you. If Violet or Daisy ever found out, they'd think I was crazier than a bedbug. And they'd probably be right."

"Not for me to judge." The widow sat down and pulled her crochet needle, thread, and a half-made doily out of her bag.

"Have you ever seen your Henryk?"

"No. 'Course, it's been so long, I probably wouldn't know the man if I tripped over him." The widow pulled the doily up to her eyes to see where she'd left off. "And I'm certainly not going to go looking. If I see that man in heaven, it'll be too soon. But knowing Henryk, that's a big *if*."

Grace lifted the edge of the doily to admire the pinwheel design. "How many are you up to now?"

"Twenty-five." The widow wrapped the thread around her gnarled finger.

"I can't say I ever heard of someone making favors for her own funeral. Is that how the Catholics do it?"

The widow shook her head as she started to work the hook.

"Poles?" Grace asked.

"Just thought it'd be nice if people had something to remember me by."

"How many you making?"

"Well, that's the question. I'm ninety-one years old. Not a lot of people left to bury me. I overdo it, they'll say I was proud. I come up short, they'll call me chintzy." The widow's eyes stayed focused on her work. "Guess I'll just keep at it till my time comes."

Grace watched as the widow tied off her doily. "You thinking it'll be soon?"

"Not especially."

"When my time comes, I want to die in my own bed."

"Well, if I get there first," the widow lifted her hand toward the sky, "I'll put in a good word."

"Thank you. Given any more thought to what kind of service you want to have?"

"I have lots of ideas. I put them all in a letter to Stanley. Wrote, *Smile when you think of me and do good deeds,* across the front of the envelope to keep him from wallowing when I'm gone."

"That's considerate."

"What about you?"

"Funerals are for the living. Violet and Lily can decide when I'm gone."

"That so?"

"I will say this." Grace patted the arms of her rocker. "I don't want some drawn-out affair. Just put me in the ground before I start stinking."

"The Jewish faith got that one right," the widow said.

"Speaking of . . ." Grace glanced over at her old house, "I haven't seen the Nisselbaums around this week."

"They're in Queens, New York, till Sunday, visiting her people. She asked me to take in the mail, but Myrtle got to it first," the widow groaned.

"Wonder if her ears are burning," Grace whispered, as Myrtle stepped back out onto her porch. As soon as she sat down, the telephones began ringing in unison again, giving Grace and the widow a start. Myrtle jumped up and opened her front door to listen. Two shorts and long. She looked over at Grace.

"Well, answer it," Grace said. "You know you're dying to."

"Happy to save you the steps." Myrtle darted inside.

"Save me the steps," Grace mumbled, her jaw clenched. "She's three years older than I am."

Half a minute later, Myrtle walked back out with the receiver in her hand. "It's for you."

"I know that," Grace called over. "Who is it?"

"Violet. She wants to know if you'll be okay alone for another hour or two. Daisy'll be home after that."

"She's not alone," the widow said.

Myrtle put the phone to her ear. "Johanna Lankowski's with her." She cupped the mouthpiece to keep her voice from carrying, but she was unsuccessful. "Yes. They're over there planning their funerals again. I swear, if they don't . . ." Myrtle's eye widened. "Humph." She held up the receiver. "We got cut off."

Grace smirked at the widow. "Funny how no one ever hangs up on Myrtle. They always seem to get cut off."

"I'd cut her off too if I could," the widow said and returned to her crocheting.

As traffic whizzed by the pay phone at the Texaco service station on Green Ridge Street, Violet hung up the receiver to disconnect the call, then picked it up again. Her fingers trembling, she tapped the hook switch a couple of times and fed another coin into the nickel slot. "Operator," she said, using her foot to prop open the accordion door for a breath of air, "I need the number for a Miss Zethray Long."

CHAPTER TWENTY-NINE

VIOLET JUMPED UP FROM THE TABLE to help Zethray wrestle a large box fan into the kitchen window. "This should cool things off," Zethray said, coupling the plug with a nearby extension cord. A swirl of blades drew a warm cross-breeze from an open window in an adjacent bedroom.

"I'm sorry to put you to all this trouble." Still shaky, Violet sat back down and took a sip of her iced tea.

"No trouble," Zethray said, setting a bowl of confectioners' sugar next to the strawberries she'd already put out.

"I didn't know where else to go."

"Here's fine. I knew to expect company this week." Zethray sat down, dipped a berry in the sugar, and took a bite. "Mm-mmm. Nothing sweeter." She wiped her mouth with a cloth napkin in the same shade of mint-green as the Formica tabletop. "Now about this little girl."

"My older sister. Our Daisy. It's what we call her."

"That's the one."

"Like I said on the phone, my heart nearly stopped when she walked into that river." Violet shuddered.

"She's just trying to get your attention. Our Daisy can be a bit theatrical at times."

"I don't know what you did," Violet said, "but you have to make this stop."

"What *I* did?" Zethray took a long sip of tea and washed most of the indignation from her voice. "This is all *her* doing. Rest assured."

"I'm sorry. I didn't mean . . . All this started up after I talked to you at the Globe Store. God forgive me. I don't want to see her again. It scares me."

"Then listen instead," Zethray said, rubbing her neck.

"To what?"

"Close your eyes."

"Why?"

"That child has something to say, and for both our sakes, you need to hear her out."

Violet whispered, "Can't she just tell you like before?"

"I'm trying to help you." Zethray exhaled, looked back at the bedroom doorway, and mumbled, "Cut from the same cloth."

Reluctantly, Violet closed her eyes and listened—to the box fan rattling against the window sash, a *drip drip drip* at the kitchen sink, Zethray's silence. Our Daisy's silence too. Violet's lids began to flutter open.

"Keep 'em closed," Zethray said, her voice encouraging but firm.

Violet heard Zethray scrape her chair away from the table and shuffle a few steps across the room and back before settling again. The *drip drip drip* disappeared.

"Sometimes you have to sit with the discomfort. See where it takes you." The ice cubes in Zethray's drink clinked against the glass. "What is she trying to tell you?"

"I wish I knew."

"You know."

Zethray's certainty made Violet uneasy. "I don't like this."

"You don't have to."

Violet twiddled her thumbs, first in one direction and then the other. Some part of her needed to be in motion for the rest of her to remain so still.

"What's coming to mind?"

"Nothing." Violet squeezed her eyes tighter, searching for a thought, any thought, to satisfy this woman. She shook her head, and something about that movement unearthed a string of words: "How she said I was bravest girl she knows."

"That's right." Zethray took another sip. "It's funny. When the dead speak through me, I usually only recall a few details, but with her, I remember almost all of it. Like she wants me to know."

"I can still see your handwriting on the Globe Store's delivery slip. Same exact message."

"Good. And how did those words make you feel?"

"Unworthy." The answer fell from Violet's mouth like a loose stone.

Zethray's chair squeaked as she shifted position. "Why's that?"

Violet opened her eyes. "Because I *am* unworthy. I haven't been completely honest with somebody."

"Daisy?"

"In a manner of speaking." Violet stared at her hands. "A different Daisy. My daughter."

"This isn't for me to hear," Zethray muttered. "I should have known as soon as I saw Johnny pull up in that Buick."

"Who?"

"Never mind." With her arms crossed, Zethray shot a look at the doorway. "What are you getting me tied up in?"

"I don't understand."

"Not you. *Her.*"

Violet followed Zethray's gaze, and to her relief saw nothing.

"You win." Zethray said before turning back to Violet. "So you were telling me about your daughter."

"And a promise I made to Lily, my baby sister, a long time ago. Twenty-five years."

"Does this have to do with you claiming that baby?"

Two months after their discussion in the Globe Store's subbasement, Violet was still unsettled over Zethray's ability to divine such a thing. "Yes." She swallowed hard. "Daisy was born to Lily, but she's my child in every way that counts."

"And you promised you'd never say a thing about it."

"That's right."

"And now you're struggling with what to do."

"I pray on it all the time."

"You gotta throw some shoes on those prayers," Zethray said. "Go tell you daughter before someone else does."

"Who?"

"Doesn't matter. Secrets always find a way out."

"What about my promise to Lily?"

"That wasn't yours to make."

"I kept this from my daughter for so long." Violet dropped her head into her hands. "What if she gets mad at me?"

"She'll get glad again."

Violet looked up at Zethray. "My mother always says that."

"My mama said it too." Zethray smiled. "Wonder what else they shared besides working as housemaids together."

Violet matched her smile. "My mother got so excited when she realized you were Ruth Jones's daughter."

"Tell Daisy your secret," Zethray said, "and she'll tell you hers."

"Hers?"

"We all have secrets."

"What's yours?" Violet's question seemed to surprise both of them. "I'm sorry, I'm overstepping."

"Hmm. No one's ever asked me that before. Everybody's always coming to me for their own answers."

"Do they help you? These . . . spirits? I know they talk through you, but do they talk *to* you? Give you peace of mind?"

"Sometimes. Mama comes, but she never speaks."

"Why's that?"

"Aren't you full of questions," Zethray said. "Always wondered about that myself." Her good foot started tapping. "How old were you when your sister passed?"

"Eight going on nine."

"Going on nine," Zethray mused, "Funny how the 'going on' matters at that age."

"How about you?"

"Fourteen."

"That's right. I remember you saying so the day we met."

"Do you carry any guilt?"

"Every day," Violet said.

"Not that you should."

"I know."

"Me too." Zethray shifted in her chair. "I'm not sure how much help I can be. For some strange reason, my story's getting all tangled up with yours tonight."

"*Your* story?"

"And Mama's. She took her own life thirty-nine years ago this month, two weeks to the day after her husband Clarence got himself killed."

"You were so young. And to think she committed . . ." Violet tried and failed to say the word. "I'm sorry."

"Me too. For both of us."

"Forty-two years for Our Daisy as of July. Doesn't seem possible."

"You think you've moved on," Zethray said, "but tragedy always pulls you back to *What if?* What if I hadn't been so moody with Mama?"

"What if I hadn't found those sparklers?"

"What if I'd been nicer to Clarence? My stepfather. Mama gave him two shiny quarters for spending money that day, but Mr. I'm Buying the Next Round wanted more. I saw him sneak two one-dollar bills out of the coffee can where Mama kept the rent money. So I told. And she got mad—at me, not him. Said I should mind my own business. What was hers was his. Sent me out on the porch for a good think."

"My father sent us outside, Our Daisy and me. We'd been arguing in the kitchen while my mother was baking, and he yelled at us to 'get out while you still can.' That's when I found the sparklers. And the matches."

"So you're carrying that burden," Zethray said.

"She suffered so. Three days in all."

"You have to forgive yourself."

"I have," Violet said. "At least a thousand times."

"Does it ever stick?"

"For a while."

"Make it a thousand and one."

Violet glanced at the empty doorframe where Zethray's eyes kept drifting. "Is she saying that?"

"Nope, *I* am. And you have to talk to your daughter."

"I know." Violet swallowed a lump of fear.

"Soon."

"This weekend. We'll both have time to sit down and sort things out." Violet locked eyes with Zethray. "And you? How can you get your mother talking?"

"Not sure she wants to."

"She wants to."

"Could've fooled me." Zethray's shoulders slumped.

"This doesn't have anything to do with you telling on Clarence. That's a kid's trick. No mother would hold that against her child."

"I still think if I'd been less sullen," Zethray said, "she never would've done it. I could've helped her through the sadness."

"It's the grief that killed your mama. Not you. Grief grabs hold with a powerful fist. Too powerful for some people. It's not your fault. And it's not hers either. I saw it with my own mother after my sister's death. And I felt it too. Grief's a mighty force."

"Ha. That's exactly what your sister said to me."

Violet found comfort in the notion that she and Our Daisy still thought alike after all this time. "Because it's true."

"Then why doesn't Mama speak?" Zethray asked. "Maybe if I'd kept my mouth shut when I saw him taking her money out of that coffee can."

"Maybe if my sister and I hadn't been running around the kitchen. Hadn't knocked that blueberry pie out of my mother's hands."

Zethray looked up, stunned. "Huckleberry," she corrected as she pushed back her chair and limped into the bedroom. A moment later, she returned to the table with a maple box. "My treasure chest. Clarence made it for me." She set it on the table and lifted the hinged lid. Inside, a folded apron sat on top of a stack of documents. "Huckleberries," she said, running her fingers across the fabric's inky embroidery. "Mama promised there'd be a huckleberry pie waiting for me after school that day. I was thrilled, huckleberries being my favorite. But there was no pie when I got home. Only a note saying how sorry she was. Then a policeman come by and took me downtown to identify her body. I saw her laid out on that table and called her a liar for not making me that pie. Can you imagine? Told her right there and then I never believed a word she said. Of course that wasn't true, but the damage was done. She never spoke another word." Zethray studied the apron. "I didn't mean it, Mama. That was the grief talking."

Violet reached across and patted Zethray's hand. "She'll speak to you now."

"Maybe." Zethray rooted through the papers in her treasure chest. "I saved everything I could to remind me of her. Newspaper articles. Insurance booklets. Recipes." She held up a scrap of paper crowded with cursive. "Mama used to write out Bible verses she wanted to memorize."

"Knock-knock, anybody home?" A tall woman with silver hair pushed through the door.

"Marcella." Zethray set the apron in the box and closed the lid. "I forgot you were stopping by."

"I can come back. I'm sure my Walter can wait a little longer."

"You're fine," Zethray said. "Take a seat. This is Violet Davies. Violet, this is Mrs. Marcella Madison. She's the choir director over at the AME church."

"What a beautiful necklace," Violet said, admiring the coral glass beads against the woman's dark skin. "I've never seen one like it."

"A gift from my first husband," Marcella said. "I thought he might appreciate seeing it on me this time."

"Well, don't let me hold you up." Violet rose. "A pleasure to meet you, Mrs. Madison."

"No need to rush off," Marcella responded before turning to Zethray. "I'm just here to find out if you learned anything else about those stars you saw that last time I was here. I've been racking my brain."

"Remind me what you're talking about," Zethray said. "I don't always remember."

"You kept seeing a bird and a big gold star and little stars on a blue background."

Zethray looked up at Violet who was still standing next to the table. "All of that mean anything to you?"

"Cornflower blue? Could be the Medal of Honor," said Violet.

"Of course!" Marcella yelled. "How could I forget? Walter wrote to me about earning a medal for valor. Then the army lost the paperwork, and I never heard another word."

"Funny how that only ever happened to the Negro units," Zethray said.

"That's not fair," Violet said. "Especially if a man served honorably."

"And he did," Marcella assured.

Zethray looked at Violet. "How'd you know what that was?"

"I hand-color photographs. Been doing it for years. Painted my fair share of soldiers during the war. Learned all their medals and ribbons."

"That makes sense. When Marcella and I couldn't figure out the bird and the stars, your sister told me to ask *you*. I thought she was pulling my leg. I guess I should've listened to her."

"Maybe we both should," Violet said.

Zethray turned, and for a moment stared at a spot beyond Marcella. "See about that medal. Walter wants what's his. And you

. . ." she shifted around and pointed a finger at Violet, "tell your daughter."

"And you," Violet pointed back playfully, "talk to your mother."

Zethray turned to Marcella. "Any chance you drove over here in that car of yours?"

"As a matter of fact, I did."

"Would you mind giving Violet a ride home? She's not too far. The Providence section of North Scranton. I'd appreciate the favor. And that'll give me time to clear my mind before I start talking to Walter."

Violet shook her head. "I don't want to put you out."

"Happy to help," Marcella said.

When Violet reached the porch steps, she could hear Zethray talking in the kitchen: "Mama, I'd give anything to hear your voice . . ."

I'm gonna cross the river Jordan,
Down by the riverside . . .

And Ruth said, Intreat me not to leave thee, or to return from following after thee: for whither thou goest, I will go; and where thou lodgest, I will lodge: thy people shall be my people, and thy God my God. Where thou diest, will I die, and there will I be buried: the Lord do so to me, and more also, if ought but death part thee and me.

—Book of Ruth, Chapter 1, Verses 16–17.

CHAPTER THIRTY

"WELL, AREN'T YOU THE EARLY BIRD." Violet eyed Daisy as she strolled into the kitchen. "I thought you went in late on Fridays."

"Beverly's sister-in-law's having the baby." Daisy kissed her grandmother who was already at the table. "She's been at the hospital since late last night. A friend of hers from beauty school is taking her customers today."

"That's exciting," Grace said. "I didn't know Beverly was expecting."

"Not Beverly, Grandma." Daisy gave Archie's ears a quick scratch. "Her sister-in-law."

Grace frowned. "Who did I say?"

"We knew what you meant." Violet squeezed her mother's shoulder. "More tea?"

"Yes, please."

Daisy bent down to see her reflection in the chrome bread box as she tied a kerchief around her neck. "So I have to get over there this morning to open up the beauty shop."

"I'll keep her in my prayers." Violet turned and busied herself by wiping off a perfectly clean counter. "What are you up to tomorrow?" She took a deep breath. "I feel like I've hardly seen you lately."

"Funny," Daisy said, "I was thinking the same thing."

"What about lunch?" Violet unwrapped the previous night's biscuits and set them on the table. "The Purple Cow has their spaghetti plate special on Saturdays."

"Perfect."

"And maybe a little window shopping."

"Is it a boy or a girl?" Grace asked.

"Not sure yet." Daisy buttered a biscuit and passed it to her grandmother. "She's still at the hospital."

"I remember Beverly when she was *this* high." Grace held her hand to her waist.

"Mother, how are you feeling?"

"Couldn't be better." Grace poured a little molasses on her plate and smacked her lips.

"I worry about leaving you alone all day," Violet said.

"I'm not alone. I have the TV to keep me company. And Lily's due for a phone call." Grace dipped her biscuit into the molasses and took a bite. "And Johanna usually comes for a visit. Or I go over there."

"I'd rather you stay home today." Violet rinsed out her teacup and set it on the drainboard. "We're getting a storm. I don't want you caught out in it."

"Will do." Grace gave a quick salute and took another bite. Violet and Daisy shared a worrisome glance.

"Call if you need us," Daisy said. "If you're in a hurry, don't bother dialing. Just pick up the receiver and ask the operator to connect you."

Grace stared over at the window. "We always got along fine without, didn't we?"

"Without what?" Violet asked.

"A telephone."

"Well, we have one now, and I'm glad for it." Violet untied her apron and draped it over her chair. "It keeps me from fretting even more."

"What's the name of the new neighbors?" Grace tapped the table to jog her memory.

"Which new neighbors?" Daisy asked.

Grace swung around.

Violet's eyes followed. "You mean the Nisselbaums next door? They've been living in our old house a few years now."

"Well they're new for Spring Street," Grace said.

"You're right about that." Daisy sighed. "Not much changes around here."

"The wife wants to get my roses going again," Grace said. "I sure hope I'm here to see that."

"You will be." Violet pointed to a list tacked on the wall next to the phone. "The number for the Lace Works is here."

"And the studio," Daisy said.

Violet nodded. "But you can also—"

"Just ask the operator," Grace said. "I heard you the first time. Now stop your fussing. I'm fine. You need to get going if you want to be on time."

"I don't have to leave for another half hour," Daisy said. "I'll make sure she's settled."

"I'm fine," Grace repeated.

"I'm trusting you to tell me the truth." Violet kissed the top of her mother's head and turned to Daisy. "It's starting to spit out," she said, giving her daughter's cheek a quick peck. "Make sure you take your umbrella."

"I'm going to be late tonight," Daisy said, "but I'll see you for lunch tomorrow."

"Tomorrow," Violet repeated and headed out the door.

Thankfully, the worst of the rain held off until Violet made it to the Lace Works. As much as she hated leaving her mother, Violet was eager to begin her eight-hour shift. *Hard to let your mind wander too far,* she thought, *with a straight knife cutter in hand.* Between yesterday's visit with Zethray and tomorrow's lunch with Daisy, Violet was a bundle of nerves. She slipped her umbrella into one of the stands near the door, punched her time card, and made it upstairs a few minutes before the other employees arrived.

Last day of my first week in the Vinylite department, Violet thought as she looked around the workroom. After Tommy passed away, she knew her life would change considerably, but she could never have imagined herself standing on a factory floor. If you'd asked her five years ago, heck, five weeks, she'd have said she was too old to learn a new skill, but here she was, cutting curtains for houses all across America. When God said, *Pride goeth before a fall*, Violet hoped He wasn't talking about work, because she took pride in providing for her family. And, to her delight, she was enjoying herself. Where else would she have met Doreen, Annie, and Babs? Even Arlene. They'd gotten off to a rocky start, but she seemed to be warming up. Violet closed her eyes and inhaled a strong stew of machine oil, floor wax, and Vinylite. The first couple of days, the fabric's chemical smell gave her a scratchy throat, but thankfully, that passed. Now if her fingers would callous up, she'd be all set.

Violet opened her eyes and found Arlene standing in front of her. "I didn't want to interrupt your . . . prayers? Anyway," she thumbed through the pages on her clipboard, "see me in my office at the end of the day."

Arlene hurried away before Violet had a chance to speak. *See me in my office.* For what? As the other employees headed toward their stations, Violet frantically searched her mind. What had she done wrong? She'd shown up on time every day. Made her quotas all week. Sure, her numbers were lower than those of the experienced cutters, but wasn't that how all the trainees started out?

Eight o'clock on the dot and the room suddenly filled with the purr, buzz, and thrum of machinery. It was hard to think in all that noise, and for that, Violet was grateful.

Somehow, she'd made it to the last hour of her shift. She'd know soon enough whatever Arlene had in store for her. Violet prayed she wouldn't cry. Why give Arlene the satisfaction? And she hoped the rest of the workers would be long gone by the time her supervisor had her say, because they didn't need to witness the firing firsthand.

"Violet," Arlene called out at the end of the day.

"Coming." Violet gave her table one more wipe. No one could ever say she didn't keep her station clean. As the rest of the workers streamed toward the exit, Violet turned around, walked into the office, and shut the door.

"I'd like you to meet Mr. Brauer from personnel." Arlene pointed to one of two men standing in the room.

"Mr. Brauer." Violet nodded.

"And Mr. Hughes. He takes the pictures for the *Lace Yarn*."

"Mr. Hughes." Violet noticed the camera dangling from his neck. "Wait. What?"

Mr. Brauer pulled an envelope out of his sport coat and passed it to Violet. "Congratulations on winning the company's 'Bright Idea' prize for your suggestion to make rain bonnets out of Vinylite scraps. Should make us a little money." He took Violet's hand and gave it an awkward shake. "Don't lose that now," he said about the envelope. "There's five bucks inside."

Violet stood stunned, her mouth open.

"I submitted your idea." Arlene beamed. "If you won, I wanted it to be a surprise."

"You got your wish." Violet half laughed, and the worry she'd been carrying seeped out like she'd opened an air valve.

"Say cheese." Mr. Hughes lifted his camera to his eye and clicked.

"Thank you," Violet said, blinking away the bright flash. "I never expected—"

Someone tapped against the glass in the door. "We're ready."

Violet turned around and saw Doreen and the girls standing at her table with a cake. "Congratulations!" the women called.

"Let's go," Arlene said. "You've earned it."

As Violet walked out, Doreen said, "We've been keeping this secret for two days. That's a new record for us."

Annie giggled. "I honestly didn't think we'd make it through lunch."

"This is a huge deal." Babs poured fruit punch into glasses. "Some people spend their whole lives working here and never win a 'Big Idea' prize."

"Is that so," Violet said, still a little shocked by the announcement.

"I've never won one," Annie said.

"Five dollars." Doreen handed Violet a knife. "That's enough money for two tickets to the dinner dance."

Violet howled, "You're too much!" As she cut the cake into perfect squares, the rain began to pound against the window.

"Don't worry," Doreen said, "that husband of mine let me take the car today. I'll give you a lift home."

"Thank you," Violet said. "This sure is my lucky day."

As Doreen pulled in front of Violet's house, water splashed up from the gutter, soaking a passerby. "Sorry!" Doreen yelled from inside the car.

The man scowled but kept scurrying up the street.

"Thank you so much for everything," Violet said as she readied her umbrella. "The ride. The cake."

"You're a good egg, Violet Davies. Glad to know you," Doreen said. "Stay safe."

"You too."

Violet slid out, opened her umbrella, and zigzagged around the puddles and up to the porch. She waved as Doreen pulled away, then hung her umbrella on the mailbox. Violet stood for a moment and listened. Her mother had the television turned up so loud she could hear it from the porch. After eight straight hours of heavy precipitation, Russ Hodges from WARM-TV was warning people about wind gusts.

"I'm home," Violet announced, pushing through the front door. A choking wave of gas flooded her senses. "Mother!" she screamed, running to the kitchen, turning off the open burner on the stove. "Mother!" Violet covered her mouth and nose with a dish towel as she ran around throwing open all the windows on the first floor. Torrents of rain blasted past the screens. "Mother!" Violet pounded upstairs, searching room by room. "Mother!" she called out one last time before running back down to the telephone.

"Come quick," Violet cried as soon as she heard Stanley pick up the receiver. "I need help."

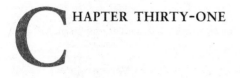

CHAPTER THIRTY-ONE

RUNNELS OF WATER POURED DOWN Market Street as Stanley coaxed his Oldsmobile over the bridge. "Listen. You can't stall out. You hear me?" He patted the dashboard as if encouraging a horse instead of an engine. "Violet needs my help." Stanley turned the corner onto North Main Avenue, and when the road leveled out, he picked up speed. "Don't fail me now." With the storm drains backing up, he was forced to plow through newly formed rivulets. Just short of Spring Street, his tires lost traction for a harrowing couple of seconds. "Come on," he said, when he regained control and caught his breath, "we're almost there." He tapped his brakes, making sure they still worked under all that water, before taking a sharp left. The rain made the road slick, and he skidded to a stop along Violet's curb.

Stanley hopped out of the car, up the steps, and into the house. In spite of the raging storm and all of the opened windows, a smell of gas hung in the air. "What happened?"

Violet stood at the bottom of the stairs, gripping the newel post as if she couldn't trust her legs to hold her. "I searched every room twice over. Even the coal bin. She's nowhere to be found."

"Who?" Stanley cast his eyes left into the kitchen and right toward the parlor. "Your mother?"

"Yes. I called the widow. She didn't come over today because of the rain, but she said they talked on the phone around one."

Stanley glanced at the clock. *Quarter to six.*

"My mother had just finished watching some soap opera and

was going to make a pot of tea. I told her not to fool around with the stove when I'm gone. That back burner . . ."

"She's not here, so she wasn't overcome with fumes. That's good."

"Anything could have happened." Violet's voice broke. "The house could have exploded with her in it."

"But it didn't." Stanley pulled Violet by the shoulders. "And your mother's fine." He took a breath to chase the tremor out of his voice. "She's probably with a neighbor, waiting out the storm. You sit tight. I'll go knock on doors."

"I'm coming with you." Violet grabbed a scarf from the coat tree in the hallway.

"No, someone should be home in case she comes back. *When* she comes back."

Stanley turned to leave, and the widow stepped inside. "I figured I'd be more useful over here." She stood on a rag rug near the threshold and brushed off the rain.

"I'm not sure it's safe," Violet said.

The widow took a good sniff of the air. "Most of it's cleared."

"Will you call Myrtle?" Stanley asked. "She'll spread the word faster than Walter Winchell."

"Already did," the widow said. "That's what took me so long to get over here. Now get going."

Violet tied the scarf around her head. "We'll cover twice as much ground together."

Stanley knew it was futile to object, so he cautioned, "Stay close," as he followed her out the door.

Howling winds blew sheets of rain sideways across the porch. "It won't help," Stanley called out as Violet tried to hand him an umbrella.

A gust of wind claimed Violet's scarf, and her hair whipped against her face. "Let's go."

Stanley pointed to the Nisselbaums' house, and the pair hurried down the steps and across both yards. After knocking at least a dozen times, Myrtle poked her head out from next door and yelled, "They're away till tomorrow!"

Stanley tried the knob just in case, but it was locked. He and Violet ran back down and over to Myrtle's. "Have you heard anything?"

"Not yet. You can skip Mildred's." Myrtle held the phone in the air. "I'm on the horn with her now, and your mother's not there."

Violet turned to Stanley. "Ready?"

Under a menacing sky, they sprinted over to the Kippycashes' house. And the Sundays'. And the Pehanicks'. The Sweets'. The Holdens'. The Kennedys'. And every other place down and up Spring Street without any luck. "What about the church?" Stanley hollered through the whistling wind.

Violet nodded, and they both dashed back to the house for Stanley's car.

The widow stepped up to the screen door and shouted, "Anything?"

"No." Stanley threw her a worried glance. "You?"

"No. Except Lily's on her way up from Atlantic City. Frankie too. Myrtle got on the call before me and spilled the beans."

"I can't think about that now." In spite of the wind, Violet turned her ear toward the sound of the telephone ringing inside, two shorts and a long.

The widow rushed to answer it. "That was Myrtle," she said a moment later. "Archie got out. He's over on the Nisselbaums' back porch. She said he's sitting on his haunches howling at their door."

"She's there!" Violet shouted. "I'm sure of it! Archie always watches out for her." She and Stanley ran next door to the Nisselbaums' and around to the backyard. "Archie!" Violet yelled as soon as she saw the dog. Instead of reacting to his name, he started scratching at the door.

Stanley turned the knob. "It's open," he said, surprised, and motioned Violet through. Archie squeezed past them and bolted straight back to her parents' old bedroom.

Violet ran down the hall. "Mother!"

In the middle of the Nisselbaums' four-poster bed, Grace's small face poked up from the blankets.

Violet rushed to the bed and touched her hand to her mother's cheek. "Are you all right?"

"Owen." Though Grace's voice was barely audible, her face shone with joy. "Look who it is. Our Violet."

"Mother, what are you doing? You can't be here."

"I want to die in my own house."

"You're not dying." Violet sat on the bed and cradled her head. "I won't let you."

"That's right," Grace said. "Will me to live a little longer." She paused to catch her breath. "I'd like to see my roses bloom another summer."

Violet pushed back the blanket. "She's soaked. We have to get her home."

"Mrs. Morgan," Stanley raised his voice so she'd be sure to hear him, "I'm going to pick you up."

Grace winced. "I'm not deaf, you know."

Stanley smiled and spoke softly: "Tell me if I'm hurting you." He pressed both arms under her body.

"Stanley," Grace said as he lifted her up, "home from school already?"

He shot Violet a look of concern. "Yes, Mrs. Morgan, I am."

"Did you hear?" Grace took a couple of shallow breaths.

"Mother, save your strength." Violet tugged Grace's nightgown over her knees. "You'll tire yourself out if you talk."

Grace kept her eyes on Stanley. "Our Violet is valedictorian. Class of 1923."

Stanley thought about Violet's medal in his pocket. "I heard something about that."

"We're very proud of our girl."

"We all are," Stanley said, carrying Grace down the hall.

Violet scooted ahead, unlocked the front door, and held it open. "The rain's letting up a bit. Hurry."

"Thank God for small favors." Stanley peered down at Grace. "Ready?"

"As I'll ever be."

Halfway across the yard, Grace's body went limp in Stanley's arms.

CHAPTER THIRTY-TWO

BY A QUARTER TO MIDNIGHT, Hurricane Connie's fury had faded to a lulling rain. Violet sat in a small armchair at her mother's bedside, listening to the rhythmic patter. "No hospital. She wants to die at home." That's what the doctor had said earlier in the evening when he'd examined her. At first, Violet couldn't understand what he was saying. Her mother hadn't regained consciousness since they'd gotten her back to the house. How could he know what she wanted? "We've spoken about it often," he'd said, squeezing Violet's shoulder. "You need to prepare."

Over the years, Violet had seen all kinds of death. A gamut, from old to young. Likely deaths to senseless ones. Quick to prolonged. Joyful, regretful, fearful. Ready, defiant, surprised. Hard-earned. Hard-fought. Hard-won. Never had she felt prepared.

Her daughter Daisy peeked into the room and whispered, "Any change?"

Violet shook her head. "The same."

"I washed all the bedding and brought it back over to the Nisselbaums'. Stanley mopped up the floors. He said to tell you he's staying with the widow tonight."

"I don't know what I'd do without you." Violet glanced at the window, anxious for her sister's arrival. They should be together now, even if it meant seeing Frankie too. "Any word from Lily?" No sooner had she spoken the name than a pair of headlights appeared out front.

"I'll go get her." Daisy disappeared into the hallway and down the steps.

Violet caught bits of tender greetings and hurried questions before a pair of feet scurried up to the bedroom. "Lily," she said, "I'm so glad you made it."

The sisters cried as they embraced, two versions of the same face, cheek to cheek.

Lily tiptoed to the other side of the bed, smoothed her mother's white hair, and whispered, "I love you so much." She looked up at Violet and mouthed, *How long?*

Violet blinked hard. "Not long. The doctor said it's only a matter of time."

Lily sat down in a cane-bottomed rocker and stroked the top of Grace's hand. "When I was little, I used to sit in church and trace these veins with my fingers." She ran her thumb over the watery lines.

"And fall asleep with your head on her lap," Violet said.

"As soon as the sermon started."

"She'd rub your back, and God help her if she stopped."

"I'd grab that hand to get it going again." Lily laughed lightly. "Worked like a charm."

"She loved you," Violet said. "Loves you. Loves *us*."

They both pressed their lips into the same cheerless smile and fell silent. Outside, the wind wound down to a whisper. *At least the roof held*, Violet thought, glancing up at the dry ceiling. Small consolation now, but she was grateful nonetheless.

She gazed at her sister, neat as a pin after hours of travel. Pencil skirt, tailored blouse, a strand of pearls around her neck. Real pearls, knowing Lily. And those kitten heels that were all the rage. A smart ensemble. High fashion compared to the housedress Violet had put on after the doctor's visit. Youthful too, with a pixie haircut framing her blue eyes. Her daughter's blue eyes.

Violet's heart dropped. She'd been so worried about confessing her secret to Daisy that she'd forgotten to forewarn Lily. "I know this is terrible timing," Violet got up and shut the bedroom door, "but I have to talk to you."

"What about?"

Violet sat back down and blurted out the words, "I'm going to tell her."

"Who?"

"Daisy." Saying her daughter's name aloud seemed to open the floodgate that had been holding back Violet's fears. "The truth about her birth is bound to come out. It'll level her if she hears it from someone else. And besides, she's old enough now. I know I made you a promise, but I have to break it. I don't have a choice. I can't lie to her anymore. I'm so sorry." Violet braced for her sister's ire.

Lily returned to watching the steady rise and fall of her mother's chest. "Not while I'm here."

"What?"

"Wait till I go home." Lily crossed her legs and folded her arms. "If she has questions, she can come to Atlantic City. I'll speak to her there."

"That's it?" Indignation cut ahead of Violet's fear. "I've protected you this whole time. I've beaten myself up over this for years, and that's your response?"

Lily scoffed, "You were always going to do what you wanted when it came to Daisy."

"What I wanted?" The muscles in Violet's neck tightened, but she kept her voice low. "Nothing's ever been about what I wanted."

"No?" Lily met Violet's agitation with calm. "Then who brought the baby home against my wishes?"

Violet grabbed her heart. "I couldn't leave her there."

Lily pressed her palm against her own chest. "And I knew I couldn't bear to keep her, so I went to the Good Shepherd." Lily shrugged. "But what I wanted never mattered to you."

"She was better off with us."

"Are you sure?"

"You were being selfish."

"Maybe. But is that any worse than being a martyr? Saint

Violet sacrifices for *our* sins." Lily wagged her finger. "And don't you forget it."

Violet's mouth dropped open. "I did what I thought was best for Daisy."

"Exactly. What *you* thought, and you alone. No one else's opinion mattered. Certainly not mine."

Violet's head hurt. She'd done what she'd thought was right, and at great cost to her own future. Why couldn't Lily see that? "But look at us now," she reasoned. "It all worked out."

"Just because it worked out doesn't mean you were right. It may have worked out the other way too. We'll never know."

"So you're saying I should have left her there?"

"I'm saying you should have asked me that question twenty-five years ago."

"There wasn't time."

"There's always time."

"Taking Daisy was the hardest decision I ever made."

"Hard doesn't mean it was yours to make."

Violet sucked in her cheeks. "Forgive me for trying to give that beautiful baby a good life."

Lily bent forward. "You gave her a wonderful life. I'm grateful for that, truly. This story has a happy ending, even if I was written out of it, but you need to remember that when you complain about never getting what you wanted in life, at least you had choices. They may not have been good choices, but there's power in being able to make your own decisions. Even your own mistakes. You took that power away from me in my most vulnerable hour."

"You're barking up the wrong tree if you think I had a choice." Violet smoothed the skirt of her housedress as she mumbled, "But I am sorry, I guess. I should have asked you."

"Yes."

"I would have taken her anyway."

Lily rolled her eyes. "Oh, I know."

"Still." Violet yanked a loose thread at her hemline. "I could have handled it better."

"I'm sorry too."

"For what?"

"Not always appreciating the sacrifices you made for our girl." Lily's eyes filled with tears. "She's lucky to have you."

"*Us*," Violet said. "Her family. Her blood."

"And you're right to tell her," Lily said. "But not till I'm gone. I don't want to talk to her about it here. It'd be too overwhelming."

"All right."

"When you tell her, make sure she knows I love her."

"I promise." Violet grabbed a box of tissues from her mother's nightstand, pulled out a few, and passed the rest to Lily. "We're quite a pair."

"Am I interrupting?" Daisy asked as she opened the door.

"Come in," Lily said. "You should be here with us."

Daisy approached the vanity and dragged the bench seat to the foot of the bed. "She looks so small."

"I always thought of Mother as a force to be reckoned with, but now . . ." Lily absently pulled at her pearls.

"Three generations of strong Morgan women in this room." Violet blew her nose.

"And well-spoken," Lily said. "Remember when she made us take elocution lessons?"

Violet's face lit up. "In the basement of the Presbyterian church."

"Elocution lessons?" Daisy covered her eyes as if embarrassed for her mother and aunt.

"Yep." Lily slapped her thighs. "We had to memorize all these silly poems."

"What was the one about doughnuts?" Violet asked.

Lily turned to Daisy. "And we had to walk around with books on our heads while we practiced them out loud."

"Why on earth?" Daisy laughed.

"To improve our posture." Violet squared her shoulders.

"And our poise." Lily said, stretching her neck.

"No kidding?"

"And then," Lily squealed, "she made us perform every poem in front of the whole congregation. I was mortified!"

"Mortified?" Violet fanned herself as beads of sweat ran down her back. "You were seven." She paused for effect. "I had nine years on you."

"Oh my Lord," Lily said, "you were sixteen years old? You must have looked like a damn fool up there."

The three laughed so hard their tears turned straight to grief.

"I still need you," Daisy said to her grandmother, rubbing her curled feet. "There's so much I have to tell you yet. So much I want you to see."

"I should've called her every day," Lily said, kicking off her heels, "to hear her voice. And I should've come home more than three or four times a year." She squeezed her mother's hand. "It's funny. Even though I don't see her often, I always take comfort knowing she's in the world."

"Mother knows how much you love her," Violet said, pulling at the top of her housedress to get some air.

"I'm just grateful Frankie drove me up here tonight. Especially in that rain."

"How is Frankie?" Violet asked.

"He's Frankie. Thought I'd traded George in for a better model. Turns out they all come with headaches." Lily looked at Daisy and quipped, "Remember that, if you're ever fool enough to marry."

Another time, Violet might have pressed Lily about her discontentment—asked questions, offered advice—but not tonight. Tonight, her mind wandered its own path. "I made the bed up in my room for the two of you."

"I won't sleep," Lily said. "And knowing Frankie, he's already conked out on the couch."

"He is," Daisy said. "As soon as you went upstairs, he turned on the TV. They started playing the National Anthem, and he fell asleep before the test pattern came on. I threw the afghan over him."

The room fell silent, each woman lost in her own thoughts.

"Almost," Violet murmured. She closed her eyes to concentrate.

"Almost what?" Lily asked.

"It's on the tip of my tongue." Violet shook her head as she tried to remember, and then a look of delight spread across her face. She opened her eyes and singsonged, "*I asked my pa a simple thing.*"

"That's it!" Lily said. "That's the poem!"

"*Where do the holes in doughnuts go?*" Violet recited, then stalled.

Lily continued: "*Pa read his paper, then he said . . .*"

The sisters grinned at each other and finished the verse together: "*Oh, you're too young to know.*"

"This is priceless." Daisy clapped.

Now that their memories had been jogged, they managed the next verse in unison:

I asked my ma about the wind,
"Why can't you see it blow?"
Ma thought a moment, then she said,
"Oh, you're too young to know."

"Don't stop now," Daisy pressed.

"That's as far as I can go," Violet said.

Lily offered a hint: "It's the one about the jam." When Violet shook her head, Lily finished the piece:

Now, why on earth do you suppose
They went and spanked me so?
Ma asked, "Where is that jam?" I said,
"Oh, I'm too young to know."

As all three sat laughing, Violet asked, "How did you remember?"

"That's the verse where his mouth gets him into trouble. Story of my life!" Lily winked.

Grace's body twitched, and everyone jumped up.

"Maybe we're being too loud," Daisy said.

"Not at all." Violet wet a washcloth and touched it to her mother's lips. Although unconscious, she opened her mouth like a baby bird and sucked the moisture. "She likes to be in on the fun."

Instinctively, the women took each other's hands and bowed their heads. Violet started them off on the Twenty-third Psalm: "*The Lord is my shepherd . . . I shall not want.*"

Lily and Daisy joined in: "*He maketh me to lie down in green pastures: He leadeth me beside still waters . . .*"

Two verses later, they each squeezed the hands they were holding as they continued their prayer: "*Yea, though I walk through the valley of the shadow of death, I will fear no evil: for Thou art with me . . .*"

Just before sunrise, the laughter, tears, and prayers gave way to exhaustion. Violet and Lily dozed in their chairs. Daisy bent forward on the bench to lay her head on the foot of the bed.

Outside, the milkman pounded up the front porch steps, the bottles clanking inside their wire crate. Grace slowly opened her eyes and caught a glimpse of Owen filling the doorframe. "There you are," she said, smoothing her nightgown and crossing her arms. "I was starting to wonder."

Not yet, my love. He blew her a kiss and disappeared.

Grace looked around the room. "All my girls," she rasped, rousing everyone from their sleep. "What a wonderful surprise."

CHAPTER THIRTY-THREE

"You gave us quite a scare." Dr. Gustitis placed his stethoscope on Grace's chest one more time and listened. "I'm happy to report the heart's still ticking."

"Glad to hear it," Grace said, her voice still scratchy but growing stronger. "Now how about that egg?"

"Daisy's frying one up right now," Violet said, smoothing her mother's hair.

"And after that, young lady, I want you to rest." The doctor began packing up his medical case. "I'll be back in the morning to check on you."

"Assuming I'm still here."

"Mother," Lily said, "don't talk like that."

Dr. Gustitis smiled. "Mrs. Morgan, you'll probably outlive us all."

"Breakfast," Daisy announced, as she walked in the room carrying her mother's round tray with the hand-painted roses.

Lily plucked a pair of milk-glass, slipper-shaped salt and pepper shakers off the tray. She ran her fingers across the word *Scranton* painted in gold on both buckles. When she tipped the shoes back, she saw that the same hand had painted *1866* on the bottom of the salt and *1916* on the pepper.

Grace leaned forward to see better. "Your father bought those as a souvenir the year of the semi-centennial. After he took us to that parade. Lily, you were too young, but Violet, you were there."

"Yes I was." Violet loved those shakers and that day.

"They're yours now," Grace said to Lily. "A little something to remember me by."

Violet stiffened. *She'd* been the one at that parade. Those shakers were hers to pass on to Daisy. They held no sentiment for Lily.

"Oh, Mother, you mean it?" Lily said.

Violet swallowed her objections.

"Of course I mean it." Grace sat up a little taller. "Now where's that egg?"

Daisy set the tray on the nightstand. "Right here," she said, tucking a napkin into the collar of her grandmother's nightgown and kissing her cheek.

"She's got her appetite," Dr. Gustitus proclaimed. "That's a good sign."

Grace turned her ear to a sudden blast of bouncy music coming up through the floor vents. "I'm missing my programs."

"Looney Tunes." Lily rolled her eyes. "Frankie's favorite."

"A grown man," Grace said, shaking her head.

"It's Saturday, Mother." Violet pushed back the curtains and opened the windows to a beautiful blue sky. "Your shows aren't on today." She threw a worried look at the doctor.

"Says who?" Grace replied. "What about Lawrence Welk? He'll be on tonight. And I like that Edward R. Murrow fellow. He always gets me thinking."

"No flies on you, Mrs. Morgan." The doctor gestured toward Violet and Lily. "Walk me out?"

When they reached the bottom of the stairs, Lily called into the parlor, "Could you turn that down?" Frankie sneered but got up from the couch and lowered the volume on the television.

"How is she really?" Violet asked.

"Better than I could have imagined after last night, but she's not out of the woods. Her heart's failing. Could be next week, next month, next year. We just don't know. Make the most of the time you have with her." He reached over to the coat tree, grabbed his hat, and set it on his head. "I'll stop back tomorrow."

Violet and Lily stood on the porch long after the doctor had driven away. "Good news," Lily said. "I talked to Frankie. He said you can quit your job and he'll pay your bills."

"I'm not taking his money." Though Violet could never get a straight answer out of Lily, she was convinced Frankie was still tied up in the mob.

"It's *our* money."

"No."

"What about Mother? She can't be alone."

"I'll think of something." Violet stretched over the railing at the sound of Stanley's car chugging up the hill. As soon as he reached Mrs. Lankowski's house, he parked and ran around to the passenger side.

"Is she up for company?" the widow called over as she got out of the car.

"For you, yes," Violet said.

The widow handed Stanley her cane and took his arm. When they reached the sidewalk, she stopped and looked up at Violet. "After you called this morning, I said to Stanley, 'Take me to Mass. God answered our prayers, and I want to thank Him in person.'" She pulled herself up the porch steps with Stanley at her side. "We won't stay long," she said, a little out of breath. "I just need to lay eyes on her."

Lily held the door open. "Stay as long as you like."

"I better wait a minute before tackling more stairs," the widow said and shuffled into the parlor. "Well, Frankie Colangelo, I haven't seen you in a dog's age."

"Mrs. Lankowski." Frankie sat up on the couch and slicked back the sides of his duckbill haircut. "You don't look a day over forty."

"Then you need to get those eyes checked. Now scoot over," the widow said and motioned for Stanley to sit next to her. Instead, he kneeled down on one knee near the steps to pet Archie.

Lily plopped into Grace's chair. "I'm glad you're here," she said to the widow. "Maybe you can talk some sense into her." She hooked her thumb toward Violet, who was taking the seat behind the folding table.

"What's the problem?" the widow asked.

"No problem," Violet said.

"Frankie here offered to support my sister, so she could be around for Mother, but she's not having it."

"Violet's a proud woman," the widow explained.

"Too proud, if you ask me." Lily frowned. "Who's going to watch my mother? She can't be left alone."

"Do I get a say in this?" Violet asked.

"If you won't quit that job," Lily threw up her hands, "at least let us pay for someone to sit with her during the day."

"Hmm." The widow cast her eyes toward Violet and spoke confidentially, as if no one else in the room could hear her: "It's not like *you'd* be taking his money. It'd be your mother."

"Exactly," Lily said, either unaware of or unconcerned about the widow excluding her from the conversation. "What do you say? Frankie and I can stay a few days to help out until you find someone."

Frankie peered out from his paper but kept silent.

"I wouldn't know where to begin, who to hire," Violet said.

"I have an idea if you want to hear it." Everyone shifted their focus to Stanley, still kneeling near the stairs. "I know someone. Her husband lost his job when he tried to unionize the garment workers. We have a good chance of winning the case, but it'll be tied up for at least a year. She just had a baby, and they could sure use the money."

Violet cleared her throat. "The Green Stamps woman?"

"Yes." Stanley dropped his gaze. "Mrs. Hinkley."

The room fell quiet while Violet mulled the suggestion. "Only if she brings that baby of hers."

"I imagine she'd have to," Stanley said.

"Good. It'll do wonders for Mother to have a little one around." Violet smiled at Stanley. "Thank you," she said, "for everything."

* * *

By dinnertime, the plan was set. Stanley had called to say he'd talked to Mrs. Hinkley, and she could begin on Thursday morning. Lily and Frankie would stay through her first day and drive home that night, ahead of the hurricane brewing on the heels of Connie. Hurricane Diane. She looked to be fizzling out, but Frankie didn't want to risk driving through another storm. In the meantime, Grace, who was snoozing again, had started getting some color back in her cheeks.

"Soup's on," Violet called out while plating the pot roast.

"Smells delicious." Lily inhaled deeply as she poured the iced tea.

Frankie sauntered into the kitchen without bothering to turn the television off. "I'm so hungry I could eat a horse." He rubbed his belly.

Daisy glanced out the sun-filled window as she mashed the potatoes at the sink. "Your geraniums have certainly perked up."

"A soaking rain does wonders," Violet said.

"Goes to show, we can all benefit from a good stiff drink." Frankie smirked, even as Lily threw her elbow in his side. "What? Violet knows I'm kidding."

Violet put on a smile. Yes, Frankie had a way of getting under her skin, but if he could drop everything to drive up to Scranton, she could at least try to get along with him. "Anybody need anything before we sit down?"

"Vi, you outdid yourself," Lily said, as they all took their seats.

Violet's eyes traveled around the table. Her daughter had Frankie's coloring and height, but everything else was Lily. Same nose. Same eyes. Same facial expressions. It's a wonder people hadn't long ago figured out Daisy's parentage. Same sense of style too. Both women had put on pedal pushers and colorful blouses, while Violet hadn't yet changed out of her housedress from the night before.

"Who wants to say the blessing?" she asked.

"You do it," Lily said. "I love to hear a proper grace."

"If by proper you mean *long*," Frankie smirked at Daisy, "then your mother's your girl." When no one laughed, he said, "What? Violet knows I'm pulling her leg."

Violet put on her smile again, but it was less generous this time. "Let's join hands . . . Dear Lord, thank you for giving us more time with Mother. If possible, Lord, allow her to see her roses again before taking her home. And thank you for bringing Lily and Frankie safely through the storm, so Mother could wake up surrounded by all our love.

"And Dear Lord, thank you for this food and the hands that have prepared it. As we nourish our bodies, let us also nourish our souls. Teach us to lead with kindness at home and in the world. Lord, we spend our imperfect lives benefiting from your mercy and grace. Let us follow your example and extend those same blessings to others.

"Dear Lord, please lift our spirits and heal our bodies. Help us to always find joy in our days and you in our hearts.

"In Jesus's name we pray. Amen."

"Amen," Lily and Daisy repeated while Frankie made the sign of the cross.

"Beautiful," Lily said. "Mother would be proud."

Frankie took a few scoops of mashed potatoes and passed the bowl. "Well," he said, "I think we dodged a bullet."

"I have to agree," Violet said. "I really thought we were going to lose her."

"Oh, sure." Frankie pointed to the television in the other room. "But I was talking about Hurricane Connie."

Violet took a deep breath. "If you want more iced tea, there's another pitcher in the refrigerator."

Daisy pushed the onions off her piece of pot roast. "I heard the Carolinas didn't fair too well."

"Nothing more powerful than water," Violet said, as she watched Lily scrape the onions off her plate too, and onto Frankie's.

"I still think about the flood of '42. Never saw anything like it," Lily said. "The Flats in South Side got clobbered."

"That's where Mickey lives," Daisy said to her mother. "Over where Roaring Brook and the Lackawanna River meet."

"Who?" Violet responded.

"The little bowlegged boy who takes dance lessons from me."

"Dance lessons?" Frankie cringed. "A boy?"

"Yes, a boy." Daisy glared at Frankie, daring him to say another word. Lily mirrored the expression before returning to the original conversation: "Parker Street got hit pretty hard too, as I remember."

Violet nodded. "That's right. Down where the church used to baptize its members."

"Wait a minute," Frankie said. "You two got dunked in the Lackawanna?" He pinched his nose as if blocking a bad smell.

"That was well before our time." Violet glanced at her reflection in the chrome bread box and could see the irritation in her expression.

"Who was it that ended up on their roof?" Lily asked, not seeming to notice Violet's mood.

Violet consciously relaxed her face. "Susie and Eddie Hopkins."

"Members of our congregation," Lily clarified for Frankie's benefit. "As the house started flooding, they kept moving higher and higher till they got to the attic. Once the water pushed up through those floorboards, Eddie used an axe to chop a hole in the roof, and they all climbed out on to it. Even the dog."

"I saw that photo," Frankie said, his mouth full. "The one of them sitting on the peak of that house."

"*Everyone's* seen it," Daisy said.

"The *Tribune* republishes it whenever we get a hard rain," Violet said.

"So did they make it?" Frankie asked.

"Thankfully," Violet stifled a yawn, suddenly wondering how

long it had been since she'd slept, "someone came by in a rowboat and picked them up. The dog too."

"I'd have been terrified." Daisy shivered.

"You never were much for water." Lily spooned more carrots onto Frankie's plate and then her own.

"It's amazing what you can do when you're scared enough." Violet rubbed her tired eyes.

"Let's hope so," Daisy said as she got up and poured more iced tea.

By Thursday, Grace had regained some of her strength. The widow had asked Stanley to cut down one of her old canes, and with a little practice, Grace had started using it to get around. Not too far, but far enough to have her meals downstairs again and sit out on the porch. She tired easily, so she napped more often, went to bed earlier, slept a little later. Still, her mind was sharp, considering, and she seemed happy to be in the world.

With Lily and Frankie in town the last four days, Violet had been staying in her mother's room, but she'd finally be able to sleep in her own bed, and for that she was grateful. She needed to get her house back. Her life. Some sort of routine.

Suitcases packed, Lily and Frankie stood in the parlor saying their goodbyes to Violet and Daisy. Six o'clock and Grace was already asleep upstairs.

"We'll be back for Labor Day weekend." Lily embraced her sister.

"Anytime. And don't you worry," Violet said, "I'll take good care of her."

"You always do." Lily pulled Daisy into a hug. "And you. Keep an eye on your mother. Make sure she gets some sleep. She's exhausted."

"I will," Daisy said.

Frankie peeled Lily away from her family. "Time to shove off," he said. "Rain's already started."

"Not a drop all summer. Now two storms in a week," Violet said. "Be careful." She and Daisy followed them out to the porch and watched until the car was out of sight.

"Do you have a few minutes?" Violet asked.

Daisy looked at her mother's serious expression and half laughed. "Uh-oh. What did I do?"

Violet shook her head. "I just want to talk to you about something."

"Okay. I actually have some news of my own."

Violet's heart dropped. *What did Zethray say about secrets?* "Let's go inside."

As soon as they sat down on the couch, Violet spied the milk-glass salt and pepper shakers on the coffee table. "Lily's going to be kicking herself."

"Maybe she'll remember before they get too far."

"Frankie's not the type to turn around unless it benefits him. She can get them next time." Violet paused for courage. "So . . ."

Daisy blurted, "Me first."

Violet's stomach tightened, bracing for a punch.

"I met someone."

Violet's face froze. "Are you expecting?"

"No!" Daisy shrieked. "Why would you say that?"

"Because you said you had bad news."

"I said I had news. Not *bad* news. I'm not pregnant."

"But if you were," Violet's features and voice softened, "we'd get through it."

"But I'm not."

"We can tackle anything together."

"Are you hearing yourself?"

"All I'm saying is it wouldn't be the end of the world. That baby would be loved. Love is what makes a family. Nothing else."

"You really need to get some sleep."

"So it's not bad news?"

Daisy waited a beat. "It's news."

Violet took a breath. "Let's start again. You met someone. Tell me about him. What does he do?"

"He plays piano."

Violet's body started to relax. "Of course he does. What else?"

"He loves me."

"And?"

"Mom, I love him with my whole heart."

"What's his name?"

"Johnny. Johnny Cornell."

"I'd like to meet this Johnny-Johnny Cornell."

"You will. Soon." Daisy sprang up from the couch like a jack-in-the-box. "He asked me to marry him." She gritted her teeth. "And I said yes." Her fists flew to her mouth as she braced for her mother's reaction.

Violet let the words wash over her. "Is he good to you?"

"Very."

"Then that's all that matters." Violet's eyes watered. "Don't worry," she said, opening her arms for a hug. "They're happy tears."

"Wait," Daisy said. "There's something else."

"Okay . . . ?"

"He's sweet and kind and honest and loving and true," Daisy took a breath and scrunched her eyes, "and Negro."

Violet gasped at the sight of Frankie filling the doorway. "God as my witness," he hissed, "no daughter of mine is marrying a spook."

CHAPTER THIRTY-FOUR

"GET OUT!" GRACE BARKED at Frankie from the top of the stairs. "You'll not bring that poison into my house."

Her rebuke seemed to have punctured Frankie's rage. His shoulders dropped, his fists unclenched, but his lip stayed curled in contempt. "You're all alike." He spied the salt and pepper shakers on the coffee table.

Grace inhaled deeply, puffing up her frail body. "Not. One. More. Step." With each word, her features grew more menacing.

Archie bounded into the parlor and growled.

"Go to hell," Frankie sneered. "The whole pious lot of you."

Grace aimed her cane. "You first," she said, as he stomped back out and into the rain.

Gripped with anguish, Violet made her confession. About Frankie getting Lily pregnant. About accompanying her sixteen-year-old sister to the Good Shepherd Infant Asylum. About being with her when she gave birth to Daisy. Holding her. Claiming her. Never looking back. About a mother's love for her daughter, because, "God strike me dead if I'm lying," Daisy was her daughter.

"I never should have made that promise to Lily." Pressed up against the arm of the couch, Violet rubbed circles into her palm. "And I was going to tell you. Then Frankie . . ." Her voice trailed off. "It was *my* place to tell you." She stiffened with indignation.

"Then why didn't you?" At the other end of the couch, Daisy's eyes hardened into blue stones.

For so many reasons. Good reasons. Violet struggled to think of one.

"That's how things were," Grace said. "What choice did we have?" Her body looked deflated in her button-backed armchair.

"I'm so sorry." Violet took a few stuttering breaths. "About not telling you." She sat up straight. "But know this: I'm not sorry for taking you. I'd do it all over again, given the chance. You've been my greatest blessing." She leaned toward Daisy, who flinched. "But I'd tell you the truth from the start. I promise you that."

"Well," Daisy said with biting brightness, "as long as you promise."

"You're mad at me. I understand," Violet said. "But I love you, and that's never going to change."

"Everything's changed," Daisy yelped.

"How can I make this right?" Violet started to cry.

"Did Dad know?"

"Yes."

"Who else?"

"Your grandmother." Violet blinked hard but the tears kept coming. "The widow. Stanley."

"Stanley?" Daisy's mouth opened into a perfect O. "So, everyone in town but me? Ha! Wait till I tell Johnny."

"Johnny?" The quick shift in focus befuddled Violet.

"Yes, Johnny. The man I'm going to marry."

Violet looked at Daisy and blurted, "You can't."

"What did you say?"

Grace piped up: "One conversation at a time."

"No." Daisy locked eyes with her mother. "I want to hear this."

"It'll be too hard You'll ruin your life." Violet pulled at her lip. "Mixed marriages don't work. The world's not ready."

"The world or *you?*"

"That's not fair. I've spent my life being judged. I'm only trying to spare you some pain. I want you to have it easy."

"It's not about what *you* want," said Daisy.

"I'm your mother."

"Are you?"

"That's enough." Grace thumped the arm of her chair. "Daisy, you're my pride and joy, but you have no idea what this woman sacrificed for you."

"I'm sorry, Grandma, but whose fault is that?" Daisy stood up and grabbed her purse from the coffee table.

"Where are you going?" Violet asked, her voice soaked in misery.

"Anyplace but here," Daisy said, and marched out the door.

"What was your father's old saying for this kind of weather?" Stanley jumped over the puddles and up to the porch where Violet sat in a rocker.

"It's raining old wives and walking sticks."

"I can hear him now." Stanley sat in the rocker next to hers. "With that hint of a Welsh brogue."

"It's over." Violet's shoulders slumped.

"What?"

"Daisy knows. Never in a million years did I think Frankie Colangelo would be the one to tell. He never even wanted her."

"She knows? About Lily?"

"And she's furious with me."

"Is she here?" Stanley asked.

"Ran off. I don't know where. And it gets worse." Violet took a shaky breath. "Daisy says she's getting married."

"How is that worse?"

"To a Negro man."

"No. She can't marry him. They'll be shunned."

"Exactly. I told her it would be too hard, but she wouldn't listen. She's trying to make me out to be the bad guy here when everyone knows mixed marriages don't work."

"Mixed marriages?" Stanley stopped his rocker. "Your father used those very same words to keep *us* apart."

Violet shooed away the implication. "He was wrong about that. We both know it. But Daisy's situation is different."

"Is it?"

"He was talking about religion. Protestants and Catholics." Violet cradled her arms over her stomach. "This is different, right? I was just trying to look out for her best interests."

"And your father was trying to look out for yours. Doesn't make it right."

Violet gasped. "What did I do?"

"Talk to her."

"She won't listen. Not after tonight."

"She'll come around."

"Why would she?"

"Because you're the mountain she leans against." Surrounded by a steady beat of rain, Stanley reached over and took Violet's hand in his.

"Hold your horses!" Zethray yelled as she shuffled toward the ringing telephone on the kitchen wall. "Hello . . . Hello?"

"I'm sorry to bother you. This is Daisy." The line crackled with static. "Johnny's Daisy. May I speak to him, please?" The voice sounded far away, probably an effect of the storm. Zethray pressed the receiver hard against her ear.

"Daisy, he ran over to Stahler's Market to get me some lunch meat. He won't be long. Can I give him a message?"

"Would you ask him to call me?"

"Sure."

"At the studio," Daisy said. "He knows the number."

"As soon as he comes in. Everything all right?"

The phone went quiet for a few seconds. "If you'd just have him call me," Daisy's voice broke, "I'd appreciate it."

"Will do." Zethray stayed on the line until she heard the dial tone. Whatever reservations she had about the romance, she was worried for the girl.

* * *

Ten minutes later, Johnny kicked off his wet shoes at the front door and headed into the kitchen.

"Call Daisy," Zethray said. "At the studio."

"Did she say why?" Johnny tossed the lunch meat into the refrigerator before picking up the phone.

"Just said to call."

When Johnny started dialing, Zethray stepped out to the back porch and pulled the door shut behind her. The boy deserved a little privacy. Her nose did not need to be in his business. That's a lesson her mama had impressed upon Zethray as a child. "You have enough of your own faults," her mother had said, "without picking at someone else's."

Mama. She hadn't spoken yet, but Zethray felt sure she was working up to it. She'd started humming the occasional tune, and Zethray took comfort in humming along. Or singing when she knew the lyrics. Somewhere right now her mother was humming in time to the beat of the rain on the roof:

Let me call you sweetheart.
I'm in love with you.
Let me hear you whisper
That you love me too.

Zethray knew the song well. Clarence used to sing it to her mama when he wanted to dance with her. The day Zethray got sent outside for telling on him, she'd pulled a stool up to the kitchen window and watched them glide across the linoleum floor. Mama had tugged her neckline low, an invitation for Clarence to lose himself in her bosom as she goosed his behind, laughing. Overcome with embarrassment, Zethray had turned away.

But not immediately, she suddenly realized.

Keep the lovelight glowing
In your eyes so true . . .

Zethray stood up and looked through her own kitchen window to where Johnny should have been standing. Instead, she saw Mama grabbing Clarence's behind—and his pants pocket. When she pulled her hands back, she had two one-dollar bills crumpled in her left fist.

Zethray's eyes popped. By all accounts, Clarence had pulled a knife on a man for stealing his money, and died in the attempt.

But now, as she looked at her mother, sitting alone in that kitchen, bereft, Zethray understood why she'd taken her own life.

It was Mama who'd stolen the money back from Clarence before he'd ever left the house. It was Mama who'd gotten Clarence killed.

Kenny dropped Johnny off in front of the studio. "I'll be back to pick you up at quarter of."

That would give Johnny almost an hour to calm Daisy down before heading over to the Ron-Da-Voo in South Side for a nine o'clock set. With any luck, he'd convince her to go with him. He didn't want to leave her alone. Not in her state. "Thanks again for the ride," Johnny said before making a mad dash through the rain and into the studio.

"Daisy," he called as soon as he hit the top step. Across the room, she sat on the couch, knees to her chest, face buried in her hands. "It's going to be okay." He ran over and dropped alongside her. "None of this matters. Not really." He lifted her chin. "You're still the same beautiful girl."

"My whole life is a lie." Daisy had sounded frantic on the phone, but now her words sounded measured, resigned.

"Not us."

"My own mother didn't want me."

"*I* want you. Let's get married this weekend. We don't need

Scranton. We can to go New York, get an apartment, start making those dimpled babies."

"I'm Aunt Lily's daughter," Daisy said, her speech halting, like she was practicing another language. "Why didn't they tell me?"

"They must've had their reasons."

"What reasons?"

"I don't know. People always find reasons to feel righteous." He put his arm around her shoulder.

"I can't stay in Scranton," she said, chewing her lip.

"You don't have to."

"You know, it's crazy. Here I was feeling guilty all this time about keeping you a secret from my moth—" Daisy tried again, and the word lifted into a question: "Mother? Aunt?" She sidestepped the issue in favor of finishing her original point. "Turns out she had a secret of her own." Daisy rolled her eyes. "And a real doozy, at that."

"It didn't work out the way you'd hoped," Johnny stroked her cheek, "but I'm proud of you for telling her about us. I know that wasn't easy."

"Do you?" Daisy pulled away. "How'd your mother handle it when you told her the news?"

Johnny bristled, though he held his tongue.

"I'm sorry," she said. "None of this is your fault."

"I'm going to tell her. Soon. We'll go to Atlantic City, you and me, so I can make a proper introduction. Maybe we can get married down there."

Daisy let loose a humorless string of laughter. "And while we're at it, I can introduce you to my mother. The real one."

"I know you might not want to hear this," he said gently, "but ever since I met you, all you've done is talk about how good your mother is. I know you're hurting, but I truly believe she loves you."

"You're right." Daisy scooted to the other side of the couch. "I don't want to hear it."

"Okay." Johnny changed tack: "What can I say to make you feel better?"

"Talk to me about New York."

"That I can do." Johnny settled back against the cushions. "We'll live in one of those old brownstones with the big steps out front."

"Where?"

"Harlem, Brooklyn, anyplace you want, as long as the windows face east. There's nothing more beautiful than morning sun." Johnny caught Daisy's eye. "Almost nothing."

"And?"

"In the summers, we'll make ice cream and eat it out on the stoop."

"Where we can watch people pass by."

"All kinds. People like us too."

"But no one from Scranton." Daisy pushed his knee with her foot and let it stay there.

"Not a soul."

"Only strangers."

"And Kenny."

"Kenny?"

"I've been saving the best part." Johnny rubbed his palms together. "Kenny got us those auditions at that club in the Village. He knows the guy who runs the place. Says we're a sure thing."

Daisy tensed. "And just how long have you been saving that news?"

"Not long."

"Since the night you picked Kenny up at the train station?"

"I was going to tell you, but a lot happened. Your grandmother took sick."

"Three days later."

"You're missing the point. I won't have to go looking for a job. I already have one in the bag."

"So when you said, 'I'm not going anywhere . . .'" Daisy hesitated for an uncomfortable few seconds, "right before we made love for the first time . . . you meant you weren't going anywhere that night."

"I was planning for our future."

"Knowing I wanted to stay in Scranton." Daisy's eyes narrowed into slits.

"But that's all changed. You want to leave town. Start fresh. So do I. That's what matters now."

"Is it?"

"Look, I was doing what was best for both of us."

"You're right about one thing, Johnny Cornell. People do find reasons to feel righteous." Daisy eyed the doorway. "I think you should go."

"But I—"

Someone pounded up the steps. "I need a minute to dry off," Mickey announced as he traipsed into the studio dripping wet. "It's coming down in buckets."

"Get over here." Daisy grabbed the quilt and dried him off as best she could.

Johnny studied at the boy. "What are you doing out, little man?"

"Granny dropped her insulin needle and the glass shattered. She didn't have a spare, so I had to go to Sheeley's Drug Store for another one." He reached inside his shirt and pulled out the paper bag.

"Is she okay?" Daisy asked.

"I think so. She was acting a little funny, so I gave her some orange juice before I left. That's supposed to help when her sugar drops."

Out on the street, someone leaned on a car horn. Johnny looked out the window. "It's Kenny." He turned back to Daisy and clasped his hands together. "Be right back. I just need to tell him I'm not going."

"No," Daisy said. "Go."

"But—"

"I'm all talked out tonight." She draped the quilt over the couch. "You can do me a favor, though."

"Anything," Johnny said.

"Have Kenny drop me and Mickey off at his house. I want to look in on his grandmother."

"Sure. And we'll pick you up after we're finished playing."

"No," Daisy said, "I'll find my own ride."

"Not in this weather."

"Why don't you stay over?" Mickey said. "Granny could use the company. She gets nervous after one of her spells."

"Your granny gets nervous or *you* do?" Daisy gently asked.

Mickey blushed. "A little of both."

Daisy offered the boy a smile. "I'll stay if she'll have me." When Johnny put up his hand to protest, she shook her head. "No more. Not tonight."

"Then when?"

"Let's see what tomorrow brings," she said and turned off the lights.

CHAPTER THIRTY-FIVE

DOWN IN THE FLATS, HOUSES GROANED in response to the punishing wind and rain. Just before midnight, Mickey ran through the apartment blasting his silver pea whistle. "The river's coming!" he yelled. Daisy sprang up from the couch and ran out to the second-floor porch. Under the glow of the streetlight, the neighbors stood in a few inches of water, watching Mr. Secoolish coax his old DeSoto to life. Daisy glanced at her watch, wondering if it was too late to call home to let them know where she was, and then remembered how she'd stormed out in anger.

"Granny!"

"Stop blowing that thing, you'll wake the dead." Mickey's grandmother hurried out to the parlor and asked Daisy, "What's it looking like?"

"I'd say groundwater, Mrs. McCrae." Daisy stretched over the railing to see better. "Backed-up storm drains, most likely, but we better not take any chances." She stepped inside and slipped into her sandals. "Let's see if you and Mickey can go with Mr. Secoolish. I'll walk up the hill to the studio."

"That's a mile away," Mrs. McCrae said. "Your shoes'll get soaked."

"Least of our worries." Daisy ushered them toward the stairs.

When they reached the street, Mr. Secoolish had the car running. "Mrs. McCrae," he said, "I was just coming up to get you two."

"I knew you wouldn't forget us," Mickey's grandmother said as she slid in next to his wife. Several other neighbors immediately crammed into the car.

"We won't make it up the hill with all this weight." Mr. Secoolish eyed Bertie Heerman, the local drunk with the crooked nose, wedged against a back door. "I'll drop them off and swing around for you."

Bertie gave a thumbs-up and tumbled out of the car.

"Wait," Mrs. McCrae shouted, "where's my Mickey?"

"I'll take the next ride." Mickey slapped the trunk, signaling for Mr. Secoolish to drive.

"No!" Mrs. McCrae screamed as the DeSoto lurched up the hill.

A couple of miles away, the Ron-Da-Voo's owner hopped up on the stage and took the microphone. "Sorry to stop the party, folks. Looks like Hurricane Diane is coming for us after all. Dumped a foot of rain already, and she's not letting up. Time to go home and check your cellars." Overhead, the lights started blinking. "And stay away from the bridges, they could give out any minute."

Johnny jumped up from the piano and dashed over to the pay phone near the men's room. He dialed the studio, praying Daisy had changed her mind and gone back up there. After letting the phone ring a dozen times, he decided to call Mickey's house in spite of the late hour. "Operator, I need the number for a Mrs. McCrae on Birch Street."

"Connecting," the operator said.

Johnny tapped his fingers on the wall as he waited for the phone to ring.

The woman came back on the line: "I'm sorry, sir, that number seems to be out of service. Is there another call I can make for you?"

"Violet Davies on Spring Street," Johnny said, "and hurry."

"Johnny's on his way to get her," Violet said to Stanley. "Daisy's Johnny. His buddy is driving him over."

"And where did you say this Mickey lives?"

"Somewhere down in the Flats, near Roaring Brook."

"But it hasn't flooded so far." Stanley's voice lifted with forced optimism.

"Not yet. I told him to bring everybody here, but I don't know if she'll come."

"But she's safe." Stanley nodded at Violet, as if to get her nodding too. "That's what counts. And he knows where to find her."

"Yes." Violet rubbed her worry into her hands.

"Tell me what you want to do," Stanley said. "My car's across the street. I can try to find her right now if you get me an address."

"Let's wait to hear what Johnny has to say," she said, turning on the television for news. "He promised me he'd call."

Daisy and Mickey stood on the second-floor porch watching for Mr. Secoolish to return. "I wish you'd gone with your granny."

"I wanted to keep you company," Mickey said.

Daisy studied Bertie Heerman standing near the streetlight. The man had to be six feet tall, and he stood calf-deep in water. "We better start walking while we still can," she said as calmly as she could.

"No!" Mickey screamed. In front of them, Roaring Brook heaved over its banks, flooding the streets, plunging Bertie headlong into the angry torrent before carrying him away.

Johnny hung up the phone and turned to Kenny. "I have to get to Daisy."

"Let's go." Kenny bagged his trumpet, tucked it under his arm, and pulled out his car keys.

"Roaring Brook just went over!" the Ron-Da-Voo's owner shouted, his ear pressed up to a radio at the bar. "The river's still holding, but not for long."

"We'll be right behind you," Ferdie said, waving a hand at the band. He looked around at the diehards finishing their drinks. "There's a girl needs saving. Who's coming?"

Twenty men piled into four cars and followed Kenny through the pouring rain toward the Flats. They got as far as Anthracite Plate Glass and parked at the top of the hill. That side of the road sat up higher than Mickey's house and was safe for the time being.

"There." Johnny pointed to a house on the corner of South Washington and Birch. Daisy and Mickey stood on the second-floor porch beckoning for help.

The men moved carefully on foot, and by the time they reached the middle of the four-lane road, the water was knee-high. "You can't just go in there," Kenny hollered, "the current's too strong!"

Johnny eyeballed the waterline against the house. Four, maybe five feet high.

Each man grabbed the wrist of the person in front of him, forming a human chain. At the lead, Johnny pushed through the swell, pulling the men behind him into the straightest line they could muster. As he neared the house, he saw Daisy guide the eight-year-old over the banister to a lip of porch on the other side. With the railing between them, the pair held tight to one another, waiting. Johnny pressed on as the rain fell harder and the water inched higher. A couple of feet away, he plunged forward and grabbed hold of the half-immersed porch post and looked up. Mickey let go of the railing with one hand while he fished his whistle out from under his shirt. The whoosh of rushing water kept Johnny from hearing what they were saying, but he saw the boy hand his prized possession to Daisy. She slid the chain around her neck, gave the boy a squeeze, and watched him scramble down the post and onto Johnny's back.

The water started rising faster, and Johnny felt a tug from the tether of men. "Climb down!" he screamed to Daisy, knowing his words would be lost to the punishing winds. Mickey reached his arms up as if to catch her.

Alone on that porch, shrouded by the raging storm, Daisy blew them each a gentle kiss.

Suddenly, Johnny was yanked back through the water, half

walking, half drowning, with Mickey holding on. As soon as they hit Anthracite Glass, someone shrieked, "Get to higher ground!" Drenched to the bone, the men raced up to their cars.

"Take the boy!" Johnny hollered to Kenny. "I'm going back!"

"Not without me!" Mickey shouted, locking his legs around Johnny's waist.

Just as Johnny was about to object, he felt the ground rumble under his feet. Over near the slaughterhouse at the far end of Birch, the Lackawanna River thundered over its banks, uprooting trees and telephone poles, dragging trucks and streetlights in its wake. Crackles of electricity from swinging wires lit up the night as an uncoupled boxcar smashed sideways into Mickey's house, sending it flying off its foundation. "Hold on tight, little man!" Johnny yelled as he outran the rushing water.

When they'd made it to safety at the top of the hill, Johnny lowered the boy to the ground, took his hand, and turned back around. The pair squinted through the curtain of rain and the unlit sky in search of the familiar. Instead they found a neighborhood half-drowned, rivers for roads, buildings as islands. Johnny's eyes swept past the empty spot where Mickey's house once stood, hoping to find it lodged up against another house or an embankment. He knew he'd never see Daisy again. He knew this the moment they'd started running, yet he kept searching all the same. "We have to find her."

"She's gone," Kenny said, gripping Johnny's shoulders. "She's gone."

Johnny dropped to his knees and wailed.

"You don't know that!" Mickey stared up at Kenny. "And anyways, what about the others? There must be others." He grabbed hold of Johnny's arm and started to shake him. "I saw Bertie Heerman get washed away. The guy's a louse," he cried, "but his poor wife needs him."

Johnny wiped his nose with his wet sleeve. "We're not giving up, little man." They locked eyes. "You have my word." He took a few deep breaths and sprang to his feet. "Let's round up some boats!" he called out and started leading the men uphill.

CHAPTER THIRTY-SIX

SHOULDER TO SHOULDER, RIVER AND BROOK lashed out against the folly of men who'd tried to tame them. Their waters cut a vengeful course across the Flats, exerting authority over their expanding domain.

Just a few blocks up on Maple Street, Mickey and Kenny stood in front of the junior high school, double-checking supplies in the aluminum fishing boat, a fourteen-foot four-seater Kenny had borrowed from a neighbor. Soon he'd tow it to the newly formed shoreline at the bottom of the hill.

"Flashlight?" Kenny shouted over the pounding rain.

A drenched Mickey held up a red and chrome Big Beam six-volt hand lamp. "Check."

"Life jackets?"

Mickey rooted through a box. "One."

"Rope?"

"Check."

"Both oars locked in?"

"Check." Mickey ran to the other side of the boat. "And check."

Johnny came out of the junior high school carrying two Styrofoam cups of coffee. He shouted to Kenny, "I called Daisy's mother—told her I would!"

"How'd she take it?"

"Scared. Tried to tell her not to worry. Said I was going after her." Johnny handed one of the cups to Kenny.

"Where's *my* coffee?" Mickey asked.

"You're too young," Johnny said. "Besides, we're drinking this to stay awake on the water."

"So you want me to fall asleep out there?"

"I don't want you out there at all. You're staying put. Go inside and see if someone from the Red Cross can track down your granny."

"Not a chance," Mickey said. "We've come this far together. I'm not leaving now. And besides, I've lived down here my whole life. I know this neighborhood like the back of my hand. You need me out there." He tried to shake off the rain, to no avail.

"The kid has a point," Kenny said, checking the mount on the outboard motor.

"No, he does not."

"Here." Kenny tossed the cork-filled life vest to Mickey, who eagerly buckled himself into it.

"It's too big," Johnny said.

"Only one there is."

Mickey poked his buried chin through the neck of the contraption. "Fits perfect." His arms rested over the bulky fabric with elbows jutting out like rubber hoses on either side of a gas pump.

"I don't like this," Johnny said as he tightened Mickey's straps to the point of discomfort. "Not one bit."

Choppy currents beat against the boat's aluminum hull. Kenny sat at the stern, running the motor at trolling speed to protect the propeller from debris. Mickey balanced on the edge of the seat between the oars, shining the flashlight back and forth across the water. Johnny took point at the bow, scanning for hazards, searching for people in need of rescue. Searching for Daisy, unable or unwilling to let his brain convince his heart that she was gone. "Slow down!" he yelled through the unrelenting wind and rain, carefully probing the water in front of him with an oar. He hit something solid and on closer inspection saw a chrome hood ornament poking out. "Car! Go around!"

Kenny tilted the motor up a notch and pushed the tiller for a hard left, causing the opposite side of the boat to lift out of the water. Mickey sprang up and slid across the slatted seat just as they started to roll. A few seconds later, the vessel finally surrendered to the countermotion and righted itself.

"Good thing I'm here," Mickey said.

"There!" Johnny's arm shot out. "Straight on."

Mickey aimed his light at what looked to be a small head and torso clinging to an iron fence. Kenny guided the boat within ten feet of the figure and cut the motor.

"Shove over!" Johnny shouted as he scrambled to the middle, slid the oar back into place, and began rowing.

"Hurry!" Mickey screamed as he dropped forward.

Johnny rowed till they were close enough for Kenny to grab hold of the fence. Only then could they see the figure for what it was, an old empty snowsuit, probably boxed away in someone's attic before now.

"Well, that's a relief," Kenny said.

Mickey cast his beacon twenty yards beyond the fence. "Holy hell, it's Jesus!"

Johnny and Kenny turned to find a robed man not walking on water but seemingly sitting atop it while the currents cut around him. "What the . . ." Johnny began rowing again, careful to avoid all manner of debris rushing past.

"Wait a minute." Mickey ran up to the front and trained his light on the bit of face that poked out from the covering. "That's not Jesus." He waved at the man and lost his balance. Just as he started to tumble over the bow, Johnny sprang forward, snagged a strap on the boy's life jacket, and pulled him back in.

"What're you doing?" Johnny yelled.

"It's Mr. Secoolish," Mickey said, his light now catching a glint of metal underneath the man. "He's sitting on his DeSoto."

Now a few feet away, Johnny could see the man's feet wedged into the rungs of a ladder tied to a roof rack on a mostly submerged car.

"Mickey, my boy," the man called out from the paint-splattered tarp he'd used to cover himself, "I'm hung up on a fire hydrant."

Not for long, Johnny said to himself, knowing that at any moment a downed telephone pole or some other piece of wreckage could come barreling into the back end of his car without warning. Mr. Secoolish was almost level with the boat, so Johnny rowed right up and tied onto the DeSoto's roof rack. "Careful now!" He extended his hand to the man, who then climbed aboard.

"How'd you end up out here?" Mickey asked as the man sat down.

"I went back for you and the girl and Bertie just as Roaring Brook come over," Mr. Secoolish said. "Did the other two make it out?"

Tears filled Mickey's eyes and spilled onto his rain-soaked cheeks.

Mr. Secoolish pulled the boy in. "I'm so sorry," he said, "really and truly."

I went back for you and the girl. The last two words hit Johnny like a couple of gunshots fired in succession—one to the throat, one to the heart. Equally fatal.

Nope. Johnny shook his head as he untied the rope. *Can't think about her now.* He pushed off from the car. *Later.* He rowed upstream, narrowly avoiding a cedar wardrobe being swept along in the raging waters. *Don't think.* He locked the oars into place. *Not about her eyes.* He turned toward the stern. *Her lips.* He gave Kenny the signal to press on. *Her kiss.*

The wardrobe slammed into the DeSoto, knocking it off its perch and deeper into the water.

After dropping Mr. Secoolish off on the shoreline, Johnny, Kenny, and Mickey spent the next few hours out on the water rescuing souls. A mother and child hanging out of an attic window. A couple of guys at the slaughterhouse. An elderly gentleman with two cats and a box turtle, though as Mickey pointed out, the turtle probably would have survived without their help.

They marveled as a helicopter lowered a rope to a man on a roof at what Mickey determined to be Hickory Street and brought him to safety. And they watched as a one-handed man in a nearby boat tried lassoing a drowning dog. "Well, I'll be a son of a gun!" Mickey exclaimed when the man succeeded on his third attempt and pulled the animal aboard.

But still no Daisy. Teeth clenched, eyes closed, Johnny gripped the sides of the boat, willing himself to hold back his despair as it gathered strength and pushed against hope, shouting, *She's gone! She's gone!*

"Help!" someone called out.

Daisy? His eyes now open, Johnny jumped up and grabbed the flashlight from Mickey. On the second floor of Goodman Silks, a woman stood in a doorway swinging a towel like a flag of surrender.

A woman.

Not Daisy.

Johnny dropped back on his seat and told Kenny to steer the boat in her direction.

CHAPTER THIRTY-SEVEN

HURRICANE DIANE KEPT UP ITS ONE-TWO PUNCH of wind and rain. Houses strained against the punishing current, as did mailboxes, street signs, and anything else that considered itself to be fixed in place. Some of it held. Some of it surrendered to the storm.

Bicycles. Photographs. Galvanized ash tins. Two-by-fours. Record albums. A case of Jim Beam. Roofing shingles, ladders, a brand-new refrigerator. Coal shovels, scaffolding, an outhouse door. Floor lamps, a saddle, the lid off a trash can. Suitcases, lawn mowers, two slaughterhouse steers. A wedding gown, car fender, meat grinder, seesaw. Ironing board, oil drum, football, guitar.

And Daisy.

She gasped for air as a whirlpool spit her out for the third time in as many minutes before sucking her back down toward a partially open manhole. Muscles spent, lungs on fire, she listened to the siren song. Seconds before losing consciousness, her body, independent of her will, stiffened into a bullet, and when the vortex shot her out again, Daisy landed beyond its reach, into the middle of the angry torrent.

With no fight left, she surrendered to the whims of a newly birthed tributary intent on destroying the work of human hands. Her chin barely above water, Daisy searched through the blinding rain for anything familiar. Only the charcoal night looked back at her. She blinked hard, forcing her eyes to acclimate. Up ahead, a flutter of white pierced the dark sky. A bathrobe or sheet?

Or a child's dress? Daisy squinted at what appeared to be

a little girl tucked into a shadow of something. A tree, Daisy suddenly realized in disbelief. A giant oak. She aimed her body toward a gnarled branch and managed to grab hold. As the storm kept up its assault, her feet found a foothold on a submerged limb. She wedged herself against the trunk and coughed up mouthfuls of bile and water. A minute later, still halfway immersed, she took her first full breath since being tossed off of Mickey's porch.

Overhead, the little girl in the white dress smiled. Daisy tried to speak, but her vocal cords seized up. It wouldn't have mattered, she thought, her ears now filled with the deafening tumult of destruction. And yet, inexplicably, she could hear the child start to sing:

Jesus wants me for a sunbeam,
To shine for Him each day . . .

I must be losing my mind, Daisy thought. How could she hear this little girl singing a Sunday school song over the rumble of what sounded like a hundred freight trains?

In ev'ry way try and please Him,
At home, at school, at play . . .

Forget the singing. How could a child around Mickey's age climb a tree in the middle of a flood and not ruin her white dress?

A sunbeam, a sunbeam,
Jesus wants me for a sunbeam.
A sunbeam, a sunbeam,
I'll be a sunbeam for Him.

Certain she was dying, Daisy succumbed to the madness and let the girl soothe her with another tune:

Softly and tenderly, Jesus is calling,
Calling for you and for me . . .

The child sang for what seemed like hours, hymn after hymn, the way Daisy's Aunt Daisy had done when she lay dying all those years ago. Isn't that how the story went? Her mother's sister sang hymns for three days. Numb and cold, Daisy struggled to remember. All she wanted to do was sleep. The rain slowed, and Daisy closed her eyes to dream.

Just a closer walk with Thee.
Grant it, Jesus, hear my plea . . .

That was the first song Johnny had played when he'd found Daisy's little red piano sitting out in the sun. *Let folks hear who you are,* he'd quoted his mother, looking so comical, with those long legs of his cramped under the keyboard.

Johnny Cornell, the man who'd tried to save her. She loved him for that. The man who did save Mickey. This made her love him more.

Daisy might never get to be a mother, but she'd known a mother's love and worry as she guided Mickey over that banister in the middle of the raging storm.

A mother's love. She'd learned that at home. From her own dear mother whom she adored.

A surge of warmth inched its way from Daisy's full heart to her trembling limbs. On the verge of passing out, she welcomed the relief.

The little girl stopped singing and tapped Daisy's shoulder. When she opened her eyes, a piece of moon peeked out at her from the clearing sky.

They're coming, the little girl said, *but they can't see you.*

Desperate for slumber, Daisy ignored her.

The girl poked her in time to the *putt-putt* of an approaching motor.

Only half-awake, Daisy tried to grasp the meaning of the sound. *A boat? A truck?* She closed her eyes again.

They have to hear you. The little girl poked her hard this time.

Mostly roused, Daisy tried to call out toward the sound, forgetting she'd lost her voice. She watched, stunned, as a thirty-foot duckboat passed right by them, its headlights strong enough for Daisy to read the words, *Summerlin Brothers, Good in a Pinch*, painted over a *Rocky Glen Amusement Park* banner.

The whistle! the little girl yelled as the amphibious vehicle continued up the newly formed waterway.

Daisy pulled Mickey's whistle out from inside her blouse, inhaled as deeply as her weakened lungs would allow, and blew.

Both Summerlin brothers and Bertie Heerman, whom they'd plucked off a flagpole a couple hours earlier, stood on the port side of the now anchored duckboat, staring at Daisy a few yards away. Her eyelids fluttered as her half-submerged body teetered precariously on a tree limb.

"Hang on!" the shorter brother called to her as he tried to fit a round life preserver over his shoulders. He looked at the two men on either side of him. "It doesn't fit."

"You don't wear it," the taller brother explained, "you hold onto it, so you don't sink."

The shorter brother pulled the preserver off his head, stepped into it, and wiggled it up to his waist.

"I thought it was for her," Bertie said, "so she don't drown while you're trying to save her."

The brothers shrugged as the taller one tied one end of a rope to the preserver and the other to a cleat near the bow.

"I'm going in." With the preserver around his middle, the shorter brother climbed down the ladder and pushed off the boat with enough force to cover the dozen or so feet to Daisy. As soon as he reached her, he latched onto the end of the tree limb where she'd found refuge and yelled, "I'll catch you!"

Daisy woozily slid from her perch into the water, but just as she went under, the shorter Summerlin grabbed her arm and yanked her into him. Bertie and the other brother pulled the pair back toward the ladder. It took all three of them to get her up the rungs and onto the deck of the duckboat, but as soon as she was aboard, she started to come around.

Daisy sat shivering under a blanket as the boat traveled upstream. She had no memory of the rescue or when the rain had stopped, but it had, thank God. She did remember seeing the little girl in the white dress dissolve into a million pinpoints of shimmering light as the whistle sounded. If Daisy lived to be a hundred, she knew she'd never see something so magnificent again. She'd wait to sort out whatever it really was when her mind cleared.

"You're one tough cookie," the taller brother, Frick or Frack, said as he handed Daisy another blanket. "It's going on sunrise. You musta been in that water at least six hours."

She smiled but kept her eyes trained on a pair of live horned steers tied to the other end the boat. When they seemed to stare back, she dropped her gaze. "I'll never be able to thank you," she rasped at the man, her voice barely audible.

"Don't thank us," he said. "The cows are what saved you."

Daisy looked up and whispered, "How's that?"

"Slaughterhouse is paying twenty-five bucks a head. We already had the duckboat. Got it for a steal last month. Figured, why not give wrangling a try?"

"The cows don't come along easy." The shorter brother turned away from the steering wheel long enough to show Daisy a bloody gash on his upper arm. "Can't say I blame them, though."

"Maybe we don't give them back," the tall one said. "Maybe we put them in the old barn, let them live out their days."

"They've certainly earned it," the short one said as he guided the boat out of the water, shut off the propeller, and let the six truck tires cut into the road of mud.

"It'd save us on milk," the taller brother said.

"You're a damn fool." The short one drove up the Maple Street hill and parked in front of the junior high school. "When have you known us to drink milk?" The pair eyed each other and snorted.

Bertie pulled a flask out of his shirt and took a long swig. "They make a lot more sense when I'm drunk."

A fireman slapped the side of the vehicle. "What've you got?"

"A girl," Bertie hollered from the truck bed. "You might wanna grab the wheelchair."

Daisy tried to stand, but after all those hours in the tree, her legs and arms still shook like Jell-O.

"Whoa, Nellie," the tall one said. "Let the Red Cross give you a hand. That's what they're here for."

"All set!" the fireman yelled from the street.

Frick or Frack scooped Daisy up in his arms and handed her over the side. "They still giving out cigarettes to the volunteers?"

"Sure are," the fireman said, as he grabbed hold of a blanketed Daisy and lowered her into the wheelchair.

Since she still couldn't speak above a whisper, she tipped her face up to the three men in the duckboat and clasped her hands in gratitude.

"You're mighty welcome," the tall one said, and saluted. "Summerlins. Good in a pinch."

The fireman started to push the chair up to the school's front doors, but Daisy motioned for him to turn her around. With the sun rising behind them, she wanted to look down at the Flats, to see in the light of day what she'd suffered through in the dark.

Her breath caught at the magnitude of the devastation. House after house after house, beaten and drowned. Businesses too. Steigmaier Brewing. Belinski's Garage. Gallagher's Café. Rescuers rowed or motored up and down city streets that had transformed into streams while residents stood on redrawn shorelines, contemplating the power of water. And covering their mouths and noses against the stench. Hurricane Diane may have gathered her punishing winds to use against another town, farther up the coastline, but even this morning's breezes were enough to carry the smell. A smell that reminded Daisy of fishing with her father so many years ago.

He'd trained her up right. She could put her own worm on the hook, take her own fish off the line without getting finned, and clean her own catch for dinner. He'd always have her throw all the heads and innards into a pile in the woods for the animals, and sometimes she'd come across them later in the day when she and the Wilson twins were out playing cowboys. The stink of rot would set her back on her heels, same as now.

Her eyes lifted beyond the horizon to the morning sky. A cloudless backdrop against the ruin. A blue-white balm for the heart. A promise of hope, even without the rainbow.

"That's enough," Daisy whispered, patting the arms of the chair. The fireman swung her toward the school. She lowered her eyes to avoid the glare of the sun and caught a pair of muddied Keds running toward her.

"We've been looking all night for you!" Mickey cried as he threw himself on Daisy's lap and hugged her. "We just came back to see if Granny showed up yet, and here you are." He squeezed her tighter. "Our hearts were broken. We found ten people with Kenny's boat, but none of them was you."

Daisy tipped the boy's head back. "I knew I'd see you again." She reached for his whistle. "You saved my life with this."

Mickey beamed.

The sun's rays pulsed more brightly, blinding Daisy to the scene surrounding her. As she lifted a hand to her brow for relief, a figure stepped in front of the light, sparing her eyes. *Johnny*. Mickey scrambled off her lap as Johnny pulled her out of the chair and into his arms.

"Tell me you're real," he said.

"I'm real."

"I love you."

"I know. I really do." She squeezed him as hard as her tired arms would allow. "I love you too."

"I thought I'd lost you. My life was over. Nothing mattered without you."

Daisy noted the weight of Johnny's arms around her. The sound of his heartbeat. The love in his glistening eyes. "*Everything* matters," she said.

Inside the junior high school, Violet washed cups and saucers in the back of the cafeteria while Zethray dried. They'd shown up after Johnny had called each of them to report Daisy missing. As soon as Zethray saw Violet, she apologized for not mentioning her connection to Johnny sooner. "I didn't think it was my place."

"We're all doing our best," Violet had said and hugged her. "I'm happy to have a friend here."

At first they'd sat in the gymnasium with all the other waiting families, but soon enough they'd migrated to the kitchen, both needing something to do with their hands.

"So you really don't have any kind of feeling about this?" Violet asked as she set another cup and saucer in the dish drainer. "No voice telling you where she is?"

"Doesn't work that way." Zethray dried each dish and stacked them on the table with the others. "They tell me what they want me to know. Be real nice if they wanted me to know how to find her, though."

"But you're not feeling heavy like she's—" Violet stopped speaking.

"Crossed over already? Wish I could say I had a feeling one way or the other, but I'm as clueless as you are."

"It must be hard."

"What's that?"

"Not being able to count on your gift in times like these."

"Better to count on our faith." Zethray reached over and squeezed Violet's wet hand.

"You're a comfort. I don't know what I'd do without you here."

Behind them, Stanley clomped into the room, defeated and wet. He'd been out on the water all night with Mrs. Hinkley's husband, Howie, and her brother, Carl, who owned a boat. They'd rescued half a dozen people and the same number of dogs, but no Daisy. "Nothing yet," he said before Violet had a chance to turn around and see the disappointment in his face. "Not giving up though. Just grabbing a cup of coffee."

Violet's shoulders slumped, but she kept at the dishes.

"I don't suppose you ran into Johnny," Zethray said.

"Not that I know of, but if you want me to go back to the gym and ask around, I'd be happy to."

"Drink your coffee," Zethray said. "He'll find us when he knows something."

"Mom!" Daisy called out in as loud a voice as her hoarse throat would allow.

Violet gripped the front of the sink and slowly turned, knowing her legs would give out if her ears had deceived her. "Daisy?" At the sight of her daughter coming through the door in a wheelchair, Violet slid to the floor. "My baby!"

Daisy threw off the blanket, bent forward, and hugged her mother.

"My baby, my baby, my baby." Violet leaned back without letting her go. "Let me look at you. Are you hurt?"

"I'm fine. Exhausted," Daisy rasped, her lips trembling as she spoke, "but none the worse for wear."

"God is good." Violet glanced at Zethray, then up toward the ceiling with a quick prayer of thanks. "Mighty good," she said. A moment later, unbridled sobs started rolling through her. "I'm so sorry." She buried her face in Daisy's shoulder.

"I know."

"I. Never. Meant. To. Hurt. You." Each word preceded another heaving breath. "Truly."

"I know." Daisy patted her mother's back till her breathing evened out. Once Violet calmed down, Daisy held her at arm's length. "I love you. Everything else can wait."

"Not everything." Violet pulled herself up and studied the man standing behind the wheelchair. Tall, dark, and soaked to the skin.

"Mrs. Davies." Johnny let go of the push handles and took a soggy step toward her. Though covered in mud from the knees down, his doting glances at Daisy belied the hardships he'd surely endured out on that water.

"Johnny," Violet said, throwing her arms around him. "Thank you. Thank you. Thank you. You saved our girl."

"I'm afraid I didn't." Johnny dropped his head. "Not from lack of trying." He tugged the blanket back over Daisy's shoulders as he spoke. "We searched for her all night, but in the end—"

Daisy jumped in: "It's a long story. I'll tell it after I've slept."

"You're a good man, Johnny. You tried," Violet said.

"He is a good man." Daisy took her mother's hand. "Now let's go home."

CHAPTER THIRTY-EIGHT

VIOLET ENDED HER CALL WITH DAISY and dialed Zethray's number. "They got there safe and sound."

"Thanks for keeping me posted," Zethray said. "Now let's just hope she remembers to take it easy while they're down there."

"She told me she was up to the trip. Complained about a sore arm, but that's from the typhoid shot. Still, it's only been four days."

"At least we know she's in good hands with Johnny," Zethray said. "And Kenny's car can make the trip to Atlantic City and back again."

Violet's gaze settled on the piece of trim on the kitchen doorway, where Daisy's heights had been marked off in pencil. "Back for how long?"

"How do you mean?"

Violet pulled a chair up to the phone and sat down. "They're talking about moving to New York City after the wedding."

Zethray went quiet for a moment. "I hope they know what they're getting into."

"They don't," Violet said, and both women laughed. "But they're in love. I'll give them that."

"I will say this," Zethray reasoned, "it's not unheard of around here, but they'll stick out like sore thumbs. A big city might be better for them."

"Better isn't the same thing as good."

"Don't I know it." On the other end of the phone, Zethray sucked in a breath through clenched teeth.

"They're young. They don't want to hear it. And Johnny's a good man. All we can do is love them."

"That's the truth," Zethray said. "Will she see Lily while she's there?"

"I asked. She's not ready yet." Violet cradled the receiver between her neck and shoulder so she could pick up the slipper-shaped salt and pepper shakers Lily had left behind. "Said they're only going to visit Johnny's mother this time." She ran her thumbs across the word *Scranton* painted in gold across each milk-glass shoe buckle. "And give her a hand. The hurricane dumped a few feet of water in her cellar."

"At least they don't have to worry about missing work. How long is the mayor shutting down the city?"

"A week. Speaking of the mayor . . ." Violet set the shakers on the counter and pressed the receiver closer to her ear. "Hold on, Zethray." She listened harder. "Myrtle, is that you? Myrtle, I can hear that cuckoo clock of yours chiming in the background. Hang up the—" The phone clicked off and the clock with it.

"Every neighborhood has a Myrtle." Zethray chortled. "So you were saying."

"I was just going to ask what Mayor Hanlon's doing about your water situation."

"They brought in tankers. I have a couple of gallon jugs here. When they're empty, I set them on the porch and the neighborhood boys fill them for me. How 'bout you? I imagine you still have tap water up in North Scranton."

"We do," Violet said. "Has to be boiled for ten minutes, but there's others worse off. Did you see they found two bodies in Scranton?"

"Read it in the paper," Zethray said, "and they're still finding bodies from that summer camp in the Poconos. Over thirty dead and counting. God rest their souls."

"So much grief. That's why I'll never complain about having to boil water. Only thing is, I have a tricky back burner that needs watching."

"You want to keep an eye on that."

"I do." Violet pulled at the coil of phone cord. "I was wondering. You wouldn't want to come over here for dinner tomorrow night, would you? I could ask Stanley to pick you up."

"He can drive without that hand?"

"He drives real good."

"Well, isn't that something," Zethray said.

"I just thought since you don't have running water . . ." When Zethray still didn't respond to the invitation, Violet added, "And you don't have to go to work the next day."

"That's true." Zethray spoke the words slowly as if buying time while considering her answer.

"Think about it."

"I'll bring my corn bread," Zethray declared.

"Wonderful. Six o'clock?"

"Six is fine. And next time you'll come here. Bring Daisy. She must have questions about that little girl."

"I'd say so. I know I do."

"Haven't seen her and that pretty white dress since before the flood," Zethray said. "But that's not a bad sign. Could be she did what she came to do and went on home. Time will tell. Truth is," she dropped her voice, "I kind of miss her."

"But your mother's still around?"

"She is," Zethray said.

"Has she spoken?"

"Not yet. Then again, Mama never did do anything till she was good and ready."

"She will. I'll bet she was just waiting for the storm to pass, so she'd have your full attention."

"Funny. I had the same thought."

A delivery truck pulled up in front of Violet's house and started to unload. "I'm going to have to call you back. Someone's dropping something off. Must have the wrong address."

"Go," Zethray said. "I'll see you tomorrow. And thank you for the invite."

Both women hung up and Violet headed out to her front porch. "What in the—"

"Where do you want it?" a man yelled up from the road with a brand-new electric range strapped to a dolly.

"I didn't order . . ."

With Stanley by her side, the widow walked past the truck and pointed her cane at the house. "You'll need to take the old one out first," she told the man. "Go around back. The doorway's wider."

Violet scowled at Stanley. "You know I can't accept—"

Stanley drew an *X* over his heart. "I had nothing to do with this."

"This is my doing," the widow called out, "and I don't want to hear a word about it. It's my gift to your mother, so she doesn't gas herself again." She pulled herself up the porch steps. "If you're lucky, she'll let you use it," she said as she limped into the house.

Violet dropped into one of the rockers and gestured for Stanley to take the other. "How'd she even find a stove? The whole city's shut down."

"You know Babcia," Stanley said. "She always knows a man."

"Yes she does."

A monarch butterfly with colorful wings swooped onto Violet's geraniums. Weeks earlier, she'd given them up for dead, but now, revived by the recent rains, fists of scarlet buds defied her expectations, still blooming in spite of the late season. Still attracting butterflies.

"I'm not looking to be saved," Violet said.

Stanley shifted in his rocker to face her. "What are you looking for?"

"I don't know." Violet touched the quarter-sized age spot near her left temple. "I'm scared."

"That makes two of us." Stanley reached in his pocket. "I've wanted to give this to you for a long time."

"No," Violet said, "I'm not ready."

Stanley uncurled his fingers. Violet's valedictorian medallion rested in his palm. "I think this belongs to you."

Stunned, she picked up the gold medal and ran her finger over the date. *Class of 1923.* "How did you . . ."

"I always intended to give it back," Stanley said. "Just took me a little longer than expected."

"I didn't think I'd ever see this again." Violet turned it over in her hand.

"Wait a minute," Stanley said. "What did you mean when you said you're not ready?"

"Never you mind, Stanley Adamski." Violet kept her eyes on the medallion.

"Did you think I had a ring?"

Violet blushed. "Everything's crazy here today. Daisy's off to Atlantic City. Someone's delivering a stove I didn't order."

Stanley rubbed his chin. "Interesting."

"What?"

"You said you're not ready."

Violet's eye narrowed. "Don't go looking for something that's not there."

Stanley smiled. "I can wait."

"I like how things are," Violet said. "I'm finally learning to take care of myself, and it feels good."

"Can't we take care of each other?"

"I don't know." Violet stood up and walked to the edge of the porch.

"It's good to have you back in my life." Stanley got his rocker going at an easy pace. "That's enough for now."

The deliveryman came around from the back with the old stove on the dolly. Violet's stove. Her mother-in-law's stove before that. It had served them well over all these years, but, yes, it was time for a change.

Violet kept her eyes forward but cast her voice in Stanley's direction: "There's a dinner dance next Saturday night at the Jermyn Hotel."

The creak of Stanley's rocker slowed. "Is that so?"

"In the Arabian Ballroom." She tried for a casual tone. "Have you ever been?"

"Violet Morgan, are you asking me out on a date?"

"That all depends on how you answer."

Stanley beamed. "Nothing in this world I'd rather do than dance with you."

EPILOGUE

I'm gonna talk with the Prince of Peace,
Down by the riverside . . .

The moment I heard about my Clarence, I knew I'd follow him to glory. Guilt played a role, but it was mostly Grief. Of course, you don't lay a burden like that at your child's feet. You carry it with you. A mama can't just up and say, "I didn't want to go on living without him." That's of no help. Not at first.

But you're grown now, Zethray, and between you and me, that was the truth of it. Lord, I loved that man.

Then the second I saw myself lying in that river, I cried out. There ain't no relief in leaving your baby behind. That's disrespecting yourself 'cuz she's a part of you. What's done is done, but the knowledge sure weighs heavy.

I still don't know how to make sense of it except to say Grief knew my ways. That trickster with his thorned teeth and burred eyeballs, he'd watched me over the years. He'd seen what I'd already given up for love. My joy of reading. My big laugh. My bigger opinions.

I once knew a man who told me I'd be beautiful if I just kept my stomach pulled in. That's a thing that's harder than it sounds. Takes some of your breath away, but you can get used to it. I did. Keep it up long enough, you come to think of it as breathing, in the same way you start believing sacrifice is love.

But then you meet a man like Clarence who asks your opinion and brings you books and kisses your soft belly. A man who prides himself on getting you to laugh so hard your sides start hurting. In the middle of all that, you forget you ever called anything else love.

So when Clarence died, Grief got right in my ear, reminding me what I'd given up for lesser men. Telling me how my husband deserved a far bigger sacrifice.

Then he showed me that bridge.

Now, Daughter, here's what I want you to know. Grief *will* come calling. He always does, but if you hold on long enough, the sun will shine again. God set His bow in the clouds for a reason. That's not to say Grief won't keep after you. He will. Best to get ahead of him when you can. And when you can't, sit with him a spell. Just, not too long. Set yourself on a hard chair and heed the discomfort when it comes. That's how you find your way back to living.

The End

Acknowledgments

"Vaccinated with a Victrola needle." That's what my grandfather used to say when I'd pepper him with questions. Thank goodness he encouraged my curious nature, because all these years later, I cannot write without asking questions. Lots of them. Too many.

As such, I owe a debt of gratitude to Valerie Black, Shari Chambers, Cathy Hardaway, Zethray Hudson, Glynis Johns, Jeff Mackie, Jason Smeltzer, Doug Smith, and Gail Waters. You graciously allowed me to interview you about Scranton's history, culture, music scene, and so much more. The book and I are better for having met you.

And thank you, James "Chimesy" Williams. Years after your passing, I discovered your *Northern Fried Chicken* books at the Albright Memorial Library, and your stories sparked my imagination.

I'm also grateful to Jolene Lane, Maxine Libenson, and Pat Riley. All of you gave me stories and details that found their way into *Rain Breaks No Bones*.

And many thanks to Jaclyn Fowler and Aileen Mack for your powerful insights into the other side.

Laurel Radzieski, thank you. Every time I needed a little inspiration, I'd read the "spontaneous poem" you wrote for me as prayer.

Thanks to Jeff Aukscunas, Michael Bonser, Jane Baugess, Carol Kochis, Ann Lehman, Kim Mancini, Christopher West, Roxanne West, Barbara Holmes, and Maria Trozzolillo, for answering still more questions. Maria, I'm sorry the book took me so long to write.

And to Dawn Leas. I'm grateful for all the times you walked across the hall for brainstorm sessions. We had a pretty good run at Chapin, my friend.

And Nathan Summerlin. Thank you for taking it upon yourself to "walk the dog" so I would know how long it would take for Stanley's arms to tire out. That's going above and beyond.

I'm also indebted to my brother-in-law, Jimmy McGraw, for answering my texts every time I needed to know how something worked. And to my sister, Alice McGraw, for the countless trips down memory lane.

Thank you to Jaclyn Fowler (again!), Julie Sidoni, and Lauren Stahl, my fellow workshoppers who got me to the finish line. Very simply, this book wouldn't exist without you.

And to Vylinda Bryant, Andre Carter, Kristin Ivey, Monique Lewis, Ann Reeves, and Kate Sotiridy, my outside readers, thank you for such invaluable feedback.

Rain Breaks No Bones is the last book in a trilogy that I never intended to write until I met Chris Tomasino, my wonderful agent and friend. The first time you read a draft of *Sing in the Morning, Cry at Night*, you suggested my characters might have more to say. The idea overwhelmed me, and yet, here we are because of your guidance. I'll always be grateful.

And thank you to publisher Johnny Temple and everyone at Akashic Books for believing a schoolteacher from Scranton had something to say worth reading. I'm proud to publish with Akashic and Kaylie Jones Books.

In 2006, I met a woman who scared me a little and changed my life forever. Kaylie Jones—mentor, editor, publisher, friend extraordinaire—simply put, I am a writer because of you, and that's everything.

Finally, I'd be remiss if I didn't mention my dad, Carl Taylor. Although you passed before I started writing *Rain Breaks No Bones*, this book, like all the others, is brimming with the research we collected together. We did it, Dad. You and me.